FOOLS
AND
MORTALS

BY

B E R N A R D   C O R N W E L L

HarperCollins*Publishers*

HarperCollins*Publishers*
1 London Bridge Street
London SE1 9GF

www.harpercollins.co.uk

Published by HarperCollins*Publishers* 2017

1

Copyright © Bernard Cornwell 2017

Bernard Cornwell asserts the moral right to
be identified as the author of this work

A catalogue record for this book is available from the British Library

HB ISBN: 978-0-00-750411-4
TPB ISBN: 978-0-00-750412-1

Part One illustration: 17th century view of London © Private Collection/Bridgeman Images;
Part Two illustration: Elizabethan theatre scene © Lebrecht Music and Arts Photo Library/
Alamy; Part Three illustration: The Globe Theatre from 'Old and New London' by Edward
Walford © Montagu Images/Alamy; Part Four illustration: Scene from an Elizabethan
playhouse © Chronicle/Alamy; Endpapers: Elizabethan theatre performers from 'Drolls' by
Francis Kirkman © Granger/Bridgeman Images; Section from William Shakespeare's last
will and testament © Ian Dagnall/Alamy

This novel is entirely a work of fiction. The names, characters and incidents portrayed in it,
while at times based on historical figures, are the work of the author's imagination.

Set in 12/15pt Adobe Caslon

Printed and bound by CPI Group (UK) Ltd, Croydon, CR0 4YY

MIX
Paper from
responsible sources
FSC
www.fsc.org
FSC™ C007454

This book is produced from independently certified FSC paper
to ensure responsible forest management.

For more information visit: www.harpercollins.co.uk/green

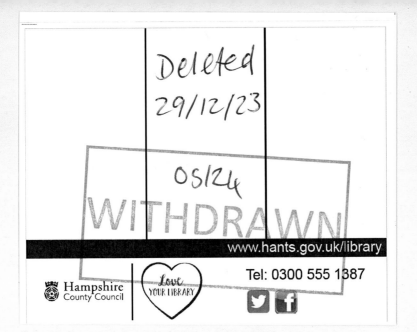

Fools and Mortals
is dedicated, with affection,
to all the actors, actresses, directors,
musicians and technicians of the
Monomoy Theatre

St Giles

Fleet River

Smithf.

Holborn

The Strand

Fleet Street

Ludgate Hill

Charing Cross

Newgate

Blackfriers

Whitehall
Palace

River Thames

Lambeth
Palace

London
1590

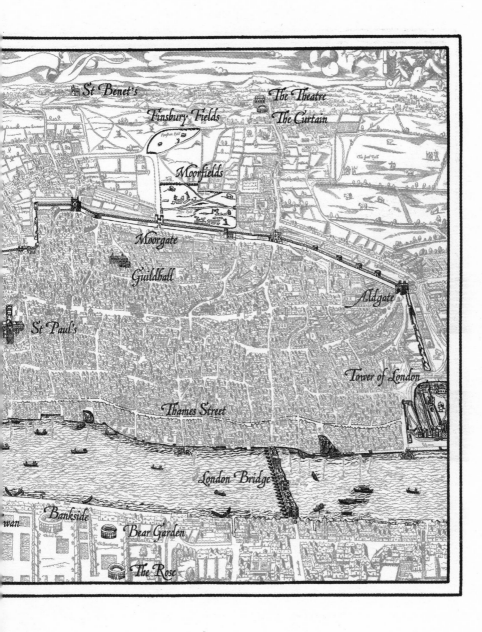

PUCK: Lord, what fools these mortals be!

A Midsummer Night's Dream
Act III, Scene 2, line 115

HIPPOLYTA: This is the silliest stuff that ever I heard.
THESEUS: The best in this kind are but shadows; and
the worst are no worse, if imagination amend them.
HIPPOLYTA: It must be your imagination then, and
not theirs.
THESEUS: If we imagine no worse of them than they
of themselves, they may pass for excellent men.

A Midsummer Night's Dream
Act V, Scene 1, lines 207ff

PART ONE

EXCELLENT MEN

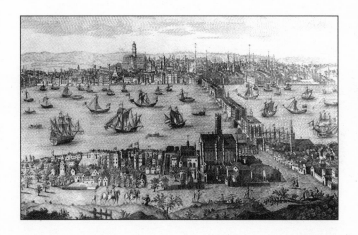

ONE

I DIED JUST after the clock in the passageway struck nine.
There are those who claim that Her Majesty, Elizabeth,
by the grace of God, Queen of England, France, and of Ireland,
will not allow clocks to strike the hour in her palaces. Time is
not allowed to pass for her. She has defeated time. But that
clock struck. I remember it.

I counted the bells. Nine. Then my killer struck.

And I died.

My brother says there is only one way to tell a story. 'Begin,'
he says in his irritatingly pedantic manner, 'at the beginning.
Where else?'

I see I have started a little too late, so we shall go back to five
minutes before nine, and begin again.

Imagine, if you will, a woman. She is no longer young, nor is
she old. She is tall, and, I am constantly told, strikingly handsome. On the night of her death she is wearing a gown made
from the darkest blue velvet, embroidered with a mass of silver
stars, each star studded with a pearl. Panels of watered silk,
pale lavender in colour, billow through the open-fronted skirt

as she moves. The same expensive silk lines her sleeves, the lavender showing through slits cut into the star-studded velvet. The skirt brushes the floor, hiding her delicate slippers, which are cut from an antique tapestry. Such slippers were uncomfortable, as tapestry shoes always are unless lined with linen or, better, satin. She wears a ruff, high at the back and starched stiff, and above it her striking face is framed by raven-black hair, which is pinned into elaborate coils and rolls, all looped with strings of pearls to match the necklace that hangs down her bodice. A coronet of silver, again decorated with pearls, shows her high rank. Her pale face shimmers with a strange, almost unearthly glow, reflecting the light from the flames of a myriad candles, while her eyes are darkened, and her lips reddened. She has a straight back, and throws her hips forward and pushes her shoulders back so that her silk-clad bosom, which is neither too large nor vanishingly small, draws the eye. She draws many eyes that night for she is, as I am frequently told, a hauntingly beautiful woman.

The beautiful woman is in the company of two men and a younger woman, one of whom is her killer, though she does not yet know it. The younger woman is dressed every bit as beautifully as the older, if anything her bodice and skirt are even more expensive, bright with pale silks and precious stones. She has fair hair piled high, and a face of innocent loveliness, though that is deceptive, for she is pleading for the older woman's imprisonment and disfigurement. She is the older woman's rival in love, and, being younger and no less beautiful, she will win this confrontation. The two men listen, amused, as the younger woman insults her rival, and then watch as she picks up a heavy iron stand that holds four candles. She dances, pretending that the iron stand is a man. The candles flicker and smoke, but none goes out. The girl dances gracefully, puts the stand down, and gives one of the men a brazen look. 'If thou

4

would'st know me,' she says archly, 'then thou would'st know my grievance.'

'Know you?' the older woman intervenes, 'oh, thou art known!' It is a witty retort, clearly spoken, though the older woman's voice is somewhat hoarse and breathy.

'Thy grievance, lady,' the shorter of the two men says, 'is my duty.' He draws a dagger. For a candle-flickering pause it seems he is about to plunge the blade into the younger woman, but then he turns and strikes at the older. The clock, a mechanical marvel that must be in the corridor just outside the hall, has started striking, and I count the bells.

The onlookers gasp.

The dagger slides between the older woman's waist and her right arm. She gasps too. Then she staggers. In her left hand, hidden from the shocked onlookers, is a very small knife that she uses to pierce a pig's bladder concealed in a simple linen pouch hanging by woven silver ropes from her belt. The belt is pretty, fashioned from cream-coloured kidskin with diamond-shaped panels of scarlet cloth on which small pearls glitter. When pricked, the pouch releases a gush of sheep's blood.

'I am slain,' she cries, 'alas! I am slain!' I did not write the line, so I am not responsible for the older woman stating what must already have been obvious. The younger woman screams, not in shock, but in exultation.

The older woman staggers some more, turning now so that the onlookers can see the blood. If we had not been in a palace, then we would not have used the sheep's blood, because the velvet gown was too rich and expensive, but for Elizabeth, for whom time does not exist, we must spend. So we spend. The blood soaks the velvet gown, hardly showing because the cloth is so dark, but plenty of blood stains the lavender silk, and spatters the canvas that has been spread across the Turkey carpets. The woman now sways, cries again, falls to her knees, and, with

5

another exclamation, dies. In case anyone thinks she is merely fainting, she calls out two last despairing words, 'I die!' And then she dies.

The clock has just struck nine times.

The killer takes the coronet from the corpse's hair, and, with elaborate courtesy, presents it to the younger woman. He then seizes the dead woman's hands, and, with unnecessary force, drags her from view. 'Her body here we'll leave,' he says loudly, grunting with the effort of pulling the corpse, 'to moulder and to time's eternity.' He hides the woman behind a tall screen, which mostly hides a door at the back of the stage. The screen is decorated with embroidered panels showing entwined red and white roses springing from two leafy vines.

'A pox on you,' the dead woman says softly.

'Piss on your bollocks,' her killer whispers, and goes back to where the audience is motionless and silent, shocked by the sudden death of such dark beauty.

I was the older woman.

The room where I have just died is lit by countless candles, but behind the screen it is shadowed dark as death. I crawled to the half open door and wriggled through into the antechamber, taking care not to disturb the door itself, the top of which can be seen above the rosy screen.

'Gawd help us, Richard,' Jean said to me, speaking softly. She brushed a hand down my beautiful skirt that was stained with sheep's blood. 'What a mess!'

'Will it wash out?' I asked, standing.

'It might,' she said dubiously, 'but it will never be the same again, will it? Pity that.' Jean is a good woman, a widow, and our seamstress. 'Here, let me wet the silk.' She went to fetch a jug of water and a cloth.

A dozen men and boys lounged at the room's edges. Alan was sitting close to two candles and silently mouthing words he was

6

reading from a long piece of paper, while George Bryan and Will Kemp were playing cards, using one of our tiring boxes as a table. Kemp grinned. 'One day he'll stick that knife right through your ribs,' he said to me, then grimaced, pretending to die. 'He'd like that. So would I.'

'A pox on you too,' I said.

'You should be nice to him,' Jean said to me as she began dabbing ineffectually at the sheep's blood. 'Your brother, I mean,' she went on. I said nothing, just stood there as she tried to clean the silk. I was half listening to the players in the great chamber where the Queen sits on her throne.

This was the fifth time I had played for the Queen; twice in Greenwich, twice at Richmond, and now at Whitehall, and folk are forever asking what is she like, and I usually make up an answer because she is impossible to see or describe. Most of the candles were at the players' end of the hall, and Elizabeth, by the grace of God, Queen of England, France, and Ireland, sat beneath a rich red canopy that shadowed her, but even in the shadow I could see her face white as a gull, unmoving, stern, beneath red hair piled high and crowned with silver or gold. She sat still as a statue except when she laughed. Her face, so white, looked disapproving, but it was evident she enjoyed the plays, and the courtiers watched her as much as they watched us, looking for clues as to whether they should enjoy us or not.

Her bosom was white like her face, and I knew she was wearing ceruse, a paste that makes the skin white and smooth. She wore her dresses low like a young girl enticing men with a hint of pale breasts, though God knows she was old. She did not look old, and she glowed in her expensive fabrics, which were studded with jewels that caught the candlelight. So old, so still, so pale, so royal. We dared not look at her, because to catch her eye would break the illusion we offered her, but

7

I would snatch a glimpse when I could, seeing her paste-white face above the perfumed crowd, who sat on the lower seats.

'I might have to sew new silk into the skirt,' Jean said, still talking softly, then she shivered as a gust of wind blew rain against the antechamber's high windows. 'Nasty night to be out,' she said, 'raining like the devil's piss, it is.'

'How long before this piece of shit ends?' Will Kemp asked.

'Fifteen minutes,' Alan said without looking up from the paper he was reading.

Simon Willoughby came through the door from the great hall. He was playing the younger woman, my rival, and he was grinning. He is a pretty boy, just sixteen years old, and he tossed the coronet to Jean then twirled around so that his bright pale skirts flared outwards. 'We were good tonight!' he said happily.

'You're always good, Simon,' Will Kemp said fondly.

'Not so loud, Simon, not so loud,' Alan cautioned with a smile.

'Where are you going?' Jean demanded of me. I had gone to the door leading to the courtyard.

'I need a piss.'

'Don't let the velvet get wet,' she hissed. 'Here, take this!' She brought me a heavy cloak and draped it around my shoulders.

I went out into the yard where rain seethed on the cobbles, and I stood under the shelter of a wooden arcade that ran like a cheap cloister about the courtyard's edge. I shivered. Winter was coming. There was a deeply arched gateway on the yard's far side where two torches guttered feebly. Something dark twitched in the arcade's corner. A rat perhaps, or one of the cats that lived in the palace. A pox on the palace, I thought, and a pox on Her Majesty, for whom time does not exist. She likes her plays to begin in the middle of the afternoon, but the visit of an ambassador had delayed this performance, and it would be a wet, dark and cold journey home.

'I thought you needed to piss?' Simon Willoughby had followed me into the courtyard.

'I just wanted some fresh air.'

'It was hot in there,' he said, then hauled up his pretty skirts and began to piss into the rain, 'but we were good, weren't we?' I said nothing. 'Did you see the Queen?' he asked. 'She was watching me!' Again I said nothing because there was nothing to say. Of course the Queen had been watching him. She had watched all of us. She had summoned us! 'Did you see me dance with that tall candle-stand?' Simon asked.

'I did,' I said curtly, then strolled away from him, following the cloister-like arcade about the courtyard's edge. I knew he wanted me to praise him because young Simon Willoughby needs praise like a whore needs silver, but there could never be enough compliments to satisfy him. Other than that he is a decent enough boy, a good actor and, with his long blond hair, pretty enough to make men sigh when he plays a girl.

'It was my idea,' he called after me, 'to pretend the candle-stand was a man!'

I ignored him.

'It was good, wasn't it?' he asked plaintively.

I was at the courtyard's far side now, deep in the shadows. No hint of the flames guttering in the archway could reach me here. There was a door to my right, barely visible, and I opened it cautiously. Whatever room lay beyond was in even deeper darkness. I sensed it was a small room, but did not enter, just listened, hearing nothing above the wind's bluster and the rain's ceaseless beat. I was hoping to find something to steal, something I could sell, something small and easily hidden. In Greenwich Palace I had found a small bag of seed pearls which must have been dropped and lay half obscured beneath a tapestry-covered stool in a passageway, and I had hidden the small bag beneath my skirts, then sold the pearls to

9

an apothecary who ground them small and used them to cure insanity, or so he said. He paid me far less than they were worth because he knew they were stolen, but I still made more money in that one day than I usually make in a month.

'Richard?' Simon Willoughby called. I kept silent. The dark room smelled foul, as if it had been used to store horse feed that had turned rotten. I reckoned there would be nothing to steal and so closed the door.

'Richard?' Simon called again. I remained silent and did not move, knowing I would be invisible in my dark cloak. I liked Simon well enough, but I was in no mood to tell him over and over how good he had been.

Then a door on the courtyard's far side opened, letting a wash of lantern-light into the rain-soaked courtyard. At first I thought it would be one of the players, come to let us know we were needed, but instead it was a man I had never seen before. He was young and he was rich. It is easy to tell the rich from their clothes, and this man was dressed in a doublet of shining yellow silk, slashed with blue. His hose was yellow, his high boots brown and polished. He wore a sword. His hat was blue with a long feather, and there was gold at his throat and more gold on his belt, but what stood out most was his long hair, so palely blond that it was almost white. I wondered if it was a wig. 'Simon?' the young man called.

Simon Willoughby answered with a nervous giggle.

'Are you alone?'

'I think so, my lord.' Simon had heard me open and close a door, and must have thought I had gone into the palace. Then the far door closed, plunging the newcomer into shadow. I was utterly still, just another shadow within a shadow. The young man walked towards Simon, and the guttering torches in the gate arch threw just enough light for me to see that his boots had heels like those on women's shoes. He was short and wanted to look taller. 'Richard was here,' I heard Simon say, 'but he's gone. I think he's gone.'

The man said nothing, just pushed Simon against the wall and kissed him. I saw him haul up Simon's skirts and I held my breath. The two were pressed together.

There was nothing surprising in this, except that his lordship, whoever he was, had not waited till the play's ending to find Simon Willoughby. Every time we had played at one of the Queen's palaces, the lordlings had come to the tiring room, and I had watched Simon disappear with one or other of them, which explained why Simon Willoughby always appeared to have money. I had none, which is why I needed to thieve.

'Oh yes,' I heard Simon say, 'my lord!'

I crept nearer. My tapestry slippers were silent on the stones. The wind fretted loud around the palace roofs, and the rain, already relentless, increased in vehemence to drown whatever the two said. There was just enough light from the becketed torches to see Simon's head bent back, his mouth open, and, still curious, I crept still nearer. 'My lord!' Simon cried, almost in pain.

His lordship chuckled and stepped back, releasing Simon's skirts. 'My little whore,' he said, though not in an unkind voice. I could see that even with the women's heels on his boots he was no taller than Simon, who is a full head shorter than me. 'I don't want you tonight,' his lordship said, 'but do your duty, little Simon, do your duty, and you shall live in my household.' He said something more, though I could not hear it because the wind gusted to drive hard rain on the cloister's roof, then his lordship leaned forward, kissed Simon's cheek, and went back to the tiring room.

I stayed still. Simon was leaning against the wall, gasping. 'So who is the dwarf?' I asked.

'Richard!' he sounded both scared and alarmed. 'Is that you?'

'Of course it's me. Who is his lordship?'

'Just a friend,' he said, then he was saved from answering any more questions because the antechamber door opened again, and Will Kemp leaned out. 'You two whores, come,' he snarled. 'You're needed! It's the ending.'

My brother was evidently speaking the epilogue. I knew he had composed it specially, draping it onto the play's end like ribbons on the tail of a harvest-home horse, and doubtless it smothered the Queen with compliments.

'Come!' Will Kemp snapped again, and we both hurried back inside.

When we are at the playhouse, we end every performance with a jig. Even the tragedies end with a jig. We dance, and Will Kemp clowns, and the boys playing the girls squeal. Will scatters insults and makes bawdy jokes, the audience roars, and the tragedy is forgotten, but when we play for Her Majesty, we neither dance nor clown. We make no jokes about pricks and buttocks, instead we line like supplicants at the edge of the stage and bow respectfully to show that, though we might have pretended to be kings and queens, to be dukes and duchesses, and even gods and goddesses, we know our humble place. We are mere players, and as far beneath the palace audience as hell's goblins are beneath heaven's bright angels. And so, that night, we made obeisance, and the audience, because the Queen had nodded her approval, rewarded us with applause. I am certain half of them had hated the play, but they took their cue from Her Majesty, and applauded politely. The Queen just stared at us imperiously, her bone-white face unreadable, and then she stood, the courtiers fell silent, we all bowed again, and she was gone.

And so our play was over.

'We shall meet at the Theatre,' my brother announced when, at last, we were all back in the antechamber. He clapped his hands to get everyone's attention because he knew he needed to speak swiftly before some of the lords and ladies from the audience came into the room. 'We need everyone who has a part in *Comedy*, and in *Hester*. No one else need come.'

'Musicians too?' someone asked.

'Musicians too, at the Theatre, tomorrow morning, early.'

Someone groaned. 'How early?'

'Nine of the clock,' my brother said.

More groaning. 'Will we be playing *The Dead Man's Fortune* tomorrow?' one of the hired men asked.

'Don't be an arsehole,' Will Kemp answered instead of my brother, 'how can we?'

The urgency and the scorn were both caused by a sickness that had afflicted Augustine Phillips, one of the company's principal players, and Christopher Beeston, who was Augustine's apprentice and lodged in his house. Both were too ill to work. Fortunately, Augustine was not in the play we had just performed, and I had been able to learn Christopher's part and so take his place. We would need to replace the two in other plays, though if the rain that still seethed outside did not end then there would be no performance at the Theatre the next day. But that problem was forgotten as the door from the hall opened and a half-dozen lords with their perfumed ladies entered. My brother bowed low. I saw the young fair-haired man with the blue-slashed yellow doublet, and was surprised that he ignored Simon Willoughby. He walked right past him, and Simon, plainly forewarned, did nothing except offer a bow.

I turned my back on the visitors as I stepped out of my skirts, shrugged off the bodice, and pulled on my grubby shirt. I used a damp cloth to wipe off the ceruse that had whitened my skin and bosom, ceruse that had been mixed with crushed pearls to make the skin glow in the candlelight. I had retreated to the darkest corner of the room, praying no one would notice me, nor did they. I was also praying that we would be offered somewhere to sleep in the palace, perhaps a stable, but no such offer came except to those who, like my brother, lived inside the city walls and so could not get home before the gates opened at dawn. The rest of us were expected to leave, rain or no rain. It was near midnight by the time we left, and the walk home around the city's northern edge took me at least an hour. It still rained, the road was night-black dark, but I walked with three of the hired men, which was company enough to deter any footpad crazy enough to be abroad in the foul weather. I had to wake Agnes, the maid who slept in the kitchen of the house where I rented the attic room, but Agnes was in love with me, poor girl, and did not mind. 'You should stay here in the kitchen,' she suggested coyly, 'it's warm!'

Instead I crept upstairs, careful not to wake the Widow Morrison, my landlady, to whom I owed too much rent, and, having stripped off my soaking wet clothes, I shivered under the thin blanket until I finally slept.

I woke next morning tired, cold, and damp. I pulled on a doublet and hose, crammed my hair into its cap, wiped my face with a half-frozen cloth, used the jakes in the backyard, swallowed a mug of weak ale, snatched a hard crust from the kitchen, promised to pay the Widow Morrison the rent I owed, and then went out into a chill morning. At least it was not raining.

I had two ways to reach the playhouse from the widow's house. I could either turn left in the alley and then walk north up Bishopsgate Street, but most mornings that street was crowded with sheep or cows being herded towards the city's slaughter-houses, and, besides, after the rain, it would be ankle deep in mud, shit, and muck, and so I turned right and leaped the open sewer that edged Finsbury Fields. I slipped as I landed, and my right foot shot back into the green-scummed water.

14

'You appear with your customary grace,' a sarcastic voice said. I looked up and saw my brother had chosen to walk north through the Fields rather than edge past frightened cattle in the street. John Heminges, another player in the company, was with him.

'Good morrow, brother,' I said, picking myself up.

He ignored that greeting and offered me no help as I scrambled up the slippery bank. Nettles stung my right hand, and I cursed, making him smile. It was John Heminges who stepped forward and held out a helping hand. I thanked him and looked resentfully at my brother. 'You might have helped me,' I said.

'I might indeed,' he agreed coldly. He wore a thick woollen cloak and a dark hat with an extravagant brim that shadowed his face. I look nothing like him. I am tall, thin-faced, and clean shaven, while he has a round, blunt face with a weak beard, full lips, and very dark eyes. My eyes are blue, his are secretive, shadowed, and always watching cautiously. I knew he would have preferred to walk on, ignoring me, but my sudden arrival in the ditch had forced him to acknowledge me and even talk to me. 'Young Simon was excellent last night,' he said, with false enthusiasm.

'So he told me,' I said, 'often.'

He could not resist the smallest smile, a twitch that betrayed amusement and was immediately banished. 'Dancing with the candle-stand?' he went on, pretending not to have noticed my reply. 'That was good.' I knew he praised Simon Willoughby to annoy me.

'Where is Simon?' I asked. I would have expected Simon Willoughby to be with his apprentice master, John Heminges.

'I . . .' Heminges began, then just looked sheepish.

'He's smearing the sheets of some lordly bed,' my brother said, as if the answer were obvious, 'of course.'

'He has friends in Westminster,' John Heminges said,

sounding embarrassed. He is a little younger than my brother, perhaps twenty-nine or thirty, but usually played older parts. He is a kind man who knows of the antagonism between my brother and I, and does his ineffectual best to relieve it.

My brother glanced at the sky. 'I do believe it's clearing. Not before time. But we can't perform anything this afternoon, and that's a pity,' he gave me a sour smile, 'it means no money for you today.'

'We're rehearsing, aren't we?' I asked.

'You're not paid for rehearsing,' he said, 'just for performing.'

'We could stage *The Dead Man's Fortune?*' John Heminges put in, eager to stop our bickering.

'Not without Augustine and Christopher,' my brother said.

'I suppose not, no, of course not. A pity! I like it.'

'It's a strange piece,' my brother said, 'but not without virtues. Two couples, and both the women enamoured of other men! Space there for some dance steps!'

'We're putting dances into it?' Heminges asked, puzzled.

'No, no, no, I mean scope for complications. Two women and four men. Too many men! Too many men!' My brother had paused to gaze at the windmills across the Fields as he spoke. 'Then there's the love potion! An idea with possibilities, but all wrong, all wrong!'

'Why wrong?'

'Because the girls' fathers concoct the potion. It should be the sorceress! What is the value of a sorceress if she doesn't perform sorcery?'

'She has a magic mirror,' I pointed out. I knew because I played the sorceress.

'Magic mirror!' he said scornfully. He was striding on again, perhaps attempting to leave me behind. 'Magic mirror!' he said again. 'That's a mountebank's trick. Magic lies in the . . .' he paused, then decided that whatever he had been about to say

16

would be wasted on me. 'Not that it signifies! We can't perform the play without Augustine and Christopher.'

'How's the Verona play?' Heminges asked.

If I had dared ask that same question I would have been ignored, but my brother liked Heminges. Even so he was reluctant to answer in front of me. 'Almost finished,' he said vaguely, 'almost.' I knew he was writing a play set in Verona, a city in Italy, and that he had been forced to interrupt the writing to devise a wedding play for our patron, Lord Hunsdon. He had grumbled about the interruption.

'You still like it?' Heminges asked, oblivious to my brother's irritation.

'I'd like it more if I could finish it,' he said savagely, 'but Lord Hunsdon wants a wedding play, so damn Verona.' We walked on in silence. To our right, beyond the scummed ditch and a brick wall, lay the Curtain, a playhouse built to rival ours. A blue flag flew from the staff on the Curtain's high roof announcing that there would be an entertainment that afternoon. 'Another beast show,' my brother said derisively. There had been no plays at the Curtain for months, and it seemed there would be no play at the Theatre this afternoon either. We had nothing to perform until other players learned Augustine and Christopher's parts. We could have performed the play we had presented to the Queen, except we had done it too often in the past month. Perform a play too often, and the audience is liable to pelt the stage with empty ale bottles.

We came to the wooden bridge that crossed the sewer ditch and which led to a crude gap in the long brick wall. Beyond the gap was the Theatre, our playhouse, a great wooden turret as tall as a church steeple. It had been James Burbage's idea to build the playhouse, and his idea to make the bridge and pierce the wall, which meant playgoers did not have to walk up muddy Bishopsgate to reach us, but instead could leave the city through Cripplegate and stroll across Finsbury Fields. So many folk made that journey that there was now a broad and muddy path running diagonally across the open ground. 'Does that cloak belong to the company?' my brother asked as we crossed the bridge.

'Yes.'

'Make sure it's returned to the tiring room,' he said snidely, then stopped in the wall's gap. He let John Heminges walk ahead, and then, for the first time since we had met at the ditch's edge, looked up into my eyes. He had to look up because I was a full head taller. 'You are going to stay with the company?' he asked.

'I can't afford to,' I said. 'I owe rent. You're not giving me enough work.'

'Then stop spending your evenings in the Falcon,' was his answer. I thought he would say no more because he walked on, but after two paces he turned back to me. 'You'll get more work,' he said brusquely. 'With Augustine sick and his boy sweating? We have to replace them.'

'You won't give me Augustine's parts,' I said, 'and I'm too old to play girls.'

'You'll play what we ask you to play. We need you, at least through the winter.'

'You need me!' I threw that back into his face. 'Then pay me more.'

He ignored the demand. 'We begin today by rehearsing *Hester*,' he said coldly, 'we'll only be working on Augustine and Christopher's scenes. Tomorrow we'll perform *Hester*, and we'll play the *Comedy* on Saturday. I expect you to be here.'

I shrugged. In *Hester and Ahasuerus* I played Uashti, and in the *Comedy* I was Emilia. I knew all the lines. 'You pay William Sly twice what you pay me,' I said, 'and my parts are just as large as his.'

'Maybe because he's twice as good as you? Besides, you're my brother,' he said, as if that explained everything. 'Just stay through the winter, and after that? Do what you will. Leave the company and starve, if that's what you want.' He walked on towards the playhouse.

And I spat after him. Brotherly love.

George Bryan paced to the front of the stage, where he bowed so low that he almost lost his balance. 'Noble Prince,' he said when he recovered his footing, 'according as I am bound, I will do you service till death me do confound.'

Isaiah Humble, the bookkeeper, coughed to attract attention. 'Sorry! It's "till death me confound". There's no "do". Sorry!'

'It's better with the "do",' my brother said mildly.

'It's crapulous shit with or without the "do",' Alan Rust said, 'but if George wants to say "do", Master Humble, then he says "do".'

'Sorry,' Isaiah said from his stool at the back of the stage.

'You were right to correct him,' my brother consoled him, 'it's your job.'

'Sorry, though.'

George swept off his hat and bowed again. 'Something, something, something,' he said, 'till death me do confound.' George Bryan, a nervous and worried man who somehow always appeared confident and decisive when the playhouse was full, had replaced the sick Augustine Phillips. The rehearsal was to bind him and Simon Willoughby, who had replaced Christopher Beeston, into the play.

John Heminges acknowledged George's second bow with a languid wave of a hand. 'For a season we will, to our solace, into our orchard or some other place.'

Will Kemp bounded onto the stage with a mighty leap. 'He that will drink wine,' he bellowed, 'and hath never a vine, must send or go to France. And if he do not he must needs shrink!' On the word shrink he crouched, looked alarmed, and clutched his codpiece, which sent Simon Willoughby into a fit of giggling.

'Do we go to the orchard?' George interrupted Will Kemp to ask.

'The orchard, yes,' Isaiah said, 'or some other place. That's what it says in the text, "orchard or some other place".' He waved the prompt copy. 'Sorry, Will.'

'I'd like to know if it is the orchard.'

'Why?' Alan Rust asked belligerently.

'Do I imagine trees? Or some other place without trees?' George looked anxious. 'It helps to know.'

'Imagine trees,' Rust barked. 'Apple trees. Where you meet Hardydardy.' He gestured towards Will Kemp.

'Are the apples ripe?' George asked.

'Does it matter?' Rust asked.

'If they're ripe,' George said, still looking worried, 'I could eat one.'

'They're small apples,' Rust said, 'unripe, like Simon's tits.'

'Isn't this a tale from the scriptures?' John Heminges put in.

'My tits aren't small,' Simon Willoughby said, hefting his scrawny chest.

'It's from the Old Testament,' my brother said, 'you'll find the story in the Book of Esther.'

'But there's no one called Hardydardy in the Bible!' John Heminges said.

'There bloody well is now,' Alan Rust said. 'Can we move on?'

'Book of Esther?' George asked. 'Then why is she called Hester?'

'Because the Reverend William Venables, who wrote this piece of shit, didn't know his arse from his shrivelled prick,' Alan Rust said forcefully. 'Now will you all be quiet and let Will speak his lines?'

'If it's so bad,' George asked, 'why are we doing it again?'

'Can you think of another play we can fit by tomorrow?'

'No.'

'Then that's why.'

'Go on, Will,' my brother said tiredly.

'There's a loose board here,' George said, stubbing his toe at the front of the stage, 'that's why I almost fell over when I bowed.'

'I lack both drink and meat,' Will Kemp appealed to the empty galleries of the Theatre, 'but, as I say, a dog hath a day, my time is come to get some!'

'Get some!' Simon Willoughby almost peed himself with laughter. He had arrived at the Theatre before me, and looked surprisingly sprightly and alert. 'You didn't go home last night?' I had asked him, but instead of answering he just grinned. 'Did he pay you?' I asked.

'Perhaps.'

'You can lend me some?'

'I'm needed onstage,' he had said, and hurried away.

'Shouldn't that be "meat and drink"?' George now interrupted the rehearsal again.

'It's my line,' Will Kemp growled, 'why should you care?'

Isaiah peered at the text. 'No,' he said, 'Will got it right, it's "drink and meat", sorry.'

I was feeling tired, so I wandered out of the yard and through the shadowed entrance tunnel where Jeremiah Poll, an old soldier who had lost an eye in Ireland, guarded the outer gate. 'It's going to rain again,' he said as I passed, and I nodded. Jeremiah said it every time I passed him, even on the warmest, driest days. I could hear the clash and scrape of blades, and emerged into the weak sunlight to see Richard Burbage and Henry Condell practising their sword skills. They were fast, their blades darting, retreating, crossing, and lunging. Henry laughed at something Richard Burbage said, then saw me, and his sword went upwards as he stepped back and motioned with his dagger hand for the practice to stop. They both turned to look at me, but I pretended not to have noticed them and went to the door that led to the galleries. I heard them laugh as I stepped through.

I climbed the short stairs to the lower gallery, from where I glanced across at the stage where George was still fretting about apples or loose planks, then, as the sound of the swords started again, I lay down. I was playing Uashti, a queen of Persia, but my lines would not be needed for at least an hour, and so I closed my eyes.

I was woken by a kick to my legs and opened my eyes to see James Burbage standing over me. 'There are Percies in your house,' he said.

'There are what?' I asked, struggling to wake and stand up.

'Percies,' he said, 'in your house. I just walked past.'

'They're there for Father Laurence,' I explained, 'the bastards.'

'They've been before?'

'The bastards come every month.'

Father Laurence, like me, lived in the Widow Morrison's house. He was an ancient priest who rented the room directly beneath my attic, though I suspected the widow let him live there for free. He was in his sixties, half crippled by pains in his joints, but still with a spry mind. He was a Roman Catholic priest, which was reason enough to have most men dragged on a hurdle to Tyburn or Tower Hill and there have their innards plucked out while they still lived, but Father Laurence was a Marian priest, meaning he had been ordained during the reign of our Queen's half-sister, the Catholic Queen Mary, and such men, if they made no trouble, were allowed to live. Father Laurence made no trouble, but the Pursuivants, those men who hunted down traitorous Catholics, were forever searching his room as if the poor old man might be hiding a Jesuit behind his close-stool. They never found anything because my brother had hidden Father Laurence's vestments and chalices among the Theatre's costumes and properties.

'They'll find nothing,' I said, 'they never do.' I looked towards the stage. 'Do they need me?'

'It's the dance of the Jewish women,' James Burbage said, 'so no.'

On the stage Simon Willoughby, Billy Rowley, Alexander Cooke and Tom Belte were prancing in a line, goaded by a man who carried a silver-tipped staff with which he rapped their legs or arms. 'Higher!' he called. 'You're here to show your legs. Leap, you spavined infants, leap!'

'Who's that?' I asked.

'Ralph Perkins. Friend of mine. He teaches dancing at the court.'

'At the court?' I was impressed.

'The Queen likes to see dancing done well. So do I.'

'One, two, three, four, five, leap!' Ralph Perkins called. 'It's the galliard, you lumpen urchins, not some country dump dance! Leap!'

'Goddam ill fortune about Augustine and his boy,' James Burbage grumbled.

'They'll recover?'

'Who knows? They've been purged, bled, and buggered about. They might. I pray they do.' He frowned. 'Simon Willoughby will be busy till Christopher recovers.'

'That'll please him,' I said sourly.

'But not you?' I shrugged and did not answer. I was frightened of James Burbage. He leased the Theatre, which made him the owner of the building if not the land on which it stood, and his eldest son, called Richard like me, was one of our leading players. James had been a player himself once, and, before that, a carpenter, and he still had the muscular build of a man who worked with his hands. He was tall, grey-haired, and hard-faced, with a short beard, and though he no longer acted, he was a Sharer, one of the eight men who shared the expenses of the Theatre and divided the profits among themselves. 'He drives a hard bargain,' my brother, another of the Sharers, had once told me, 'but he keeps to it. He's a good man.' Now James frowned at the stage as he talked to me. 'Are you still thinking about leaving?'

I said nothing.

'Henry Lanman,' Burbage said the name flatly, 'has that bastard been talking to you?'

'No.'

'Is he trying to poach you?'

'No,' I said again.

'But is your brother right? He says you're thinking of walking away from us. Is that true?'

'I've thought about it,' I said sullenly.

'Don't be a fool, boy. And don't be tempted by Lanman. He's losing money.' Henry Lanman owned the Curtain playhouse that lay just a brief walk to the south of ours. During our performances we could hear their audience cheering, the beat of their drummers, and the sound of their trumpeters, though of late those sounds had become scarcer. 'He's showing sword fights these days,' Burbage went on, 'sword fights and bear baiting. So what does he want you to do? Piss about in a frock and look pretty?'

'I haven't talked to him,' I insisted truthfully.

'So you've a lick of sense. He's got nobody to write plays, and nobody to play in them.'

'I haven't talked to him!' I repeated testily.

'You think Philip Henslowe will hire you?'

'No!'

'He's got plenty of actors.' Henslowe owned the Rose play-house, south of the Thames, and was our chief rival.

'Then there's Francis Langley,' James Burbage went on relentlessly, 'has he talked to you?'

'No.'

'He's building that monstrous great lump of a playhouse on Bankside, and he's got no players, and he's got no plays either. Rivals and enemies,' he said the last three words bitterly.

'Enemies?'

'Lanman and Langley? Lanman hates us. The landlord here hates us. The bloody city fathers hate us. The lord mayor hates us. Do you hate us?'

'No.'

'But you're thinking of leaving?'

'I'm not making any money,' I muttered, 'I'm poor.'

'Of course you're bloody poor! How old are you? Twenty? Twenty-one?'

'Twenty-one.'

'You think I started with money?' Burbage asked belliger-ently. 'I served my apprenticeship, boy, I earned my money, saved money, borrowed money, bought the lease here, built the playhouse! I worked, boy!'

I gazed out into the yard. 'You were a joiner, yes?'

'A good one,' he said proudly, 'but I didn't start with money. All I had was a pair of hands and a willingness to work. I learned to saw and chisel and augur and shape wood. I learned a trade. I worked.'

'And this is the only trade I know,' I said bitterly. I nodded towards my brother. 'He made sure of that, didn't he? But in a year or so you'll spit me out. There'll be no more parts for me.'

'You don't know that,' he said, though he did not sound con-vincing. 'So what parts do you want?'

I was about to answer when Burbage held up a hand to silence me. I turned to see that a group of strangers had just come into the playhouse and were now standing in the yard, staring at the prancing boys on the stage. Four were grim-looking men, all with scabbarded swords and all wearing the white rose of Lord Hunsdon's livery. The men stood, foursquare and challenging, to guard four women. One of the women was older, with grey hair showing beneath her coif. She signalled the men to stay where they were, and strode towards the stage, straight-backed and confident. My brother, seeing her, bowed low. 'My lady!' he greeted her, sounding surprised.

'We have been inspecting an estate at Finsbury,' her ladyship said in brusque explanation, 'and my granddaughter wished to see your playhouse.'

'You're most welcome,' my brother said. The boys onstage had all snatched off their caps and knelt.

'Stop grovelling,' her ladyship said sharply, 'were you dancing?'

'Yes, your ladyship,' Ralph Perkins answered.

'Then dance on,' she said imperiously, before gesturing to my brother. 'A word, if you please?'

I knew she was Lady Anne Hunsdon, the wife of the Lord Chamberlain, who was our company's patron. Some nobles showed their wealth by having a retinue of finely-clothed retainers ever at their heels, or by owning the swiftest deerhounds in the kingdom, or by their lavish palaces and wide parks, while some, a few, patronised the acting companies. We were Lord Hunsdon's pets, we played at his pleasure, and grovelled when he deigned to notice us. And when we toured the country, which we did whenever a plague closed the London playhouses, the Lord Chamberlain's name and badge protected us from the miserable Puritan town fathers who wanted to imprison us, or, better still, whip us out of town. 'Come, Elizabeth,' Lady Hunsdon ordered, and her granddaughter, for whose marriage my brother had been forced to abandon his

Italian play and write something new, went to join her grand-mother and my brother. The two maidservants waited with the guards, and it was one of those two maids who caught my eye and stopped the breath in my throat.

Lady Anne Hunsdon and her granddaughter were cloaked in finery. Elizabeth Carey was glorious in a farthingale of cream linen, slashed to show the shimmer of silver sarsenet beneath. I could not see her bodice because she was wearing a short cape, light grey, embroidered with the white roses that were her father and grandfather's badge. Her hair was pale gold, covered only with a net of silver-gilt thread on which small pearls shone, her skin was fashionably white, but she needed no ceruse to keep it that way, for her face was unblemished, not even touched with a hint of rouge on the cheeks. Her painted lips were full and smiling, and her blue eyes bright as she stared with evident delight at the four boys who had started dancing again to Ralph Perkins's instructions. Elizabeth Carey was a beauty, but I stared only at her maid, a small, slim girl whose eyes were bright with fascination for what happened on the stage. She was wearing a skirt and bodice of dark grey wool, and had a black coif over her light brown hair, but there was something about her face, some trick of lip and bone, that made her outshine the glowing Elizabeth. She turned to look around the playhouse and caught my eye, and there was the hint of a mischievous smile before she turned back towards the stage. 'Dear sweet Jesus,' I murmured, though luckily too softly for the words to reach any of the women.

James Burbage chuckled. I ignored him.

Elizabeth Carey clapped her gloved hands when the dance finished. My brother was speaking with her grandmother, who laughed at something he said. I stared at the maid. 'So you like her,' James Burbage said caustically. He thought I was staring at Elizabeth Carey.

'Don't you?'

'She's a rare little kickshaw,' he allowed, 'but take your bloody eyes off her. She'll be married in a couple of months. Married to a Berkeley,' he went on, 'Thomas. He gets ploughing rights, not you.'

'What is she doing here?' I asked.

'How the hell would I know?'

'Maybe she wants to see the play my brother's written,' I suggested.

'He won't show it to her.'

'Have you seen it?'

He nodded. 'But why are you interested? I thought you were leaving us.'

'I was hoping there's a part for me,' I said weakly.

James Burbage laughed. 'There's a part for bloody everyone! It's a big play. It has to be big because we need to do something special for his lordship. Big and new. You don't serve up cold meat for the Lord Chamberlain's granddaughter, you give her something fresh. Something frothy.'

'Frothy?'

'It's a wedding, not a bloody funeral. They want singing, dancing, and lovers soaked in moonbeams.'

I looked across the yard. My brother was gesticulating, almost as though he were making a speech from the stage. Lady Anne Hunsdon and her granddaughter were laughing, and the young maid was still staring wide-eyed around the Theatre.

'Of course,' Burbage went on, 'if we perform a play for her wedding then we'll need to rehearse where we'll play it.'

'Somerset House?' I asked. I knew that was where Lord Hunsdon lived.

'Bloody roof of the great hall fell in,' Burbage said, sounding amused, 'so like as not we'll be rehearsing in their Blackfriars house.'

'Where I'll play a woman,' I said bitterly.

He turned and frowned at me. 'Is that it? You're tired of wearing a skirt?'

'I'm too old! My voice has broken.'

Burbage waved to show me the whole circle of the playhouse. 'Look at it, boy! Timber, plaster and lath. Rain-rotted planks on the forestage, some slaps of paint, and that's all it is. But we turn it into ancient Rome, into Persia, into Ephesus, and the groundlings believe it. They stare. They gasp! You know what your brother told me?' He had gripped my jerkin and pulled me close. 'They don't see what they see, they see what they think they see.' He let go of me and gave a crooked grin. 'He says things like that, your brother, but I know what he means. When you act, they think they see a woman! Maybe you can't play a young girl any more, but as a woman in her prime, you're good!'

'I've a man's voice,' I said sullenly.

'Aye, and you shave, and you have a cock, but when you speak small they love it!'

'But for how long?' I demanded. 'In a month or so you'll say I'm only good for men's parts, and you've plenty of men players.'

'You want to play the hero?' he sneered.

I said nothing to that. His son Richard, who I had seen crossing swords with Henry Condell, always played the hero in our plays, and there was a temptation to think that he was only given the best parts because his father owned the playhouse's lease, just as it was tempting to believe he had been made one of the company's Sharers because of his father, but in truth he was good. People loved him. They walked across Finsbury Fields to watch Richard Burbage win the girl, destroy the villains, and put the world to rights. Richard was only three or four years older than I, which meant I had no chance of winning a girl or of dazzling an audience with my swordplay. And some of the apprentices, the boys who were capering onstage right now, were growing taller

29

and could soon play the parts I played, and that would save the playhouse money because apprentices were paid in pennies. At least I got a couple of shillings a week, but for how long?

The sun was glinting off the puddles among the yard's cobblestones. Elizabeth Carey and her grandmother, holding their skirts up, crossed to the stage, and the boys there stopped dancing, took off their caps, and bowed, all except Simon, who offered an elaborate curtsey instead. Lady Anne spoke to them, and they laughed, then she turned, and, with her granddaughter beside her, headed for the Theatre's entrance. Elizabeth was talking animatedly. I saw that the hair had been plucked from her forehead, raising her hairline by a fashionable inch or more. 'Fairies,' I heard her say, 'I do adore fairies!'

James Burbage and I, anticipating that the ladies would walk within a few paces of the gallery where we talked, had taken off our caps, which meant my long hair fell about my face. I brushed it back. 'We shall have to ask our chaplain to exorcise the house,' Elizabeth Carey went on happily, 'in case the fairies stay!'

'Better a flock of fairies than the rats in Blackfriars,' Lady Anne said shortly, then caught sight of me and stopped. 'You were good last night,' she said abruptly.

'My lady,' I said, bowing.

'I like a good death.'

'It was thrilling,' Elizabeth Carey added. Her face, already merry, brightened. 'When you died,' she said, letting go of her skirts and clasping her hands in front of her breasts, 'I didn't expect that, and I was so . . .' she hesitated, not finding the word she wanted for a heartbeat, 'mortified.'

'Thank you, my lady,' I said dutifully.

'And now it's so strange seeing you in a doublet!' she exclaimed.

'To the carriage, my dear,' her grandmother interrupted.

'You must play the Queen of the Fairies,' Elizabeth Carey ordered me with mock severity.

The young maid's eyes widened. She was staring at me, and I stared back. She had grey eyes. I thought I saw a hint of a smile again, a suspicion of mischief in her face. Was she mocking me because I would play a woman? Then, realising that I might offend Elizabeth Carey by ignoring her, I bowed a second time. 'Your ladyship,' I said, for lack of anything else to say.

'Come, Elizabeth,' Lady Anne ordered. 'And you, Silvia,' she added sharply to the grey-eyed maid, who was still looking at me.

Silvia! I thought it the most beautiful name I had ever heard.

James Burbage was laughing. When the women and their guards had left, he pulled his cap onto his cropped grey hair. 'Mortified,' he said. 'Mortified! The mort has wit.'

'We're doing a play about fairies?' I asked in disgust.

'Fairies and fools,' he said, 'and it's not fully finished yet.' He paused, scratching his short beard. 'But mayhap you're right, Richard.'

'Right?'

'Mayhap it's time we gave you men's parts. You're tall! That doesn't signify for parts like Uashti, because she's a queen. But tall is better for men's parts.' He frowned towards the stage. 'Simon's not really tall enough, is he? Scarcely comes up to a dwarf's arsehole. And your voice will deepen more as you add years, and you do act well.' He climbed the gallery to the outer corridor. 'You act well, so if we give you a man's part in the wedding play, will you stay through the winter?'

I hesitated, then remembered that James Burbage was a man of his word. A hard man, my brother said, but a fair one. 'Is that a promise, Mister Burbage?' I asked.

'As near as I can make it a promise, yes it is.' He spat on his

31

hand and held it out to me. 'I'll do the best I can to make sure you play a man in the wedding play. That's my promise.'

I shook his hand. 'Thank you,' I said.

'But right now you're the Queen of bloody Persia, so get up onstage and be queenly.'

I got up onstage and was queenly.

TWO

S ATURDAY.
  The weather had cleared to leave a pale sky in which the
early winter sun cast long shadows even at noon, when the bells
of the city churches rang in jangling disharmony. High clouds
blew ragged from the west, but there was no hint of rain, and
the fine weather meant that we could perform, and so, when
the cacophony of the noon bells ended, our trumpeter, standing
on the Theatre's tower, sounded a flourish, and the flag, which
displayed the red cross of Saint George, was hoisted to show we
were presenting a play.

The first playgoers began arriving before one o'clock. They
came across Finsbury Fields, a trickle at first, but the trickle
swelled, as men, women, apprentices, tradesmen, and gentry,
all came from the Cripplegate. Others walked up from the
Bishopsgate and turned down the narrow path that led by the
horse pond to the playhouse, where one-eyed Jeremiah stood
at the entrance with a locked box that had a slit in its lid, and
where two men, both armed with swords, cudgels, and scowls,
guarded the old soldier and his box. Every playgoer had to drop
a penny through the slot. Three whores from the Dolphin tavern

were selling hazelnuts just outside the Theatre, Blind Michael, who was guarded by a huge deaf and dumb son, was selling oysters, and Pitchfork Harry sold bottles of ale. The crowd, as always, was in a merry mood. They greeted old friends, chatted, and laughed as the yard filled.

Richer folk went to the smaller door, paid tuppence, and climbed the stairs to the galleries, where, for yet another penny, they could hire a cushion to soften the oak benches. Women leaned over the upper balustrade to stare at the groundlings, and some young men, often elegantly dressed, gazed back. Many of the men who had paid their penny to stand in the yard had no intention of staying there. Instead they scanned the galleries for the prettiest women, and, seeing one they liked, paid more pennies to climb the stairs.

Will Kemp peered through a spyhole. 'A goodly number,' he said.

'How many?' someone asked.

'Fifteen hundred?' he guessed. 'And they're still coming. I'm surprised.'

'Surprised?' John Heminges queried. 'Why?'

'Because this play is a piece of shit, that's why.' Will stepped away from the spyhole and picked up a pair of boots. 'Still,' he went on, 'I like being in plays that are shit.'

'Good Lord, you do? Why?'

'Because then I don't have to watch the damn things.'

'Jean,' someone called from the shadows, 'this hose is torn.'

'I'll bring you another.'

The trumpeter sounded his flourish more often, each cascade of notes being greeted by a cheer from the gathering crowd. 'Remind me what jig we're doing today?' Henry Condell asked.

'Jeremiah,' Will Kemp answered.

'Again?'

'They like it,' Will said aggressively.

George Bryan was shivering in a corner of the room. Not shivering with cold, but nervousness. One leg twitched uncontrollably. He was blinking, biting his lip, trying to say his lines in a low voice, but stuttering instead. George was always terrified before a play, though once on the stage he appeared the soul of confidence. Richard Burbage was stretching in another corner, loosening his arms and legs for the acrobatics to come, while Simon Willoughby, resplendent in an ivory-panelled skirt and with his hair piled high and hung with glass rubies, swirled back and forth in the tiring room's centre until Alan Rust growled at him to be still, whereupon Simon sulkily retreated to the back of the room, sat on a barrel, and picked his nose. My brother came down the stairs, evidently from the office where the money boxes were taken to be emptied. 'Seven lordlings on the stage,' he said happily. It cost sixpence to sit at the stage's edge, so the Sharers had just earned three shillings and sixpence from seven hard stools. I was lucky to earn three shillings and sixpence in a week, and soon, when the winter weather closed the playhouse down for days at a time, I would be lucky to earn a shilling.

Jean, our seamstress, shaved me. It was my second shave that day, and this one, with cold water, stung as she scraped my chin, upper lip, cheeks, and then my hairline to heighten my forehead. She used tweezers to shape my eyebrows, then told me to tip my head back. 'I hate this,' I said.

'Don't be a fusspot, Richard!' She dipped a sliver of wood into a small pot. 'And don't blink!' She held the sliver over my right eye. A drop of liquid fell into my eye, and I blinked. It stung. 'Now the other one,' she said.

'They call it deadly nightshade,' I said.

'You're being silly. It's just juice of belladonna.' She shook a second drop into my left eye. 'There. All done.' The belladonna, besides stinging and making my vision blurry for a time, dilated my pupils so that my eyes seemed larger. I kept them closed as Jean covered my face, neck, and upper chest with ceruse, the paste that made my skin look white as snow. 'Now the black,' she said happily, and used a finger to smear a paste of pig's fat and soot around my eyes. 'You look lovely!'

I growled, and she laughed. She took another pot from her capacious bag and leaned close. 'Cochineal, darling, don't tell Simon.'

'Why not?'

'I gave him madder because it's cheaper,' she whispered, then smeared my lips with her finger, leaving them red as cherries. I was no longer Richard, I was Uashti, Queen of Persia.

'Give us a kiss!' Henry Condell called to me.

'Dear sweet God,' George Bryan muttered, and bent his head between his knees. I thought he was going to vomit, but he sat up and took a deep breath. 'Dear sweet God,' he said again. We all ignored him, we had seen and heard it before, and knew he would play as well as ever. My brother held a breastplate to his chest and let Richard Burbage buckle the straps.

'There should be a helmet too,' my brother said, shrugging to make the newly buckled breastplate comfortable. 'Where's the helmet?'

'In the fur chest,' Jean called, 'by the back door.'

'What's it doing there?'

'Keeping warm.'

I climbed the wooden stairs to the upper room where most of the costumes and the smaller pieces of stage furniture were stored, and where the musicians were tuning their instruments. 'You look lovely, Richard,' Philip, who was the chief musician, greeted me.

'Put your lute up your arse,' I told him, 'and give it a twist.' We were friends.

'Give us a kiss first.'

'Then give it another twist,' I finished. I peered through the balcony door. The musicians would play on the balcony that afternoon, and a tabour player was already standing there. 'Nice big audience,' he told me, then tapped his drumsticks on the tabour's skin, provoking a cheer from the crowd below.

I turned back into the room and climbed the ladder to the tower roof. I was clumsy in my long dark skirts, but I hoisted them up and slowly mounted the rungs. 'I can see your arse!' Philip called.

'You lucky musician,' I said, then clambered through the trapdoor onto the platform, where Will Tawyer the trumpeter stood.

Will grinned at me. 'I was waiting for you,' he said. Will knew I would join him, because climbing to the rickety platform before a performance was my superstition. Every time I played in the Theatre I had to climb the tower. There was no reason I knew of, except a firm belief that I would play badly if I did not struggle up the ladder in my heavy and cumbersome skirts. All the players had their superstitions. John Heminges wore a hare's foot on a silver chain, George Bryan, in between his shivering and twitching, would reach up to touch a beam in the tiring room ceiling, Will Kemp would force a kiss on Jean, the seamstress, while Richard Burbage would draw his sword and kiss the blade. My brother tried to pretend he had no ritual, but when he thought no one was looking, he made the sign of the cross. He was no papist, but when he was challenged by Will Kemp, who accused him of kissing the filthy arse of the Great Whore of Babylon, my brother had just laughed. 'I do it,' he explained, 'because it was the very first thing I ever did on a stage. At least, the very first thing that I was paid to do on a stage.'

'And what part was that?'

'Cardinal Pandulph.'

'You were in that piece of crap?'

37

My brother nodded. 'First play I ever performed. At least as a paid player. *The Troublesome Reign of King John*, and Cardinal Pandulph was forever crossing himself. It signifies nothing.'

'It signifies Rome!'

'And does your kissing Jean signify love for her?'

'God forbid!'

'You could do worse,' my brother had said, 'she works hard.'

'Too hard!' Jean had overheard the conversation. 'I need someone to help me. One woman can't do everything.'

'She can try,' Will Kemp growled.

'Bleeding animal,' Jean said under her breath.

The superstitions, whether it was climbing the tower, making the sign of the cross, or kissing the seamstress, were hardly meaningless, because we all believed that they kept the devils away from the playhouse; the devils that made us forget our words or brought us a sullen audience or made the trapdoor in the stage stick, which it sometimes did after damp weather.

I stood for a moment longer on the tower's platform. A breeze gusted, fretting the red-crossed flag on its pole above us. I looked south and saw there was no flag and no trumpeter on the Curtain playhouse, which meant they were not even presenting a beast show on this fine afternoon. Beyond the empty playhouse, the city was dark beneath its ever-present smoke. I flinched as Will Tawyer blew another fanfare to rouse the groundlings, who dutifully cheered the sound. 'That woke them up,' Will said happily.

'It woke me up too,' I said. I stared north, past the tower of Saint Leonard's church, to the green hills beyond the village of Shoreditch where cloud shadows raced across woods and hedges. The noise of the audience rose from the yard and galleries. The playhouse was almost full, which meant the Sharers would have six or seven pounds in coins this day, and I would be paid a shilling.

I clambered down the ladder. 'Do you have a ritual?' I asked Phil.

'A ritual?'

'Something you must do before every performance?'

'I look up your skirts!'

'Besides that.'

He grinned. 'I kiss Robert's crumhorn.'

'Really?'

Robert, Phil's friend, raised the instrument, which looked like a shepherd's short crook. 'He kisses it,' he said, 'and I blow it.'

The other musicians laughed. I laughed too, then went down the stairs and saw Isaiah Humble, the bookkeeper, pinning a paper by the right-hand stage door. 'Your entrances and exits, masters,' he called, as he always did. We all knew our entrances, but it was comforting to know the list was there. It was even more comforting to see Pickles, the playhouse's bad-tempered cat, waiting by the same door. Everyone using that door had to touch Pickles to keep the demons at bay and if Pickles lashed out with a spiteful claw and drew blood, that was regarded as an especially good omen.

'I need a piss,' Thomas Pope said. He always needed a piss before a play.

'Piss in your breeches,' Will Kemp growled, as he also always did.

'Jean! Where's the green cloak?' John Duke called.

'Where it always is.'

'Sweet Jesus,' George Bryan said. He was visibly shaking, but no one tried to calm or encourage him because that would bring ill-luck, and besides, we all knew that George's whimpering nerves would vanish the moment he went through one of the stage doors, and the mouse turned into a lion.

The white-faced, red-lipped, black-eyed boys in their pretty dresses gathered by the left-hand door, their tresses bulked out with hair-rolls and ribbons. Simon Willoughby stared into a polished piece of metal nailed by that door and admired his reflection. Then Will the trumpeter, far above us, blew six high and urgent notes that sounded like a call on the hunting field. The first city church had just struck two o'clock.

'Wait,' my brother said, as he always did, and we stood silent as one after another the churches rang the hour, filling the sky with their bells. The last bell tolled, but no one moved and no one spoke. Even the waiting crowd was silent. Then, somewhere to the south of the city, a distant church sounded the hours. It tolled a good minute after all the others, but still we did not move.

'We still wait,' my brother said quietly. He had his eyes closed.

'Dear God,' George Bryan whispered.

'I really do need a piss!' Thomas Pope moaned.

'Keep the words moving!' Will Kemp snarled, as he always did. 'Keep them moving!'

And then, after what seemed an eternity, Saint Leonard's rang two o'clock. The church, just to the north of us in Shoreditch, was always the last, and the crowd, knowing that its bells were the signal for the play to begin, cheered again. Footsteps sounded above us as the musicians went onto the balcony. There was a pause, then the trumpet flourished a final time, and the two drums began beating.

'Now!' my brother said to the waiting boys, and Simon Willoughby threw open the left-hand door and the boys danced onto the stage.

We were players and we were playing.

'The fretting heads of furious foes have skill,' I said, 'as well by fraud as force to find their prey!' I spoke small, meaning I pitched my voice as high as I could and still kept it loud enough to reach the folk leaning over the upper gallery's balustrade. 'In smiling looks doth lurk a lot as ill,' I piped, 'as where both stern and sturdy streams do sway!'

In fairness I have to say my brother had not written this hodge-pudding of nonsense, though God knows he has written enough idiocies that I have declaimed onstage. We were playing *Hester and Ahasuerus*, so I was Uashti, Queen of Persia, though I was dressed in fine modern clothes, the only concession to the biblical setting being a great cloak of fur-trimmed linen that swirled prettily whenever I turned around. The cloak was a very dark grey, almost black, because I was a villainess, the heroine being the nose-picker Simon Willoughby, the plump little sixteen-year-old, who played Hester in a pale cream cloak. God only knows why the role was named Hester, because her name was Esther, but whatever she was called, she was about to become Queen of Persia in my place. The story is from the Bible, so I have no need to retell it here except to explain where the play has changed the tale. In our version, Uashti tries to poison Hester, fails, has a skin-the-cat moment of fury, then relinquishes her crown and licks Hester's plump arse, which is what I was now doing. I was kneeling to the smirking little bastard. 'Be still, good Queen,' I said, and gave the word 'still' a lot more force than it needed because Willoughby, the preening little slut, was flicking a fan of peacock feathers to keep the audience's eyes on his over-painted face, 'their refuge and their rock,' I went on, 'as they are thine to serve in love and fear. So fraud nor force nor foreign foe may stand against the strength of thy most puissant hand!'

The groundlings love this stuff. Some cheered as I prostrated myself in front of Hester, while the richer folk in the galleries clapped their hands. They knew they were not really watching a tale from the Bible. Uashti might be Queen of Persia, but she represented Katherine of Aragon, while Hester was Queen Anne Boleyn, and the whole piece was an arse-sucking flattery

41

of Elizabeth, which pretended that the popish Katherine had respected the rightful status of Elizabeth's Protestant mother. We did the play rarely because, even though audiences seemed to like the tale, it truly was dross, but when the dross is written by a royal chaplain it has to be performed now and then. That chaplain, the Most Reverend William Venables, was in the lower gallery, beaming at us, convinced he had written a masterpiece. He thought we were performing the play because of its brilliance, but in truth we were currying royal favour because the city's aldermen were having another of their attempts to close the playhouses. The Theatre was built outside the city's boundaries, so they had no authority over us, but they did possess influence. They said we were sinks of sin, and cockpits of corruption, 'which is wholly accurate, of course,' my brother liked to say.

'Thou, to a convent will conveniently convey,' my brother, playing Mordechaus, kicked me in the ribs, 'there to contemplate and in constance pray.' And with that two Persian guards wearing burgonets and breastplates and both armed with mighty halberds hauled me to my feet and took me to the tiring room. The play was ending.

'Oh, Richard,' Jean said, then tutted, 'look at your bodice. All torn! Let me pin it for you.'

'It was George Bryan,' I said, 'he bloody mauled me.'

I sometimes wonder about the Most Reverend William Venables. In the biblical story, Haman, the villain, is accused of assaulting Esther, but that wasn't good enough for the reverend, who added a scene where Uashti is half raped by the bastard. The scene made no sense because Haman and Uashti are supposedly allies, but the groundlings adored it anyway. George Bryan, all nervousness gone, had been clawing at me, much to the audience's joy. They were urging him to drag up my skirts and show them my legs, but I managed to get a knee between his thighs and jerk it up hard. He went very still, and the audience probably thought he was having a moment of even greater joy, and I pushed him off while I screamed my next line, which provoked a cheer.

The audience liked me. I knew that. I know it still. Even when I play the villain they cheer me on. There are always a few who are coarse, shouting at me to show my tits, but they are swiftly silenced by others. The coarser members of the audience have their moment at the play's end, when we perform the jig, a separate play altogether, and one designed to send the groundlings home happy. They applauded when our play ended, then shouted for the players to return to the stage. Phil and his musicians gave them a jaunty tune, but the calls for our return got louder, then there was a raucous cheer as the big central door from the tiring room was thrown open and the boys danced onto the stage.

There was a roar of welcome when Simon Willoughby joined the jig, still costumed as Queen Hester, but the roar was twice as loud when I danced onto the stage. I played to the grinning faces, whirling around at the stage's front, lifting my skirts and winking at some red-faced butcher who was gazing raptly up at me. This jig was called *Jeremiah and the Milk Cow*, and it had been written by Will Kemp, who played a soldier who had been blinded in the wars and had returned home and was searching for his wife, who had run off with a farmer played by my brother. The farmer kept offering other girls to the soldier. Jeremiah, though blind, realised none of the offered girls was his missing wife, until, in the end, my brother offered Bessie the cow, who was played by me. I made horns with my fingers, and mooed, and ran away from Will Kemp, who finally caught me by the hips, turned me about and gave a massive jerk of his loins, which got the crowd cheering again. 'I'd know this arse anywhere!' Will Kemp roared, I bellowed as he jerked again, the crowd was laughing, and Will slammed his body into mine time after time and kept shouting that he had found his wife at last. He finally let go of me and rattled off a string of bawdy jokes as I went back to join the dance with the other players. I managed to step on Simon's cloak, which made him miss his step and half fall. The playhouse does have its compensations.

'You were, you were,' the Reverend Venables had come to the tiring room after the play and now waved his hands as if he could not find the words he wanted. He was talking to all the half-undressed players. 'You were magnificent!' he said. 'Quite magnificent! Richard, my dear,' he darted at me, and, before I could evade, put his hands on my cheeks and kissed my lips, 'the best I have ever seen you! And you, dear sweet Simon,' off he went to buss Willoughby, 'I shall tell Her Majesty of your loyalty,' the reverend said, beaming at us, then looked to my brother. 'I've written another piece. *Judith and Holofernes.*'

There was a beat before my brother responded. 'I am replete with happiness,' he said drily.

'And young Richard,' the reverend's fingers brushed my shoulder, 'would be superb as Judith. While dear Simon can play her sister.'

'Judith had a sister?' my brother asked, evidently puzzled.

'She doesn't in the Vulgate,' Venables said coyly, 'but in my play? One cannot have too many darlings, can one?' He smiled at Simon, who duly wriggled and smiled back.

My brother just looked tired. 'Doesn't Judith cut off Holofernes's head?' he asked.

'With a sword!'

'Beheadings,' my brother warned, 'are monstrous difficult to do onstage.'

'But you can do it!' Venables exclaimed. 'You are all magicians. You are all . . .' he hesitated, looking pained as if he could not find the right word to do us justice, 'you are all sorcerers!'

What is it about the playhouse that turns men and women into quivering puppies? All we do is pretend. We tell stories. Yet after the play the audience lingers at the tiring-house door wanting to see us, wanting to talk to us as if we are saints whose very touch could cure their sickness. But what sickness? Dullness? Boredom? The Most Reverend William Venables was evidently entranced by us, by the playhouse, and by what he believed was some kind of benign magic. He touched my elbow. 'Dear Richard,' he murmured, 'a word?' He gripped my upper arm and pulled me towards the stage door. I resisted for a heartbeat, but for a small, thin man he was surprisingly strong, and he dragged me away as Simon Willoughby smirked and my brother looked surprised.

The reverend took me through the left-hand door onto the stage, where he stopped and gazed into the courtyard where Jeremiah was sweeping hazelnut and oyster shells from the cobbles. Pickles the cat lay in a patch of weak sunlight and began licking a battered paw. 'I hear you might leave the company,' the reverend said, 'is that true?'

The sudden question confused me. 'I might,' I muttered. In truth I had no plans, no offers of other employment, and no future. My threat to walk away from the Lord Chamberlain's Men was nothing but pique, an attempt to gain some sympathy from my brother in hopes that he would give me men's parts and a larger wage. 'I don't know, sir,' I added sullenly.

'Why would you leave?' he asked sharply.

I hesitated. 'I want to grow a beard,' I finally said.

He laughed at that. 'What a shame that would be! But I do understand.'

'You do?'

'Oh, dear boy, isn't it obvious? You're getting too old. Your voice is just passable for an older woman, but how long will that endure? And what men's parts are there for you? Richard and

45

Henry won't make way for you, will they? They are our young and handsome heroes, are they not? And Alexander and Simon are snapping at your heels, and they're both so exquisitely talented.' He gave me a pitying smile. 'Perhaps you can run away to sea?'

'I'm no sailor,' I said. I had seen the sea once, and that once was enough.

'No, you're not,' Venables said forcefully, 'you're a player and a very good one.'

'Am I?' I asked, sounding like Simon Willoughby.

'You have grace onstage, you have been blessed with beauty, you speak clearly.'

'Thank you, sir,' I said in Uashti's voice, 'but I have no beard.'

'You don't need a beard,' he said, and took my arm again, steering me towards the front of the stage.

'I can't grow one yet,' I said, 'because I still have to play the women's parts. But James has promised me a man's part soon.'

He let go of my arm. 'James Burbage has promised you a man's part?' his tone was surprisingly harsh.

'Yes, sir.'

'What part?'

'I don't know.'

'And in what play?'

He still spoke harshly, and I remembered my brother saying that it was easy to underestimate the Reverend William Venables. 'He might appear a light fool,' my brother had said, 'but he keeps his place in the royal court, and Her Majesty likes neither clergymen nor fools.'

'She doesn't like clergymen?' I had asked, surprised.

'After the way her sister's bishops treated her? She despises them. She believes churchmen stir up unnecessary trouble, and she hates unnecessary trouble. But she likes Venables. He amuses her.'

The Very Reverend William Venables was not amusing me. He was gripping my elbow again and leaning too close. I tried to pull away, but he kept hold of me. 'What play?' he demanded a second time.

'It's a wedding play,' I told him, 'for the Lord Chamberlain's granddaughter.'

'Ah! Of course.' He relaxed his grip and smiled at me. 'A new play, how exciting! Do you know who is writing it?'

'My brother, sir.'

'Of course he is,' he said, still smiling. 'Tell me, Richard. Have you heard of Lancelot Torrens?'

'No, sir.'

'Lancelot Torrens is the third Earl of Lechlade and a quite remarkable young man.' I sensed that this was why he had drawn me out onto the empty stage where no one could overhear what we said, and that impression was intensified when Venables lowered his voice. 'His grand-daddy became rich under gross Henry, gave the fat king money, and suddenly a leather merchant from Bristol is translated into an earl. Almighty God moves in a stupefying way sometimes, but I must confess young Lancelot graces the rank, and young Lancelot also has money.' He paused, smiling slyly at me. 'Do you like money, young Richard?'

'Who doesn't?'

'Your brother tells me you're a thief.'

I blushed at that. 'It's not true, sir,' I said, too forcefully.

'What young man isn't? And onstage you steal our hearts!' He smiled brightly. 'You are good.'

'Thank you,' I said awkwardly.

'And Lancelot Torrens, third Earl of Lechlade, would like to possess a company of actors, and the young man has money, a great deal of money. He would, I think, regard you as a most valued member of any company that was fortunate enough to boast of his patronage.' He watched me, waiting for me to

47

speak, but I had no idea what to say. 'He knows of you,' he added coyly.

I laughed at that. 'I'm sure he doesn't, sir.'

'And I assure you he does, or rather his man of business knows of you. I supplied him with a list of players fit for his new playhouse.'

'He has a playhouse?'

'Of course! A company needs a playhouse, and only the finest will satisfy young Lancelot. Who do you think is paying for that monstrosity on Bankside?'

I tried to remember the name of the man building the new playhouse, the one James Burbage had been worried I might have talked to. 'Francis Langley?'

'Langley has money, but if he owned every brothel in Southwark it wouldn't be sufficient. The little earl is paying.'

'Little?' I asked.

'He has beauty, but lacks stature,' the reverend explained, 'while you, my dear, have both.'

I had a sudden memory of Simon Willoughby being pinned against the palace courtyard wall as the rain fell. 'The earl,' I said, then hesitated.

'Richard?'

'Is he fair-haired?'

'Fair-haired?' The Reverend William Venables smiled seraphically. 'I should rather say that his locks were spun from the palest gold on the distaff of an angel.' So it was the Earl of Lechlade who had accosted Simon that night? I could not be sure, of course, but it seemed most likely. 'Why do you ask?' the reverend demanded.

'I wondered if I'd seen him, that's all.'

'You'd remember him if you had.'

'Are you writing for him?' I asked.

Venables looked hurt. 'Your brother won't stage any more

48

plays of mine. *Hester* brings in the crowds, but will he perform *Susannah and the Elders*? No! Or *David and Bathsheba*? No!'

'And Langley will?' I asked.

'Francis and the earl recognise quality,' he said stiffly, 'but they need other plays.' He turned to look me straight in the eyes. 'If you were to take Langley your brother's new play I think you would find that you never need steal again!'

I just stared at him, too shocked to speak.

'You should talk to Langley,' the reverend said.

I did not know what to say. His proposal was so dishonest, so shocking, that I could not find the words. A playhouse's scripts are among its most precious possessions because if another company could find a copy of a play then that company could present that play. Sometimes, when plague closed the play-houses, a company would publish one of its scripts to make some money, and then that play became the property of anyone who wanted it. That was how we had secured *The Seven Deadly Sins*. We needed to pay no money to its author, we just performed it when we liked, though too many performances would soon see an empty playhouse. If the Earl of Lechlade's company came by a copy of the wedding play, or of the new play set in Verona that my brother was still writing, they could perform the plays and so steal our audience. A play script is precious, worth eight, nine, or ten pounds each, and so they are locked safely away. To steal one would be to betray the company, and so I hesitated, stammered, and finally evaded an answer by saying I had prom-ised to stay with my brother's company through the winter.

'Promises in playhouses,' the Reverend William Venables said airily, 'are like kisses on May Day. They don't count. Go and talk to Langley.'

Because the earl had money.

And I had none.

*　　*　　*

49

I did not go to find Francis Langley. London might be a mighty city, but the players in the playhouses all know each other. I feared that if James Burbage or my brother discovered I had been talking with Langley, then their promise of a man's part in the new play might vanish like a summer mist. I was tempted, but for once I did not yield to temptation.

Then the Percies came on Monday.

We call them the Percies, but they are really Her Majesty's Pursuivants, black-dressed retainers whose job is to hunt down and root out those Roman Catholics who would slaughter the Queen and take England back to the Roman church. Their prize quarry are the Jesuits, but any Roman priest or anyone who shelters such a priest can expect the Percies to come calling and on the Monday they came to the Theatre.

We were rehearsing the *Comedy*, or, to give the play its full title, *The Comedy of Errors*. We knew the play well, but on Sunday George Bryan had tripped over the lintel of Saint Leonard's church and broken his nose. 'We are cursed,' my brother had said, delivering the news, 'first Augustine, now George.'

The rehearsal was not going well. A hired man called Robert Pallant had to take George's part. Pallant was a middle-aged man with a paunch, a spade beard, and a hangdog face. He was nervous because he was playing Egeon, a merchant, who opened the play with an immensely long speech that Pallant had memorised, but kept mangling. Everyone else was just bad-tempered. 'Let's start again,' my brother had suggested, after Pallant stammered to a halt for the fourth or fifth time.

The six players all went to the back of the stage as if they had just come through the doors from the tiring room. 'The trumpet sounds,' Alan Rust said, 'it ends, and you enter.'

Pallant walked towards the front of the stage. 'Proceed,' he began and got no further.

'Jesu! You walk as if you've got a bone up your arse!' Alan Rust bellowed. Pallant stopped and looked astonished.

'What?' he began.

'What's your first line?' Rust growled.

'Um . . .'

'Christ on his silver-painted cross! If I ever hear the word "um" on this stage I will kill! I will kill! What's your goddamned line?'

'"Proceed, Solinus, to procure my fall and by the doom of death end woes and all."'

'End our woes. Christ grant us that blessing! And to whom are you speaking? Pray tell me?'

'The duke.'

'The duke! So why are you wandering like a constipated goose to the front of the goddamned stage? The duke is there!' He pointed to my brother, who was standing on the right-hand side of the stage.

'The speech . . .' Pallant began weakly.

'I've read the goddamned speech,' Rust snarled. 'It took a week of my life, but I read it! God in His feather-stuffed bed, man! There isn't time to watch you waddle as well as listen to the endless stuff. Say the words to the duke! This is a god-damned play, not a bleeding sermon in Saint Paul's. It needs life, man, life! Start again.'

Alan Rust was new to the company. He had been playing with Lord Pembroke's men, and James Burbage and my brother had persuaded the other Sharers to let Rust join us. 'He's very good,' my brother had explained to the company, 'and the audiences like him. He's also very good at staging. Have you noticed?'

'No,' Will Kemp said. He alone among the Sharers had opposed Rust, suspecting that the newcomer had a character as forceful as his own. Kemp had been out-voted, and so Rust

51

was here to tell us what to do on the stage; where to move, how to say the words, how to do all the things that previously the Sharers had squabbled about. They still squabbled, of course, but Rust had imposed some order on the chaos.

'Jesus on his jakes,' Rust now shouted at Robert Pallant, 'what in Christ's name are you doing?'

'Going towards the duke,' Pallant said hopefully.

'You move like a constipated nun! If you're moving,' Rust spoke from the yard where the groundlings stood to watch the plays, 'then for Christ's sake move! And talk at the same time! You can do that, can't you? Go back to the duke's last line. What is it?' he demanded of my brother, who played Duke Solinus.

'"Well, Syracusian, say in brief . . ."' my brother began.

'In brief? Jesus in a rainstorm! Brief? The speech is longer than the book of Genesis! And you,' he pointed at me, 'what are you smiling at?'

'Simon Willoughby just farted,' I said.

'At least that's more interesting than Egeon's speech,' Rust said.

'I did not fart!' Simon squealed. The rest of us wore our usual clothes, but little Simon had put on a long skirt for the rehearsal. He flounced towards the front of the stage. 'I did not!'

'Can we proceed, gentlemen?' Rust asked sourly.

So we did, but slowly. I was sitting at the edge of the stage because I would not be needed for some time. I was playing Emilia, wife to Egeon. It was not a large part, my words scarcely filled a sheet of paper, but we had not performed the *Comedy* for some weeks, and I had forgotten many of the lines. '"Most mighty duke,"' I kept saying to myself, trying to relearn the words, '"behold a man much wronged!"'

'Go and mutter somewhere else,' Rust snarled at me, 'somewhere I can't hear you.'

I went to the lower gallery, where I had talked with James

Burbage. There were at least a score of people already in the gallery because the Sharers never minded folk watching the rehearsals. There were the girlfriends of some of the players, two boyfriends, and a happy gaggle of girls from the Dolphin. The Dolphin is a fine tavern which sells ale, food, and whores, and the girls earned a few pence more by selling hazelnuts to the groundlings before each performance, and then earned shillings by climbing to the galleries and selling themselves. Three of them were now giggling on the front bench, and they gave me coy looks as I settled just behind and above them. Jeremiah, the sour old soldier who guarded the front door, was fond of the girls, and had given them each a small bag of hazelnuts that they cracked under their heels while Robert Pallant laboriously told the story of his shipwreck.

The tale had always seemed most unlikely to me. Egeon, the merchant, had been at sea with his wife, his twin sons, and twin boy servants, when the ship had hit a rock and they had all been thrown into the stormy waves, and the wife, one son, and one servant had drifted one way, while Egeon, with the other son and servant, had drifted the other. It took Pallant forever to tell the story. I closed my eyes, and a moment later a voice said, 'Open your mouth.'

'Hello, Alice,' I said, without opening my eyes.

'Nut for you,' she said. I opened my mouth, and she put a hazelnut on my tongue. 'Are you a girl again?' she asked.

'I'm a woman. An abbess.'

She tucked her arm through mine and nestled into me. 'Can't see you as an abbess,' she said. It was chilly, but at least it was not raining. 'But you do look lovely as a girl,' she went on.

'Thank you,' I said, as ungratefully as I could.

'You should come and work with us.'

'I'd like that,' I said, 'but what happens when some bastard lifts my skirts?'

'Just roll over, of course,' she said.

'Your hands will be tied behind your back,' Rust shouted at poor Pallant, 'so don't gesture!'

'Does he find his wife again?' Alice asked me.

'I'm his wife,' I said, 'and yes. He finds me at the end of the play.'

'But you're an abbess! How could an abbess be married? They were nuns, weren't they?'

'It's a long story,' I said.

'But he does find her?'

'He does,' I said, 'and his long lost son too.'

'Oh good! I was worried.'

She was sixteen, perhaps fifteen or maybe seventeen, a slight girl from Huntingdonshire, with very fair hair, a narrow face, squirrel eyes, and a weak chin, but somehow the parts added up to a delicate beauty. She could play an elf, I thought, or a fairy, except the surest way to rouse the fury of the Puritans was to put a girl on the stage. They already accused us of being the devil's playthings, purveyors of evil and the spawn of Satan, and if we did not have the protection of the Queen and of the nobility, we would have been whipped out of town on hurdles long ago.

'It's so sad,' Alice said.

'What's sad?'

'That he was shipwrecked and lost his wife.'

'It's poxy stupid,' I said. 'If they'd all drifted, they'd have drifted in the same direction.'

'But it didn't happen that way,' she protested. 'Poor old man.'

'Why don't you go home?' I asked her.

'To the Dolphin?'

'No, to Huntingdon.'

'And milk cows? Churn butter?' she sounded wistful. 'I was shipwrecked. So were you.'

'By my bastard brother,' I said vengefully.

'By my bastard lover,' she echoed. She had been seduced by a charming rogue, a man who wandered the country selling buttons and combs and needles, and he had enticed her with a vision of a happily married life in London, and the silly girl had believed every word only to find herself sold to the Dolphin, in which she was half fortunate because it was a kindly house run by Mother Harwood, who had taken a liking to the waif-like Alice. I liked her too.

Hoofbeats sounded in the outer yard, but I gave them no thought. I knew we were expecting a cartload of timber to make repairs to the forestage, and I assumed the wood had arrived. I closed my eyes again, trying to remember my second line, then Alice uttered a small squeal. 'Oooh, I don't like them!' she said and I opened my eyes.

The Percies had come.

There were five Pursuivants. They strutted through the entrance tunnel, all dressed in black, with the Queen's badge on their black sleeves, and all with swords sheathed in black scabbards. Two stayed in the yard, while three vaulted up onto the stage and walked towards the tiring room. 'What the hell are you doing?' Alan Rust demanded.

They ignored him, going instead into the tiring room. The two remaining Percies stood in the yard's centre, and Rust turned on them. 'What are you doing?'

'The Queen's business,' one snarled.

They turned to look around the Theatre, and I saw the two men were twins. I remember thinking how strange it was that we were rehearsing a play about two sets of twins and here was the real thing. And there was something about the pair that made me dislike them from the first. They were young, perhaps a year or two older than me, and they were cocky. They were not tall, yet everything about them seemed too big; big rumps, big noses, big chins, with bushy black hair bulging under their black velvet caps, and brawny muscles plump under their black hose and sleeves. They looked to me like bulbous graceless bullies, each armed with a sword and a sneer. Alice shuddered. 'They look horrible,' she said. 'Like bullocks! Can you imagine them . . .'

'I'd rather not,' I said.

'Me too,' Alice said fervently, and made the sign of the cross.

'For Christ's sake,' I hissed at her, 'don't do that! Not in front of Percies.'

'I keep forgetting. At home, see, we had to do it.'

'Then stop doing it here!'

'They're horrible,' Alice whispered, as the twins turned back to stare at the girls from the Dolphin. They sauntered towards us. 'Show us your tits, ladies,' one said, grinning.

'They're not ladies, brother,' the other said, 'they're meat.'

'Show us your tits, meat!'

'I'm leaving,' Alice muttered.

The girls fled through the back, and the two young men laughed. The players, all but my brother and Will Kemp, had retreated to the edges of the stage, unsure what to do. Kemp stood at the stage's centre, while my brother had followed the Percies into the tiring room. The twins strolled towards the stage and saw Simon Willoughby in his long skirt. 'He's a pretty boy, brother.'

'Isn't he?'

'Are you a player?' one of them demanded of Simon.

'Show us your duckies, pretty boy,' the other one said, and they both laughed.

'Give us a treat, boy!'

'What,' Will Kemp demanded belligerently, 'are you doing here?'

'Our duty,' one of the twins answered.

'The Queen's duty,' the other one said.

'This playhouse,' Rust said grandly, 'lies under the protection of the Lord Chamberlain.'

'Oh, I'm terrified,' one of the twins said.

'God help me,' the other said, then looked at Simon, 'come on, boy, show us your bubbies!'

'Leave!' Kemp bellowed from the stage.

'He's so frightening!' One of the twins pretended to be scared by hunching his shoulders and shivering. 'You want to make us leave?' he demanded.

'Oh, I will!' Alan said.

One of the twins drew his sword. 'Then try,' he sneered.

Alan Rust snapped his fingers, and one of the men who had been guarding the prisoner Egeon understood what the snap meant and tossed Rust a sword. Rust, who was standing close to the bulbous twins, pointed the blade at their smirking faces. 'This,' he snarled, 'is a playhouse. It is not a farmyard. If you wish to spew your dung, do it elsewhere. Go to your unmannered homes and tell your mother she is a whore for birthing you.'

'God damn you,' the twin with the drawn sword said, but then, just before any fight could begin, the right-hand door opened and two of the three Percies who had evidently searched the tiring room came back onto the stage. One was carrying clothes heaped in his arms, while the second had a bag, which he flourished towards the twins. 'Baubles!' he said. 'Baubles and beads! Romish rubbish.'

'They are costumes,' Will Kemp snarled, 'costumes and properties.'

'And this?' the Pursuivant took a chalice from the bag.

'Or this?' His companion held up a white rochet, heavily trimmed with lace.

'A costume, you fool!' Kemp protested.

'Everything you need to say a Romish mass,' the Pursuivant said.

'Show me the nightgown!' the twin whose sword was still scabbarded demanded, and the Percy tossed down the rochet. 'Oh pretty,' the twin said. 'Is this what papists wear to vomit their filth?'

'Give it back,' Alan Rust demanded, slightly raising his borrowed sword.

'Are you threatening me?' the twin with the drawn blade asked.

'Yes,' Rust said.

'Maybe we should arrest him,' the twin said, and lunged his blade at Alan.

And that was a mistake.

It was a mistake because one of the first skills any actor learns is how to use a sword. The audience love combats. They see enough fights, God knows, in the streets, but those fights are almost always between enraged oafs who hack and slash until, usually within seconds, one of them has a broken pate or a pierced belly and is flat on his back. What the groundlings admire is a man who can fight skilfully, and some of our loudest applause happens when Richard Burbage and Henry Condell are clashing blades. The audience gasp at their grace, at the speed of their blades, and even though they know the fight is not real, they know the skill is very real. My brother had insisted I take fencing lessons, which I did, because if I had any hope of assuming a man's part in a play I needed to be able to fight. Alan Rust had learned long before, he had been an attraction with Lord Pembroke's men, and though what he had learned was how to pretend a fight, he could only do that because he really could fight, and the twins were about to receive a lesson.

Because by the time the second twin had pulled his blade from its scabbard, Alan Rust had already disarmed the first, twisting his sword elegantly around the first clumsy thrust and wrenching his blade wide and fast to rip the young man's weapon away. He brought the sword back, parried the second twin's cut, lunged into that twin's belly to drive him backwards, and then cut left again so that the tip of the sword threatened the first twin's face. 'Drop the rochet, you vile turd,' Rust said, speaking to one twin while threatening the other, and using the voice he might have employed to play a tyrant king; a voice that seemed to emerge from the bowels of the earth, 'unless you want your brother to lose an eye?'

'Arrest him!' one of the twins called to the Pursuivants. His voice was pitched too high, too desperate.

Just then the last of the Pursuivants came from the tiring room, his arms piled with papers. They were our play scripts that had been locked in the big chest on the upper floor. 'We have what we want,' he called to his companions, then frowned when he saw the discomfited twins. 'What . . .' he began.

'You have nothing,' my brother interrupted him. He looked angrier than I had ever seen him, yet he kept his voice calm.

For a heartbeat or two no one moved. Then Richard Burbage and Henry Condell both drew their swords, the blades scraping on the throats of their scabbards. 'Not the scripts,' Burbage said.

'Not anything,' Rust said, his sword's tip quivering an inch from the twin's eyeball.

'We are here on the Queen's business . . .' the Pursuivant carrying our scripts began, but again was interrupted by my brother.

'There has been a misunderstanding,' my brother said. 'If you have business here,' he spoke quietly and reasonably, 'then you must make enquiries of the Lord Chamberlain, whose men we are.'

'And we are the Queen's men,' the tallest of the Pursuivants on the stage insisted.

'And the Lord Chamberlain,' my brother still spoke gently, 'is Her Majesty's cousin. I am sure he would want to consult her. You will give me those,' he held out his hands for the precious pile of scripts. 'A misunderstanding,' he said again.

'A misunderstanding,' the Pursuivant said, and meekly allowed my brother to take the papers. The tall man dropped the costumes. He had seen the ease with which Alan Rust had disarmed one man, and he gave a wary glance at Richard Burbage, whose sword was lifted, ready to lunge. I doubted it was the swords that had persuaded him to stand down, despite Rust's display of skill. I suspected it was the mention of Lord Hunsdon, the Lord Chamberlain, which had convinced him. 'We're leaving,' he called to his fellows.

'But . . .' one of the twins began a protest.

'We're leaving!'

They took nothing with them, instead, trying to hold onto their damaged dignity, they stalked from the Theatre, and I heard the hoofbeats as they rode away.

'What in the name of God . . .' Richard Burbage began, then shook his head. 'Why would they dare come here? Don't they know Lord Hunsdon is our patron?'

'Lord Hunsdon can't protect us from heresy,' my brother said.

'There's no heresy here!' Will Kemp said angrily.

'It's the city,' my brother sounded weary. 'They can't close us because we're outside their jurisdiction, but they can hint to the Pursuivants that we're a den of corruption.'

'I should bloody well hope we are,' Will Kemp growled.

'They'll be back,' Alan Rust said, 'unless Lord Hunsdon can stop them.'

'He won't like it,' my brother said, 'but I'll write to his lordship.'

'Do it now!' Will Kemp said angrily.

My brother bridled at the aggressive tone, then nodded. 'Indeed now, and someone must deliver the letter.'

I hoped he would ask me because that would give me a chance to visit the Lord Chamberlain's mansion in Blackfriars, and it was there that the grey-eyed girl with the impish smile was employed. Silvia, I said the name to myself, Silvia. Then I said it aloud, 'Silvia.'

But my brother asked John Duke to carry the message instead.

And I went back to Ephesus to play Emilia.

THREE

IT WAS TWO weeks later that Henry Carey, Lord Hunsdon, the Lord Chamberlain and our patron, came to the Theatre himself. He did not come to watch a performance, indeed he had never seen a play in the Theatre, but instead arrived unexpectedly during a morning rehearsal. The first we knew of it was when four of his retainers, all wearing dark grey livery with the Carey badge of the white rose bright on their shoulders, strode into the yard. They wore swords, they came confidently, and those of us onstage went very still. The four men were followed by an older man, limping slightly, with a harsh, life-battered face, and a cropped grey beard. He was stocky, with a broad chest, and wore simple clothes, undecorated, but dyed a deep black, betraying their expense. He had a gold chain about his neck and a golden badge on his black velvet cap. If it had not been for the gold and the expensively dyed clothes, a man might have mistaken him for a tradesman, one who had spent his working life wrestling with timber or stone, a hard, strong man, and certainly not a man to cross lightly. 'Master Shakespeare,' he addressed my brother, 'I received your message.'

'My lord,' my brother snatched off his hat and went down onto one knee. We all did the same. No one needed to tell us who the hard-faced older man was. The badge on his retainers' shoulders told us all we needed to know. A fifth retainer, a slim man also in the dark grey livery that displayed the Carey badge, had followed the older man and now stood respectfully a few paces behind his lordship with a satchel in his hands.

'No need to kneel, no need to kneel,' Lord Hunsdon said. 'I have business in Hampstead, and thought I might as well look at the place you fellows lurk.' He turned to stare at the Theatre's high galleries. 'It reminds me of an inn yard.'

'Very like, my lord,' my brother agreed.

'So this is a playhouse, eh?' His lordship looked around with evident interest, gazing from the galleries to the stage's high canopy supported by its twin pillars. 'You think they'll last?'

'Last, my lord?'

'There were no such things when I was a young man. Not one! Now there's what? Three of them? Four?'

'I think they'll last, my lord. They're popular.'

'But not with the Puritans, eh? They'd have us all singing psalms instead of watching plays. Like those bloody Percies.'

My brother stiffened at the mention of the Pursuivants. 'We managed to avoid blooding them, my lord.'

'A pity,' Lord Hunsdon said with a grin. Simon Willoughby, wearing a skirt over his hose, had fetched a chair from the tiring house and jumped off the stage to offer it, but the courtesy only provoked a scowl from Lord Hunsdon. 'I'm not a bloody cripple, boy.' He looked back to my brother. 'There's a disgusting man called Price. George Price. He's the chief Pursuivant, and a pig in human form. Heard of him?'

'I have heard of him, my lord, yes. But I don't know him.' My brother was doing all the talking for the company. Even Will Kemp, who was usually so voluble, was stunned into silence by the Lord Chamberlain's arrival.

'He's an eager little bugger, our Piggy Price,' Lord Hunsdon said. 'He's a Puritan, of course, which makes him tiresome. I don't mind the bloody man finding Jesuits, but I'll be damned if he'll interfere with my retainers. Which you are.'

'We have that honour, my lord.'

'You're unpaid retainers too, the best sort!' Lord Hunsdon gave a bark of laughter. 'I told the bloody man to leave you alone.'

'I'm grateful to your lordship.'

'Which he might or might not do. They're an insolent pack of curs, the Percies. I suppose insolence goes with the office, eh?'

'It frequently does, my lord,' my brother said.

'And the Queen likes her Pursuivants,' the Lord Chamberlain continued. 'She doesn't want some bloody Jesuit slitting her throat, which is understandable, and Piggy Price is damned good at sniffing the buggers out. He's valued by Her Majesty. I told him to leave you alone, but the moment he smells sedition he'll let loose the dogs, and if they succeed in finding it then even I can't protect you.'

'Sedition, my lord?' my brother sounded puzzled.

'You heard me, Master Shakespeare. Sedition.'

'We're players, my lord, not plotters.'

'He claimed you're harbouring copies of *A Conference*.' The accusation was hard and sharp, spoken in a quite different tone to his lordship's previous remarks. 'He has been informed, reliably he tells me, that you distribute copies of the damned book to your audiences.'

'We do what, my lord?' my brother asked in amazement.

We are players. We pretend, and by pretending, we persuade. If a man were to ask me whether I had stolen his purse I would give him a look of such shocked innocence that even before I offered a reply he would know the answer, and all the while his purse would be concealed in my doublet.

Yet at that moment we had no need to pretend. I doubt many of us knew what his lordship meant by '*A Conference*', and so most of us just looked puzzled or worried. My brother plainly knew, but he also looked puzzled, even disbelieving. If we had been pretending at that moment then it would have been the most convincing performance ever given at the Theatre, more than sufficient to persuade the Lord Chamberlain that we were innocent of whatever sin he had levelled at us. My brother, frowning, shook his head. 'My lord,' he bowed low, 'we do no such thing!'

James Burbage must have known what '*A Conference*' was because he also bowed, and then, as he straightened, spread his hands. 'Search the playhouse, my lord.'

'Ha!' Lord Hunsdon treated that invitation with the derision it deserved. 'You'll have hidden the copies by now. You take me for a fool?'

My brother spoke earnestly. 'We do not possess a copy, my lord, nor have we ever possessed one.'

His lordship smiled suddenly. 'Master Shakespeare, I don't give the quills off a duck's arse if you do have one. Just hide the damned thing well. Have you read it?'

My brother hesitated, then nodded. 'Yes, my lord.'

'So have I. But if Piggy Price's men do find a copy here, you'll all end up in the Marshalsea. All of you! My cousin,' he meant the Queen, 'will tolerate much, but she cannot abide that book.'

The Marshalsea is a prison south of the Thames, not far from the Rose playhouse, which is home to the Lord Admiral's men with whom our company have a friendly rivalry. 'My lord,' my brother still spoke slowly and carefully, 'we have never harboured a copy.'

'I can't see why you should.' Lord Hunsdon was suddenly cheerful again. 'It's none of your damned business, is it? Fairies and lovers are your business, eh?'

'Indeed they are, my lord.'

Lord Hunsdon clicked his fingers, and the thin retainer

unbuckled his satchel and took out a sheaf of papers. 'I like it,' Lord Hunsdon said, though not entirely convincingly.

'Thank you, my lord,' my brother responded cautiously.

'I didn't read it all,' his lordship said, taking the papers from the thin man, 'but I liked what I read. Especially that business at the end. Pyramid and Thimble. Very good!'

'Thank you,' my brother said faintly.

'But my wife read it. She says it's a marvel. A marvel!'

My brother looked lost for words.

'And it's her ladyship's opinion that counts,' Lord Hunsdon went on. 'I'd have preferred a few fights myself, maybe a stabbing or two, a slit throat perhaps? But I suppose blood and weddings don't mix?'

'They are ill-suited, my lord,' my brother managed to say, taking the offered pages from his lordship.

'But there is one thing. My wife noticed that it doesn't have a title yet.'

'I was thinking . . .' my brother began, then hesitated.

'Yes? Well?'

'*A Midsummer Night's Dream*, my lord.'

'A midsummer night's what?' Lord Hunsdon asked, frowning. 'But the bloody wedding will be in midwinter. In February!'

'Precisely so, my lord.'

There was a pause, then Lord Hunsdon burst out laughing. 'I like it! Upon my soul, I do. It's all bloody nonsense, isn't it?'

'Nonsense, my lord?' my brother enquired delicately.

'Fairies! Pyramids and thimbles! That fellow turning into a donkey!'

'Oh yes, all nonsense, my lord,' my brother said. 'Of course.' He bowed again.

'But the womenfolk like nonsense, so it's fit for a wedding. Fit for a wedding! If that bloody man Price troubles you again without cause, let me know. I'll happily strangle the bastard.'

His lordship waved genially, then turned and walked from the playhouse, followed by his retainers.

And my brother was laughing.

'It is nonsense,' my brother said. As ever, when he talked to me, he sounded distant. When I had run away from home and had first found him in London, he had greeted me with a bitter chill that had not changed over the years. 'His lordship was right. What we do is nonsense,' he said now.

'Nonsense?'

'We do not work, we play. We are players. We have a play-house.' He spoke to me as if I were a small child who had annoyed him with my question. It was the day after Lord Hunsdon's visit to the Theatre, and my brother had sent me a message asking me to go to his lodgings, which were then in Wormwood Street, just inside the Bishopsgate. He was sitting at his table beneath the window, writing; his quill scratching swiftly across a piece of paper. 'Other people,' he went on, though he did not look at me, 'other people work. They dig ditches, they saw wood, they lay stone, they plough fields. They hedge, they sew, they milk, they churn, they spin, they draw water, they work. Even Lord Hunsdon works. He was a soldier. Now he has heavy responsibilities to the Queen. Almost every-one works, brother, except us. We play.' He slid one piece of paper aside and took a clean sheet from a pile beside his table. I tried to see what he was writing, but he hunched forward and hid it with his shoulder.

I waited for him to tell me why I had been summoned, but he went on writing, saying nothing. 'So what's a conference?' I asked him.

'A conference is commonly an occasion where people confer together.'

'I mean the one Lord Hunsdon mentioned.'

He sighed in exasperation, then reached over and took the top volume from a small pile of books. The book had no cover, it was just pages sewn together. 'That,' he said, holding it towards me, 'is *A Conference*.'

I carried the book to the second window, where the light would allow me to read. The book's title was *A Conference About the Next Succession to the Crowne of Ingland*, and the date was printed as MDXCIIII. 'It's new,' I said.

'Recent,' he corrected me pedantically.

'Published by R. Doleman,' I read aloud.

'Of whom no one has heard,' my brother said, writing again, 'but he is undoubtedly a Roman Catholic.'

'So it's seditious?'

'It suggests,' he paused to dip the quill into his inkpot, drained the nib on the pot's rim, then started writing again, 'it suggests that we, the people of England, have the right to choose our own monarch, and that we should choose Princess Isabella of Spain, who, naturally, would insist that England again becomes a Roman Catholic country.'

'We should choose a monarch?' I asked, astonished at the thought.

'The writer is provocative,' he said, 'and the Queen is enraged. She has not named any successor, and all talk of the succession turns her into a shrieking fury. That book is banned. Give it back.'

I dutifully gave it back. 'And you'd go to jail if they found the book?'

'By "they",' he said acidly, 'I assume you mean the Pursuivants. Yes. That would please you, wouldn't it?'

'No.'

'I am touched, brother,' he said acidly, 'touched.'

'Why would someone lie and say we had copies of the book at the Theatre?' I asked.

He turned and gave me a look of exasperation, as if my question was stupid. 'We have enemies,' he said, looking back to the page he was writing. 'The Puritans preach against us, the city council would like to close the playhouse, and our own landlord hates us.'

'He hates us?'

'Gyles Allen has seen the light. He has become a Puritan. He now regrets leasing the land for use as a playhouse and wishes to evict us. He cannot, because the law is on our side for once. But either he, or one of our other enemies, informed against us.'

'But it wasn't true!'

'Of course the accusation wasn't true. Truth does not matter in matters of faith, only belief. We are being harassed.'

I thought he would say more, but he went back to his writing. A red kite sailed past the window and settled on the ridge of a nearby tiled roof. I watched the bird, but it did not move. My brother's quill scratched. 'What are you writing?' I asked.

'A letter.'

'So the new play is finished?' I asked.

'You heard as much from Lord Hunsdon.' *Scratch scratch.*

'*A Midsummer Night's Dream?*'

'Your memory works. Good.'

'In which I'll play a man?' I asked suspiciously.

His answer was to sigh again, then look through a heap of paper to find one sheet, which he wordlessly passed to me. Then he started writing again.

The page was a list of parts and players. Peter Quince was written at the top, and next to it was my brother's name. The rest looked like this:

Theseus	*George Bryan, if well*
Hippolita	*Tom Belte*
Lisander	*Richard Burbage*

Demetrius	*Henry Condell*
Helena	*Christopher Beeston, if well*
Hermia	*Kit Saunders*
Oberon	*John Heminges*
Tytania	*Simon Willoughby*
Pucke	*Alan Rust*
Egeus	*Thomas Pope*
Philostrate	*Robert Pallant*
Nick Bottome	*Will Kemp*
Snout	*Richard Cowley*
Snug	*John Duke*
Starveling	*John Sinklo*
Francis Flute	*Richard Shakspere*
Pease-blossome	
Moth	
Cobweb	
Mustard-seede	

The last four names had no actors assigned to them, and they intrigued me. Pease-Blossome . . . Cobweb . . . I assumed they were fairies, but all I really cared about was that I was to play a man! 'Francis Flute is a man?' I asked, just to be sure.

'Indeed he is,' my brother wrote a few words, 'so you will have to cut your hair. But not till just before the performance. Till then you must play your usual parts.'

'Cut my hair?'

'You want to play a man? You must appear as a man.' He paused, nib poised above the paper. 'Bellows menders do not wear their hair long.'

'Francis Flute is a bellows mender?' I asked, and could not keep the disappointment from my voice.

'What did you expect him to be? A wandering knight? A tyrant?'

'No,' I said, 'no. I just want to play a man.'

'And you shall,' he said, 'you shall.'

'Can I see the part?' I asked eagerly.

'Isaiah is copying it, so no.'

'What's the play about?'

He scratched a few more words. 'Love.'

'Because it's a wedding?'

'Because it's a wedding.'

'And I mend bellows at a wedding?'

'I would not recommend it. I merely indicated your trade so you will know your place in society, as must we all.'

'So what does Francis Flute do in the play?'

He paused to select a new sheet of paper. 'You fall in love. You are a lover.'

For a moment I almost liked him. A lover! Onstage it is the lovers who strut, who draw swords, who make impassioned speeches, who have the audience's sympathy, and who send folk back to their ordinary lives with an assurance that fate can triumph. A lover! 'Who do I love?' I asked.

He paused to dip the quill in his inkpot again, drained the nib carefully, and began writing on the new page. 'What did the Reverend Venables want of you?' he asked.

'Venables?' I was taken aback by the question.

'Some weeks ago,' he said, 'after we performed his piece of dross, the Reverend Venables had words with you. What did he want?'

'He thought I played Uashti well,' I stammered.

'Now tell me the truth.'

I paused, trying to gather my thoughts. 'He'd heard that I might leave the company.'

'Indeed. I told him so. And?'

'He wanted me to stay,' I lied.

The pen scratched. 'He didn't suggest you join the Earl of

Lechlade's new company?' I said nothing, and that silence was eloquence enough. My brother smiled, or perhaps he sneered. 'He did. Yet you have promised me to stay with the company through the winter.'

'I did promise that.'

He nodded, then laid the quill down and sifted through the pile of papers. 'You are always complaining that you lack money.' He found the sheets he wanted, and, without looking at me, held them towards me. 'Copy the part of Titania. I will pay you two shillings, and I want it done by Monday. Pray ensure it is legible.'

I took the sheets. 'By Monday?'

'We will begin rehearsing on Monday. At Blackfriars.'

'Blackfriars?'

'There's an echo in the room,' he said, handing me some clean sheets of paper. 'Lord Hunsdon and his family are wintering in their Blackfriars mansion. We shall perform the play in their great hall.'

I felt another surge of happiness. Silvia was there! And there was a second pulse of joy at the thought of playing a man at last. 'Who is Titania?' I asked, wondering if she would end up in my arms.

'The fairy queen. Do not lose those pages.'

'So the play is about fairies?'

'All plays are about fairies. Now go.'

I went.

I enjoyed copying. Not everyone likes the task, but I never resented it. I usually copied a part I would play, and writing the lines helped me to memorise them, but I was happy to copy other actors' parts too.

Every actor received his part, and no other, which meant that for this wedding play there would be fifteen or so copied parts, which, if they were joined together, would make the whole play. Isaiah Humble, the bookkeeper, would have a complete copy, and usually another would be sent to the Master of the Revels, so he could ensure that no treason would be spoken onstage, though as our play would be a private performance in a noble house that permission was probably unnecessary. Besides, Sir Edmund Tilney, the Master of the Revels, was appointed by the Lord Chamberlain, who had already approved the play.

I worked in Father Laurence's room. He lived just beneath my attic in the Widow Morrison's house. His room had a large table beneath a north-facing window. The room was also much warmer than mine. He had a hearth in which a sea-coal fire was burning, and beside which he sat wrapped in a woollen blanket, so that, with just his bald head showing, he looked like some aged tortoise. 'Say it aloud, Richard,' he encouraged me.

'I'm only just starting, father.'

'Aloud!' he said again.

I had written down the words immediately before Titania's entrance, the last two lines that Puck said, followed by a line from a fairy whose name was not given. Then came a stage direction which brought Oberon and Titania onstage. '"Ill met by moonlight, proud Titania,"' I said aloud.

'Who says that?'

'Oberon, King of the Fairies.'

'Titania! A lovely name,' Father Laurence said, 'your brother took it from Ovid, didn't he?'

'Did he?'

'From the *Metamorphoses*, of course. And Oberon, Oberon?' he frowned, thinking. 'Ah! I remember, I had a copy of that book once.'

'A copy of what, father?'

'It's an old French tale,' he chuckled, 'Huon of Bordeaux had to fulfil some dreadful errands, rather like the labours of

Hercules, and he was helped by the King of the Fairies, who was called Oberon. Read on, Richard, read on!'

"'What, jealous Oberon?'" I read, "'Fairy skip hence, I have forsworn his bed and company.'"

I worked in Father Laurence's room because the window gave good light and because the Percies, whatever else they stole, had left the old man his ink and a sheaf of quills. Besides, I liked Father Laurence. He was ancient, gentle, wise, and had long ceased to struggle against the enmity of Protestants. 'I just want to die in peace,' he would say, 'and I'd prefer not to be dragged to the scaffold on a wicker hurdle to have my belly ripped open by some Smithfield butcher.' He was crippled, and could scarcely walk without the help of a companion. The Widow Morrison, I think, let him live rent-free, and I suspected she made confession to him too, but it was best not to ask about things like that, yet most days I would hear footsteps on the lower stairs and the creak of his door and the mutter of voices, and suspect that some person had come to confess their sins and receive absolution. The parish constables must have known too, they were not fools, but he was a harmless old man, and well loved. The new minister of the parish was a fierce young zealot from Oxford who cursed all things of Rome, but when a parishioner lay dying it was often Father Laurence who was summoned, and he would limp down the street in his ancient, threadbare cassock, and local people greeted him with a smile, all but the Puritans, who were more likely to spit as he passed. When I had money I would take him food, coal, or firewood, and I always helped tidy his room after the Percies had ransacked it. 'Read more to me,' he said now. 'Read more to me!'

"'These are the forgeries of jealousy,'" I read aloud,

'And never since the middle summer's spring
Met we on hill, in dale, forest, or mead,

74

By pavéd fountain or by rushy brook,
Or in the beachéd margent by the sea,
To dance our ringlets to the whistling wind.'

Father Laurence sighed, a small noise. I looked across the room to see his head had fallen against the high back of his chair, his eyes were closed, and his mouth open. He did not move, made no more sound, and I half started to my feet, thinking he had died. Then he spoke. '"To dance our ringlets to the whistling wind"'!' he said very softly. '"To dance our ringlets"'! Oh, how perfect.'

'Perfect?'

'I remember, when I was a very young priest, seeing a girl dance. She had ringlets too, and her name was Jess.' He sounded sad. 'She danced beside a stream did my Jess, and I watched as she danced her ringlets to the whistling wind.' He opened his eyes and smiled at me. 'Your brother is so clever!'

'Is he?' I asked dourly.

'You must be more generous, Richard. He speaks with the tongue of an angel.'

'He doesn't like me.'

'Which is sad,' Father Laurence said. 'Perhaps it's because you're young and he's not?'

'He's not old!'

'Thirty-one, you told me? He's in his middle age, Richard. And he dislikes you because you have what God never granted him. Good looks. His face is blunt, his chin weak, and his beard sparse. You, on the other hand ...' He left whatever he was about to say unfinished.

'They call me pretty,' I said resentfully.

'But pretty in a boy grows to handsome in a man, and you're a man now.'

'Not according to my brother.'

'And he dislikes you too,' Father Laurence went on, 'because you remind him of Stratford.'

'He likes Stratford,' I protested. 'He keeps telling me he'll buy property there.'

'You tell me he was born in Stratford, that he grew up and married there, but I wonder if he was ever happy there. I think he became a different man in London, and he doesn't want to be reminded of the old, unhappy William.'

'Then why would he buy property there?'

'Because when he returns, Richard, he would be the biggest man in town. He wants revenge on his childhood. He wants the respect of the town. Saint Paul tells us that when we were children we spoke as children, we understood and thought as children, but when we become men we put away childish things, but I'm not so sure we ever do put them away. I think the childish things linger on, and your brother craves what he wanted as a child, the respect of his home town.'

'Did he tell you that, father?'

He smiled. 'He doesn't visit me often, but when he does, we talk. He's an interesting man.'

'I just wish he'd help me more,' I said resentfully.

'Richard, Richard! In this life we can look to God for help, but God also expects us to look to ourselves. You must be a good player, a good man, and your brother will see it in the end. Don't look to your brother for help, be a help to him.'

I laughed at that, not because it was funny, but because I could not think what to say, then I dipped the quill in ink again and went on copying. As ever, when I used a pen, I remembered Thomas Mulliver, one of the ushers in the school at Stratford, and the man who had taught me to read and write. He carried a stick, which he rapped across our skulls if he detected inattention or a mistake. 'Writing raises us above the beasts,' he would chant. 'Are you a beast, boy?' And the stick would whistle

76

through the air, and the sharp pain slice through the skull. He liked to quote Latin to us, even though most of us struggled with the strange language. '*Audaces fortuna iuvat*,' he would chant. 'And what does that mean? It means fortune favours the brave! Are you brave, boy?' And the stick would hiss again. He was kinder in the afternoon, when his breath smelled richly of ale, and he would tell us jokes and even slip us a small coin if our work pleased him. I liked him well enough, but then he was discovered behind Holy Trinity Church with his hand up the skirt of Mistress Cybbes, wife of the bailiff, and that was the end of Thomas Mulliver.

I had followed not long after. I hated Stratford. I hated my father's sullen anger and my mother's tears. My brother had left his wife and three small children in the house, the children cried, and Anne screamed at my mother, who wept and worried. No one was happy. Bad harvests had made food cruelly expensive, the summers were wet, the winters were cold, and my father plucked me from school because, he insisted, they could no longer afford to educate me nor feed me. I was fourteen when he told me my schooldays were over and that I was to learn a trade. 'Thomas Butler has agreed you'll be his apprentice. It's a good opportunity.' Butler was a carpenter, and by becoming his apprentice I would have to live in his house and thus be one less mouth for my mother to feed. I remember my father marching me around to the Butler house on a Thursday morning. 'It's a good trade, carpentry,' he told me as we walked under the elms of Henley Street. 'The blessed Virgin's husband was a carpenter, God bless him.'

'Why me?' I asked. 'Why not Gilbert or Edmund?'

'Don't be daft, boy. Gilbert's already apprenticed. And your younger brother's not old enough. Your sister is working, why shouldn't you?'

'I don't want to be a carpenter!'

77

'Well, that's what you'll be. And be glad you can read, write, and sum! That's more schooling than most boys get. Doesn't do no harm to know your letters and numbers, and now you can learn a trade too.' I carried a bag with a change of clothes, which I clung to as my father stood in the Butler kitchen and drank a pot of ale with my new master, and as Agnes Butler, a surly creature, eyed me suspiciously. They had no children of their own, though Bess, an orphan who was just eleven years old, was their maid. She was a skinny little thing, with wide brown eyes, lank red hair, and a dark bruise on her forehead. Agnes saw me looking at her. 'Take your lusting eyes off her, boy!' she snapped. 'He must sleep in the workshop,' she added to her husband.

'He shall,' my new master said, 'so he shall.'

Then my father patted me on the head. 'He's a good boy, most of the time. Behave yourself, Richard.' And with that he was gone.

'I'll teach you a useful trade,' Thomas Butler promised me, though all he ever taught me was how to stack firewood. 'Winter's coming,' he told me, 'time to split timber and slaughter hogs.' When he deemed I had not worked hard enough, he hit me and he hit hard, sometimes using a piece of wood. He hit Bess too, and sometimes his wife, who hit back. They shrieked at each other. I hated them and missed my home. My father, when he was sober, was jovial, and my mother, when she was not distraught with worry, was loving. She had told us stories, weaving fantasies of castles and gallant knights, of animals that could talk, and of the spirits who haunted the green woodlands. I cried once after she had visited me, and Agnes Butler slapped me about the head. 'You can't go back home,' she snarled, 'we bought you! Seven years' labour you owe us, and seven years' labour you will give us.'

They fed me stale bread and weak slops, and made me sleep

in the workshop, which was a shabby, dank shed in their yard. I was locked in at night, with no candles, and forbidden to feed the small fire on which Thomas Butler melted his glue. He found the ashes warm one morning, and I was beaten for that even though I had not fed the fire, which had simply burned longer than usual. Thomas Butler had hit me, then flourished an awl in my face. 'Do that again, boy, and I'll take out an eye. You won't be so pretty then, will you?'

Seven years' labour, and it lasted three weeks.

It ended on a Saturday morning when I accidentally knocked over the glue pot. 'You little bastard,' Thomas snarled, and picked up a length of beechwood waiting by the lathe, 'I'll beat you senseless.' He ran at me, and, in panic, I snatched up a heavy wooden maul that I swung at him.

It hit. It slammed into the side of his skull, and he went down like a stunned ox. I remember he twitched among the wood shavings for a brief moment, then went still. A trickle of blood oozed from his ear, and I stood, whimpering, remembering that they hanged murderers. Thomas Butler did not move. A purse hung from his belt, and when he fell some coins had rolled out of it. Three shillings and eight pennies, which I stole. They hanged thieves too, but I reasoned they could not hang me twice.

I could not go home. The constables would look for me in Henley Street, but nor could I stay. I was not thinking properly. The panic that had made me snatch up the wooden hammer was still making me shake. I was fourteen and a murderer. So I ran. I was crying, I remember that, crying as I ran into the world.

Fate is strange, but real. I was told, much later, that I had been born under a lucky star, while my mother, God save her soul, believed the angels watched over us, one angel to every person, and my angel was watchful that morning. I fled the yard and turned north towards Warwick. Why Warwick? Perhaps because the thought of hanging was still tormenting me, and Warwick was where murderers were hanged, but within a few yards I saw Peg Quiney, a friend of my mother's who would have recognised me, and so I turned and ran the other way. I ran blindly, not stopping to catch my breath until I had crossed the bridge and was on the road to Ettington. Sheep bleated in a field beyond a ditch and hedge. Two horsemen came from the south and I hid deep in a great bunch of cow parsley. The horsemen passed without seeing me. I was shaking still, trying not to sob.

The horsemen went towards the town, and I fell asleep. That still surprises me, that in my terror I slept, and Lord knows for how long. Maybe an hour? Maybe two, but then I was woken by a dog licking my face, and I heard a familiar and friendly voice. 'Hiding, boy?' It was Edward Sales, a Stratford carrier and a kindly man, sitting high on his wagon with his two brindle horses, Gog and Magog, in the wagon's harness. The wagon's bed was heaped with sacks and crates. Edward had once carried woolsacks to London for my father, back when there was money in the house. 'Come here, Lucifer!' he called to his dog. 'I wouldn't have spied you,' he said, 'if Lucifer hadn't smelled you out.' Lucifer, a great ugly hound, looked terrifying, but I knew of old that he was more likely to lick a man to death than bite him. 'They're looking for you, Richard,' Edward went on, 'hue and cry, uphill and down dale.'

'I didn't mean to kill him,' I stammered.

'What? Kill Tom Butler!' He laughed. 'He's not dead. He'll have a pain in his skull for a month, and serve the miserable old bugger right. But you didn't kill him. He's got a noddle like an oak stump.'

'He's alive?'

'Alive and spitting curses.'

'He'll kill me if I go back,' I said.

'More than like, yes he will. Not a forgiving man, is he? Nor would I be, married to that shrew. She'd claw the eyes out of an angel, that one, then piss in the sockets.'

I climbed out of the ditch. 'I can't go home either.' I had stolen money. I was a thief, and thieves are hanged.

Ned seemed to know what I was thinking, because he grinned. 'They won't hang you, boy. Maybe brand you? A big T on your forehead? But most like your father will pay Tom Butler some silver and send you back to him.'

I hesitated for a moment, then asked the question that changed my life. 'Where are you going, Ned?'

'London, boy. Down to the big stink.'

'I have money,' I pulled two of the shillings from my pocket and brushed the sawdust from them, 'can I come?'

Ned stared at me for what seemed a long time. One of his horses, either Gog or Magog, grazed the thick roadside grass. 'He'll get wind eating that,' Ned said, and jerked a rein. 'And what will you do in London, Richard?'

'My brother's there.'

'So he is. Well, hop up, then, hop up.'

I went to London.

London!

Ever since my brother had gone to London I had been fascinated by the city, by the stories men and women told of it, and of its glory that was so much greater than Warwick or Kenilworth, let alone little Stratford. Ned Sales had often talked of it when sitting in our kitchen. 'I saw the Queen herself once,' I remember him saying, 'and she had a thousand horsemen carrying lit torches that flamed all around her. She glowed! Like a ruby, all red and shiny! Of course they cleaned the city for her,' he had chuckled. 'They hung tapestries and flags over the windows. Sometimes just bed sheets.' He had sipped his ale and looked at me. 'That's to stop folk chucking their turds and piss out the window. Wouldn't do to have a common turd spattered on Her Majesty's hair.'

'Don't talk so,' my mother had said, but with a smile.

''Tis true, Mistress Mary, I swear it.' He had made the sign of the cross, which made my mother tut, but again with a smile.

'I've never been to London,' she had said wistfully.

'It's full of strangers. From France, the Netherlands, the Germanies, even blackamoors! And the buildings . . . My sweet Lord, but you could cram all Stratford into Saint Paul's and have room left over for Shottery!'

'I worry about my Will being there,' my mother had said.

'He's thriving, mistress. I saw him last week when he gave me that missive.' Ned had brought a letter from my brother, along with two gold eagles wrapped in a scrap of linen. 'He's thriving,' he said again. 'He has silver aiglets on his laces!'

My mother had toyed with the golden coins. 'They say the plague strikes harder in London.'

Ned had made the sign of the cross again. 'Everything's bigger, better, or worse in London. That's just the way of it.'

Now, riding Ned's wagon behind the big rumps of Gog and Magog, I had a whole week to ask more questions. 'It's a dirty city, boy,' he told me as we trundled slow between wide Oxfordshire pastures and fields of growing barley, 'filthy like you've no idea. And the city smells . . . shit underfoot and smoke overhead, but there's gold between the shit and the smoke. Not for the likes of us, of course.'

'My brother sends gold . . .'

'Aye, but your Will is a clever one. He always was.'

'Mother says he should go back to his school-teaching.'

'Mothers are like that, boy. They think you mustn't rise too high in case you fall too far.'

I knew what my mother thought because I had usually

written her letters as she dictated them, and in every one she had pleaded with my brother to return to his old job as an usher in a Warwickshire school.

'But he won't,' Ned said with a grin, 'he's having a high time, he is. Just you wait and see.'

At that time my brother had lodgings in the Dolphin, the tavern just north of the Bishopsgate, and that is where Ned took me. 'I'm not letting you walk through London, boy, I'd rather let you loose in hell.' He stopped his wagon beneath the huge inn sign on which a grotesque fish leaped out of the water, and gave me the newest letter my mother had dictated, a letter that had probably been written by Gilbert or by Edmund, then tossed me one of the two shillings I had given him. 'Look after yourself, boy. It might be a grand city, but London can be dangerous.'

I jumped down from the wagon, but before I could even walk to the tavern door a man seized my arm with a grip as tight as Thomas Butler's big vice. 'Spare charity for an old soldier, master,' he said. His one hand held me, the other was groping inside my jerkin, scrabbling for a purse or trinket that might be hanging around my neck.

Ned's whip cracked, the tip flicking the man's cheek to draw an instant bead of blood. 'Leave the boy alone,' Ned growled, and cracked the whip again. 'Get inside, Richard,' he said. 'Get inside.'

I hesitated. For a heartbeat I was tempted to beg Ned to take me home. I would be beaten bloody, and I might even be branded as a thief, but I would be safe. I stood, fearful and irresolute, then remembered Thomas Mulliver hitting me with his stick as he quoted Latin, 'Audaces fortuna iuvat, you horrible child!' Fortune favours the brave, and so the horrible child turned and walked into the Dolphin.

I would stay.

*   *   *

My brother was not there. 'Don't know exactly where he is, darling,' Nell told me. She was in my brother's bed, though all I could see of her was a mass of red hair spread on a pillow. 'You're his brother?'

'Yes.'

She pulled the blanket off her face and peered at me. 'You're a pretty one. What's your name?'

'Richard.'

'And how old are you?'

I hesitated, then lied. 'Seventeen.'

'And I'm a virgin, darling,' she said with a smile. 'Have you run away from home?'

I hesitated again, then nodded. 'Yes.'

'I did that too,' she said, then yawned. 'Your brother went to some place in Sussex, darling, to play in some big house. Lord somebody or other. They should all be back tomorrow.'

I was embarrassed. By now I could see her naked shoulders and the upper swell of her pale breasts. She was pretty. She had bright green eyes, a generous mouth, and that tangle of red hair. She was probably no more than sixteen or seventeen, but she made me feel very young and very awkward. 'Do you . . .' I began, then faltered.

'Do I live here? Not in this room, darling, but his bed is a lot more comfortable than mine. I suppose you'll want it tonight?'

I did not know what to say, so instead looked around the room that was furnished with the bed, a close-stool, a clothes chest, a wide table under a north-facing window, and a solid chair. The table was covered in papers. There were three ink wells and a pewter jar holding a sheaf of quills. There was a small hearth in which there was a pile of ashes. 'I can sleep on the floor,' I muttered.

'Don't be so daft. There's room for two in the bed.' She saw me blush and laughed. 'Don't worry, darling, you can have the bed, and I'll go back to the attic.'

'You . . .' I began, and faltered again. I had been about to suggest that of course she could stay, then lost all my courage.

'Yes?' she asked, knowing full well what I had been about to say, then she laughed again, pushed the blanket away, and swung her legs to the floor. She was naked. She did it on purpose, of course, knowing that I would blush even more deeply. She pulled a robe over her shoulders and stood. 'You look like a sweet boy, Richard,' she said, not unkindly. 'When did you last eat?'

'Last night.'

'I'll take you down for some supper later, if I get a minute's peace. Now turn your back, I need to piss.' I stared at the wall, still blushing. She was a whore, of course, I knew that, but I had also been taught that whores are the devil's creatures. There were women in Stratford who were called whores, and no one mentioned them without angry disapproval, but they fascinated us boys, of course. I remember Susan Fletcher being stood up in church and accused of adultery, and I had gazed at her wide-eyed. 'Behold a depraved woman!' the Reverend Bramhall had declared. 'A creature of Satan!' But Susan did not look depraved nor satanic, she looked pretty, and she dressed like every other goodwife in Stratford, which did not stop the Reverend Bramhall from reducing her to tears with his savage preaching.

So Nell was another creature of Satan, but I had liked her instantly. More than liked her, I had hoped she would stay in my brother's bed one more night, in which hope I was disappointed, though she did feed me bread, pease pudding, and ale that afternoon. 'Isn't he a pretty one?' she asked Meg, another of the girls who lived and worked in the Dolphin. 'You should keep your teeth white, Richard,' she added to me.

'I clean them,' I mumbled.

'How? By licking them? No, darling, grind up cuttlefish bones and mix them with salt and vinegar.'

'Or soot,' Meg said, showing me her white teeth. 'Soot cleans teeth.'

'Tastes like shit,' Nell said.

'It works though!' Meg said.

'Cuttlefish bones, salt and vinegar is better,' Nell said. 'Mix it up then rub it in. Rub it hard! I expect you know how to rub, don't you?' Both girls burst out laughing, and I, of course, blushed.

My brother returned the next day. I heard his footsteps on the stairs, then the door was thrown open, and he just stopped and frowned at me. 'God in His holy heaven,' he finally said. 'What in Christ's name are you doing here?' He dropped a heavy bag onto the floor, threw his hat on the bed, and strode to the window, which he threw wide open. 'It stinks like a tannery in here. Did you empty the stool?'

'No,' I backed away from his anger, 'I didn't know where.'

'Downstairs, take the passage to the back, go into the yard and follow your nose. Rinse the bucket with water from the horse trough, then come back here and explain yourself.'

I did as he ordered, then, haltingly, nervously, explained myself. He sat at the table looking through his papers as I spoke. He had not looked at me once as I told my tale, and still he did not turn from his papers. 'You can't stay here,' he finally said, still reading.

I did not know what to say, so blurted out, 'I met Nell.'

'Nell has nothing to do with it, and when you're back in Stratford, you'll not mention her name.'

'I'm not going back!'

'You're not staying here, and you insist you're not going home,' he at last turned to look at me, 'so what are you going to do?'

'I thought you'd help me . . .'

'Don't start crying, for Jesu's sake.' He slapped his hand onto the table. 'You can't stay here. I won't abide it. You need somewhere to sleep, somewhere to eat, somewhere to learn a trade.'

'I won't be a carpenter,' I said sullenly.

'What then?' he asked, but the question seemed addressed to himself rather than to me. He gazed at me, frowning, and I thought how he had changed in the last few years. He was broader in the shoulders, his face was harder, his hair thinner, and his manner harshly decisive. 'What do you want to do?' he demanded.

'Be a player,' I muttered, 'like you.'

He laughed. 'Sweet Christ, half the idle youth in London want to be players! Are you good at it? Can you speak clearly? Dance? Fence? Tumble?'

'I can learn,' I said.

'You should have started learning eight years ago.' He turned back to his papers, then suddenly paused. 'Sir Godfrey,' he said.

'Sir Godfrey?'

He looked back at me. 'You can't stay here,' he said, 'and you insist you will not go home. So I will give you one chance. That chance is called Sir Godfrey. Do you have any baggage?'

'Who's Sir Godfrey?' I asked.

'Do you have baggage?' he asked again, irritably. I had none. 'Then follow me,' he said, and led me through the streets of London.

Chaos! That had been my impression when Ned had driven me through the crowded streets, edging his wagon past carriages and carts, and now, following my brother, who resolutely strode ahead of me, I was terrified. People! More people than I had ever seen, and the noise, as hawkers bellowed, horses neighed, and dogs howled. There were women wearing pattens that kept their shoes out of the shit, and small boys scooping up the dog turds that they would sell to the tanners who worked

87

alongside the River Fleet. A church bell tolled for a funeral. Apprentices wearing their blue caps stood at the doors of their masters' shops and watched the passers-by, accosting any who looked wealthy enough to buy their wares. They carried cudgels. Other men, wealthier, wore swords, and people made way for them. We turned down alleys, threaded streets, and my brother did not speak to me once until we reached Cheapside, a broader street, where a black-robed preacher stood on the steps of a tall stone cross and bellowed at the crowd. 'This is a mark of Satan!' he shouted. 'Papist excrement! Repent your sins and pull down this cross!'

My brother, his broad hat pulled low, stood and listened to the harangue. He seemed amused. I stood beside him, timid, listening as the angry preacher denounced all crosses as images of the devil. 'London is cursed!' the man spat. 'It allows crosses, whorehouses, and playhouses! It must be cleansed! We must be washed in the blood of the lamb.'

'Dear sweet God,' my brother said, then acknowledged my company. 'Come on, don't dawdle.' He paced on ahead of me, and I followed, not knowing where he took me, nor why. He did not speak again till we reached a tall stone house next to a small church. The house had a heavy, studded door. 'We're in Blackfriars,' he said, as if that explained everything, then rapped on the door.

A huge man, built like a bull, opened the door. He had a broad, flat face with a broken nose and scars around his eyes. He scowled at us. 'What is it?' he growled.

'Is Sir Godfrey home, Buttercup?' my brother asked.

Buttercup? I could not believe my ears, but my brother's use of the name made the huge man pause. 'I know you,' he said uncertainly.

'You do indeed,' my brother said brusquely, 'and we wish to see Sir Godfrey.'

88

The big man looked at me. He frowned. 'You'd better come in,' he said, pulling the heavy door wide.

Two minutes later I was standing in front of Sir Godfrey.

And two days later I wished I had stayed with Thomas Butler.

'You haven't written a word since Saint Leonard's struck ten,' Father Laurence chided me, 'and that must be ten minutes ago.'

'I was thinking,' I said, and dipped the pen's nib into the ink.

'I could see that. What was the last line you copied?'

'"The seasons alter,"' I read aloud, '"hoary-headed frosts fall in the fresh lap of the crimson rose."'

'Oh dear, that is a little florid,' he said with a chuckle. 'Florid, rose,' he explained the joke, then sighed when I did not smile. 'So what would you do, Richard, if you left the company?'

'Join another?'

'The Admiral's men?'

I shook my head. 'They don't need players. But I hear a new company is forming.'

'Oh?'

'The Earl of Lechlade.'

'That must be the new earl,' Father Laurence said, 'and I trust the son is not like the father.'

I turned to look at him. 'You knew his father?'

'I knew about him, and he was a very nasty man.' His claw-like hand appeared from inside the blanket and sketched the sign of the cross on his breast. 'Sins of the flesh,' he said bleakly.

'He liked women, father?' I asked with a smile.

'Women, boys, girls, children. Did he like them? He liked to hurt them. It's just rumour, of course. Perhaps I do the man wrong, but the rumours were very persistent, and the Queen banished him from court. So the son is starting a company?'

'I'm told so.'

'I wish him well. I wonder who will write his plays?'

89

'I don't know.'

'They say he's rich. His father was. Indeed, his father purchased himself out of trouble time and again, or so it was said. He's currying favour, isn't he?'

'Currying favour?'

'The new earl. The Queen loves her plays, how better to please her than by offering her a new company and new plays. Perhaps it's an opportunity for you?'

'I've promised to stay at the Theatre a few more weeks, father,' I told him, and felt a pulse of pleasure that, at last, I would play a man's part. 'And maybe I'll stay after that.'

Then I remembered that we would start our rehearsals on Monday, and those rehearsals would be in the Lord Chamberlain's great hall at Blackfriars. And my pleasure turned into excitement as I thought of Silvia, the maid. I turned the pages I still had to copy and saw a couplet that made me smile.

And thy fair virtue's force doth move me
On the first view to say, to swear, I love thee!

On Monday, I swore, the world would begin anew. I would play a man.

PART TWO

REASON AND LOVE

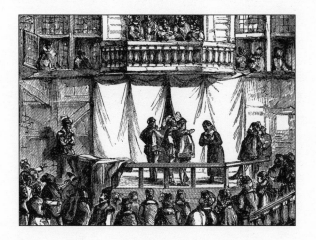

And yet, to say the truth, reason and love keep little company together nowadays.

A Midsummer Night's Dream
Act III, Scene 1, line 138

FOUR

I PREPARED CAREFULLY on Monday. I woke early and felt a shiver of anticipation, not just because I was at last to start rehearsals for a man's part, but because we would be rehearsing at the Lord Chamberlain's mansion in Blackfriars, and that was where Silvia worked. I tried to summon a picture of her in my imagination, but though I could remember her grey eyes, her wide mouth, her light brown hair, and her mischievous smile, I could not see the whole face. My mind would not make the picture, yet today I might see her again. Silvia!

I washed with a damp cloth, then cleaned my teeth, rubbing the cuttlefish bone paste so hard that my gums bled. I wore clean linen, newly washed by Agnes the maid, who blushed every time she met me on the stairs or in the kitchen at the back of the Widow Morrison's house. Agnes was a year or two older than me, with pock-marked skin, scrawny brown hair, and a limp. I sometimes helped her carry water from the parish pump, and she would stutter thanks and blush scarlet.

I wore my cleanest stockings, dark grey, gartered with ribbons of white silk, and over them a pair of black padded breeches that I had borrowed from the Theatre's tiring room.

All black clothes were expensive because of the dye, and my breeches were handsome, though they had been much mended and sometimes patched with a dark blue cloth which was almost black. I wore a clean white linen shirt, and over it a doublet of grey and yellow stripes, the sleeves laced to the shoulders with white string, tipped with silver points. Silver aiglets! I smiled as I remembered Ned the carrier telling my mother about my brother's silver aiglets, though doubtless his points had been honestly bought, while mine were stolen from the tiring room. The doublet, like the hose, belonged to the Theatre, and I hoped the Sharers had forgotten all about the garments, just as I hoped they had forgotten about the sleeveless mustard-coloured jerkin, decorated with a row of silver buttons, which I wore over the doublet. The buttons were purely for show because the jerkin was worn loose, and above it I laced a white falling band instead of a ruff. I brushed dust from a wide-brimmed hat of dark grey felt, buckled a black leather belt about my waist, and hung my sheathed knife beside the buckle, then pulled on my best boots, which were knee-high to keep the mud from the hose.

'Good Lord above!' the Widow Morrison said when she saw me in the kitchen. 'Look what the cat threw up! Are you off to a wedding, Richard?' She reached out and straightened the falling band. 'Getting married, are you?'

I put a shilling on the table. 'I know I owe you more,' I said.

'You do.' The shilling vanished like magic. 'You could pawn those clothes, Richard.'

'He looks nice,' Agnes muttered.

'I don't know how he can afford to look nice,' the widow said. 'He can't pay his rent, but he can dress up. I suppose you want a crust too?' she said to me. 'Wouldn't want you dying of starvation before you've paid me, would I?'

'Please,' I said humbly.

The widow cut a piece of bread. 'You rehearsing today?'

'At the Lord Chamberlain's house,' I said casually, as though I rehearsed there every day. 'At his mansion in Blackfriars.'

'Oh!' She brightened. Any mention of the aristocracy got the widow's attention, while an account of a performance before the Queen was worth a whole week's rent. 'That's nice, dear,' she said, and rewarded me by slathering some dripping onto the bread. 'You'll have to tell me all about it.'

'He's the Queen's cousin,' I said, pushing my advantage.

'I know that, dear,' she said. The Widow Morrison is a striking-looking woman, black-haired, and brusque, who had been married to a player. 'I met his lordship,' she said, 'when my husband was alive, God rest his soul.' She made the sign of the cross. 'A very gracious man, he was.'

'Your husband?'

'Of course he was gracious. Goodness, I look at these new players and wish to God my Mister Morrison was still alive. He could set the stage on fire with a gesture.' She sniffed. 'And his voice! He could summon an angel from heaven with that voice. None of this shuffling and mumbling that passes for playing these days. And his lordship was gracious too. And thank you for the rent, dear.'

I had delivered the copied part of Titania to my brother the day before, and, to my surprise, he had given me the promised two shillings without needing to be asked. He had leafed through my work first and had grunted approval. 'You copy well,' he had said, and then, surprisingly, he had asked whether I had liked what I had copied. I doubt he truly cared about my opinion, but had just wanted to hear something complimentary.

'I did,' I said, then remembered Father Laurence's advice to be kinder to my brother. 'I especially liked ...' I began, but faltered.

'Yes?'

'"To dance our ringlets to the whistling wind,"' I quoted.

He had smiled at that. 'Sometimes,' he said, 'the words come and you have no idea where they come from. I like that line too.' He added my copied pages to the stack of papers on his table. 'Thank you, and I shall see you tomorrow.'

I had pointed at the papers. 'Is Francis Flute's part there?'

'All the parts are there.'

'Please, can I see it?'

'You can see it tomorrow,' he had said, and his voice was back to its usual curt tone, 'and don't be late.'

Be late? With Silvia at Blackfriars? If I could, I would have walked to Blackfriars on Sunday and waited all night for another glimpse of Silvia, but instead I was up early on Monday, and now, dressed to impress, I thanked the widow, took the offered bread and dripping, swallowed some weak ale, and hurried out. I jumped the sewer ditch without falling in, then followed the path beaten by playgoers across Finsbury Fields, where the windmills creaked to a small southerly wind. The day was cold, but the sun was shining, and that seemed a good omen. Laundresses had draped heavy flax sheets across the ground to dry, the sheets guarded by small boys with big dogs. There was a thick haze of smoke above the city, as there always was, but the sun still cast sharp shadows from the Moorgate's battlements. Once through the gate I had to walk more slowly because the streets were crowded. My borrowed finery made me look wealthy, and apprentices shouted at me, offering me silver plate, linen, saddlery, gloves, or fine French lace. I ignored them, walking the city confidently, but always remembering my constant fear when I had first arrived. No one accosted me now, no one threatened me, because after seven years I had become a Londoner. I had a Londoner's eye for the newcomers, who clutched their purses too tightly and looked around with nervous eyes. They shrank from the beggars, many of whom were grievously wounded from the wars in Ireland or the Low Country, and almost all of them starving.

It was a long walk. The Theatre lay to the north of the city on its eastern side, while Blackfriars was on the river close to the western walls. I hated Blackfriars, and, after skirting the looming bulk of Saint Paul's, I walked down to Carter Lane and spat towards Addle Hill. That was where Sir Godfrey lived, in his great stone house next to Saint Benet's church. One day, I dreamed, I would have the pleasure of sliding a blade into his belly. I thought of that often, thought of watching his terrified eyes as I ripped the blade upwards, thought of him begging me for forgiveness, and of my smile as I refused to spare him. Then I forgot all about Sir Godfrey as I turned down Saint Andrew's Hill to where the Lord Chamberlain had his city mansion. The great house had once been a monastery, and stood on the western side of the street, just above the river. I had not been to the house before, but it was not difficult to find because a great stone rose, painted white, was carved above the main gate that was crowded with petitioners and guarded by two liveried men carrying halberds. One of the guards accosted me after I had made my way through the clutching hands of the beggars. 'Where are you going?' he demanded.

'I am . . .' I began.

'Are you one of the players?' he interrupted me. He was a grim-looking beast, his bearded face framed by a close-fitting helmet.

'I am.'

'Then go round the back, lad.' He sneered as he looked me up and down, plainly unimpressed by my fine clothes. 'Round the back,' he said again, very slowly. He shifted his weight, and the halberd's blade reflected the sunlight. 'There's a servants' entrance in Water Lane,' he added, jerking his helmeted head, 'and that's where you're going.'

I turned, but was again interrupted. 'We are his lordship's retainers!' a voice boomed. 'We enter his lordship's house as we wish, where we wish, and by what gate we wish.' It was Alan Rust, who now seized my arm and turned me back towards the imposing archway.

'You will . . .' the grim guard began.

'Inform his lordship of your impudence,' Rust finished the sentence for the guard. 'Your name, fellow?' Both guards looked confused. 'We are summoned, fellow,' Rust said to the man who had turned me away, 'we are summoned by his lordship, who will not be best pleased when he hears you have detained us. The gate, if you please!' He pointed to a small wicket gate set in one of the two massive leaves. 'Now, fellow! Now!' He used his tyrant king voice, and the grim-faced guard hurried to open the wicket gate rather than argue. 'Go ahead, Master Flute,' Rust ordered me.

I stepped through into a sunlit courtyard. Alan Rust followed, letting the guard close the wicket gate behind him. He was smiling. 'That was what I call an entrance,' he said. 'Use a servants' gate in Water Lane indeed! Who does he think we are? His lordship's scullions? Now where the hell do we go?'

I could see only one door into the mansion from the courtyard, and I pointed to it. 'There, I suppose.'

'I suppose so too.' He crossed the cobbled yard. 'The sun shines! I'd forgotten what it looked like. Sunlight and no rain!'

'No rain,' I agreed happily. The summer and autumn had been cold and wet, which meant the harvest had again been meagre. Folk were starving, and I had heard muttering in the streets about ransacking the homes of the rich. Prices were rising, and there were rumours that one London riot had already been savagely suppressed by troops and the ringleaders summarily hanged. Yet the playhouses were still full.

The door, set in an imposing archway approached by a brief flight of stone steps, was bolted. Alan Rust beat on it with his fist, then looked me up and down. 'I see you've dressed for the occasion, Richard?'

'It seemed polite,' I said vaguely.

'Polite!' He sounded amused. 'God send us all such courtesy. Where are these bloody people?' He hammered on the door again, and still no one answered. 'You must be happy to be playing Francis Flute.'

'Very.'

'It's a good part,' he said enthusiastically.

'He's a lover, my brother tells me?' I said, making it into a question in hope that he could tell me more about the character.

'Flute is a lover indeed,' Rust said gravely, 'and if the play were not a comedy we might almost say he is a tragic lover.'

'Tragic?' I was intrigued.

Rust beat on the obstinately closed door. 'Are they all asleep?'

And just then we heard bolts being shot back. The door opened, and a nervous woman peered out. 'Masters?' she asked.

'We are summoned to the great hall, woman,' Rust said grandly.

'Yes, master,' she said, and pulled the door fully open. She was an older woman carrying a birch-twig broom, and, seeing my clothes, she bobbed me a curtsey.

'And where is the great hall, my good woman?' Rust demanded, stepping through into a large stone-flagged chamber hung with tapestries.

'Straight on, master,' the woman said, pointing to a wide passageway. 'Down there.'

'We shall remain for ever in your debt,' Rust said, and led me down the passage, which ended at a large double door. He threw both leaves open, then stopped abruptly. 'My,' he said after a long pause. 'Oh my!' We had reached the great hall, and were evidently the first of the company to arrive. 'Oh my!' Rust said again.

The hall was vast, shadowed and grand. Elegantly curved oak beams supported the high roof, each beam decorated with carved roses painted white and edged with gold leaf. The walls were panelled, and hung with great tapestries showing hunting scenes, and between the tapestries were ancient swords, spears, and axes, all hung to make patterns.

We had entered on one of the hall's long sides. Opposite us was a gaping hearth, the jambs and mantel shelf were of carved white marble surrounding a fire-blackened space in which an ox could have been roasted. No fire burned there, there were just two enormous black iron firedogs, which stood in a great pile of ash. In the centre of the hall was a long table surrounded by high-backed chairs. I counted them; thirty-six, while to our left was a minstrels' gallery, beneath which a pair of doors led into the rest of the mansion. At the opposite end of the hall, facing south, was a big oriel window that jutted out from the panelled wall and was reached by a pair of carved wooden staircases. 'That must overlook the river,' Rust said. There was a cushioned seat the width of the oriel, which was the only window in the cavernous hall. 'Only one window?' Rust said. 'Think what they must spend on candles!' He walked to the dark space beneath the minstrels' gallery, where he turned to look down the length of the hall. 'Let there be light!' he said loudly, then grunted. 'There's an echo. Still, fill the place with wedding guests and it won't be so bad. Have you ever performed in a wedding play?'

'No.'

'I hate them,' he growled, 'hate them.'

'Why?'

'Because the audience is drunk, that's why. The bastards start drinking in the forenoon, and by the time we play in the evening they're either tottering or stupefied. It's like playing to a room full of farting corpses.' He walked the length of the hall, his footsteps loud on the flagstones, then climbed the brief stairs to the oriel window through which he stared into the smoke-hazed sunlight above the Thames. 'And they're privileged, Richard. You can't tell them to be quiet. If they're bored they'll talk the whole play long. The only thing that keeps them quiet is if the Queen is present and enjoying the play. Then they'll be quiet.'

'Will the Queen be here?'

He shrugged. 'Who knows? She's Lord Hunsdon's cousin, so maybe. I hope so, I can't abide performing to a hall full of chattering lordlings.'

'Why hire us if they don't watch us?' I asked.

'To show they can afford us, of course. We are pearls cast before sleeping swine.'

I followed him up the stairs. Sunlight glittered on the river that was thick with watermen's wherries. A big sailing barge was headed downstream, presumably bringing grain or vegetables from far inland. Swans paddled between the craft. On the southern bank I could see the bull-baiting arena, which looked uncannily like the Theatre, while to the west was the new playhouse that was being built by Francis Langley. The building loomed over the small houses on the river's south bank, yet its flintstone walls were still unfinished and were surrounded by a dense web of wooden scaffolding. 'Just look at the size of it,' Rust said scornfully. 'It's going to take three thousand people to fill that!'

'He'll need players,' I said, thinking of my conversation with the Reverend Venables.

Rust appeared not to hear me. He was gazing at the far scaffolding. 'Twenty years ago,' he said ruminatively, 'there wasn't a playhouse in London. Nor anywhere else either. We played inn yards, three a week. Monday in Gloucester, Wednesday in Worcester, Saturday in Warwick, and the same piece of rubbish could be played in all three places. Now we play to the same audience week after week after week, and we need what? Thirty, forty plays a year? Where's Langley going to find them? He doesn't need players, players are a dozen a groat, he needs men who can write plays, and those men don't grow on trees. If you want to make money, son,' he punched me lightly on the arm, 'don't waste your time prancing about onstage, write the damn plays! That's where the money is.'

'I can't write.'

'Thank Christ your brother can. I just wish he'd write more. The beast has to be fed.'

'The beast?'

'The playgoers. The great mongrel beast that always wants something new.'

The other players were arriving now, coming through the doors beneath the minstrels' gallery. I heard their exclamations of awe as they looked about the great hall. Kit Saunders and Simon Willoughby climbed onto the long table and danced up and down its length, linking arms and whirling about, laughing whenever they almost fell off. Isaiah Humble, the bookkeeper, was shuffling papers at the table's end and gave a feeble protest when Simon Willoughby danced too close to his carefully arranged piles. Alan Rust went down to join my brother and Will Kemp, who were standing beside the dead fire, heads together, where a dignified grey-haired man in the white rose livery of Lord Hunsdon had joined them. The man turned to frown at Kit and John. 'Now, my young masters,' he said sternly, 'that table is polished. Have a care of it!'

'He means get your poxy feet off the table,' Will Kemp growled.

I watched the two boys from the oriel's height and felt a surge of pleasure. At last I was to play a man! I was no longer a boy. I was a player, a man, one of the Lord Chamberlain's Men! Till now I had been neither fish nor fowl, neither an apprentice nor a proper hired man. I had simply been tolerated as the younger brother of a Sharer, but now I had a real part, and I went down the short stairs determined to show I was worthy of the trust. I would make the Sharers value me.

'We need candles,' Isaiah Humble said tentatively, 'if it's possible? Sorry, but it's very dark.'

'Candles are coming,' the liveried man said. He wore a dark grey robe trimmed with fur, and had a chain of office about his neck.

'And a fire?' my brother asked. 'It's cold.'

'I'm sure his lordship will allow you a fire.'

'I thank you,' my brother said, then slapped the table to gain everyone's attention. 'Seat yourselves, seat yourselves! And thank you all for being here so early in the day.' A murmur of laughter sounded. The company was seating itself, the Sharers at one end, the boys at the other, and the hired men in between. I sat between John Duke and John Sinklo, both hired men. 'I wanted us to meet here,' my brother continued when the scraping of chairs had ended, 'so that you can see our playing space. It will look quite different, of course. His lordship has given us permission to make a stage.' He turned and looked at the grey-haired man in Lord Hunsdon's livery, who nodded affirmation. 'Let me name Walter Harrison, his lordship's steward, who will look after his lordship's interests while we are here. You wish to say something?' he asked the steward.

Harrison had remained standing beside the hearth, but now stepped forward and looked at us sternly. 'His lordship welcomes you,' he began, 'and you have the free use of this hall for your practices.'

'Rehearsals,' John Sinklo said irritably, but not loud enough for the steward to hear.

'You will come and go through the Water Lane gate,' Harrison went on, 'and you will approach the hall through the scullery passage, not by the main passage as some of you did today.'

'Guilty,' Alan Rust said cheerfully.

'The scullery passage brings you to those doors,' Harrison pointed to the two doors beneath the musicians' gallery. 'Behind those doors there are stairs to the minstrels' gallery and you may use those. I understand you wish to use the gallery too?' he asked my brother, who nodded. 'And that is all,' Harrison said very firmly. 'You can use the stable yard, the scullery passage, the hallway beyond those doors, the gallery, and this hall. The rest of the house is forbidden to you.'

'So where do we piss?' Will Kemp asked brusquely.

'The stable yard,' Harrison said.

'What do we use for a tiring room?' George Bryan asked with a frown. His broken nose was mended, though it was still swollen and the bruising had not quite subsided.

My brother answered. 'His lordship has agreed that we can make a new wall beneath the gallery, so much of the space beneath the gallery will become our tiring room. The stage will be in front of that new wall. There will be three doors. A large central door, and two smaller ones flanking it.'

'Just like the Theatre,' John Heminges put in.

'Just like the Theatre,' my brother agreed.

'It's a big play,' Will Kemp intervened, standing up to address us all. He liked to show his authority. He was a Sharer, of course, and my brother had talked quite long enough for Will's taste. 'There are a lot of parts. That means some of you will be sitting around with nothing to do but fart while others rehearse, and you'll keep yourselves quiet! I'm looking at you apprentices . . .'

'May I?' Walter Harrison looked enquiringly at my brother, but it was Will Kemp who answered.

'Speak, master steward!'

'His lordship,' Harrison said, 'has given instructions, very strict instructions, that none of the household are to witness your practices. He and her ladyship have read the play, of course, and they like it, but he wishes it to be a surprise to the rest of the household on the day of the wedding. I know the Lady Elizabeth came and talked to you at the Theatre, but she doesn't know what the play is about and she mustn't know. If you see any servant listening, perhaps from the gallery, you will ask them to leave. You will insist that they leave,' he said forcefully, and I grimaced. I had dressed carefully in hope of seeing Silvia, Elizabeth Carey's maid, but it seemed that hope was vain. 'The only exceptions,' the steward went on, 'are the tutors who will accompany the small boys.'

'Small boys?' Will Kemp asked in a horrified voice.

'There'll be music,' my brother said, 'and his lordship's choristers will sing as a fairy choir.'

'God bloody help us,' Will Kemp growled.

'Does the fairy choir dance?' Ralph Perkins, who trained the dancers at the Theatre, asked.

'They will dance, Ralph, and you'll show them how. Now,' my brother took a step forward, subtly asserting his authority over Will Kemp, 'we don't have all the time we'd wish because we need to be at the Theatre just after midday, but we'll read as far as we can. You may keep your parts, keep them and learn them.'

'Con them well,' Will Kemp snarled.

'And do not lose the parts,' my brother also snarled.

'Say what the play treats on,' Will Kemp, still standing, said to my brother.

'It's a wedding play,' my brother said, 'and all the action takes place during one night in Athens.'

'Athens?' George Bryan asked. He frowned. 'Why Athens?'

'Because it doesn't bloody rain in Athens,' Will Kemp said.

'It rains everywhere.'

'Is Athens in France?' Simon Willoughby asked.

My brother thumped the table to stop the chatter. 'We'll begin by fitting the play,' he said, meaning we would start by giving each player his part, 'and the tale begins in the palace of Theseus, Duke of Athens, who is marrying Hippolyta, Queen of the Amazons.'

'That's me,' Thomas Belte said brightly from the apprentices' end of the table.

'Mister Humble, please?' my brother said, and Isaiah carefully selected two sheaves of paper from the pile on the table and placed the first in front of George Bryan. All of us tried to judge from the number of pages how large the part of Theseus was. It looked substantial.

'I have to learn all this?' George said, looking through the pages.

'Unless you'd rather play Mustard-Seed?' my brother said.

'I'm Queen of the Amazon,' Thomas Belte, a skinny freckled boy, said happily as Isaiah gave him a thinner sheaf.

It took some minutes to distribute the parts, and as they were placed on the table my brother described the play, which, to me, sounded very tangled. There was the duke and Hippolyta, who were getting married, and then two pairs of lovers from Duke Theseus's court. One of the two girls, Hermia, which was Kit Saunders's part, was supposed to marry Demetrius, who would be played by Henry Condell, but was really in love with Lysander who was Richard Burbage. Meanwhile Helena, now played by Alexander Cooke, was also madly enamoured of Lysander, and all four lovers wander into a moonlit wood where they become even more confused by a magical potion given to them by Alan Rust, playing a character called Puck, who, in turn, served Oberon, King of the Fairies, who was John Heminges.

Richard Burbage was leafing through his part, which,

naturally, looked large. 'Why do we go into the wood, Will?' he asked.

'You're eloping with Hermia.'

'And this fellow Puck does what?'

'Causes confusion.'

'Shouldn't I play Puck?' Will Kemp demanded.

'No,' my brother said shortly. 'Meanwhile,' he went on, 'a group of Athenian tradesmen also go to the wood to rehearse a play which they hope to perform before the duke on his wedding night.'

'It's a busy wood,' Will Kemp growled.

'Why don't they rehearse in a barn?' George Bryan asked plaintively. 'Or at home? Why go to a wood?'

'It's all explained in the play,' my brother said patiently.

'Which we'd like to know about,' Alan Rust snarled, 'so will you all be quiet and let Will tell us?'

My brother continued, explaining how Nick Bottom, a weaver played by Will Kemp and one of the tradesmen, was transformed into an ass, and Titania, the Queen of the Fairies, played by Simon Willoughby, fell in love with him thanks to Puck's magical potion. My brother described all this, and I tried to sort out the different stories and also listened for any mention of Francis Flute or the woman he loved. I heard nothing that enlightened me, and supposed I must wait until I received my part.

We paused as two servants brought candles, which were placed along the table and lit so that we could read the pages. Walter Harrison, the steward, nodded approval when the candles were burning. 'We shall leave you alone,' he said, and ushered the two serving men from the hall.

'Now for the mechanicals,' my brother said.

'"Mechanicals"?' Will Kemp interrupted. 'What in God's name are "mechanicals"?'

'They're tradesmen of Athens,' my brother said curtly. 'I shall play Peter Quince, a carpenter.'

'Wasn't there a Peter Quince with a workshop in Cow Lane?' John Heminges asked.

'There was,' my brother said. 'Will, you already have Bottom's part, yes?'

'He was a carpenter,' John Heminges said.

'He was a wheelwright!' Henry Condell corrected him. 'It was his brother James who was the carpenter.'

'They both died of the plague, God rest them,' John Heminges said.

'Have you finished?' Will Kemp glared at them. 'And yes, Will, I've got the part.' He flourished some sheets of paper.

'Richard,' my brother looked at Richard Cowley, not at me, 'you'll play Snout, a tinker.' He waited as Isaiah put Snout's part in front of Cowley. 'John?' he looked at John Sinklo next to me, 'you're Robin Starveling, a tailor.'

'Starveling!' Simon Willoughby said, and laughed. The name fitted, because John Sinklo was impossibly thin.

'John Duke?' my brother looked around the table. 'There you are. You're Snug, a joiner.'

Isaiah put a single sheet of paper in front of John Duke. Someone sniggered, and John Duke, one of the hired men, frowned. 'It's a very small part,' he said plaintively.

'A lot of it is extempore,' my brother said, 'you'll be roaring.'

'Roaring?' Duke was puzzled.

'I can roar!' Will Kemp put in eagerly, and immediately demonstrated by roaring like a mad beast. Simon Willoughby giggled and tried to roar himself.

'Enough!' My brother slapped the table. 'Snug roars, and only Snug!' He glared at Will Kemp, who just grinned back. 'And the last of the mechanicals,' my brother went on, 'is Francis

Flute, a bellows mender. And that part,' he smiled at me, he actually smiled, 'that part is all yours, Richard.'

Isaiah put the last sheaf of papers in front of me. There were four or five sheets, and that meant it was a substantial enough part, and certainly a lot longer than some of the other mechanicals. My brother began to explain the play's first scene, which was set in Theseus's palace, but I did not listen. Instead I was eagerly reading Flute's opening lines, looking for the character with whom I would fall in love. This was my first proper part as a man! I was excited.

Then I came to Francis Flute's third line, and my heart sank. I just stared. For a moment I could not believe what I was seeing, then I looked back to the top of the page and read the opening cues and lines again. The bastard, I thought, the utter bastard!

'So let's begin,' my brother said, 'George? You have the first line.'

The bastard!

I wanted to stand up and walk out. Instead I sat seething. The play's opening droned past me with the usual long speeches. 'Full of vexation,' I heard Thomas Pope say, and that was nowhere near strong enough to describe how I felt. I was full of vexation and humiliation, I was angry and scorned. Get up, I told myself, stand up and walk away, but a common loaf was a whole penny these days, and I needed money. I had to endure the scorn or starve.

The play went on. No one seemed particularly excited by what they were hearing. The duke threatened to kill Hermia if she refused to marry Demetrius, but what did I care? I knew my face had reddened, I was staring at the page on the table, not daring to look up and catch my brother's eye.

'"Is all our company here?"' my brother's voice broke in.

"'You were best to call them generally, man by man, according to the scrip,'" Will Kemp, playing Nick Bottom, at last put some energy into the reading. Men perked up, looking forward to Will Kemp's wit. I guessed my part was coming and so kept my eyes on the first line on my first page.

"'Here is the scroll,'" my brother read, "'of every man's name which is thought fit through all Athens to play in our interlude before the Duke and the Duchess, on his wedding night.'"

"'First, good Peter Quince,'" Will Kemp interrupted vigorously, "'say what the play treats on, then read the names of the actors, and so grow to a point.'"

Men laughed, because Nick Bottom's interruption and harrying of Peter Quince was so like the way Will Kemp interrupted and harried the other Sharers whenever we rehearsed a play. Kemp understood the joke and grinned, 'Grow to a point, Will!' he called.

"'Marry!'" My brother was also grinning, taking energy from Will's enthusiasm, "'Our play is *The Most Lamentable Comedy, and Most Cruel Death of Pyramus and Thisbe.*'" This time the laughter was louder, the players around the table were enjoying the dialogue.

The Most Lamentable Comedy, and Most Cruel Death of Pyramus and Thisbe was the play that the tradesmen of Athens wanted to perform for the duke's wedding. It would doubtless prove a mockery of the sort of performance that we had all witnessed from tailors, carpenters, and ploughmen putting on an entertainment of a winter's night back home.

"'A very good piece of work, I assure you,'" Will Kemp said heartily, "'and a merry! Now, good Peter Quince, call forth your actors by the scroll. Masters, spread yourselves!'"

"'Answer as I call you,'" my brother said. "'Nick Bottom, the weaver?'"

I knew my lines must come soon. I stared at the paper.

All around me men were laughing as Will Kemp delivered a bombastic speech. Nick Bottom had the part of Pyramus in the play the mechanicals would perform, but was pleading with Peter Quince to be given an even more heroic part. Men grinned, recognising that Nick Bottom was a portrait of Will Kemp, and Kemp himself enjoyed the jest. "'This is Ercle's vein,'" he finished, "'a tyrant's vein. A lover is more condoling!'"

"'Francis Flute?'" my brother said, "'the bellows mender?'"

That was the first line on my sheet of paper.

"'Here, Peter Quince,'" I read lifelessly. The Sharers were looking at me, grinning in the candlelight. They knew what was coming.

"'Flute,'" I could hear the suppressed amusement in my brother's voice, "'you must take Thisbe on you.'"

"'What is Thisbe?'" I read, still tonelessly, "'a wandering knight?'"

"'It is the lady Pyramus must love,'" my brother said, unable to hide his amusement, and with those words the whole room burst into raucous laughter.

'Oh, that's good, Will, that's very good!' John Heminges said.

"'It is the lady Pyramus must love!'" Simon Willoughby squeaked, and I could have throttled the little turd.

'Speak up, Thisbe,' Will Kemp said with savage enjoyment, 'let's hear you!'

"'Nay, faith,'" I read, "'let me not play a woman.'" And at that line they all started laughing again. I waited, but the laughter did not stop, so I raised my voice angrily to finish the line. "'I have a beard coming.'"

'He's got a beard coming!' Simon Willoughby crowed.

"'That's all one,'" my brother did not look at me as he spoke his lines, "'you shall play it in a mask, and you may speak as small as you will.'"

'In a mask!' Richard Burbage said, covering his face with his hands to imitate the masks high-born women wore to prevent the summer sun darkening their skin.

'And speak small, Richard!' Simon Willoughby shrieked happily. 'Speak small!'

'You're playing a man,' Rust said, 'you always wanted to!'

'Who plays a woman,' Simon Willoughby said, just in case anyone around the long table had failed to see the jest.

Will Kemp, or rather Nick Bottom, interrupted to demand that he play Thisbe instead of me, and that started yet more merriment, because Kemp was famous for wanting to play other parts beside his own. The company was beginning to enjoy the play, and there was a growing excitement in the room as it continued, but I just sat simmering with an angry resentment. Alan Rust was right, I was playing a man, but the man I played had to pretend to be a woman. And there was nothing I could do about it.

I had been cozened by my grinning brother.

Then, as the rehearsal broke up, I thought there was something I could do about it.

We never finished reading the play that day, time was too short. As the city churches mangled the air by striking eleven, my brother commanded us to take care of our parts, to learn them, and to assemble at the Theatre next morning to finish the reading. 'All those who appear in *The Seven Deadly Sins* should go to the Theatre now,' he said.

'Why aren't we rehearsing here tomorrow?' George Bryan demanded.

'Peter Strete will be here tomorrow,' my brother explained. Strete was a carpenter who did most of the Theatre's work. 'We will rehearse here most days,' my brother went on, 'but tomorrow they're moving all the timber in for the new stage and wall, and we'll have no peace.'

I had no part in *The Seven Deadly Sins*, and so was not

needed. My brother, deep in conversation with John Heminges and Henry Condell, ignored me as he left. Alan Rust, though, sought me out. 'You're being a fool,' he said.

'Why?'

'Because Flute is a good part. The whole notion is that you play a woman badly! The audience will know you're a man.'

'They already know that,' I said sullenly.

'Christ on his silver-painted cross! What kind of a fool are you? When you play Uashti, the audience doesn't see a man dressed as a woman, they see a queen! They even hear a queen! We deceive them, Richard! But Flute? The whole conceit is that you don't deceive them. That you are what the play says you are, a man playing a woman. So you play the woman like a man, and you play her badly. It's a jest, and it's a very fine one.' He had led me out through one of the two doors beneath the minstrels' gallery, but now hesitated, unsure which way to choose. 'This must be the scullery passage.'

It was indeed the scullery passage, and led to the stable yard where a pair of carriage horses were being washed and combed. 'I dare say,' Rust said, looking at me, 'that your last scene with Will Kemp will be the funniest in the play. It's a good part! You should be happy.'

'I have to fall in love with Will Kemp?' I said savagely.

'Not easy, I agree, but you're a player. You pretend. Really, Richard, you should be happy.'

I was anything but happy. Rust was right, it was a jest, but the jest was on me, and, to make my misery worse, I had seen no glimpse of Silvia.

We left the stable yard, and, once on Water Lane, Rust turned uphill, going towards the Theatre, but I turned left towards the river. I had a handful of coins in my purse, and, much as I resented losing any, I had decided to take a wherry across to the Paris Garden Stairs on the south bank of the Thames.

I had nothing else to do that day except, perhaps, learn Francis Flute's lines, and I had no enthusiasm for that.

There were a half-dozen watermen waiting at the stairs at the lower end of Water Lane, but before I could hail a boat I was hailed myself, or rather I was distracted by a gasp that made me turn, and there, to my sudden surprise and pleasure, was Silvia. She had evidently followed me down Water Lane, going, as I was, to the river stairs. She was dressed in a long grey cloak and hood, and carrying a basket covered with a clean linen cloth. She was smiling, which was gratifying. 'You're the player!' she said.

'Francis Flute,' I said impulsively. Why? I had no idea, and, to cover my confusion, I offered her a bow. 'At your service.'

She giggled at my elaborate bow. 'You're crossing the river?'

'I am.'

'You can come with me, then!' she said cheerfully. 'That end boat.' She pointed to the far end of the pier where two watermen sat in a wherry.

'Why that boat?'

"'Cos the big man at the stroke is my father.' She grinned.

The waiting watermen all knew her. They called to her in greeting, either by name or by calling her 'darling' or 'sweetheart'. 'Got yourself a handsome lad, darling?' one shouted.

'He's Mister Flute to you, Billy,' she called back.

'Going to blow him, darling?'

I thought she would be embarrassed, but she turned and grinned at the man. 'No good relying on your strokes, Billy!'

The watermen cheered, while her father, grinning proudly, stood to help her down into his boat. She gave him a respectful nod, then tilted her head so he could kiss her cheek. 'Usual?' he asked.

'The usual,' she said, then gave me a worried glance. 'Is the Paris Garden Stairs all right for you?'

'It's where I was going,' I said, stepping into the boat.

'This is Mister Flute,' Silvia introduced me to her father. 'He's one of Lord Hunsdon's men, a player!'

'Honoured to meet you, sir,' her father said, obviously impressed by my borrowed finery. 'I'm Joe Lester.'

'I'm honoured to meet you, sir,' I replied, then sat beside Silvia in the wide thwart at the stern of the boat. She waved at the other watermen as we pulled away.

'I've known them since I was a child,' she said to me, explaining her familiarity, then she grinned at her father, a big man hauling on a big oar. 'Gawd,' she said, 'it's good to get out of there!'

'You're lucky to have the position, Silvia,' he said, 'you and your brother.'

'You have a brother?' I asked.

'Two of them! Great lunks they are. Yes, Ned works for his lordship. I know I'm lucky, Pa, and they're good to us, but oh my gawd, there are times we just sit about doing nothing while her ladyship reads. Well, maybe not nothing, but how many unicorns can a girl embroider in a day?'

'That's what a lady's maid does,' her father said.

'This one would rather be working,' she said. I stole a glance at her. How had I forgotten that face? Just looking at her was to be struck by Cupid's arrow. She stopped the breath in my throat, turned my blood to smoke, struck me senseless. I remembered a line of Titania's that I had copied, and I muttered it under my breath. "'O how I love thee! How I dote on thee!'"

'What did you say?' Silvia asked.

'Nothing, nothing.'

'So you're a player,' her father said to me. 'Do you play at the Rose?'

'We're at the Theatre,' I said, 'the Rose is the Lord Admiral's company.'

'We go to the Rose sometimes,' Joe said happily. 'We saw *Friar Bacon and Friar Bungay* last. I laughed!'

'It's a funny play.'

'It'll be nice when the new playhouse opens,' Silvia said, nodding towards the monstrous pile looming over the small cottages of the southern bank. 'It'll be right on your doorstep, Pa!'

'With all the bloody drunks too,' her father said. 'No offence, sir.' He glanced over his shoulder to judge his progress against the current and the tide. 'It's bad enough with the Ugly Duck right there.'

'The Ugly Duck?'

'It's a tavern,' Silvia explained. 'It's close to Ma and Pa's house. I used to work there.'

'Work there?' I asked, surprised.

'Not like that!' she said, laughing, and I was embarrassed that she had divined my meaning, though neither she nor her father seemed to have taken offence. 'No,' she went on, 'when I was little I used to wash their pots.'

'She's a hard worker, our Silvia,' her father said proudly.

'Is that why you're crossing the river?' she asked me. 'To see the new playhouse?'

'I want to see it,' I said awkwardly.

'Me too!'

'You have to see Nurse Dodds,' her father said strictly.

'That's what I'm doing, Pa, that's what I'm doing,' Silvia said, then looked at me. 'Milly Dodds is Sir George's old nurse,' she explained.

'Sir George?' I asked, puzzled.

'He's Lord Hunsdon's son,' she said, 'and father to the bride. Nice man, isn't he, Pa?'

'Sir George Carey is a proper gentleman,' her father said.

'So at midday on every Monday I take her comfits and

sweetmeats,' Silvia said, indicating the basket. 'Sir George insists. He sometimes goes himself.'

'A proper gentleman,' her father said again, hauling on the loom of his oar.

'They've given her a nice little cottage,' Silvia went on. 'Well, they haven't given it to her, but they let her live there. She's a lovely old lady. On Thursdays I take her to the bear baiting! She loves that little outing. Do you like marchpane?'

'I've never eaten it.'

'Never eaten marchpane! Lord above! Here,' she lifted the linen cloth and brought out a yellow-coloured square, soft enough for her to pull into four separate parts. 'Nurse Dodds don't like marchpane, but I don't tell Sir George that on account that I love it, here, one piece for you, one for me, one for Father and one for Tom.' Tom was evidently the bow oarsman, who had said not a word since I climbed into the wherry. 'It's only almonds, rosewater, and sugar,' she said. 'And we add egg whites, not everyone does, try it. It's like nibbling a bit of heaven!'

The boat swung into the current and eased alongside the Paris Garden Stairs. I stepped off first, then held out a hand to help Silvia. The touch of her fingers! 'I'll look for you, darling,' her father said.

'About one o'clock, Pa,' she said, 'and thank you, Tom.'

Tom, a heavyset young man, just nodded.

'Should I pay?' I asked her father.

'Get on with you, lad!' he said. He had called me 'sir' when I first stepped into the boat, but the short crossing of the river had evidently persuaded him of my true status.

I thanked him, then climbed the stone stairs with his daughter. I had so wanted to be with her, but now found I had nothing to say, or rather my mind went blank. I had rehearsed a hundred lines to impress her, but I could remember none of them. That had happened to me at the Theatre once, I had been playing the Queen in my brother's *Richard II*, a part I knew so well, yet one afternoon the words just vanished like dew under the sun. John Duke, a hired man, turned to the left of the stage, "'Here comes the Duke of York,'" he'd said, and George Bryan, wearing a gorget, had entered, and I should have spoken immediately.

> *'With signs of war about his aged neck:*
> *O, full of careful business are his looks!*
> *Uncle, for God's sake, speak comfortable words.'*

Instead I had stammered incoherently, and Isaiah Humble, who should have called the words to me, had gone out the back for a piss. George Bryan had just gaped at me for a moment, and the groundlings had started to jeer. 'Learn your words!' one shouted, and an apple core soared out of the crowd and knocked my gilt-bronze coronet over my ear. George had finally spoken his next line, which began, "'Should I do so,'" after a ghastly pause, and the words made no sense because I had been reduced to a stuttering, helpless fool, and that was how I felt with Silvia as we climbed the Paris Garden Stairs.

'He's lovely, my old pa,' Silvia said.

'He seemed nice,' I said lamely.

'He's kind,' she said. 'He pretends not to be, but he is. Soft as a bubble, really.'

I tried to think of something to say, anything! 'Can I carry that?' I blurted out, pointing to her basket.

'I'm almost there,' she said, nodding at the nearby cottages. She gave me a smile bright as the sun. 'If you want a boat back, then my pa will be here when the clocks strike one.'

'I'd like that,' I said.

'Till then,' she said, and off she went.

'My name's Richard,' I called after her.

'I know,' she said without turning around, 'but I like Francis Flute!' She whistled a pair of notes, and, still without turning, waved goodbye.

I watched her go to the door of a small cottage, watched her go inside, then I walked towards the new playhouse. They wanted players.

The marchpane had been sweet, delicious, heavenly.

And how had she known my name was Richard?

FIVE

I WALKED SOUTH from the river, cursing myself for having been tongue-tied with Silvia. What had happened to all those clever words I had dreamed of saying? I promised myself I would say them all at one o'clock when I shared the wherry back to Blackfriars.

The houses on this south bank were all built close to the Thames on either side of a lane that followed the riverbank. I took another lane that led inland, past a moss-covered stone cross that had half fallen, and within forty or fifty paces I had left the houses behind and was walking between dark hedgerows bordered by sour ditches thick with nettles. Scrawny cows grazed in small pastures. The few leafless trees were stunted and dark, while the lane was rutted and damp so that I had to leap across puddles to keep my boots from clogging with mud. The new playhouse loomed to my right, approached through a decaying gate that had been left open. The field around the new building was stacked with timber and heaped with masonry. A dozen men were busy high on the scaffolding, two of them winching up a precarious platform laden with roof tiles.

It was large. Larger than the Theatre, and larger than the

Rose playhouse, which lay to the east, close to the southern end of London Bridge. This new playhouse, I thought, would attract folk from Westminster as well as from London, almost all of them paying pennies to the watermen for bringing them to the Paris Garden Stairs. Silvia's father might complain about the noise the playhouse would bring, but it would also bring him customers. A rough-coated dog woke as I edged between the timber piles, and started barking furiously. It leaped towards me, but was jerked to a halt by a chain fastened to a staple at the playhouse entrance. 'Sultan!' a voice shouted from the scaffolding. 'Stop your poxy noise!' The dog growled and whined, but let me pass.

'Don't mind Sultan, master. He won't touch you unless Jem tells him to.' The speaker was a craftsman who was perched high on a ladder where he was smoothing white plaster on the arched ceiling of the entrance tunnel. 'And watch yourself, master,' he added as a splatter of plaster fell from his trowel. 'You're mixing it too wet!' he growled at his apprentice, a small boy half bent over a large barrel. 'Safe now, master,' he added to me, and I threaded my way between barrel and ladder and so into the huge yard.

Where I stopped and gasped. The new playhouse was built much like the Theatre, but everything was on a larger scale and far more richly decorated. Men were gilding the balustrades of the three galleries, which, unlike the two at the Theatre, were entered by gated stairways from the big yard. Two labourers were laying flagstones onto a sand and gravel base. No one, I thought, could hurl a flagstone at the stage, while the Theatre's stage was vulnerable to the yard's cobbles. Will Kemp had once demanded that the cobblestones be replaced. 'I don't mind the bastards throwing soft things,' he said, 'but cobblestones hurt!'

'Regard the cobblestones as reason enough to please our

audience,' my brother had retorted, and the cobblestones had stayed.

The front edge of the stage jutted deep into the yard and was hung with cloth embroidered with swans swimming among reeds. A tiled canopy covered the rear half of the stage, and beneath it, immediately above the three doors through which the players would make their entrances and exits, was a pillared gallery, which, I supposed, was where the wealthiest customers could look down on the stage. Two massive pillars supported the high canopy, and a painter, perched on a scaffold, was turning the bare wood of the right-hand pillar into the smoothest marble. He was evidently working his way down the pillar, because the lower half still looked like wood, while the upper part gleamed like a cream-coloured stone veined with grey. It was extraordinary. I walked closer and could have sworn the top half of the pillar was made of the most expensive marble. The painter, a lugubrious man who wore a scarf around his head instead of a hat, saw my interest. 'You like it?' he asked, though without any enthusiasm.

'It's wonderful!' I said in genuine admiration.

The painter took a half step back on his scaffold and frowned at his work. 'It's a playhouse,' he said flatly.

'Of course it is,' I said, puzzled by his response.

'A place of deception,' he said angrily.

'You don't approve?'

'Do I approve of pretence? Of falsehood? No, sir, I do not approve. Of flattery? Of lies? How can I approve? Of blasphemy? Of licentiousness? I abhor it, sir, I abhor it, but a man must live.' He turned back to his careful work. 'A man must live,' he repeated, this time resentfully, speaking to himself.

'Mister Timothy Nairn is a Puritan,' a voice spoke from behind me, 'yet he stoops to decorate our house of satanic pleasures.'

'In these hard days, Mister Langley,' the painter said, 'I am grateful that Almighty God sends me work to keep my family in bread. And it is God who will decide the fate of this place, not I.'

'I'm surprised God doesn't strike you dead for painting my pillars.'

'All that I do is for His glory,' Timothy Nairn answered dourly, 'even in this den of iniquity.'

'Iniquity!' Langley sounded amused.

I had turned to face him, seeing a stout, hard-faced man with a short brown beard. He wore rich clothes of dark blue wool slashed with yellow silk, clothes that belied his face that was knowing, scarred and battered. A formidable man. I knew he was a member of the Goldsmiths, but his money, it was rumoured, came not from fine jewellery but from the half-dozen brothels he owned. I offered him a respectful bow. 'Mister Langley,' I said, 'I'm . . .'

'I know who you are, lad. I saw you at the Theatre.' He frowned, evidently trying to remember. 'You played a daft mort who fainted. What was the piece called?'

'*Two Gentlemen of Verona*, sir?' I suggested, though I had pretended to faint in half a dozen other plays. 'I played Julia.'

'That might have been it. A shallow piece, whatever it was,' he said scornfully, 'but you were good. Who was the other lad?'

'Simon Willoughby, sir. He played Silvia.' The very thought of Simon Willoughby playing a character called Silvia now filled me with dismay. He was not worthy!

'Simon Willoughby, aye.' Something about the name amused Langley, because he gave a snort of laughter. 'So why are you here?'

'Curiosity, sir.'

'Curiosity!' he sneered at the word. 'Let's hope you're not a puss cat, eh? Now get up onstage, boy, see how you like it.'

I ran two or three steps and vaulted onto the high stage that was nearly as tall as a man. The stage, I now saw, had three trap-doors, which could be used as graves, as gateways to and from hell, or just for surprise entrances. At the Theatre we only had one trapdoor, approached through the stinking space beneath the stage where Pickles the cat waged a relentless war against rats and mice. I walked under the canopy, or the heavens as some players called it, and looked up to see cunningly painted clouds white against a blue sky. There were two trapdoors in the cloudy ceiling, and behind them, I knew, would be the flights; the windlasses used to lower players from the sky. Gods, god-desses, and angels had to hook themselves to the rope, pull up the trapdoor, and hope that the man turning the flight's handle was sober. I turned to look back at the entrance and thought how big this house was with its towering galleries and its yard half as big again as the Theatre.

'I had a fool here last week,' Langley said, 'who told me the place was too big. That his voice couldn't reach the top gallery. Say something, lad, but don't shout. Just speak as if you were playing natural.' He turned and looked up, 'Ben, are you up there?'

'I'm here, sir!' Ben, whoever he was, was hidden in the upper gallery from where I could hear the intermittent sound of a saw biting through timber.

'Listen close, Ben,' Langley called, 'and tell me if you can hear the lad.' He looked back to me. 'Go on, boy, speak.'

My mind had gone blank. I fumbled for words and found none.

'Go on, lad! Ben's listening.'

'"As for thee, boy,"' I suddenly remembered some lines, '"go get thee from my sight; Thou art an exile, and thou must not stay!"' I did not shout the words, but spoke them as loudly as I would have done at the Theatre, and, mindful that an audi-ence would be behind me as well as in front, I turned slowly as I gave the lines, which were from the second play I had performed with my brother's company. In that play I had been a girl called Lavinia who was vilely raped and had her tongue cut out and her hands severed, but the words I spoke now had been George Bryan's, who had played my father, a Roman called Titus Andronicus. "'And if you love me, as I think you do,'" I went on, finishing my turn, "'let's kiss and part, for we have much to do.'"

'Kiss and part!' Langley repeated, amused. 'Did you hear that, Ben?'

'Every blessed word, Mister Langley!'

'Aye, I thought that poxy piece of slug shit last week was deaf.'

'If the playhouse was full though . . .' I began, then faltered.

'Go on, lad, say up!'

'If it's full, sir, the sound will be softened. Especially if it's been raining.' I was trying to sound like an expert, repeating things I had heard from the likes of Alan Rust, my brother, and James Burbage. It was true, though. If the groundlings were in damp clothes we had to speak louder.

'The buggers will have to shout then,' Francis Langley said. 'Too late to shrink the place.'

"'For we have much to do!'" another voice sounded, loud and angry. 'Did you hear that, Langley? "We have much to do."' The voice seemed to come from above the stage, from the pillared gallery just under the heaven's cloudy canopy. 'Is that a player?'

'Aye, it is, Mister deValle.'

'Then bring the culley up!'

Langley used a short ladder to reach the stage. 'Be respectful when we get up there,' he muttered to me under his breath, then led me through one of the three doors into the tiring house. He left the door open to let some small light into the room, which had no windows. It was large, twice the size of the Theatre's tiring room, and smelt of new-cut timber. 'I've spent almost three hundred pounds on costumes,' Langley said bitterly. 'Three hundred pounds! He insists, you see. This way, lad.' He led me through a door into a corridor from which steps led upwards. 'This goes to the lordlings' chamber,' he explained, climbing.

'Lordlings?'

'A place for the rich to hear the plays,' he said hungrily, 'sixpence a seat, at least. Maybe even a shilling.'

'Who'd pay a shilling for a play?' I asked.

'Whoever sits up here, of course. And it won't just be a play, boy,' we had paused on a small landing and he winked at me, 'there'll be morts as well. So if they don't like the play they can have the whore. I tell you, lad, whores are cheaper. You don't have to buy costumes for whores, do you?'

A second flight of stairs, narrower and steeper, climbed from the landing, presumably to the platform where trumpeters would sound their fanfare to announce a performance, but Langley ignored it, instead opening a richly carved door into the lordlings' chamber. He beckoned me inside.

I gasped. I might have grown up in a modest house, and now lived in a decaying attic with no comforts, but I knew luxury. We had played in the Queen's banqueting hall in Whitehall, had amused her at Greenwich, and entertained her among the candlelit splendours of her Richmond palace, and this lordlings' chamber would not have been out of place in any of those mansions. The walls were carved panels, painted with a dark resin that made them gleam. The smell of the resin filled the room, despite the open gallery that overlooked the stage. The floor gleamed with the same rich shine, while the ceiling had been painted with naked angels that flew among celestial clouds. I wondered if Mister Nairn, the Puritan painter, had been asked to depict the winged and shameless women who looked down on a large table set at the room's centre. The table was smothered with plans of the new playhouse, while on the back wall was a great stone fireplace, almost as ornately carved as the one in the Lord Chamberlain's great hall, only this marble mantel was supported by a pair of naked women, carved from a milky white stone, their arms folded above their heads as they flanked a brick hearth in which a fire burned. To the left of the fire was a settle, draped in a tapestry, on which a girl was sprawled. She looked drunk, or at least asleep. She had auburn hair, a mass of freckles on a pale face, her mouth was open, and she lay with her legs wide parted, one on the settle and the other on the floor. So far as I could see she wore nothing but a brief shift.

'So who is he?' a man asked belligerently. He had been sitting at the table, but now stood. He was as tall as I and far more elegantly dressed. He wore a rapier, its hilt a swirl of silver around a grip wrapped in red leather, while on his right shoulder was an elaborate badge showing a swan wreathed in lilies. I guessed he was in his thirties, full of confidence and swagger. He wore a short fair beard that jutted from his chin, while his moustaches flared wide with an upturned flourish. He saw me gazing at the girl. 'Don't mind Becky,' he snarled, 'mind me.'

'Sir,' I said, bowing.

'So who are you?'

'Richard Shakespeare, sir.'

'Are you the writer?' he sounded intrigued. 'The one who owns a share of Langley's whorehouses?'

I was so surprised by the second question that I said nothing. My brother was a partner to Francis Langley? He owned brothels? Surely that was not true!

'Well?' deValle demanded.

'Richard is his brother, Mister deValle,' Langley said, without denying the business connection.

'Brother to your whore partner,' deValle spoke to Langley, and spoke savagely, 'and he won't write plays for you, is that true?'

129

'He writes for his own company, Mister deValle.'

DeValle sniffed and then gazed at me for a few seconds as a man might stare at a heifer he was wondering whether to purchase. 'My name's Christopher deValle,' he finally said, 'and don't you dare think that name is French. The deValles are not French. The deValles detest that nation of pox-ridden slime-toads. The deValles are made of English oak from scalp to arsehole. We are Berkshire born, Berkshire bred, and loyal subjects of our Queen, long may she reign and God bless her snow-white bubbies. I manage the Earl of Lechlade's affairs.'

'Yes, sir,' I said, because he seemed to expect some sort of a reply.

'Are you good?' deValle demanded peremptorily.

'He is good, sir,' Francis Langley answered for me, 'he's famous for the women he plays.'

'Women!' deValle seemed horrified.

'I play men's parts now, sir,' I intervened hastily. 'When I was a boy I played women,' I added, trying not to let my nervousness show, 'but now I'm given men's parts.' Which, I supposed, was near enough true. Francis Flute was a man.

'Becky!' deValle shouted. 'Wake up, bitch!' The girl stirred and sat up, pushing her red hair away from her face. She looked wordlessly at deValle, who pointed at me. 'Tell me what you think,' he ordered.

She yawned, stretched, then stood and sauntered around the table to look at me. I looked back. I guessed she was about my age, but she had a knowingness that made her seem older. Her eyes were green, like a cat's, her face was freckled, and her hair a tangle of thick curls. She was attractive, no man could look at her and not be stirred, but the knowingness made her more than a little frightening. She reached out a hand and stroked my cheek. 'He's pretty.'

'Pretty!' deValle spat.

'Handsome then.' She smiled and flicked a finger across my nose. 'I like him.'

'If he could afford you,' deValle said sourly, 'he wouldn't be here. Why are you here?'

And what was I to say to that? That I was poor, owed rent, and needed employment? Or that I wanted revenge on my brothel-owning brother who had cozened me by offering me a man's part only for me to discover that Francis Flute played a woman? My anger at that betrayal had brought me across the river, but this was no time to tell that truth. 'I hear you want players, sir,' I said, with as much dignity as I could muster.

DeValle grunted at that. 'You have employment now?'

I nodded. 'At the Theatre, sir.'

'So why leave?'

'I'm a hired man, sir,' I said, 'and they have plenty of those already.'

'So you don't get used much, is that it?'

'I'd like to be busier, sir,' I said.

'He is good, Mister deValle,' Francis Langley said eagerly. When we had met on the stage, Langley had been full of bluff confidence, but now, in deValle's presence, he was humble.

'So are the others we've seen,' deValle said, 'or so you say.'

'They're not as handsome as this one,' Becky said.

'Put some wood on the fire, girl,' deValle said, 'then keep your whore-mouth shut.' He was gazing at me still, an expression of dislike on his face. 'I'm told,' he said, 'that players need to be swordsmen, is that true?'

'If the play demands it, sir, yes.'

'And most plays do?'

'The crowds like to watch swordplay,' I said.

'Then let us see if they would like to watch you,' deValle said, and went to a chest that stood among the shadows on the far wall. He lifted the lid, rummaged among its contents for a moment, and plucked out a sword, which he shook from its scabbard. He tossed me the sword, and I let it drop to the floor rather than try to catch it by the blade. I picked it up to find it was an old backsword, its foreblade blunt and the leather of its hilt ragged. The weapon was ill-balanced and clumsy. DeValle smiled at my expression and drew his rapier with its elaborate silver guard, the long blade sliding from its scabbard with a barely audible hiss. 'We'll try a pass,' deValle said, 'and see if you're good enough to entertain our crowds.'

'Mister deValle,' Francis Langley said nervously.

'Quiet, Langley,' deValle said, keeping his eyes on me. Becky looked excited. 'First blood?' deValle suggested, meaning that the fight would end when one of us was wounded.

'Maybe I should just yield now then,' I said. I was holding the sword clumsily, the point down.

'Not if you wish employment here,' deValle answered savagely, and raised the rapier.

He was proposing a match between an old, ill-balanced sword, and a rapier. Onstage the fights were usually with swords, made for cutting as well as lunging, because such fights took less room than the long-bladed rapiers needed, and because the crowds liked to see sweeping cuts as well as elegant lunges. A rapier could not cut; it was designed solely to pierce. It required as much skill as a sword, but the skill was different. Henry Condell and Richard Burbage, who performed most of our fights at the Theatre, could fight with either weapon, but Signor Mancini, in whose hall I trained at least once a week, had only taught me the backsword. 'You learn this sword first,' he liked to tell me in his liquid accent, 'because the rapier is easy afterwards.'

I pretended to know nothing as I faced deValle. I suspected he was a good swordsman, proud of his skill and eager to inflict a wound, but I was not as clumsy as I pretended to be. I was a player, so I played being an awkward, unskilled, frightened man. I stood flat-footed, square on to deValle who was poised elegantly, his right foot forward and his blade angled upwards. 'Ready?' he asked.

'Sir?' I said uncertainly.

'First blood, boy,' he said, and stamped forward, his long blade coming for my face, and I flicked it aside, using the weak outer end of my blade, the foible. I staggered backwards and looked alarmed.

'Not his face, Mister deValle,' Francis Langley said, 'please, sir, not his face! He's a player!'

DeValle ignored the plea. He had retreated, smiling. He thought that my parry was a lucky chance, because no swordsman would parry with the foible if he could help it. He stamped forward, long blade lunging, and immediately stepped back. It was a feint, but I twitched my blade and stumbled two steps backwards as if in panic, and he laughed. 'Maybe you should only play women, Mister Shakespeare,' he said.

'Cut him, Kit,' Becky said savagely.

'Not his face!' Langley pleaded again.

'Not his face,' deValle said, 'then I'll mark his thigh.'

I knew he would come for my face. He was a bully, sure of his skill, and he wanted to humiliate me. He was a bad player, though, because he had told the lie about marking my thigh without any conviction. He simply wanted to mislead me, then draw blood from my cheek and, just as I expected, he looked at my legs, lowered his blade slightly, then smiled and stamped forward. Sure enough the long blade flicked up, aiming for my face, and I stepped to my left, cut hard and fast to the right to beat the rapier down, and slashed the blade inwards to slice it onto his exposed forearm. The blade struck, and he looked alarmed. I was no longer hesitant, no longer clumsy. I was moving lightly, I had turned him, his rapier was off to my right

133

and the length of the blade meant he had to step backwards to use it, but I gave him no chance, stamping forward, lunging, and stopping the blade an inch from his beard. 'First blood, sir,' I said, nodding at his forearm, where a seep of red was staining the lace cuff of his sleeve.

For a heartbeat he looked furious, then he forced a smile. 'Clever,' he said.

'Beginner's fortune, sir,' I said, lowering the blade, and then, to show I meant the fight to be over, handed the sword to Francis Langley.

'Beginner's fortune, eh?' deValle asked. He sheathed his blade. 'I think not. I think you are cunning, Mister Shakespeare. I think you're a weasel. I think you're sly. But you drew first blood.' He pulled up his sleeve. My blunt blade had broken the skin, little more, but there was blood there, and he would have a bruise to remember me by. He spat on the blood, rubbed it, and let the sleeve fall again. 'Who trains you?'

'Signor Mancini.'

'In Silver Street,' deValle said. 'He's good,' he added grudgingly.

I could not afford fencing lessons, but I had no chance of being a player of men's parts unless I had the skills of the sword. Signor Mancini liked me, which meant he let me owe him money, but how long would he be patient? I thought how desperately I needed coins. I had to pay rent, I had to buy food, I had to live. And the Theatre was scarcely open now, as the winter deepened and the weather worsened. I faced penury, and how long before the Widow Morrison threw me onto the street?

'Sit down.' DeValle indicated one of the chairs at the table. I sat, and deValle took the chair opposite me. My back was to the open gallery, so the winter light was on his face. He stared at me, still with dislike. 'So you can fight,' he said.

'Stage-fighting,' I said disparagingly, 'where we try neither to wound nor hurt.'

'The Earl of Lechlade, my master,' he said, ignoring my words, 'desires to have a company of players. I do not understand his desire, but he will not be denied. Players, as you have just shown me, are full of deception.' He paused to pour himself a cup of red wine. 'My task is to find his lordship players who will practise their deceptions in Mister Langley's playhouse.'

'The Swan,' Francis Langley put in.

'So named,' deValle said, 'because his lordship's emblem is a swan.' He touched the badge on his shoulder. 'But we're not telling anyone that name yet. We'll announce it when we announce the first play.' He gave Francis Langley a look of pure malevolence, then glanced back at me. 'Would you like to play at the Swan, Master Shakespeare?'

'Yes, sir,' I said, though I was by no means certain of that answer.

'What do you earn now?' he asked.

'It depends, sir,' I said, 'on whether I'm needed in a play, and whether the Theatre is open. In bad weather we don't perform. And it's winter now, sir, so some weeks we don't perform at all.'

'I did not ask for a lecture,' he said. 'What do you earn now?'

'In a bad week, sir? Nothing. In a good week? Three shillings, four shillings. Most weeks just a shilling or two.'

'A pittance. We will pay more to the players who wear his lordship's swan, is that not so, Mister Langley?'

'If you say so, sir,' Langley said. He looked alarmed, and I had the sense that the cost of building the Swan playhouse was running out of control, driven by the Earl of Lechlade's promises and demands. The nobility was famous for not paying its debts, or for delaying their payments for months or even years, and doubtless his lordship was expecting ever more fake marble, ever more painted naked ladies, and ever more lavish amounts of gold leaf, and Francis Langley was providing it at his own expense and praying that he would be repaid.

'We will pay well,' deValle told me. His blue eyes, scornful and unfriendly, were fixed on me. 'But I should tell you that players are not hard to find. Turn over any stone in London and a player crawls out.' He paused as if expecting me to protest, but I held his gaze and said nothing. 'You are, Becky says, handsome,' he went on grudgingly, 'and God knows she's seen enough men to make a judgement.'

'He's a good-looking boy,' Francis Langley said.

DeValle ignored him. 'You can dance?'

'Yes,' I said.

He hesitated, perhaps irritated that I had not called him 'sir'. 'So we should consider him, should we not, Mister Langley?'

'Consider him? Yes, sir. He's good! People like watching him.'

'But what use are players?' deValle asked. 'What use is a play-house?' He asked the questions and left them hanging. No one answered. The fire crackled in the hearth, then spewed sparks as a log dropped.

'A playhouse is no use,' deValle continued scornfully, 'and players are a waste of money, unless there is a play. We have a playhouse, and Christ knows we can find players, but where is the man who writes the plays?'

Francis Langley shuffled his feet. 'I've been talking to the Reverend . . .'

'Don't talk to me of Venables! Who performs his plays?'

'The Lord Chamberlain's Men did,' Langley said, 'well, they performed one.'

'*Hester and Ahasuerus*,' I said.

'And?' deValle asked.

'A piece of shit,' I said.

He gave a genuine smile at that. 'We don't want shit! We want plays!'

'Tom Nashe has agreed to write something,' Francis Langley said weakly.

'Have you seen it?'

'Well, I don't think he's started yet. He said he'd start soon. And Ben Jonson, you haven't met him, sir, but Ben said he'd be willing to think of something . . .' his voice trailed away.

'Ben writes for the Rose,' I pointed out.

'And demanded twenty-five pounds for a play,' deValle snarled.

'Yes, sir,' Langley said.

'His lordship is not a cow to be milked,' deValle said angrily. It was plain that the Swan had its stage and it would doubtless have players, but it had no plays. DeValle stood and walked to the balustrade from where he gazed at the stage below. 'When will the playhouse be finished, Langley?'

'End of January, sir. If there's money.' He added the last three words in a tone of despair.

DeValle ignored the despairing tone. 'So we can put on a play at January's end?'

'If the weather's good, sir, yes.'

'But we have no play!' DeValle turned on Langley savagely. 'We have no play!'

'We will, sir.' Langley did not sound convincing. 'And we can always do *The Seven Deadly Sins*, folk like that one.'

'For Christ's sake that is old! That is tired! His lordship does not expend funds so you can fart some ancient piece of nonsense that half London has seen before. Would you open a new whorehouse with nothing but old poxed ingles pissing on moth-eaten mattresses?'

'No, sir.'

'Your customers want new whores. Fresh meat. Not half-eaten tarts like Becky.'

'Thank you,' Becky said.

DeValle ignored her, turning back to look out into the play-house. 'When is the wedding?' he asked abruptly.

'Sir?' Langley asked, puzzled.

'I wasn't asking you.' DeValle still had his back to us.

'Wedding?' I asked uncertainly.

'The Lord Chamberlain's granddaughter is marrying Thomas Berkeley,' deValle said menacingly, 'when?'

'February, sir,' I said.

'February,' deValle said, 'and in the court there is much talk of that wedding. The Lord Chamberlain and his wife have even boasted of the play that will be performed there. A comedy, his lordship said. A fine piece of writing, she said. Have you seen it?'

I hesitated. 'Parts of it,' I finally admitted. I did not say that I had listened to most of the play that morning.

'What is it called?'

'My brother is still searching for a title, sir,' I lied.

'Is he now?' DeValle turned and stalked back to the table's far side. He sat, felt in a purse hanging from his belt, and brought out a handful of gold coins. He spun one of the coins on the table's top. I stared at the glitter, Becky gazed, and Langley looked hungry. 'Bring me that play,' deValle said softly.

I looked up to meet his gaze. 'Sir?'

'Bring . . . me . . . that . . . play,' he repeated, leaving a pause between each word.

I said nothing. I felt alarm, fear, danger. 'Is the play good, Richard?' Francis Langley asked nervously.

'I don't know.'

'Lady Anne Hunsdon says it's good,' deValle said slyly. 'She praised it to the Queen. She said she'd never read a finer comedy.'

'I know she's read it,' I said, 'but her husband is paying for it, and if another playhouse were to perform it first . . .'

'We have friends at court too,' deValle interrupted me harshly. 'The Lord Chamberlain's displeasure is our affair, not yours.'

'How many players, Richard?' Langley asked.

'A lot, sir!' I said, hoping that would deter him. 'At least a dozen.'

'Expensive then,' Langley said.

DeValle ignored that. 'Are you frightened, boy?'

'I don't know that I can steal a copy, sir. The pages are guarded.'

'Your brother wrote it?'

'Yes, sir.'

'Then who better to steal it than you?' He rolled one of the coins across the table, and I was forced to trap it before it fell to the floor. 'Keep that one, boy,' deValle said, 'and I'll give you six more when you bring me the pages.' I stared at the precious coin that lay enormous, heavy and gleaming in my hand. An unflattering portrait of the Queen graced one side; her crown was perched precariously on long flowing hair, and she stared off to one side over a beaked nose that somehow made her look petulant. I turned it over to see the royal coat of arms flanked by the letters E and R. 'That is a sovereign, boy,' deValle said, 'a gold sovereign. Have you held a sovereign before?'

I shook my head. I had never even seen a sovereign before. It was said to be made of almost pure gold, and, though its value was set at twenty shillings, it was rumoured to be worth far more. I put the coin on the table, took a deep breath, and pushed it back towards deValle. 'The pages are guarded, sir.'

'So you don't want employment here?'

If the moment in the ditch on the road from Stratford to Ettington had changed my life, that moment when I had asked Ned Sales where he was going and impulsively asked him to carry me to London on his wagon, this moment was another. I had a choice. I could accept deValle's gold and betray my brother. I could steal *A Midsummer Night's Dream*, and even, perhaps, the new play he was writing that was set in Verona.

I would be rich! I would have employment. It would be a sweet revenge for the part of Francis Flute, for the years of misery with Sir Godfrey, but Father Laurence's words haunted me too. 'Don't look to your brother for help, be a help to him.' I stared at deValle, who glared back at me. 'Well, boy?'

'You want me to steal my brother's play, sir?'

'Sweet suffering Christ, how daft are you? Isn't that what I just said?'

I took a very deep breath. 'If that's the price, sir, no.'

'Then get out,' he snarled. 'Get out, now!'

No one spoke as I stood. My chair scraped loud on the chamber's floor. DeValle glared at me, Francis Langley frowned at the table, Becky smiled, and still no one spoke as I crossed to the door.

I fled down the stairs, through the tiring room, and out onto the stage.

Where a tall man dressed in black, as lanky and thin as a human daddy-long-legs, his greasy black hair showing beneath a wide-brimmed black hat, a black spade beard long on his chest and his deep-lined face grinning and malevolent. He put an arm out to stop me. 'Look who we have here,' he said with a sneer worthy of deValle. 'It's little Richard, only you're not so little any more, are you?'

I slapped his arm away, took one horrified look into his gaunt and grinning face, jumped from the stage, and walked away. I wanted to run, but I walked because I would not pay this man the compliment of running away from him.

It was Sir Godfrey. And his mocking laughter followed me out of the playhouse.

Sir Godfrey Cullen was no knight. The 'sir' was a courtesy given to ministers of the Church of England, and Sir Godfrey was the parish priest of Saint Benet's in Blackfriars. He was also the proprietor of Scavenger's Yard which lay just north of the city in Clerkenwell, and which provided bears, dogs, and other beasts for London's entertainment, but chiefly he had been the owner and chief predator of Saint Benet's Choir School for Boys.

It was to Saint Benet's and to Sir Godfrey's care that my brother had consigned me on my arrival in London. I joined twenty-three other boys, most of them much younger than me, who lived in a malodorous shed in the burial ground behind Saint Benet's church, and next door to an old monastic hall that had been turned into a playhouse that could seat two hundred and seventy people. The Puritan fathers of London might detest the playhouses and had banned them from within the city's walls, but they had no power to ban a choir school, and if the choir school chose to present plays as part of the boys' education, then the city council had to swallow their rage and endure the indignity. There were three such boys' playhouses within the city walls, of which Saint Benet's was the smallest, and all were hugely popular, attended by eager crowds of playgoers willing to pay three or four pence to watch small boys prance, pose, and perform.

'He's a pretty boy,' Sir Godfrey had said, inspecting me on my first visit. We were in Saint Benet's vestry, where Sir Godfrey sprawled long-legged behind a table on which was a Bible, two tall candles, and a flagon of wine. I stood opposite him, wondering what lay in store.

'He ran away from home,' my brother had said, 'and perhaps I should send him back?'

'Perhaps,' Sir Godfrey had replied, staring at me. He had a gaunt face, deep lined, with sardonic black eyes. 'Perhaps,' he had said again, 'but he is pretty. How old is he?'

'Fourteen.'

'Fourteen!' Sir Godfrey had shuddered. 'I like my boys

younger. It's simpler to train a puppy. Old dogs and new tricks, Mister Shakespeare, as you well know. Can you read, boy?'

'Yes, sir,' I had said.

'You can't be a player if you can't read.'

'I can read, sir.'

'Prove it to me,' he had said, and drew the Bible towards him, looked for a page, then pushed it across the table. A dirty fingernail showed me what verse he wanted me to read.

'"Thou shalt not lie with mankind as with womankind,"' I read, and almost faltered because the verse was unfamiliar and surprised me, '"it is an abomination. Neither shalt thou lie with any . . ."'

'Enough!' Sir Godfrey was cackling with amusement. 'So he can read. And he has a pleasant enough voice.'

'He's a clever boy,' my brother had said grudgingly, and I remember how that had surprised me because I had never thought of myself as clever.

Sir Godfrey had gazed at me for a few heartbeats. 'Clever and mischievous, eh? Yes, mischievous! You ran away from home. Clever and mischievous. Not a happy conjunction. But he is pretty, very pretty,' he had said hungrily. 'But training lads takes money, Mister Shakespeare, it takes money.'

My brother had paid him. I don't know how much, I just heard the chink of coins being paid, which meant I had been sold to Saint Benet's and to Sir Godfrey much as I had been sold to Thomas Butler in Stratford. And so I had donned a much darned grey robe and a half-starched ruff and begun my real schooling. The place was supposed to be a choir school, and every Sunday we put on surplices and sang psalms in Saint Benet's church, but in truth we were being trained to be players because that was where the greatest part of Sir Godfrey's money came from, from performances in the playhouse in the old monastic hall.

By law we were restricted to one performance a week, but we often played three or more, and because we performed indoors the weather did not matter. Our stage was lit by candles. The youngest players were eight or nine years old, I was among the older boys, and, because I was tall and because Sir Godfrey discovered I had a talent for playing, I soon had leading parts. I was King Cyrus in *The Wars of Cyrus*, and Phaon in *Sappho and Phaon*. Phaon was a humble ferryman who was granted exquisite beauty by Venus so he could seduce Queen Sappho. 'He was born to play the part,' I remember Sir Godfrey telling some lordling who visited a rehearsal. 'Is he not pretty?'

'Exquisite, Sir Godfrey,' the lordling had said. 'Where is the play set?'

'In Sicily, my lord.'

'And you know, of course, that Sicilian ferrymen work unclothed?'

'Do they so, my lord?'

'They do, Sir Godfrey. A strange habit, I confess, but true.'

'A remarkable habit, my lord,' Sir Godfrey had said. It had been obvious that he did not believe a word that the lordling had spoken, but he liked the lie. He had smiled at me, or rather offered a grimace with his blackened teeth. 'Undress, boy.'

Yet even Sir Godfrey did not dare have me naked at a public performance, so instead I played the part wearing a skimpy loincloth and with my skin pasted thick with ceruse and powdered penis so that in the candlelight my body appeared to shimmer. Sir Godfrey raised the price of entry for that play, which we ran for over sixteen performances, all of them to packed benches.

I played men's parts because I was tall, yet all of Sir Godfrey's choristers were required to learn the skills of playing a girl. I was the moon goddess Cynthia in *Endymion*, wafting about the candlelit stage in a gown of silvery gauze. I was good.

143

I knew I was good. And I wanted to be good, because to perform well was one way to avoid Sir Godfrey's savage beatings, or the whippings administered by his two ushers.

I stayed three years. Not willingly, but I had nowhere else to go, and when a boy did flee Saint Benet's he was inevitably returned by the constables, who were in Sir Godfrey's pay. It was not till I was seventeen that I dared run, and by then Sir Godfrey seemed happy to see the back of me. I was too old for him by seventeen. I went back to my brother, who had seen me play a dozen parts in Sir Godfrey's hall, and he relented and let me play in *Two Gentlemen of Verona*. 'You're too old to be an apprentice,' he had said, 'so I suppose you're a hired man. Or a hired boy. You can't live with me. There's a widow on Bishopsgate Street who lets rooms cheaply. Her husband was a very fine player, poor man. We miss him.'

So I escaped Sir Godfrey, but in those three years I had learned so much.

I had learned the gestures that express rage, sorrow, pleasure, and lust.

I had learned to dance the jig, the coranto, and the galliard.

I had learned to fight with a sword, for swordplay was frequent upon the stage in Saint Benet's hall.

I had learned to speak clearly so that my high voice could be heard by the folk standing in the cheap space at the back of the hall and in the gallery above.

I had learned to play the lute, though never well, just well enough to sing a song onstage.

I had learned to sing.

I had learned to disguise my face so that men looked on me with lust.

I had learned to thieve.

I had learned that the ash rods held by Sir Godfrey's two ushers hurt like biting serpents, that they drew blood. 'Not his face!' Sir Godfrey would command. 'Not his face! His buttocks, beat his buttocks. Let me see blood!'

I had learned to lie so that I could avoid the savage beatings.

I had learned how to be a girl. We were made to dress as girls and walk in the streets, and if a man did not try to kiss us or feel under our skirts then we had failed the test, and failure meant another thrashing. Buttercup would follow us. His real name was John Harding, but from somewhere he had fetched the name Buttercup. He was a churchwarden at Saint Benet's, and Sir Godfrey's helper in everything; a huge man, muscled like an ox and slow of thought and speech, but strangely well-spoken. Rumour said Buttercup was of gentle birth, and perhaps that was true.

I had learned that to be summoned to the vestry at any time, but especially after evensong, was to become Sir Godfrey's plaything. And sometimes a wealthy patron, all velvet and pearls, perfume and satin, would be waiting there. 'Go, boy,' Sir Godfrey would say, 'and I want a good report of you.'

He made money by such assignations. Inevitably the patron would reward us, but we were searched as soon as we returned to Saint Benet's, and the coins taken from us. 'It's for the poor of the parish,' Sir Godfrey would leer. Sometimes those patrons were gross fat creatures, slack-mouthed and sweating, and we would be terrified. 'Go, boy, Buttercup will fetch you in the morning,' Sir Godfrey would say, and there would follow the chink of coin as we were taken away to be educated.

I had learned so much. From the innocence of Stratford, which had bored me, my brother had sent me to the stew of Saint Benet's, which had opened my eyes to the world. Now, though I hate Sir Godfrey more than I hate any other creature on God's earth, I am grateful for the education he gave me. I can sing, dance, speak, fight, thieve, lie, and dissemble. I am a player.

*　　*　　*

145

Buttercup was waiting outside the playhouse like a mastiff waiting for his master. He smiled happily when he saw me. 'It's Master Richard!'

'Buttercup,' I acknowledged him warily.

He cracked a hazelnut in one massive hand. 'Did you see Sir Godfrey?'

'I had that pleasure, yes.'

'Stop it!' This abrupt command was to Sultan, the dog, which had growled, but now subsided, recognising that Buttercup was a far more formidable beast. 'Good dog,' Buttercup said, then smiled at me. 'How fares you, Master Richard?'

'Well enough. What brings you here?'

'They want boys,' Buttercup said, nodding through the entrance tunnel where the plasterer was taking down his ladders. He cracked another nut between a massive finger and thumb, then offered me one. He loomed over me, his face flat as a malt shovel with a broken nose, jagged teeth, a scar on his forehead, and another on his cheek. He had enormous hands, tree-trunk legs, and a chest like a barrel. He was all bone and muscle dressed in drab wool and buff leather. 'Boys,' he repeated.

'I thought the choir school had closed,' I said.

'It did, yes, it did,' Buttercup frowned as if the closure of Saint Benet's school was hard to remember. I had heard that the playhouse roof had collapsed, its ancient timbers rotted, and Sir Godfrey had been fortunate that the old hall had been empty at the time. 'But Sir Godfrey still has boys,' Buttercup went on, 'seven boys now, just enough for a choir. Not like the old days, Master Richard. But we have the beasts too!'

'You'll do beast shows here?' I asked.

He frowned again as if he did not understand the question, then nodded. 'Mister deValle is hiring us to do the beast shows. We can give him dogs, the bear, and the cocks, but the cockerels aren't as popular as the dogs. I do miss the old plays!

But we have the choristers, so we can do boys and beasts.' He brightened when he said that. 'Boys and beasts!' He laughed, then cracked another nut. 'We saw you!'

'Saw me?'

'In that play about Hester,' he said. 'You were good in that. The way you shrivelled away when that bastard tried to rape you. I liked that.'

'He did rape me,' I said.

'I liked that bit,' he said, 'and you were good.' He paused, then offered me a smile. 'You're still the prettiest girl on the stage, Richard.'

'I'm too old.'

'No, no, no! You're lovely. And the voice is good.'

'My voice broke long ago, Buttercup.'

'I like it all throaty and husky. Another nut?'

'No, thank you.'

'Now your brother . . . he mumbled.'

'He had a sore throat.'

'And he looked stiff. He walked like a duck.'

'He was playing a villain,' I said, for lack of anything else to say.

'But I liked you,' Buttercup said warmly. 'So are you playing here?'

'No,' I said firmly. Even if I had been tempted by deValle's gold I would have refused his offer once I learned that Sir Godfrey was a part of his schemes. 'I just came to look at the place,' I offered as explanation. The church clocks began to strike one all across London. 'And I must go, Buttercup.'

'And the other boy was here too,' Buttercup went on.

'Other boy?' I asked. The sound of bells was thickening as more and more churches struck the hour.

'The one whose feet you kissed, that one,' he said, meaning the moment when Uashti had grovelled at the feet of

Hester. So Simon Willoughby had visited this playhouse? And I remembered the lordling who had accosted him at the palace in Whitehall. The fair-haired lordling who was buying a playhouse, hiring players, but had no plays. 'He's a pretty boy, that one,' Buttercup added wistfully.

'I must go,' I said.

'Then God go with you,' Buttercup said dutifully.

I hurried down the lane to the river and ran along the bank to the Paris Garden Stairs. Swans were thick around the wharf, where two watermen waited. 'Need a boat, young sir?' one asked.

I shook my head. I could see Silvia was already halfway across the river. She had her back to me as her father rowed her towards the Blackfriars Stairs and I felt an immense sadness. I had missed her by minutes. I was a laughing stock in my brother's company. I was lonely, abandoned, poor and miserable. I walked east, going to the bridge, and though I should have been thinking about Simon Willoughby, a song was running through my head instead, a song from my brother's play *Two Gentlemen of Verona*. It had been my very first part in a play with the Lord Chamberlain's Men, and now, looking back, I wondered if it had been an omen. I had been playing Julia, disguised as a boy, and Henry Condell, playing the tavern keeper, had sung to me.

Who is Silvia? what is she,
That all our swains commend her?
Holy, fair, and wise is she;
The heaven such grace did lend her,
That she might admirèd be.
Is she kind as she is fair?
For beauty lives with kindness.
Love doth to her eyes repair,

To help him of his blindness;
And, being helped, inhabits there.

Then to Silvia let us sing,
That Silvia is excelling;
She excels each mortal thing
Upon the dull earth dwelling;
To her let us garlands bring.

SIX

I DID NOT want to laugh.

I was still bitter about the deception my brother had played on me, yet resentful as I was, I found myself reading Flute's lines with ever more enthusiasm. No wonder, I thought, that the Lord Chamberlain's wife had boasted of the play in court, because by the time we read the final scenes it was difficult to keep going through the laughter.

Duke Theseus and his bride, Hippolyta, wanted to be entertained on their wedding night, and perversely chose to watch a play offered by a group of Athenian tradesmen, the mechanicals as my brother had called them, of whom Francis Flute was one. The duke had been warned that the mechanicals' play was bad, that it was indeed atrocious, but he insisted on seeing it, and so we performed *Pyramus and Thisbe*.

Time had forced us to abandon the first reading of *A Midsummer Night's Dream* at the Blackfriars mansion, so we finished two days later perched on uncomfortable stools set around the chilly stage at the Theatre, and, as we read it, I remembered my brother's very first play. I had been ten years old at the time, and he had been twenty, just two years married, and teaching in a village school near Stratford. Sir Robert Throckmorton, a great landowner at nearby Coughton, wanted what he called an 'interlude' for his granddaughter's wedding, and my brother obliged by writing it. The interlude, really a short play, was called *Dido and Acerbas* and was performed by my brother, who played the villain Pygmalion, by one of his pupils who played Dido herself, by a wool merchant from Alcester who was the doomed Acerbas, and by a half-dozen other local men, all craftsmen. They rehearsed for at least three weeks, and, because Sir Robert was generously open-handed, folk from the surrounding villages were invited to watch the performance.

The story, as everyone who has been to school knows, is a tragedy that ends with Dido committing suicide by hurling herself onto a blazing fire. What persuaded my brother that it was a good idea to celebrate a wedding with a play about death is a mystery, but the tragedy, instead of provoking tears, was first greeted by nervous laughter, which grew and grew until folk could not contain their mirth and the whole audience, gentry and commoners alike, had tears running down their cheeks. Sir Robert, far from being angry at the disaster, declared it the best entertainment he had ever seen, but my brother was mortified. I asked him once whether he had kept a copy of the play, and he had scowled at the question, then muttered darkly that it had shared Dido's fate. 'I burned it.'

The interlude had ended with the heroine's fiery death. My brother had first thought of using iron braziers filled with burning logs to create the crucial scene, but Sir Robert had feared for the safety of his great house, and so, instead, six of my brother's pupils, none older than ten, were dressed in red cloaks, red hoods, and red gloves. 'We are flames!' one of them announced as they filed onto the makeshift stage where they crouched at the platform's edge and then slowly rose, swaying from side to side and waving their hands above their heads as they chanted over and over, 'We are flames! We are fire! Fiery flames and flaming fire!' Meanwhile the heroine, clothed in a white gown far too big for the player's small body, writhed in her death agony and tried to make her lines of defiance heard above the chanting flames. Like the rest of the company, the boys had been brave, forging ahead with their lines despite the laughter filling the hall, and all of them, boys and men alike, were richly rewarded by Sir Robert with coins. My mother laughed with everyone else, though Anne, my brother's wife, was furious, asserting that her husband had shamed the family.

Yet in his new play, written for the Lord Chamberlain's granddaughter, my brother had turned the dross of *Dido and Acerbas* into the gold of *Pyramus and Thisbe*. I half remembered the Pyramus tale from my Latin lessons in Stratford, knowing it was about a pair of doomed lovers who were forbidden to marry by their respective parents, but who secretly met on either side of a wall, which separated their houses. The wall had a crack through which the severed lovers whispered, or in our case bellowed, their declarations of undying devotion.

I had to play Thisbe against Will Kemp's Pyramus, and I had been dreading it because Will Kemp was a bully. To the groundlings in the yard and to the folk who greeted him on the streets he seemed a jovial, open-hearted man who was quick with a smile and a quip, but in the company, far away from his adoring admirers, he could be sullen and savage. He was also good, so good that my brother wrote parts especially for him, knowing that folk would pay more than once to watch Will Kemp clown, sing, and caper. Kemp was always angry if the company performed a play that had no comic part suited to his talents because he believed the audience came to see him, not Richard Burbage. But in Nick Bottom, the weaver, he understood he had found a jewel, and, for once, he neither grumbled nor argued, but threw himself into the character with enthusiasm. When we came to the play's ending, and the trades-men of Athens at last presented their interlude of *Pyramus and Thisbe* to the duke, Kemp could no longer sit and read. He had to stand and move. He carried the pages with him, reading as he acted.

> '*O grim-look'd night! O night with hue so black!*
> *O night, which ever art when day is not!*
> *O night, O night, alack, alack, alack.*'

He played the silly speech in a mock heroic tone, bemoan-ing that his love, Thisbe, had not arrived at the wall until, at last, she did. I stood and minced across the stage. Will Kemp had snatched Richard Cowley, the hired man who played Tom Snout, off his stool and placed him at the stage's centre. 'You're the wall,' he told him, and pulled out one of Cowley's hands and made him hold his fingers apart. 'The chink in the wall,' Kemp explained, then nodded at me, 'go on, Dick.'

'"O wall!"' I cried, '"full often hast thou heard my moans, For parting my fair Pyramus and me."' I was pitching my voice ludi-crously high. I had taken off my hat to shake my long hair free, I swayed my hips, took tiny steps, and, because I had already learned the words, had my hands free so I could clasp them in front of my breast. "My cherry lips have often kissed thy stones,"' I wailed, then leaned forward and gave Cowley's out-stretched hand a slobbery kiss. The whole company laughed, only now they were not laughing at me, but at Francis Flute, who was playing a woman so grotesquely.

Kemp took the scene yet higher by making every gesture more pronounced, by using wildly exaggerated faces and stress-ing the stupidity of the words. '"I see a voice!"' he exclaimed, eyes wide, '"now will I to the chink,"' he strode with clumping steps to the wall, '"to spy,"' he leaned down, sticking his rump far out, then turned an astonished face towards the yard, "'and I can hear my Thisbe's face! Thisbe?'"

I gasped with joy, clasped my hands again, twirled around, looked coy, and made my voice higher still. "'My love thou art, my love I think!'"

Kemp puckered his lips and jammed them against Cowley's hand, then made his voice into a bestial, hungry growl. "'O kiss me through the hole of this vile wall!'"

I dashed to the 'wall', stooped, and kissed the hand. "'I kiss the wall's hole,'" I moaned, "'not your lips at all!'"

Everyone onstage was laughing. Will Kemp straightened. 'Wouldn't hole be better?' he suggested to my brother.

'Hole?'

Kemp imitated my woman's voice. "'I kiss the wall's hole,'" he piped, "'not your hole at all!'"

Again there was laughter. 'It is better,' my brother agreed, 'but the Lord Chamberlain might not be persuaded of that. And his wife certainly won't.'

'A good point, Will, a good point!' For once Will Kemp was not arguing. 'Leave it as it is,' he told me.

A few moments later it was Will Kemp again who dreamed up a small change to the script. It was his death scene. He believed, wrongly, that Thisbe was already dead, and so he stabbed himself again and again with a sword. The death, of course, made us laugh. He stabbed himself so often, so dramatically, writhing and falling, then rising again to fall once more. His last words as Pyramus were gasped in his death throes; "'Now die, die, die, die . . .'" he declaimed, then paused, evidently lost on the page. He frowned, plainly unable to remember or find the next word. He frowned at the page, looking for the word, and still he paused until, at last, Isaiah Humble, the bookkeeper, prompted him, 'It's "die", Will.'

"'Die!'" Will bellowed.

And we all laughed, just as he had meant us to. Even my brother, who could be irritated by Will Kemp's alterations to his words, laughed. 'We'll keep that,' he said, 'thank you, Will.'

'Ah,' Will Kemp said, beaming, 'we are good!'

The faces of our company were eager. The play had captured us, we knew it would work, we already anticipated the laughter of the crowd, the bursts of applause, the excitement as new audiences clamoured to hear the play.

And across the wintry river men were planning to steal it from us.

Next day it rained. And the day after. And on it went, relentless, pouring, flooding the streets and cascading from London's roofs. It was cold too, so cold that on the third day the rain turned to sleet, driven by a vicious north wind. The Theatre was closed. We sometimes played in bad weather, though we tended to hurry the plays if it began to rain, but there was no chance of playing in this wet blast, and so no flag hung from the tower and no trumpet summoned the playgoers across Finsbury Fields.

I wanted to stay indoors, to go downstairs to Father Laurence's room and shiver in front of his fire, but I wanted to see Silvia even more, and so I invented an excuse. Alan Rust, seeing the clouds gather before the rain came, had announced that the company would rehearse the final scenes in Blackfriars. 'On Monday,' he said, 'we'll begin with the courtiers. That's Duke Theseus, Hippolyta, the four lovers, and Philostrate.' The mechanicals, though they appeared in the ducal court at the play's end, were not summoned, but I still walked across London wrapped in a great cloak that was sodden before I had even reached Moorgate.

'You look like a drowned rat,' my brother greeted me, 'and why are you here?'

'We might reach the scene with Pyramus and Thisbe,' I suggested, knowing full well we would not.

'We won't,' he said brusquely, 'and you'll just be in the way. Go home.'

'In a while,' I said. A fire burned in the huge hearth, and I crouched beside it, letting its warmth seep through my soaked clothing. My brother hesitated, as though he was about to insist that I left, but Isaiah Humble, who was sniffing endlessly, wanted my brother to decipher some words he could not make out and I was left alone.

The great hall was busy. The courtiers were at the further end, beneath the oriel window, where Alan Rust walked them through their scenes, deciding where they should enter and where they would stand. Three carpenters were sawing and hammering beneath the minstrels' gallery, making the stage and the new screen, while Jean, our seamstress, was unrolling huge bolts of cloth on the big table. 'Come and help me, darling,' she called to me.

Jean was excited. Our costumes were motley; some were beautiful, most were threadbare, and all were much used, but it seemed that Lady Anne Hunsdon had decreed that the costumes for *A Midsummer Night's Dream* were to be flamboyant and distinctive. 'She wants it to look like a masque,' Jean told me, 'and she's given me a clever little girl to help me. Look at this!' She unrolled a bolt of shimmering silver silk. 'Lord alone knows what it costs. And this!' She pulled a roll of dark blue velvet from beneath the pile. 'And this! Oh my sweet lord!' She ran a hand across a bolt of pale yellow satin, then tugged at another bolt. 'And velvet! Thirty shillings a yard in Cheapside. And sarsenet! God only knows what you pay for sarsenet. Lace! Lawn! Taffeta! Oooh, and this.' She grimaced.

'What's that?'

'Just fustian,' she said, 'goose-turd green. I hate that colour.

156

Still, it will do nicely for your coat. Can you carry all these for me?'

'I want a silk coat.'

'Francis Flute does not wear silk, silly boy. Hold out your arms.'

I dutifully held out my arms. 'Where are we going?'

'To her ladyship's chamber,' she said as she heaped the bolts onto my outstretched arms, 'and you're not to say a word about the play.'

'I won't.'

'His lordship hopes the Queen will be here for the wedding, so everything has to be the best,' she said as she went ahead of me to open the central doors. She waited till we were in the grand hallway outside, then turned to me and lowered her voice. 'They say his lordship is the Queen's half-brother!'

I smiled. 'Gossip, Jean, gossip.'

'No, honest, swear to God! His mother was Mary Boleyn, the Queen's aunt. And Mary Boleyn was fat Harry's mistress before they married her off. Poor girl. Can you imagine a great lump like that bollocking between your legs? This way, not a word.' She hurried ahead, then stopped and turned to me again. 'But the Queen might not come to the wedding. She doesn't like the groom's mother.'

'How do you know?'

'Everyone knows!'

'I don't.'

'Lady Berkeley bought a lute that was all covered in jewels. And the Queen had set her heart on owning it, and Lady Berkeley bought it first and wouldn't give it to her, so now they won't talk to each other. If I was Lady B I'd just give her the lute and be done with it! I mean a lute's a lute, isn't it? They all go twang. Now hush. Not a word.' She was leading me through a maze of passageways that ended by a half open door where she told me to wait while she went into the room beyond. I saw her make a curtsey. 'Can Master Shakespeare enter, my lady?'

'Has he got clean feet?' a voice asked, provoking a chorus of giggles.

'Clean as they'll ever be, my lady.'

'Then we shall risk his presence.'

Jean turned and grinned at me. 'Come on, Richard.'

I had to edge into the room because the bolts of cloth were so cumbersome. The chamber was panelled, warmed by a fire, and hung with tapestries. Six women watched me enter, making me blush. Two were seated on high-backed chairs, and I made a clumsy bow in their direction. One was Elizabeth Carey, the bride, and next to her was a good-looking older woman who had the same fair hair as Elizabeth. The older woman had bright, clever eyes, and a smile that widened when I bowed to her. 'So nice to see a man being useful!' she observed.

The women all laughed. Four were servants or attendants, all seated on cushions, and among them was Silvia. I saw her looking up at me, saw the smile on her face, and I feared I would blush and looked away quickly.

'Mister Shakespeare is a player, Mother,' Elizabeth Carey said. She was dressed in pale blue, the satin of her skirt prettily embroidered with silver threads that made a pattern of ivy. Her fair hair was long, as befitted an unmarried girl. Her mother, Lady Carey, was dressed in deep red, slashed with white, and she seemed to find me amusing.

'Your brother is the poet?' she finally asked, after inspecting me.

'He is, my lady, yes.'

'How fortunate you are.'

'Put the bolts down, Richard,' Jean said, indicating a Turkey carpet at the floor's centre. A fierce fire burned behind the two tall chairs. Rain rattled on the diamond-paned windows, which looked out onto a courtyard.

'Your brother is a clever man,' Lady Carey said.

'He is, my lady,' I said for lack of anything else to say, then spilled the bolts of cloth clumsily onto the carpet.

'He might be clever,' Elizabeth Carey said mischievously, 'but not as good-looking as you!' All the girls giggled, and I, of course, blushed a deep scarlet.

'Elizabeth!' Lady Carey said, though not sternly.

'Can you find your way back to the hall?' Jean asked me.

'I think so,' I sounded dubious because the old monastery was a warren of rooms, passageways, and antechambers.

'You'll deny us Master Shakespeare's company?' Lady Carey asked. 'I was hoping he could tell us about the play. Your grandmother has read it,' she said this to her daughter, 'and she declares it to be astonishing, yet the rest of us are denied the pleasure.'

'Indeed we are denied, Mother,' Elizabeth Carey said.

'And here is Master Shakespeare himself,' Lady Carey said, 'and I command you, Master Shakespeare, to tell us of this play.' She offered me an imperious look. 'What is it about?'

'I . . .' I started, then stopped. 'It's very complicated, my lady,' I said weakly, 'and I only know the little pieces that I'm in.'

'The little pieces!' She half smiled, then turned it into a frown. 'For a player you're a very bad liar! What character do you play?'

Again I hesitated. I wanted to answer 'a lover' to impress Silvia, but thought that answer would simply provoke more unanswerable questions, then before I could say anything at all Elizabeth Carey challenged me. 'Are you a fairy?'

'No, my lady!' I said a little too vehemently.

'But there are fairies in the play?'

'Yes, my lady,' I said, knowing that my brother had already revealed that to her.

'But if you're not a fairy,' Lady Carey said, feigning puzzlement, 'what are you? An ogre? A demon?'

'I'm a bellows mender, my lady.'

159

Her eyes widened. It was plain she was enjoying herself. 'A bellows mender! Well, I suppose that's a very useful trade. Are there many bellows in the play?' I had no idea how to respond, and so said nothing. 'It seems we've learned one thing, ladies,' she went on, 'the play has a bellows mender in it! I confess I am intrigued. Do you mend bellows on the stage?'

'No, my lady.'

'So you're a bellows mender who doesn't mend bellows! How very intriguing! What do you do instead?'

'I play in a play, my lady,' I said, and that, of course, was the truest answer I gave her.

Lady Carey sighed. 'He's a very obstinate bellows mender. Silvia, show the obstinate bellows mender the way to the hall.'

'Yes, my lady.'

'And if you trip over any broken bellows, give them to him for mending. But come here first, young man.' I dutifully walked to her chair and bowed. 'I was teasing you,' she said, 'but we do look forward to your play.' And with those words she felt in her purse and took out coins that she offered me.

'My lady . . .' I began to stammer thanks.

'Go,' she said with a smile.

By chance Silvia had been the servant closest to the door and so the one selected to be my guide. I bowed to Lady Carey again, backed awkwardly away, almost tripping on the bolts of cloth, then followed Silvia through the door. She was giggling. 'A bellows mender?' she said, then plucked my sleeve to draw me out of the room's earshot. 'Lady Carey's nice,' she said.

'She is kind,' I said. She had given me four shillings. A good week's wages!

'And she loves poetry. She reads it to us sometimes. I don't understand half of it, but we have to listen. She's reading one now all about a red cross knight and a dragon. It's nice. But oh my word, it does go on.' She laughed. 'And her daughter's the same, she's always reading poetry. And, of course, they're both excited about your play. We all are. Did you see the new playhouse? What was it like?'

'Big.'

'I can see that for myself!' she said scornfully. She was walking very slowly. 'I'd love to go to a playhouse.'

'You've never been?'

'Never.'

'I'll take you,' I said awkwardly.

'If they ever let me out of here.' She laughed. 'I must get back, we're supposed to be sewing the costumes.' She still walked slowly. 'Spending money, they are! Well, they have plenty to spend.' She paused at a turning in the panelled corridor. 'I suppose I'll see the play here, won't I?'

'I hope so.'

'And you'll be here at Christmas.'

'I will?'

'They're putting on a play at Christmas. Didn't you know? That's why there's all the hurry in the hall. They have to finish the carpentry. So I'll see two plays!'

'You will,' I said, 'but it's not the same as at the playhouse.'

'No?'

'The playhouse is more raucous.'

'I like raucous,' she said, smiling.

'Not if it's a riot,' I said.

'A riot?'

'There was a riot last year,' I told her, 'some apprentices didn't like the play and started throwing things, then they climbed onto the stage and we had to drive them back with pistols and halberds. It happened at Greys Inn too. We were playing *Richard II*, and they wanted to hear *A Comedy of Errors*.'

'What did you do?'

'We did the comedy. Better that than a broken head!'

She grinned. 'We wouldn't want Francis Flute to have a broken head, would we? Be careful! It's dark down here.' The warning was because she had turned into a narrow passageway far from any window. I realised she was taking me back to the great hall by a much longer and more circuitous route than Jean had used, and now, in a dark corner where two corridors met, she stopped and looked up into my face. For a moment she said nothing, just looked at me, and the moment stretched awkwardly, and then, taking courage, I bent down and kissed her. It was an impulse. She had arranged the impulse, of course. She had stopped, she had smiled up at me, she had waited, and I had done just what she wanted. I kissed her, and she kissed me back, and then neither of us had a word to say. I was in a daze.

She was still smiling, still not moving.

'"Who is Silvia?"' I asked, '"what is she, that all our swains commend her?"'

She gazed up at me, her eyes big in the shadows. 'Did you make that up?'

'Yes,' I said.

'You're funny.' She stood on tiptoe and kissed me again. 'I must go back; you walk straight down that passageway.'

'I will see you again?' I called after her.

She waved without turning around, and then she was gone. And I was in love.

It was still raining. Once back in the hall I could see the sleet slashing past the oriel window and hear the wind moaning in the high chimney. I was still in a daze, still trying to relive the sensation of Silvia's kiss, and at the same time feeling disappointment that she would be busy with needlework now, and I would have no chance of seeing her. I had no business in the hall, but I did not want to leave. I went close to the generous fire, still trying to dry out my rain-soaked clothes. Richard Burbage,

Henry Condell, Alexander Cooke, and Kit Saunders were being rehearsed by Alan Rust, while the other players looked on. Alexander and Kit were playing the girls, and they were at the front of the imaginary stage, while the two men watched from the back. Kit was small for his age while Alexander was tall, and my brother had written words to fit their stature. '"You puppet you!"' Alexander screeched. When we had read the scene the first time people had laughed at the fight between the two girls, but the weather seemed to have dampened all our spirits, and no one seemed to have any enthusiasm.

'Move further to the left,' Rust told Kit.

A gust of wind splattered the high window with rain and flickered the flames in the hearth. '"How low am I, thou painted maypole? Speak!"' Kit shouted at Alexander. '"How low am I? I am not yet so low but that my nails can reach unto thine eyes!"' He ran across the stage, hands crooked, to claw at Alexander's eyes.

'Scream at her as you run,' Alan told Kit, 'I don't want silence! And don't let her reach you,' Alan added to Alexander. 'Let her get close, then run for your life. Take shelter behind the two men.'

'Do I follow her?' Kit asked.

'No, just stop where she was standing. Turn and face her, but you're not going to attack her while she's with the men. Now let's do it again.'

Richard Burbage, either tired or bored, fetched a chair from the big table and took it to the pretend stage. He sat. The real stage was being built at the other end of the hall, filling the big space with the sounds of saws and hammers. Alan Rust was looking over Isaiah Humble's shoulder to read the lines, when Isaiah suddenly sneezed.

'Oh, for God's sake, Isaiah!' Rust recoiled from the sneeze.

'Sorry,' Isaiah said, then sneezed again.

Rust snatched up the pages and moved away from Isaiah.

'Kit?' he called, 'go from "You juggler, you canker-blossom, you thief of love."'

'Sorry,' Isaiah said. He looked ill, but who would not feel ill in this miserable, cold, wet weather?

My brother came to the fireplace. 'We're rehearsing Titania and Oberon tomorrow,' he told me, 'and the mechanicals on Friday. Do you know your lines?'

'All of them.'

'So you don't have to stay now,' he said pointedly. 'Come back on Friday.'

'I'll wait for the rain to stop.'

'It's not going to stop. It will never stop. The sky is as black as Satan's arse.' He turned to watch Kit scream and run across the stage.

'Faster!' Alan Rust shouted. 'Run like you mean to kill her. Do it again.'

'You're having a Christmas play here?' I asked my brother. I would much rather have asked him whether it was true that he and Francis Langley were Sharers in a brothel, but I knew the question would only receive scorn and would elicit no answer.

'A play for Twelfth Night?' he said, then grimaced as though the idea was unwelcome, but then relented and answered. 'His lordship wants one, yes.'

'Which one?' I asked a little too eagerly, making him frown at me. I was hoping, of course, that it would be a play in which I had a part, anything that would bring me back to Blackfriars and Silvia.

'I was thinking about *Love's Labour's Lost*,' my brother said, 'but that's hardly tactful.'

'Tactful?'

Isaiah Humble began coughing and could not stop. Rust turned and frowned at him. 'Sorry,' Isaiah managed to say.

'God spare us the plague,' my brother said quietly.

'It's winter,' I said, 'the plague doesn't strike in winter.'

'It strikes when it will,' my brother said brusquely. 'And *Love's Labour's Lost* would not be tactful because at the end of the play the princess delays the marriage for a year, and I don't suppose Lady Carey would take that as a good omen for her daughter's wedding. And Christmas plays need to be short. Most of the audience is drunk, asleep, or both, so we must give them something light and quick.'

'*Love's Labour's Won*?' I suggested.

'We did that for his lordship two years ago,' he said, staring into the fire with a frown. 'Maybe *Fair Em*? We haven't played that here.'

'I thought you didn't like it?'

'It's written with a shovel,' he said derisively, 'but it's short, folk seem to like it, and his lordship hasn't seen it.'

I had not seen *Fair Em, the Miller's Daughter* either. 'Is there a part for me?' I asked, hoping that I would have reason to come to the mansion for the Christmas revels.

'No,' he said, without hesitation.

Isaiah sneezed, coughed and moaned. He found a handkerchief and buried his nose in it, then sneezed again. 'For God's sake,' Rust snarled at Isaiah, 'take your coughing away. Go home. Get better.'

'Or die!' Will Kemp added.

'Sorry!' The poor man stood and fled past the carpenters and out through the door.

'If you're going to stay here,' my brother said to me sourly, 'then be the bookkeeper till Isaiah gets back.'

'You'll pay me?'

'For God's sake, yes,' he said irritably, 'we'll pay you. Now sit down.'

I had a job. In Blackfriars! I sat at Isaiah's place, took the pages back from Alan Rust, and hid my happiness.

Is she kind as she is fair?
For beauty lives with kindness.
Love doth to her eyes repair,
To help him of his blindness.

They hang thieves. Any sizable town has a gallows, and London has several, though the only hangings I had seen were at Smithfield. The condemned, their hands tied behind their backs, were brought to their death on a cart, the ropes were tightened around their necks, and the cart dragged away so that they fell a foot or so, jerked to a stop, and started dancing. If they had friends, and if the constables and the hangman stood back, they might die quickly by having those friends drag down on their ankles, but that was never popular with the crowd, who liked to see the spasms and the dancing legs and the piss dripping off their bare feet. Their feet were almost always bare; they might be thieves, but they were always poor. 'Rich thieves,' my brother had told me more than once, 'don't end up on the gallows. They live in Grays Inn or at the Middle Temple and wear black robes.'

Sir Godfrey had liked to take us to a Smithfield hanging. When I was an unwilling pupil at Saint Benet's there were usually between fourteen and twenty of us, and we would walk in procession, dressed in our grey robes, and Sir Godfrey, resplendent in his priestly cassock, would demand a path through the crowd, a path made easier by the looming presence of Buttercup, who only had to growl to frighten folk. 'Behold,' Sir Godfrey would preach to us when we reached the front of the eager crowd, 'the fate of malefactors. Witness the wages of sin!'

When a hanging man's bladder began to empty he would push us forward. 'Crawl beneath the piss, boy, crawl! Be baptised again!' He believed, as other folk did, that to be christened by a dying man's piss would keep us from a similar fate.

Yet if the wages of sin were death by hanging, Sir Godfrey had no compunction about keeping us from sin. When he tested our ability to pass as girls he would insist that we minced down Cheapside or some other crowded street and so tempt men to follow us. If it was Cheapside, we would vanish into Cooper's Alley that was dark even on the brightest summer's day. The alley led beneath overhanging houses, then turned sharply right into a dank evil-smelling courtyard where Buttercup and George Harrowby, one of the school's two ushers, would be waiting. The man would follow, lured by a smile and by a wave of small fingers, then find himself trapped in Buttercup's fearful grip. 'What do you want with my little sister?' Buttercup would growl.

The man would protest, but a protest uttered when you are rammed against a wall with ham-like fingers tightening on your throat is futile. Some men would grope for a knife or even a sword, but George Harrowby would have his own dagger ready. 'You like the taste of steel?' he would ask, rat face grinning and dagger's point pressed against the victim's ribs. They always paid.

'You're a good boy,' Buttercup would tell us. He would sometimes slip us a coin if Harrowby was not watching. 'Hide it, boy, hide it.' The constables knew what we were doing, but Sir Godfrey was generous to them, and they ignored us.

At first I had been scared to walk London's streets dressed as a girl, but I had learned to enjoy it. It is different being a girl. A man can walk London's streets, and no one will notice him unless he is a lordling with lace, satin, silk, and a sword, but a girl, even a girl drably dressed as a servant, is watched all the time. I was always aware of the appraising glances, some brazen, some furtive, but constant. Men called to us. 'Come to me, sweetheart, I've got something special for you!' They laughed, they touched us. Every young woman, except the well-born who were escorted by retainers, was prey to any man. My height deterred some, but others found it exciting. 'Wrap those long legs round me, puss!' they would say, and I would offer them a coy glance, a smile, and lead them into the alley where Buttercup and Harrowby lurked. I would help relieve them of their purses. I became a thief.

I learned that money was the object of life, and I wanted money. I wanted the servants, the fine clothes, the respect in the street, and a horse of my own. I wanted to ride into Stratford and spit on Thomas Butler and his sour wife, to spit on all those who had told me to work harder, work harder, work harder. To work harder for what? To become a carpenter? A cobbler? A glove maker or a ditch-digger? To be someone who was forever pulling my forelock? To be always bowing, snivelling and flattering? And so I began to thieve, and I found I was good at it. Sir Godfrey rewarded me by not whipping me. I had a skirt with a slit that opened to a deep pocket, and I became adept at dropping small valuables into that hiding place. One of the other boys, dressed like me, would distract the shopkeeper or his apprentices, and I would slide a small silver cup or perhaps a trinket into the pocket; anything that Sir Godfrey could sell. The trick of it, I learned, was to linger in the shop after stealing the item, to make myself pleasant, to smile, and always leave unhurriedly. By sixteen I was an accomplished thief.

And they hang thieves.

And at seventeen I became a player with my brother's company, playing small parts that grew larger, and though by playing I made money honestly, it was never enough, and I became a thief of opportunity, no longer dressed as a girl, but now a hunter of London's alleys. My victims were drunks who were helpless, or perhaps a newly arrived bumpkin who failed to guard his baggage, and on one glorious day a nobleman, whose purse contained sixteen shillings. His lordship had been at the

Theatre, paying for one of the precious stools at the edge of the stage, and he had brought a bottle of wine with him, though he was drunk enough when he first sat down. By the end of the play the bottle was empty and he was slumped against the stage's back wall, asleep. He woke after the audience had left, and, in a slurred voice, demanded that two of us help him home. He had no servant, which was unusual for a lordling, but Simon Willoughby and I steered him across Finsbury Fields to the Moorgate where he suddenly demanded that we leave him at the Spanish Lady, a tavern just inside the gate. We helped him to a seat, where he fumbled in an embroidered purse and gave me a coin. 'Wine, boy, get me good wine, and a tobacco pipe. Go fetch!'

He was asleep within moments. Simon and I looked at each other, I put a finger to my lips, then quietly, stealthily, I unbuckled his purse. We left the Spanish Lady, each of us eight shillings richer, and I never saw the man again. I sold the purse, a fine one with silver thread and silver buckles, for another shilling.

Simon Willoughby, being younger than me, had been over-excited by the theft, and I had to snarl at him to keep silent when we returned to the Theatre. I never stole with him again, though sometimes he would look at me with a raised eyebrow as if to suggest we should try another such adventure. He was John Heminges's apprentice, and his wages, such as they were, went to his master who might or might not give him a portion, though Simon probably did not care. He was a pretty boy, and, as my brother had said, he had smeared half the beds of Whitehall with his joy. He was not short of money, I knew. He was a good player, too eager for praise, but reliable onstage, and much loved by our audiences, yet that Christmas season, as we rehearsed *A Midsummer Night's Dream*, he behaved strangely.

He was playing Titania, Queen of the Fairies, and it was one of the larger parts. She and Oberon, the fairy king, had quarrelled over an orphan boy that each wanted as a companion and whom Titania would not surrender. In revenge, Oberon played a trick on her, pouring onto her eyelids the juice of a magic flower that would cause her to fall helplessly in love with the very first creature she saw on waking. "'What thou seest when thou dost wake,'" John Heminges intoned, leaning over Simon Willoughby's sleeping body, "'Do it for they true love take;

> *'Love and languish for his sake.*
> *Be it ounce, or cat, or bear,*
> *Pard, or boar with bristled hair,*
> *In thy eye that shall appear*
> *When thou wak'st, it is thy dear.*
> *Wake when some vile thing is near.'*

And the vile thing was Will Kemp, playing Nick Bottom, whose human head had been magically changed into an ass's head. "'Bless thee, Bottom, bless thee!'" my brother, playing Peter Quince, exclaimed, "'Thou art transformed!'"

It was nonsense, of course! It was, as Hippolyta says of *Pyramus and Thisbe*, 'the silliest stuff that ever I heard'. But somehow the nonsense worked. It is one of the marvels of the playhouse that whatever you lay in front of the groundlings, they believe. 'They want to believe,' my brother once explained. 'They do half our work for us. They come wanting to be amused, to be impressed, to be awed, to be frightened. And they have imaginations too, and their imaginations amend our work.'

But the imaginations of the wedding party would need to work hard if they were to amend Simon Willoughby's work, for he could not remember his lines, nor remember where onstage he was supposed to be as he spoke them. He was nervous and often close to tears, especially when Will Kemp became annoyed with him. It was not like Simon, who, for all his flirtations and silliness, was assiduous in learning his lines and proud of his ability to play them. He, like most of the boys, wanted to remain a player, and dreamed of being a Sharer one day, yet now, day after day in the great hall of Blackfriars, he stumbled and stammered his way through the rehearsals.

There was a moment when Nick Bottom came onto the stage just after Puck had transformed his head into that of an ass. We mechanicals all fled in terror, leaving him alone except for Titania who had been sleeping, unseen by any of us, at the back of the stage. Nick Bottom, puzzled by his companions' terror and unaware that he had been turned into a monster, walked up and down singing.

> *'The ousel cock so black of hue*
> *With orange tawny bill,*
> *The throstle with his note so true,*
> *The wren with little quill.'*

'I'm sorry, Will,' John Heminges interrupted. He was talking to my brother. '"The ousel cock"? "Orange bill"? Doesn't the cock ousel have a black beak?'

'Who the hell cares?' Will Kemp erupted.

'The hen bird has the orange . . .' John Heminges began, then backed hurriedly away from Kemp's anger.

'No one bloody cares!' Kemp shouted. 'Black beak, blue beak, green arse, red arse, any colour arse you bloody want! Can we keep going?'

'Keep going,' Alan Rust said quietly. 'Just sing the last line again.'

Will growled the last line, and Titania woke, saw the grotesque figure singing, and spoke: '"What angel wakes me from my bed?"'

'Flowery bed,' I corrected Simon.

171

'Oh shit,' Simon said.

'Do it again,' Alan Rust said patiently.

Simon got it right next time. Will Kemp went on singing as Titania's fairy court came onstage. Four of the fairies had speaking parts, and they were played by apprentices, while the other three were small boys from Lord Hunsdon's chapel choir, and all seven gently joined in Will Kemp's song.

> *'The finch, the sparrow, and the lark,*
> *The plain-song cuckoo grey*
> *Whose note full many a man doth mark*
> *And dares not answer no.'*

Titania was fully awake now and gazing at the ass-headed human with wide eyes. She had fallen in love instantly, provoked by the magic potion. Will finished his lines and waited. And waited. Silence. Except that the carpenters were still working on the stage. A saw sang and a hammer banged. 'Titania,' I said softly, 'your line.'

'Sorry.'

'"I pray thee, gentle mortal, sing . . ."' I gave him his line.

'"I pray thee, gentle mortal,"' Simon hurried to interrupt me, '"sing again. Mine ear is . . . mine ear is . . ."' He faltered again.

'"Much enamoured."'

'"Much enamoured of thy note, so is mine eye enthralled to thy shape."' Simon looked about to cry as he went silent again.

'For sweet Jesu's sake,' Will Kemp snarled.

'I'm sorry.'

'Who gives a duck's turd for your sorrow? Learn the damned lines, you prickless little horror.'

'The children!' one of Lord Hunsdon's retainers, responsible for the small boys, remonstrated.

'Give Simon the page,' my brother suggested quietly.

I gave Simon the page. 'Start from "though he cry cuckoo",' Alan Rust said.

And Simon, despite having the page in his hand, faltered again, which only prompted a volley of impious and filthy oaths from Will. 'I can't read it,' Simon complained, 'it's too dark in here.'

It was indeed dark in the great hall, the only light coming from the high oriel window beyond which the Surrey sky was shrouded by smoke beneath the dark winter clouds. I had four candles on the table to help me read the lines, but it was deep shadowed where Simon, Will, and the fairies rehearsed.

'Richard,' my brother said, looking at me, 'read it through with Simon. Up on the window bench.'

The rest of the players gathered about the fire smouldering in the big hearth while Simon and I climbed to the oriel window. I read Nick Bottom's lines, and Simon spoke his. He remembered them all except two. 'I do know them,' he said to me.

'You do.'

'But when Will's there they keep running away from me,' he said miserably.

'Will can be scary,' I said, 'but Bottom isn't. He's wearing an ass's head! Let's do it again,' I suggested, but he was no longer listening, staring instead across the river at the vast playhouse being built by Francis Langley. The scaffolding on the outside had been taken down, the tiled roof evidently finished.

'It's not just Titania,' Simon still sounded miserable. 'I have to learn Em's lines too. She has a lot!'

Fair Em, the Miller's Daughter was the play that the company would present in the great hall on Twelfth Night as part of Lord Hunsdon's Christmas celebrations. I had sat through the rehearsals, thankful that Isaiah Humble was still coughing in his lodgings, and was glad I was not performing in the play. It was clumsy compared to the *Dream*. 'Em's a good part,'

I said, telling the lie to encourage Simon. He did not respond, he did not even look at me, but instead went on gazing across the river to where the new playhouse was outlined against a dark sky. 'It's big,' I said, and Simon just nodded, and I remembered him being held against the wall in the palace courtyard by a young lordling with bright hair. I watched him. 'I wonder,' I said, 'what they're going to call it?'

'The Swan,' he said, almost without thinking, still gazing across the grey, slow river. It was low tide, and thin slabs of ice gleamed on the mud banks.

'The Swan?' I asked. 'How do you know?'

He looked at me with some alarm. 'I just heard someone say that,' he said, but blushed as he spoke. 'Maybe they'll call it something else. Let's read it again, please?'

'The Swan?'

'Go from where I wake up,' he said.

'I hear they're looking for players,' I pressed him.

'"What angel wakes me from my flowery bed?"' he said. There were tears in his eyes.

I read Nick Bottom's next line, and Simon responded and this time he knew all the lines. Knew every one. He smiled when we finished. 'See, I'm good, aren't I?'

'You're good,' I said.

'I knew I could do it!'

'Do it with Will now,' I said, and he nodded. I called down to my brother, who was with the other players by the fire. 'He knows the lines.'

'Richard.' Simon had seized my sleeve. His pleasure at saying all the lines without any mistake had gone, replaced by a look of terror again.

'What is it?'

'Come down, then,' my brother called.

'Is there another door to the mansion?' Simon asked me in a

low voice. He was leaning close to me, and I could see a trace of red madder caked in his lips.

'The main gate on Saint Andrew's Hill,' I said.

'The guards won't let me out. I need another door.'

'Are you two lovebirds coming?' Will Kemp snarled.

'There's someone I don't want to meet,' Simon hissed at me.

'I don't know another door,' I said to Simon.

'Boys!' Alan Rust shouted impatiently.

'He knows the lines,' I called again to placate Alan. And Simon did know them. Titania, Queen of the Fairies, fell in love with Nick Bottom, a weaver with an ass's head, without forgetting a word.

And Titania had known the new playhouse would be called the Swan.

Lord Hunsdon was generous. Each day, as well as ordering that the hall be warmed by a vast log fire, he had his household send us ale, bread, and cheese. He or his son, Sir George, sometimes came to inspect the work being done by Peter Strete, our carpenter, who, with his four men, had finished the stage, which stood five feet high. They were working now on the false wall that hid a space beneath the minstrels' gallery. 'We thought, my lord,' my brother spoke to the Lord Chamberlain on the day after Simon Willoughby had asked me about another door leading from the mansion, 'that we would shroud the wall and the front of the stage with cloth.'

'With cloth?'

'And instead of doors, my lord, we'll curtain the three entrances.'

'Cover the wall with cloth?' Lord Hunsdon asked. 'I thought you were going to panel it all.'

'We could do that, my lord, and stain the wood as we first proposed, but the smell won't be gone by Christmas.'

'Ah,' Lord Hunsdon said. 'Well, we don't want a stinking Christmas, do we? So you want me to buy cloth?'

'Common cloth, my lord, say dyed wool?'

'What does the damned stuff cost?'

'A stick of dark purple, my lord, sixpence. We'd prefer the yellow, which is a penny more.'

'And how many sticks?' A stick was a roll of material.

'Thirty, my lord, at least.'

'Good Lord in His cradle! It's damned expensive, your play-making!'

'Spend or stink, my lord,' my brother said.

Lord Hunsdon laughed. 'Then we'll have to spend, eh? The womenfolk want this play, and what the womenfolk want we have to supply, eh? Talk to Harrison. I'll tell him to have the sticks delivered.'

Walter Harrison, the steward, must have been eager to save his master's money because he came to the great hall that afternoon saying there was already some blue cloth in the house, and asking whether that could be used to disguise the raw wood scaffolding at the front of the stage. It seemed it could, because an hour later two servants brought the two sticks which they were asked to store beneath the stage. To my surprise and pleasure Silvia came with them. She shot me a secret grin, then curtseyed to my brother. 'Her ladyship asks if we can sew white roses and red crosses to the blue cloth, sir,' she said.

My brother nodded absently. 'Of course. Yes, of course.' Then he frowned. 'Red crosses?'

'The badge of the Berkeley family, sir,' Silvia said.

'Ah, the groom. Yes, of course.'

'I'll look to it, sir,' she said, curtseying again, then offered me the slightest jerk of her head as she climbed the temporary steps to the stage and vanished.

176

'I need a piss,' I said, though no one took any notice. The Sharers were arguing about how the play's ending should be staged. My brother wanted the fairies to be on the gallery, and Alan Rust worried about providing enough candles to light that space, and they took no notice of me as I followed Silvia.

She was standing at the back of the hall, in the dark space beneath the minstrels' gallery, a space that would become our tiring room. Her face was pale in the shadows. 'I just wanted to see you,' she said.

'And I you.'

I kissed her, and she clung to me. 'We're just so busy, what with Christmas round the corner,' she said. 'It's sew this and sew that. Be better when it's over.'

I held her, then remembered Simon's question. 'Is there another way in and out of the mansion?' I asked her. 'I mean besides the main gate and the one in the stable yard?'

She leaned back to look up at me. 'Are you planning to sneak in and find me, Richard Shakespeare?'

'Of course.'

She laughed. 'There's a door onto the river alley. But it's bolted at night.'

'Show me?'

'Best be quick,' she said, 'her ladyship's expecting me. Come on!'

She led me down a narrow corridor that led from the scullery passage. We passed storerooms heaped with firewood, and others stacked with ale butts, and at the corridor's end was a stout wooden door secured by an enormous iron bolt. 'There,' she said. 'We're allowed to use it, but Harrison always sends a servant before nightfall to check that it's bolted.'

'I'd better come when it's light then,' I said.

She giggled, stood on tiptoe, kissed me, and ran.

I stayed a moment, unbolted the heavy door and pulled it

open, and saw that it looked into a narrow alley that led to Water Lane and so down to the river.

The sleet had turned into snow. I watched the heavy flakes sift down to the greasy wet floor of the alley where they melted, but the snow was falling thick and it would settle soon enough. It rarely snowed before Christmas. In January and February it was common enough, but before Christmas? I shivered, closed the heavy door, slid the bolt shut, and went back to the hall. 'It's snowing hard,' I said.

'God help us,' Will Kemp growled.

'Can we continue?' Alan Rust demanded.

We were rehearsing two plays now. *Fair Em* and *A Midsummer Night's Dream*. We were able to use the finished stage, rehearsing by the light of lanterns that now hung from the minstrels' gallery. Christmas was a week away, and the mansion was busy as servants stocked the storerooms, hung hams, and rolled in vats of wine. Manservants draped the great hall with holly and ivy, and a vast yule log was brought to the hearth. The log would be lit on Christmas Day, and it was hoped that it would burn through the twelve days of the holiday or else there would be misfortune in the house. It rested close to the fire, and wood-lice, woken by the heat, crawled out from the bark.

'We can't use the mansion during the twelve days,' my brother announced, 'except for one rehearsal on the morning of the performance. Remember your parts!' He glared at Simon Willoughby as he said the last three words. 'The costumes will stay here, and the scripts stay here too.'

'Can I take my scripts?' Simon Willoughby asked. He was still nervous, still frightened of Will Kemp, but he was struggling through the rehearsals, and there had been small need for me to feed him lines.

'You can take *Fair Em* home,' my brother said, 'but not Titania.'

'Oh.' Simon looked disappointed.

'You have plenty of time to learn Titania before we do the wedding play,' John Heminges consoled him. 'Just make sure you know Em's part.'

'Does anyone know how Isaiah is?' I asked.

'Coughing up blood and spit, last time I heard,' Will Kemp said with unholy delight. 'He might be dead and buried by Twelfth Night!'

'So be here on Twelfth Night,' my brother said to me. He glanced up at the oriel window, though it was so gloomy outside that he could see little. 'We'd best go home before the snow gets worse. Enjoy your Christmas season, masters.'

Enjoy your Christmas season.

I went home alone.

SEVEN

WILLIAM THE CONQUEROR sees the picture of a princess on the shield of the Marquess of Lubeck, who is in England for a tournament. The King falls in love with the girl whose portrait is painted on the shield, and, learning that she is Princess Marianne of Sweden who is being held hostage at the court of King Zweno of Denmark, he sails across the North Sea to woo her.

Princess Marianne, though, is in love with the Marquess of Lubeck, and has no interest in the King of England and so rejects his suit, but her friend, Princess Blanche, who is the daughter of King Zweno of Denmark, falls in love with the Conqueror. Unfortunately for Blanche the Conqueror does not return her love, so Princess Marianne and Princess Blanche concoct a plan. Princess Blanche disguises herself as Princess Marianne, and the disguise deceives William the Conqueror, who elopes with Princess Blanche because he thinks she is really the Princess Marianne.

'Sweet Jesus Christ,' Alan Rust had said at one of the first rehearsals, 'who wrote this crap?'

'Not me,' my brother growled.

'God's blood! Where did we find it? In a sewer? Rattle it along fast. Don't give the audience time to think about it.'

William the Conqueror discovers the deception, but happily realises that he has really been in love with Princess Blanche all along, and so he marries her, while Princess Marianne weds the Marquess of Lubeck. Meanwhile, in Manchester, Em, the beautiful daughter of a humble miller, is being wooed by three men, two of whom she does not want, and so she pretends blindness to deter the first, and deafness to repel the second, but in the end the man she does want to marry proves to be unfaithful, having sworn undying love to another girl, and so Em marries Lord Valingford, the man who had thought she was blind and who she discovers she really does love after all. It turns out that her father is actually Sir Thomas Goddard, a knight who has been banished by William the Conqueror, and who, instead of fleeing the country, has taken on the disguise of a miller in Manchester, and Em is thus revealed to be of gentle birth and thus a fit wife for Lord Valingford. William the Conqueror, played by my brother, recognises the injustice of Sir Thomas's banishment and restores him to his proper estate, and so ends the play.

"And what says Em to lovely Valingford?" William the Conqueror asked.

Simon Willoughby offered my brother a deep curtsey. "'Em rests at the pleasure of your highness!'" he said, then paused, and the pause stretched, and from my vantage point above I saw the look of wide-eyed panic as the next words fled his mind.

"And would . . .'" I hissed.

"And would I were a wife for his desert,'" Willoughby squeaked too hastily.

"'Then here, Lord Valingford,'" my brother said grandiloquently, and I could hear the relief in his voice that Simon Willoughby had not forgotten too many of his lines and that the play was at last ending, "receive Fair Em.

'Here take her, make her thy espoused wife.
Then go we in, that preparation may be made,
To see these nuptials solemnly performed.'

Exeunt. Flourish of drums and trumpets. Applause.

It was listless applause. Applause that only stirred itself to tepid life when Lady Anne, the Lord Chamberlain's wife, stood and called aloud, 'Well played!' Then the rest of the guests, wishing to be polite to her ladyship, imitated her enthusiasm as the players lined the stage and made a bow to the hall. It was a deep bow, but also a brief one, and then, with as much haste as they could manage without making it look like embarrassed flight, the actors filed back into the tiring room.

'Sweet Jesus,' Phil said, 'but that was agony.'

I had listened to the play in the musicians' gallery which was not the best place to be the bookkeeper, but when we had tried putting me beneath the stage no one could hear me unless I shouted, and so I had shared the gallery with Phil and his musicians. I had occasionally peered over the balustrade to watch the players beneath me. My brother wore a crown that circled a bald spot that was slowly spreading towards the bald patch at the front so it looked as if a malevolent barber had shaved the outline of an hourglass on his pate. He, like every other player, had skipped lines, hurrying the performance because the audience had been restless. Many had been yawning and some had slept through the whole play, which was perhaps excusable because they had just finished a generous feast, and the great hall was heated by a fire worthy of the pits of hell in which the last remnants of the yule log burned bright, fed by baskets of wood to drive away the winter cold. Servants threaded the hall to serve mulled wine to those in the audience who were still awake. Wine and warmth, the enemies of players. I had

watched Silvia, who, when she was not busy evading aristocratic hands as she poured the wine, had gazed at the stage
in rapture. She, at least, had loved every moment of *Fair Em,
the Miller's Daughter of Manchester*, but most of the guests had
chatted through it, had laughed at anything except the play, and
were plainly as relieved as the actors when it was finished.

Yet now, despite the play's failure, they were laughing. Now
they were suddenly awake and attentive because Will Kemp,
who had played the miller, was back onstage. He strode to the
front, held up his big hands, and bellowed for attention. 'My
lords! My ladies! Dear gentlefolk!' The noise in the hall had
slowly subsided, and Will, after bowing low to the assembly,
had promised them something new and something better. 'We
shall present a play at the wedding. Something to please you
all! And I can assure you there will be neither millers from
Manchester nor conquerors from Normandy in our new play. It
will be a play fit for the nuptials of a beauty.' That had provoked
laughter, then applause, and Sir George Carey, Lord Hunsdon's
son, had made his daughter stand to acknowledge the accla-
mation. Elizabeth dutifully stood, pale, shy, and pretty in the
candlelight, and Will Kemp had been struck with a sudden
inspiration. 'My lords!' he cried. 'My ladies! Gentlefolk all!
I pray your attention, for I have a poem for the bride.'

'No,' Phil, the chief musician, groaned, 'no, please no. Not
the farting song, please God, not that!'

'"Can anyone tell what I ail?"' Will had changed to a woman's
voice, high and shrill.

'Thank God,' Phil breathed. 'It's not the farting song.'

'"Was ever woman's case like mine?"' Will cried,

> *At fifteen years I began to pine,*
> *So unto this plight now I am growne,*

183

I can, nor will, no longer lie alone!
If dreams be true, then ride I can,
I lack nothing but a man!'

They cheered him, Elizabeth Carey laughed, and the Lord Chamberlain roared his approval. Will Kemp bowed low to his lordship, then held up his hands to quieten the room again. He had evidently decided to compensate for the disappointment of the play by being the Lord of Misrule, the traditional maker of mischief on Twelfth Night. 'One last poem,' Will announced, 'before we all go into this good night.'

'No,' Phil said quietly, 'don't do it, Will, just don't do it!'

'"It was a young man,"' Will began.

'Oh dear God,' Phil moaned, 'he is doing it!'

'"Who lived in a town,"' Will went on, '"a jolly husband was he,

> *'But he would eat more at one set dinner*
> *Than twenty would eat at three . . .'*

Will stopped abruptly because my brother and Alan Rust had hurried onto the stage, taken Will by his elbows, and now hauled him back to the tiring room. Phil, thinking quickly, looked at his musicians. 'The flourish again! One, two, one, two, three!'

The drums and trumpets sounded, the candles guttered, the yule log collapsed into glowing cinders, and the guests were laughing.

Christmas was over.

I had not enjoyed Christmas.

There had been no feast for me, except for the remnants of the meal served to Lord Hunsdon's guests on Twelfth Night.

That was when I ate cold swan for the first time, and it tasted like tough, sour mutton. There had been marchpane too, and I ate too much, so I was feeling sick. We were a morose group, sitting at the tables where the guests had eaten and surrounded by guttering candles thick with wax and the carcasses of swans and geese. Lady Anne Hunsdon, the bride's grandmother, found us there. We all stood as she arrived, bowing awkwardly, the heavy chairs scraping on the flagstones. The servants, clearing away what was left of the feast, went onto their knees.

'Well,' Lady Hunsdon said brusquely, 'that was not what I expected. Do sit down.'

'I'm sorry, my lady,' my brother had remained standing.

'Did you write it?'

'No, my lady.'

'I thought not. It lacked wit. And you, young man,' she stared at Simon Willoughby, 'you must remember your words.'

Simon Willoughby mumbled assent. His face still bore the lustrous paste of powdered pearls and ceruse, but his blush showed through.

'The wedding play . . .' my brother began nervously.

'Is better, I know, much better,' her ladyship interrupted, 'but is it a fitting entertainment if it's done badly? Many of the same guests will be here. Perhaps they'd prefer something else. Jugglers? Tumblers?'

No one responded. I knew what the Sharers were thinking, that if we were not needed at the wedding then they would not be paid for all the work they had invested in *A Midsummer Night's Dream*. Silvia was among the servants clearing away the remnants of the Christmas feast, and she caught my eye and looked anxious.

'The music was pleasant,' Lady Hunsdon went on.

'What a good woman she is,' Phil, sitting beside me, said quietly.

'More music! More dancing!' her ladyship said. 'The Queen likes such things.'

'Her Majesty is attending the wedding?' my brother, still standing, asked.

'She has not deigned to tell us whether she will attend or not, but if she does, Master Shakespeare, she will expect something spritely and witty. Nothing vulgar and coarse.' She shot a meaningful glance at Will Kemp.

'We . . .' my brother began.

'And,' Lady Anne interrupted him, 'she will expect the players to know their words! All of them. Do enjoy your food.' She swept from the great hall.

There was a moment's silence, then Will Kemp belched loudly. 'Does that mean we're still employed?'

'It means we start rehearsals again tomorrow,' my brother said.

There had been a bone-handled knife with a silver pommel engraved with a rose left on the table, and when Lady Hunsdon had arrived and distracted everyone's attention, I had managed to slip it into my sleeve. It would sell for a shilling or two, and I needed every shilling I could find. A hard winter meant a dead playhouse, and a dead playhouse meant penury.

A dozen of us slept that night in an empty stable of the mansion because it was past curfew and we could not leave the city. I remember looking up at a candlelit window and wondering if Silvia was there, but there was no chance of finding out because the doors into the mansion from the stable yard had been bolted. And that was Christmas, 1595.

In Stratford, as a child, I had looked forward to Christmas. My mother baked shrid pies, the traditional dish, mixing shredded mutton, which represented the shepherds, with thirteen fruits and spices, which stood for Christ and his twelve apostles. She usually made four or five, each large enough to feed a dozen people, and I would help carry the unbaked pies to Hamnet Sadler, the baker in Sheep Street, where all our neighbours would take their own pastries to be cooked in his big ovens. Then, over the twelve days, we would visit each other's houses to eat the pies. There was singing, dancing, and laughter, there were wassail bowls of mulled ale, spices, and chopped apples. The worst days of winter were yet to come, when the pastures about the town would be hard with frost and the river might freeze, and the bell of Holy Trinity would toll too often to announce a death, but for twelve days there was the warmth of welcoming hearths, there was food, and there was laughter.

My mother believed that at the chimes of midnight on Christmas Eve the cattle in their stalls and the sheep in their pastures knelt to celebrate the birth of Jesus. I had once sneaked from the house to peer into the cowshed behind Goodwife Larkin's house. 'The cows didn't kneel,' I had told my mother on Christmas morning.

She laughed at that. 'Silly boy, of course they didn't! They never do if you're watching.'

We decorated the house with garlands of ivy, we welcomed the mummers who circled the town in gaudy costumes, and we forgot the dark days to come. But in London, that winter, my Christmas was dark. The Widow Morrison had baked her shrid pies, but I was forbidden to taste them. 'You owe me rent, Master Shakespeare,' she had told me on Christmas morning.

'I know, mistress.' I had paid her two of the shillings that Lady Elizabeth Carey had so generously given me, but it had not been enough.

'A shilling and threepence! By Plough Monday, or I'll put you on the street!'

'Yes, mistress.'

'On the street, in the snow!'

The snow had melted by Plough Monday, and I was still in

the attic, I suspected because Father Laurence had paid what rent I owed. 'Did you, father?' I asked him.

'I'm going deaf, Richard, going deaf. How was your rehearsal yesterday?'

'It went badly, father.'

'Young Willoughby again?'

'He knows the words,' I said, then shrugged, 'well he did know them before Christmas. But now? As soon as he has to say them to Will Kemp he forgets them again.'

'Poor boy.'

But Father Laurence was the only one feeling sorry for Simon Willoughby, who, as December ended and January brought in more sleet and bitter cold, struggled with Titania's lines. Isaiah Humble returned for a few days, but then began coughing again. Augustine Phillips and his apprentice were still sick, and the company's mood grew even worse when my brother announced that he had finished his new play.

That should have been good news. We all knew he was excited by the tale and had resented breaking off its composition to write the wedding play, and he was in an ebullient mood when he arrived in the great hall one morning and dropped a thick sheaf of papers on the big table. 'The story, my masters,' he announced, 'of Romeo and Juliet.'

'And who in the devil's arsehole are they?' Will Kemp demanded.

'Star-crossed lovers,' my brother said.

'That's good, Will, that's good!' Richard Burbage responded immediately.

'Tell me I'm Romeo,' Will Kemp growled.

'You . . .' My brother was plainly astonished by the demand, as was everyone else, yet it was equally plain that Will Kemp had not been jesting. 'Romeo will be Richard,' my brother spoke firmly, nodding at Richard Burbage, 'and Juliet—' He stopped abruptly. I suspected he had been about to name Simon Willoughby for the part, but Simon had been so feeble in the last few days that my brother dared not suggest him. 'If Christopher Beeston is recovered, then he'd be an excellent fit for Juliet.'

'But I thought . . .' Simon Willoughby began, and looked close to tears.

'Christopher would be an excellent choice,' Alan Rust said savagely. 'He can remember his lines.'

'Don't we Sharers fit the plays?' Will Kemp demanded.

'Juliet is thirteen,' my brother said, ignoring the question, 'so Romeo can't be much older. Seventeen? Eighteen, perhaps? And he's beardless.' He looked at Richard Burbage, who wore a short brown beard.

'I can shave,' Burbage said.

Kemp growled unhappily, grudgingly accepting that his age prevented him from playing Romeo, but he was still in a belligerent mood. 'So what part do I play?'

My brother looked pained. 'There's a servant called Peter.'

'A big part?'

'It's not a comedy,' my brother said evasively.

'How many lines?

'As I said, it's not a . . .'

'How many lines?'

'As many as I wrote,' my brother snarled.

'Folk don't come to the playhouse to be miserable,' Kemp said forcibly. 'They want to laugh.'

'Peter is a good part,' my brother said unconvincingly, and that left Will Kemp in a foul mood for the rest of the day, and when Kemp was unhappy the rest of us suffered.

We finished early on those winter afternoons. Those of us who lived beyond the city's gates had to be outside the walls before the curfew sounded, and those who lived inside the city were supposed to be home before full dark. The constables rarely bothered those who disobeyed, but no one liked to walk the night-time streets unless they were in company, and armed company at that.

We finished early that afternoon, the same afternoon in which Kemp had grumbled at the part of Peter. The church clocks were striking four as my brother put the scripts inside the big wooden chest that stood to one side of the great hall's hearth, though this day he put two plays into the chest, *A Midsummer Night's Dream*, and the new play. 'Does it have a name?' Alan Rust asked.

'*Romeo and Juliet*, I think.'

'*Romeo, Juliet, and Peter*,' Will Kemp suggested harshly.

'*Romeo and Juliet*,' my brother said firmly, 'for certain.' He closed and locked the chest, then put the key back in its hiding place on the high carved mantel. 'We all meet here tomorrow,' he went on.

'If we can get here,' John Heminges said gloomily, 'it looks like snow again.'

'Just get here!' my brother snapped. The day's rehearsal and Will Kemp's unhappiness had left us all in an irritable mood.

We gathered by the fire to pull on our cloaks that had been set there to dry. Simon Willoughby left first. 'I need to piss,' he announced.

'You need to learn your lines,' Will Kemp growled.

'I'll wait for you in the yard,' Simon said, then fled across the stage and out into the scullery passage.

'Tomorrow morning,' my brother called up to the musicians on the gallery, 'same people, same time. We'll carry on from where we stopped today.'

We all left together, heading towards the Water Lane gate and the winter dusk. No one spoke much, no one cared to say much until we filed into the stable yard where Will Kemp cursed. 'Goddamned weather!' The sleet was falling hard.

'It will turn to snow before nightfall,' John Heminges said to me, 'and you'd better hurry if you're to leave the city before dark.' He frowned as he looked around the yard. 'Where's Simon?'

'He was pissing,' Kemp said, 'one of the few talents he has left.'

'Simon!' Heminges called. 'Simon!' There was no answer. A stable hand peered from one of the doors, then vanished. 'Simon!' Heminges called again, but there was still no answer. 'He said he'd wait for us here, didn't he?' Heminges asked plaintively.

'Maybe he was meeting someone,' Richard Burbage suggested, 'and he didn't want the rest of us to know whose bed he'll be wetting tonight.'

'I give the boy too much freedom,' Heminges said. 'Half the time I don't know where he is at night.'

'He's never late for rehearsal,' I said.

'What use is that,' Will Kemp snarled, 'if he can't remember his part?'

John Heminges looked pained, because any criticism of an apprentice reflected badly on the master. 'He's usually reliable,' he said to me, letting the other players walk on ahead, 'but I don't understand why he's so nervous.'

'Titania's a big part.'

'He's had larger. Much larger. The spoiled little beast!' He said the last four words vengefully.

'He'll be here in the morning,' I said, trying to placate him.

Heminges frowned at me. He was a Sharer, of course, and a kind man too, but that cold evening he was angry. 'Do I wait for him or not?' he asked. He expected young Simon to accompany him back to the comfortable house in Saint Mary Axe where he lived with a young wife and three small children.

'He'll find his way home,' I suggested.

'He'll have to,' Heminges said, then shivered. 'You'd better hurry.'

The city's gates were closed at nightfall, which came early on those dark, wintry days, and the guards on the gates were notoriously surly with anyone trapped on either side. If I was to get home I needed to use the closest gate, and use it quickly. I followed the other players out into Water Lane and looked up and down the hill, but if Simon Willoughby had come this way he had long disappeared. It was possible, of course, that he had used the door that led into the River Alley, a door I had shown him the day before, and it was certain, at least to me, that whoever Simon was avoiding was a person he did not want the rest of us to see. And that, surely, meant someone from a rival company, from the Swan, and I remembered the lordling lifting Simon's skirts at the palace. 'I'll see you tomorrow,' I said to John Heminges.

'Fare you well,' he said, 'and hurry!'

The church bells would be ringing the curfew soon, announcing the slamming of all the city's gates, and so I left by the nearest, Ludgate, and followed the course of the wall first north and then east around the city. I was cold, wet, and miserable. The curfew sounded as I passed Newgate, and by the time I reached Smithfield I was sopping wet, and there was still the Aldersgate, Cripplegate, and Moorgate to pass. The sleet seemed to harden, driven by a spiteful wind, and some time after dark it turned to a thin snow that caked on my sodden cloak. I was alone, but no footpad would be abroad on this frozen night.

I did not go home. The attic had no fire, it would be cold as ice, and I needed warmth. Father Laurence might or might not be awake, and if he was awake he might have the company of some secret Catholic seeking to make confession, but just two doors down from the widow's house was a small and cheap tavern called the Falcon, and the Falcon, for all its shoddy ways, at least kept a fire burning in winter.

The tavern's grand name belied the place. Most local people

called it the Stinking Chicken, because it lay just close enough to the sewer-ditch beside Finsbury Fields to smell like a cesspit. The Chicken had one room for drinkers, a door into Bishopsgate Street, another opening onto an alley, and a third leading to the malodorous room where the innkeeper, Greasy Harold, brewed his ale. Rickety stairs led to an upper chamber where Marie, a fading French widow, supplemented the Falcon's small earnings, or, more commonly, where travellers who failed to reach Bishopsgate before curfew could sleep in flea-ridden blankets for a penny. There were no travellers this night. I burst through the front door, shivering, whimpering, and more dead than alive, to see an almost empty room. Greasy Harold and his wife Margaret were there, with Marie, and with Dick, an old and morose man who seemed to live in the tavern. I ignored them because, thank God, there was a fire in the hearth.

I crouched by the flames, too cold to speak.

'You'll catch your death, Richard,' Margaret said. She was a kindly soul to all except her husband. 'Get that wet cloak off.'

'Snowing, is it?' Greasy Harold asked.

'What do you think?' Margaret snapped at him, then came and lifted the cloak from my shoulders. 'Look at you! Soaked through. You are a silly boy!'

'I'm cold,' I managed to say.

'Get all that wet stuff off. I'll fetch you a blanket. Pour him some humptey, you bullock.'

'If he pays,' Harold said.

'I'll pay,' I stammered, through chattering teeth. I had sold the silver-hilted knife for a shilling and threepence, a good price.

The evenings were always the dullest time of my day. Mornings were often spent in rehearsal, the afternoons were for performances when the weather allowed, but evenings, especially winter evenings, were empty. In summer there were always folk on Finsbury Fields, a few shooting at the archery butts, some playing bowls or skittles, a noisy bunch of apprentices kicking a ball, and most just lazing in the long twilight, but in winter the cold clamped down and the dark came early and the curfew locked the city tight. I hated going back to the cold attic, alone and lonely, and it was frustrating to sit in the Dolphin, even though the ale was better, because the Dolphin's whores were pretty, and I rarely had enough money to afford such company. Nell was gone, sadly, killed by the plague two years before, but Alice, the pretty elfin girl from Huntingdonshire, was still there, and she would sometimes sit with me until a customer demanded her. 'Round and round the mulberry bush,' she would always say when a man beckoned to her. 'Roly-poly time!'

The Stinking Chicken was cheaper. The ale was watery and the conversation stupid, if there was any conversation at all, but there was company, there was warmth, there were candles that someone else had paid for, and there was Margaret, motherly and kind, always ready to cosset me. She hung my outer garments over two chairs close to the fire and brought me a mug of humptey, which was ale into which her husband had grudgingly poured a thimbleful of brandy. Margaret had heated a poker in the fire and now dipped it into the mug to mull the humptey. The poker hissed. 'Drink that, Richard,' she said.

'Good brandy, that,' Greasy Harold remarked from the back of the room, 'not cheap rubbish.'

'Don't mind him,' Margaret said. Flecks of ash floated on the scummy surface of the ale, but it was warm, and I drank it. I was still shivering, but beginning to feel alive again.

'I saw your brother yesterday,' Dick said.

I kept silent as Margaret draped a blanket around my shoulders. 'He used to drink here,' she said, 'but not now.'

'He's gone bald,' Dick said. 'I know, because his hat blew off.'

We all contemplated that news. Conversations in the Chicken were often like this, though Margaret was happiest if I came of an evening after being at the palace. Then, just like her friend the Widow Morrison, she wanted to know every detail of what the Queen had been wearing, of what the Queen had said, and who had sat near the Queen. Somehow, in her head, I was an intimate friend of Elizabeth, by the grace of God, Queen of England, Ireland, and France.

'His hat blew off,' Dick said again, worried that the rest of us had not fully comprehended his news, 'and he was bald.'

'It was windy yesterday,' Margaret said encouragingly.

'He's not all bald,' Dick elaborated, 'but he will be soon.'

'*Votre frère est chauve, oui?*' Marie asked.

'He's bald,' I said, guessing at her meaning. He's also the clever one, the bastard. No, probably not a bastard, but maybe I am because I look nothing like my three brothers.

'You should speak English,' Greasy Harold frowned at Marie, 'like a Christian.'

'I can speak English,' she said, 'and I am Christian.'

'You're French,' Harold said, 'not the same, is it?'

'You think Jesus didn't die for the French too?' Margaret challenged him.

'Not if he had any bleeding sense, he didn't.'

'I was surprised,' Dick said. 'His hat blew off in the street and he was bald!'

'Like some others I know,' Margaret added, looking at her husband, who scowled. Greasy Harold was fat as a hog and had a head like a baby's bum; white, hairless, and full of shit.

'He's not very old, is he?' Dick asked.

'Thirty-one,' I said.

'That's not old, not really. I'm forty-seven!'

'He's in his prime,' Margaret said. 'Make another humptey, Harold.'

'If he pays,' Harold responded sullenly.

'I'll pay,' I said.

195

'Bald!' Dick said, trying to revive a conversation that seemed to have exhausted itself because the room stayed silent except for the sound of the wind and the crackle of pine logs in the fire. Dick was a scavenger, one of the men paid by the parish to clean the streets, and he considered himself an expert on fires, perhaps because they burned the collected rubbish in the Spital Field, and he was constantly warning Harold about burning pine. 'You'll have a fire in your chimney, and then it will be goodbye to the house,' he liked to say, but Harold liked cheap wood as much as he liked warmth.

Margaret brought me the second humptey. 'I knew there was something I meant to tell you,' she said, 'the Percies were here again today.'

'Not again,' I said.

'This forenoon,' she said. 'Poor old Father Laurence, they should leave him alone. He doesn't do nobody no harm.'

'He's a bloody Catholic,' her husband said.

'He's a harmless old soul,' Margaret said, 'and I'm sure he loves the Queen as much as the rest of us.'

I doubted that, but said nothing.

'I love the Queen,' Marie said.

'God bless her,' Dick said, knowing that if he said anything bad about the Queen then Margaret would make sure he never drank in the Chicken again.

'They were in the Theatre too,' Harold said.

'The Queen was?' Dick asked.

Everyone ignored him. I turned to look at Harold. 'The Percies? In the Theatre?'

'I saw them. Saw their bloody great horses in the yard.'

Lord Hunsdon had promised he would speak to the Pursuivants and warn them against searching the Theatre again, yet if Harold was right they had returned, and at a time when we were all in Blackfriars. 'Are you sure?' I asked.

196

'Of course I'm bleeding sure,' Harold said, enjoying my discomfort. 'There were five of the bastards, it was just before noon, and they went from the widow's house to the Theatre. I saw them!'

'The silly fools,' Margaret said happily, 'they won't find any Jesuits in the Theatre. You don't keep Jesuits there, do you, Richard?'

'Not even one,' I said.

But we did keep our scripts there. Our precious scripts.

That someone wanted to steal.

My brother hit me next morning. He was surprisingly strong, and the blow hurt. It was an open-handed slap across my head and made my ears ring. 'Go,' he snarled, 'just go and don't ever come back! You gross lout! You piece of shit!' He hit me again.

'Will!' John Heminges said, then louder, 'Will! Stop it!'

I had arrived at Blackfriars late. The morning had dawned bright and cold, and London was layered with a few inches of snow that glittered in the sun. The church bells told me I should hurry if I was to reach Blackfriars on time, but instead of heading for the Bishopsgate I had gone to the Theatre. My boots crunched in the snow as I walked. I headed down the alley, past the frozen horse pond, and turned into the Theatre's outer yard where I saw that the door to the tiring house was open and the hasp that had held the padlock was broken.

I climbed the three steps into the tiring room. Snow had blown through the open door and lay on the floor. Nothing appeared to be missing. Cloaks, doublets, dresses, gowns, and shirts hung thick on their usual wooden pegs, and the big chests were still filled with hose, boots, and skirts. I climbed the stairs and threw open the balcony doors to let in the snow-brightened morning light.

The big tabours were still there, along with the candlesticks, the harp that needed strings, the goblets and dishes, and all the other properties that were used onstage. At first glance it seemed nothing had been touched, but then I noticed the door that led into the box office, so called because the boxes that took the playgoers' pennies was emptied on the table inside. The lock of the door had been forced, and I could see splintered wood around the keyhole. I pushed the door open. It was dark inside, but I could see the two boxes still standing on the table. There would have been no money in either of them, so no coins could have been stolen. Then I saw the chest in the small room's far corner. Like the door, it had been forced, the lock broken and the lid prised open. I crossed the room, and, with dread, looked into the chest.

It was empty.

'Who's there?' a wary voice called from the tiring room.

'Jeremiah?' I called. 'It's me, Richard.'

Jeremiah, the one-eyed soldier whose job was to guard the Theatre, climbed the stairs. He was holding a pistol. 'Only hemp seed,' he said, meaning that the gun was charged with seeds that would sting and not kill. He crossed to the box office, stopped in the doorway, and stared at the chest's opened lid. 'Jesus in Jewry,' he said, aghast.

'You'll need His help,' I said grimly.

He laid the pistol on the table and cautiously approached the chest. He gazed into it as if hoping that the missing contents would miraculously reappear. Then he swore. 'They got them all?'

'Every last one,' I said.

'All the scripts?' He was having trouble understanding the disaster that had befallen us.

'Everything,' I said, 'and the Sharers won't be happy.' That was an understatement. The chest had contained all our plays, all the parts, all the scripts. I was not sure whether my brother had locked a copy of *A Midsummer Night's Dream* or of his new

Italian play into the heavy chest, but everything else had been there. 'You weren't here?' I asked Jeremiah.

'It was too cold yesterday,' he explained. He was usually gruff and even sullen, but the sight of the ravished chest had driven the bluster from him. 'And the snow was coming down,' he went on, 'and I reckoned no Christian would be out and about in a goddamned blizzard, so I went home. There's a fire at home, you see? There's no fire here.' His voice tailed away. He knew he would lose his job because of this.

'Greasy Harold said it was the Percies,' I said.

'The Percies!' he looked indignant. 'What do those bastards want with plays?'

'God knows.'

He picked up the pistol. It was a German weapon, its powder ignited by a wheel lock, its barrel chased with silver, and the heavy pommel on the hilt made of the same metal. It belonged to the Theatre, one of the guns we used to make a noise off-stage during battle scenes. 'If it was the Percies,' Jeremiah said slyly, 'then I couldn't have stopped them, could I?'

'No.'

'The bloody Percies can do what they bleeding like. This wouldn't have helped, would it?' He hefted the pistol. 'They'd have just killed me!'

'They would, yes.'

'So it isn't my fault!' He glared at me, wanting my agreement, but I just shrugged. 'So what do we do?' he asked.

'You stay here,' I suggested. 'I have to go to Blackfriars, and I'll tell the Sharers. They'll send someone to mend the doors.'

'Tell them it wasn't my fault. Tell them I was here,' he pleaded. 'Tell them I couldn't stop them. They're Percies!'

'I'll tell them you couldn't stop the Percies,' I promised him.

'Tell them I was here,' he said again. 'Jesus, Mary, and Joseph couldn't have stopped those buggers. It's not my fault!'

199

I left him still pleading with me, then hurried towards the Bishopsgate. The visit to the Theatre had made me late, as did the snow in the streets, which was already turning to a grey sludge. I slipped on ice in Water Lane, landing painfully on my hip and skinning my right hand. I was shivering. The beggars who usually gathered outside the big houses were all gone, sheltering God knows where. I could see that the Thames was part frozen, the channel running grey between sheets of ice. The watermen had broken a channel through to the Paris Garden Stairs, but few boats were waiting for customers. The usual guard who stood at the gates of the Lord Chamberlain's stable yard was missing, but I found him inside, where he was watching the yard's entrance from the small shelter of a horse stall.

I had expected to find the company rehearsing, but instead they were gathered around the fire in the great hall. They were arguing loudly, interrupting each other, plainly angered, but as I arrived, they immediately went silent and watched me. I saw a half-dozen bearded faces, all grim, all staring at me, along with the boys, who stood apart and just looked scared. I was too cold to sense the antagonism. I only wanted to reach the fire and give them my news. 'I've just come from the Theatre,' I said. 'The Percies were there yesterday, and they took all the play scripts. All of them! They . . .'

'They took nothing!' my brother interrupted me.

'I was there this morning,' I insisted. 'They were there yesterday, and broke the door of the box office.'

It was at that moment he strode to meet me, and, without warning, hit me across the face. Simon Willoughby, standing with the other boys, gasped. I was relieved to see Simon. Whatever adventure had prompted him to leave the mansion before the rest of us the previous evening had plainly ended.

'They took nothing!' my brother repeated, and hit me again. 'Whereas you . . .'

'Will, no!' John Heminges came to intervene.

'You goddamned thief!' my brother spat into my face. 'Go! Just go, and don't ever come back! Go!' He tried to turn me around and push me towards the door, and, when I resisted, he hit me a third time. 'You gross lout! You piece of shit!' He hit me again.

'Will!' John Heminges said, then louder, 'Will! Stop it!'

My brother drew his arm back to hit me again, but I got my blow in first, punching him in the chest. It was not a hard punch, but enough to drive him back a pace. 'Will!' John Heminges shouted, and seized my brother's arm, 'Will! Stop it!' He held onto my brother. 'He did not take them.'

'We only have your word for that,' my brother snarled.

'And my word isn't good enough?' Heminges, normally a mild man, was now angry himself.

'Stop it! Stop it! Stop it!' Alan Rust bellowed as he hurried towards us.

'Don't stop it!' Will Kemp called. He was grinning, enjoying the scene. 'Hit the bastard again, Will! Hit him harder! Punch his pretty face! Let's see blood!'

'Enough!' Rust shouted. He pushed between me and my brother, then thrust me hard against the big table. 'What did you see at the Theatre?' he demanded.

I described what I had seen, the forced doors, and the opened chest in the box office. 'The chest was empty,' I said, 'and all the scripts were gone.'

'Where was Jeremiah?' Henry Condell demanded angrily.

'They were Percies,' I said. 'Jeremiah couldn't stop them. He had a pistol charged with hemp seed, but if he'd used it he'd probably be dead now.' I had decided to lie for Jeremiah and not reveal that he had abandoned the Theatre before the Pursuivants arrived. The truth was that he could not have stopped them because they carried the royal warrant, and his presence or absence made not the slightest difference.

'Nothing else was taken?' Rust demanded.

'Nothing I could see.'

'Then they took nothing,' my brother said, still angry.

'They took all the . . .' I began.

'I took the valuable scripts out of the Theatre,' he snarled, 'and just left the dross. They got the pages for *The Seven Deadly Sins*, and a dozen other pieces of crap.'

'You took them out?' I asked weakly.

'Because it was obvious they might return,' he said, 'despite his lordship's help. Somebody hates us, somebody is trying to destroy us. You!' He lunged towards me again, but Alan Rust stopped him.

'The valuable scripts,' Rust explained to me, 'were brought here. They were locked away,' he nodded to the big chest beside the hearth, 'and last night someone stole the pages of *A Midsummer Night's Dream*, and *Romeo and Juliet*.'

That shocked me. I stammered for a moment as the bearded faces glowered at me. 'It was not me!' I protested.

'You went to Langley's new playhouse,' my brother accused me. 'You think I don't know? Francis Langley is a friend!'

'Because you're a Sharer in his brothels?' I retorted.

'Are you, Will?' Kemp asked eagerly.

'Is it true?' Alan Rust ignored Will Kemp and looked at me. 'Did you visit Langley's new playhouse?'

I hesitated a heartbeat, then nodded. 'I did go. I was curious. And they offered me gold, and I turned it down. I said no!'

'They offered you gold?'

'They wanted the pages of *A Midsummer Night's Dream*,' I said, 'because they don't have any plays.'

'They do now,' my brother said bitterly.

'And how could I have stolen the two plays last night?' I demanded. 'I left with the rest of you.'

'He did,' John Heminges said.

'And you say the scripts were locked here,' I said to my brother, 'but you didn't take the key?'

'It's not our chest. The household uses it. I can't take the key away.'

'So anyone could have stolen them,' I said, 'but it wasn't me.'

'Perhaps someone in the household just borrowed them?' John Heminges suggested nervously.

'No one borrowed them,' my brother snapped. 'I asked Harrison.' Harrison was his lordship's steward. 'He says only he knows where the key is hidden. It was one of us, and the plays are stolen. And you could easily have returned here last night.'

'In that snowstorm? No!'

'You still talked to Langley,' he accused me sourly.

'And you haven't visited the new playhouse yet?' I asked him, and saw, from his expression, that I was right. 'And how many others here have gone to see what they're building?'

No one answered. No one would even meet another man's eyes.

'I went there, yes,' I admitted, 'and I talked to Langley, and to a man called deValle, and he offered me the Earl of Lechlade's money. He offered me gold! And he said he'd pay me a wage if I joined the company. Langley was there, I'm sure he told you what happened.' I paused, and my brother did not respond, which meant he had indeed been told. 'And he would have told you,' I went on, 'that I said no.' I spoke the last four words very slowly and distinctly.

'The Earl of Lechlade?' Henry Condell asked.

'It's his money,' I said, 'and they'll call the new playhouse the Swan.'

'It wasn't Richard,' John Heminges stood beside me. 'He was with me when we left last night. I walked with him almost as far as Ludgate, and it was just minutes before the curfew.'

They were convinced now, I could see it, though my brother, resentful and hurt, would not meet my eye. 'Then who?' he asked sullenly.

'Who didn't leave with us last night?' I asked.

I heard John Heminges gasp. He turned and looked at the hearth where the boys, all of them frightened by the argument, still stood. I looked too, catching Simon Willoughby's eye. He stared at me, then at his master, and I saw the panic come to his face. He was a player, but at that moment all his skills deserted him. He should have pretended, he should have played the innocent, but instead he fled. He sprinted across the room, leaped onto the half built stage, jumped down at the back, and vanished into the scullery passage.

'Simon!' Heminges called, but his apprentice had already disappeared.

We all followed, but we were much too slow. Men were clambering onto the stage and crowding at the further door, while Simon Willoughby was long gone.

'This way!' Alan Rust set off down the scullery passage towards the stable yard, but I knew Simon Willoughby would have used the other corridor, the one I had shown him that led to the river alley. He had gone into wintry London. And our two new plays were gone with him.

It was a subdued rehearsal that morning, and no wonder. Titania was gone, and Oberon, her master, felt both betrayed and ashamed. Peter Quince was bitterly angry. Nick Bottom could not resist making jokes, which finally provoked my usually calm brother to another fit of rage. 'The play is lost, you bastard! That's our money lost!'

'There was no proper part for me,' Will Kemp snarled, 'so what does it matter?'

'Not every play has a fool in it.'

'The plays that make money do. Who gives a dog's fart for a pair of Italian lovers?'

'Masters!' Alan Rust intervened. Both Williams fell silent, content to glower at each other.

John Heminges, lost in misery because of his apprentice's treachery, sat hunched on a chair. 'I didn't know,' he said for the hundredth time.

'None of us knew,' Rust said brusquely.

'He's a traitor,' John Heminges said bitterly, 'but I don't understand why.'

'For money,' my brother said sourly.

'He was unhappy,' I said, 'because he wasn't chosen to play Juliet.'

'You knew that?' My brother turned on me savagely.

'We all knew that,' Will Kemp said, 'the little bastard didn't make a secret of it, did he?'

'So now he can play Juliet,' my brother said, 'at the bloody Swan!'

'Or he can play Titania,' Thomas Pope, the quietest of the Sharers, said plaintively.

'They'll perform *Romeo and Juliet*,' my brother said. 'They know we're almost ready to do the *Dream*. They want something no one else has done. It will be *Romeo*, God damn them.'

'We can still play it, can't we?' Pope suggested. 'The Swan won't be ready for weeks. We can do it first!'

'There was only one copy,' my brother said bitterly.

'Shit,' Richard Burbage commented.

'And it's lost,' my brother said.

'Not if we get the pages back,' I blurted out.

205

Why did I say that? An impulse, I suppose. I was afraid of my brother's wrath, and knew he disliked me, but at that moment I felt nothing but pity for him. I knew, we all knew, that he was proud of the new play, that he was excited for the story of the two lovers in far Verona. He had hoped to present *Romeo and Juliet* soon, perhaps at court or, if the weather relented, in the Theatre.

'Get the pages back?' my brother mimicked me cruelly, 'how?'

'You say Francis Langley is a friend,' Rust suggested.

'A friend?' my brother shrugged and looked embarrassed. 'We do business together, that's all.'

'And Francis Langley's business is brothels,' Will Kemp said enthusiastically.

'And what if it is?'

'You could appeal to him,' John Heminges said.

'He needs the plays more than he needs my friendship,' my brother said. 'He needs plays, he needs money. He's up to his ears in debt at the Swan.'

'Better get the whores working double fast,' Will Kemp said.

'He'll deny having the plays,' my brother said, ignoring Kemp, 'right up to the day they perform *Romeo and Juliet*. So no,' he swung around to look at me, 'we can't get the pages back.'

'They stole them,' I said, 'so we steal them back.'

He stared at me, and I stared at him. 'You're not that good a thief,' he finally said.

'I'm better than you think!' I spoke the words savagely, defying him, and my truculent tone took everyone by surprise. It surprised me too, because a lot of anger had spewed out with those four words. My brother took a step backwards, thinking I was about to hit him, and no one spoke for a moment until Alan Rust broke the silence.

'"Lord,"' he said, quoting from the play we were supposed to be rehearsing, '"what fools these mortals be."'

206

'Hit him, lad!' Will Kemp called.

'Can we begin?' Rust intervened. 'We have work to do.'

'But we don't have a script,' Richard Burbage said.

'We still have the parts of the *Dream*,' my brother said unhappily. 'The little bastard didn't steal those pages.'

The first work was to replace the little bastard. The Sharers huddled, and I saw them glance at me once or twice, but I glared at them, daring them to give me the part, and in the end they gave Titania to Bobby Gough, Thomas Pope's apprentice. He was a year younger than Simon Willoughby, and the choice surprised me. Bobby was skinny, very shy, very quiet, and prone to tears if anything went wrong or if he was reprimanded. In costume, with his face painted, he had a delicate beauty, but Titania, it seemed to me, was anything but delicate. She was a formidable queen, more than capable of facing down her wayward king, and Bobby, though he had a good clear voice and had played a couple of large roles well at the Theatre, seemed better suited for softer women's roles than the defiant Titania. Still, he was chosen, and my brother gave him the fairy queen's pages. 'You can read them for now,' he said.

And a day that had started badly just became worse. We were rehearsing a scene towards the end of the play in which Titania, surrounded by her fairy entourage, was cosseting the monstrous ass-headed Bottom. When we had first read the scene we had kept interrupting the lines with laughter, but today it was only misery. Will Kemp, of course, knew his lines. "I must to the barber's, monsieur,'" he declaimed, rubbing his cheek, "'for methinks I am marvellous hairy about the face, and I am such a tender ass, if my hair do but tickle me, I must scratch.'"

Bobby Gough, sitting beside Will, was looking at the script. "'What,'" he read, "'wilt thou hear some,'" he paused, peering close at the page, 'is that "sweet"?'

'"Sweet",' I confirmed.

'"Wilt thou hear some sweet music?"'

Will Kemp stretched out, luxuriating on the thick cushions that represented the fairy queen's bower. '"I have a reasonable good ear in music!"' he said. '"Let's have the tongs and the bones."'

Bobby was holding the page very close to his eyes. The light was bad, but not impossible to see by. '"Or say,"' he said hesitantly, '"sweet love."' He paused and frowned, '"what,"' another long pause, '"thou desir'st to,"' he looked at me, 'is that word . . .'

'"Eat"!' Will Kemp bellowed. 'Christ's belly, boy, it's "eat"! Can't you bloody well read?'

Bobby looked close to tears. 'I can read, sir.'

'He has bad eyes,' Thomas Pope, Bobby's apprentice master, said anxiously. 'He has to read things very close to his face, but he is diligent!'

'Bugger diligence!' Kemp stood, furious.

'Bobby,' Alan Rust took the boy's arm. 'Go to the window,' he pointed up at the high oriel where the light was best. 'Start learning your lines.'

'Yes, sir.'

Rust turned on me. 'Richard? Just stand in his place and read the lines.'

'I don't need to play the scene,' Will Kemp said sullenly, 'I know the damned lines. We can move on.'

We moved on. In misery.

Silvia and another maid came to the hall just before we ended that rehearsal. They began sewing white roses and red crosses onto the cloth that now garlanded the front of the stage, and Silvia kept glancing my way. We were rehearsing a scene towards the play's ending with George Bryan playing Duke

Theseus, and Thomas Belte, who was John Heminges's second apprentice, playing Hippolyta. Both knew their lines. I was supposedly the bookkeeper again, working with all the separate parts, which were out of order, but luckily the players, all except poor Bobby Gough, knew their lines. I glanced at Alan Rust. 'I need a piss.'

'Go,' he said distractedly, waving me away.

I climbed to the stage and went through the curtained door to the tiring room, and, sure enough, Silvia followed. She embraced me. 'Gawd, you're nice and warm!' She kept her arms wrapped around me. 'So what was all that shouting about this morning? Her ladyship thought you were killing each other.'

'We very nearly were.'

'So tell me!'

'Inquisitive, aren't you?'

She grinned. 'You keeping secrets from me, Richard Shakespeare?'

So I told her. Told her how the precious pages of my brother's new plays had been stolen from the chest in the great hall, and how Simon Willoughby must have taken them. 'And I'm a fool,' I said.

'Why?'

'I promised to steal them back.'

'You did what?'

'Promised to steal them back,' I paused, 'except I don't know where he took them.'

She gazed up at me. Her arms were still around my waist, as much for warmth as for affection. 'So you don't know where to go?'

I shook my head. 'No.'

'So how will you steal them back?'

'They could be anywhere,' I said.

'Anywhere?'

'They could be at the Earl of Lechlade's house,' I said, 'wherever that is. Or over at the new playhouse.'

'The earl? He's at Westminster,' she said.

'You know that?'

'I don't know it,' she said firmly, 'but the ladies were talking about him because he turned up at court wearing ermine!'

'Is that bad?'

'God and His angels help you! Of course it's bad! Only the Queen can wear ermine. It's the law. And he wore these silly shoes with tall heels. He's small, you see? Her ladyship says he's a right little cockerel, but he was sent packing to get rid of the ermine. She said he must have lived close by because he went and came back so quick. Out and back like a bleeding ferret, she said.'

'A cockerel and a ferret?'

'Don't you mock me, Mister Flute! Of course the little ferret could be staying at a tavern, some of the country lords do, but it'll be a Westminster tavern, one close to the palace.'

'I'm not mocking you.'

'You're not?'

'I'm kissing you,' I said, and I was, which she seemed to like. 'Or more likely,' I went on, 'Simon took the plays to the Swan.'

'The Swan?'

'The new playhouse.'

'Only if he walked all the way round by the bridge,' she said scornfully. 'No one was crossing the river by boat last night. And only halfwits were out walking in that snowstorm.'

'I was.'

'Well, that's what I said,' she grinned, 'but if the little bleeder had any sense he wouldn't walk far. Not to Westminster and not across the bridge neither. It's much too far. He took them somewhere close.'

Somewhere close. Of course! The weather alone dictated that Simon Willoughby could not have gone far, and that meant he had taken the stolen plays to some place in or very near Blackfriars. Somewhere safe.

And I knew just where the little bleeder was.

PART THREE

THINGS BASE
AND VILE

Things base and vile, holding no quantity,
Love can transpose to form and dignity:
Love looks not with the eyes, but with the mind,
And therefore is wing'd Cupid painted blind.

A Midsummer Night's Dream
Act I, Scene 1, lines 232ff

EIGHT

'TELL ME ABOUT *Romeo and Juliet*,' I said to my brother. I was walking with him. He had looked irritated when, as we left the Blackfriars mansion, I had fallen into step beside him, and had since ignored everything I had said. He had pointedly paused outside a saddler's shop to examine the wares. 'It helps to have the horse before buying the saddle,' I had said, a comment that he pretended not to hear. Instead he had paced on down Cheapside, hurrying to escape me, but I had easily kept up with him. 'Tell me about *Romeo and Juliet*,' I now said again.

'It's a play,' he said caustically, his anger at the loss overcoming his irritation at my company, 'and that shrivelling little bastard has stolen it.'

'So now I'll steal it back.'

That earned me a sneer. 'From where? From whom?'

'From whoever has it,' I answered airily.

'And whoever has it,' he snarled, 'will already be copying it.'

'It will take at least a week to copy,' I pointed out, 'and it was only stolen last night. Maybe they've copied one page by now? Perhaps two.'

We walked on in silence. My brother had the brim of his hat pulled down to hide his face so he would not be recognised. Folk did notice players as we walked around the city, and they frequently stopped us, wanting to tell us how they had enjoyed a play, though few people would want to accost us on this freezing evening. Some players welcomed the praise, while others tried to avoid it. Simon Willoughby, of course, could never receive enough compliments, and, like Will Kemp, he would prance in the street to attract attention. My brother preferred to hide. 'The plaudits of fools,' he once told me, 'are worthless. Gratifying, maybe, but ultimately without any meaning.'

'You don't enjoy being praised?' I had asked.

'If the compliment comes from a person of wit, yes. Otherwise it's just the yapping of a dog.'

Now he kept his gaze low, not just to escape recognition, but to help negotiate the frozen slush and dung that paved Cheapside. He glanced up occasionally to gauge the sky, which, always sullen with London's smoke, was now threatening with purple dark clouds. 'There'll be more snow,' he said.

'We should sleep at Lord Hunsdon's,' I said.

'I doubt his lordship would welcome that,' he remarked scathingly, 'and after *Fair Em* he probably regrets inviting us at all.' A gust of wind whirled snow from a roof, plastering it down onto our cloaks. 'Shouldn't you be out of the city before curfew?' he asked.

'I should,' I said, 'but I want to know if there's a part for me in *Romeo and Juliet*.'

He sighed, as if I were being tiresome, which I suppose I was. 'That is up to the Sharers, not me.'

'And you're a Sharer,' I said, 'and the others listen to you. So is there a part for me?'

He sighed again. 'There's a nurse you can play.'

'A man's part.'

'Let me think,' he said, his voice dripping with sarcasm. 'Richard would have played Romeo if we still had the play, and Henry would have been Mercutio. There's Juliet's father, but you're not nearly old enough for that role. But there are sundry serving men who clutter the stage. One of those, perhaps?'

'A speaking part,' I persisted patiently.

'Tybalt, perhaps?'

'What does he do?'

'Very little. Maybe twenty lines? Fewer, I think. About the same as Peter.'

I shuddered to think how Will Kemp would feel about having twenty lines or less. 'What I'm asking,' I said, 'is whether you'll give me a good part if I get the pages back?'

He had stopped beside the old stone cross that dominated Cheapside. The cross was usually surrounded by beggars, who only fled when the Puritan preacher was there to demand the destruction of the papist symbol, but on this freezing day the cross was deserted. My brother looked at me with his customary distaste. 'I have three slender hopes of retrieving the manuscripts,' he said. 'I can appeal to Francis Langley, which will do no good, but I can try. Francis would cozen his own mother for a penny. For a halfpenny! I could ask Lord Hunsdon to use his influence, but his lordship doesn't like to be concerned with trivialities, and will not take such a request happily. Besides, there's no proof I even wrote the two plays. Lawyers will involve themselves, and his lordship has a healthy dislike of lawyers. Or I can go on my knees to Sir Edmund Tilney and beg him to reject their scripts.'

'Will he?'

'Of course not. And even if he did, it wouldn't stop them performing the plays in private houses.'

Sir Edmund Tilney was the Master of the Revels, and was

appointed by Lord Hunsdon, the Lord Chamberlain. Sir Edmund summoned players to perform before the Queen, but he also had the responsibility of making sure that no play contained seditious or heretical material. Every script, whether it was to be played at court or in a playhouse or by a company touring the county towns, had to be submitted to Sir Edmund, and no play could be performed anywhere in England or Wales until he had signed his name and fixed his seal to the first page of the manuscript. I had often taken play scripts to him, and had found him to be an affable man, always ready to gossip about players. 'Have an apple,' he had greeted me once, 'it's from my garden. How's Will's ankle?'

'Much improved, Sir Edmund.' Will Kemp had sprained an ankle during a performance of *The Seven Deadly Sins*.

'He's a naughty man!' Sir Edmund had said. 'Those jigs of his, eh? You know what the rogue does? He invents new lines. He makes them up as he goes along.' He had chuckled. 'By rights I should put him in the Marshalsea, but he's funny. I confess he's funny! So what have you brought us today?'

'Another jig, Sir Edmund.'

'Saucy, is it? Let me see!'

Sir Edmund, a decent man, had the power to refuse a licence if the Swan submitted *Romeo and Juliet* and *A Midsummer Night's Dream* for his approval, which would mean the Earl of Lechlade's players could not perform either play in public, but my brother was surely right that Sir Edmund, let alone Lord Hunsdon, would not want to be tangled in lawyers' snares. So long as the plays did not insult the Queen or advocate papist heresy, then Sir Edmund would probably sign them. 'There is a fourth hope,' I said.

'What?' my brother asked. 'That the goblins of the forest will rescue the plays?'

'That I steal them back.'

He sneered at that. 'I have more faith in the goblins than in you.'

'And if I do return them,' I said, 'I want a man's part in *Romeo and Juliet*. A good part.'

'If you retrieve the plays,' he said caustically, 'you can play Romeo himself.' He gave a mirthless laugh at those words, then walked on. 'Your path lies that way, I believe.' He pointed up Wood Street.

'I'll be late for the rehearsal tomorrow,' I called after him.

'You won't if you want to be employed,' he snarled without turning. 'We're rehearsing the whole play tomorrow. We need you there, so be there.'

'Maybe very late,' I went on, 'because I'll be fetching you *Romeo*.'

That checked him. He stopped, turned, and looked at me as the first snowflakes sifted from the dark clouds. 'You're a misbegotten fool, Richard,' he said, but not in an unkind way, then he turned again and walked on.

But he had not forbidden me to try. So I would be late for the morrow's rehearsals.

'I know why Simon stole the plays,' I said that evening.

'Why?' Father Laurence was cocooned in his blankets, sitting close to the fire that I had fed with wood.

'He was upset that he wasn't given the part of Juliet.'

'So he was jealous? Poor boy. Jealousy is such a destructive thing.'

'And he was given gold,' I added.

'He suffered greed too?'

I half smiled. 'You can add lust, father.'

'My goodness! Envy, greed and lust! He does need absolution. Who does he lust after?'

'I saw him with the Earl of Lechlade. They were kissing.'

'That sort of lust? Dear me!'

'It's a sin, isn't it, father?'

'So we're told, Richard, so we're told.' He stretched his thin hands towards the fire. 'My, you have made a blaze! I hope we don't set the chimney on fire.'

The snow was falling softly. I could just see the big flakes through Father Laurence's small window. By daybreak, I thought, the frost would have etched its patterns on the glass and the day would be brittle with cold. 'There's one thing I don't understand,' I said.

'And what might that be?'

'Why the Percies went back to the Theatre. They only stole play scripts. Could they be working for the earl too?'

'It seems unlikely.'

'It does?'

'The earl's reputation is not good. Like our precious Saviour he consorts with publicans and sinners.'

'And the Percies aren't sinners?'

'Oh, they are, Richard, they are, but of a different kind. We're all sinners. We've all fallen short of God's grace, but the Percies are the most dangerous of all sinners.'

I waited for him to explain, but he just gazed into the fire. 'Dangerous?' I prompted him.

'They believe they are doing good, Richard. When men do evil and claim that they are doing God's work, then they are at their most dangerous. They are more than dangerous! They are the vilest of sinners.'

I frowned, trying to remember the sermons I had heard. 'But if priests, forgive me, father, if priests plot to kill the Queen, isn't that evil?'

'The Pope says not, though I confess I disagree with the Holy Father on that opinion. So let us agree that killing the Queen is evil, but so is ripping out a man's entrails for following his faith.

I have watched the martyrs die, Richard, I have watched them die.' He made the sign of the cross with a claw-like hand.

'And you saw the Protestants burning too?' I made it a question rather than an accusation.

'Poor souls, I did. And I prayed for them also. They were mistaken, of course, but if we burned every man and woman who was mistaken, then the fires would never end.' He sighed. 'Queen Mary, poor woman, thought she could cleanse England with fire. She couldn't, any more than Elizabeth can wash it clean with blood. Is it snowing hard?'

I peered through the window. 'Steadily, father.'

'It looks so nice, doesn't it, when it's fresh?'

'It does, father.'

'The whole world looks bright and clean after snow,' he mused, 'then sinful mankind besmirches it.' He gave a sad smile, then flinched as a log collapsed in the fire to spew sparks that I stamped out among the floor rushes. 'The Percies aren't working for the earl,' the old priest said, 'I'm sure of that. If anyone, they're working for the city.'

'They're not employed by the city,' I said.

'No, of course not! But they share the city's ambitions. No more playhouses. And many of the Percies are Puritans, and Puritans regard anyone who disagrees with them as an enemy. The Percies have run out of priests to torture, so they'll pursue the playhouses instead, and persuade themselves that they're combatting sin. Let me look.' He bent over the side of his chair to rummage in a basket where he kept those books and pamphlets that had not been stolen by the Pursuivants. 'Here!' He pulled out a tattered book that had no covers, and showed me the title page.

I read it aloud. '*A Treatise Against Dicing, Dancing, Plays, and Interludes, with Other Idle Pastimes.*'

'A Devon man wrote it,' Father Laurence said, 'a man called John Northbrooke. I met him once. A very earnest preacher.'

Father Laurence fumbled with the pages, then frowned as if recalling some memory. 'Not a nice man, not a nice man at all, but he did love dogs. It's hard to dislike a man who loves dogs, don't you think?' He chuckled, then found the page he wanted. 'The book is a dialogue,' he explained, 'between Youth and Age. Here we are, Youth asks the question, "Do you speak against those places also, which are made up and built for such plays and interludes as the Theatre and Curtain?"'

'The Theatre!' I said. 'He mentioned us?'

'Indeed he did, and here's what Age had to say about you, "Yea truly, for I am persuaded that Satan has not a more speedy way and fitter school to teach filthy lusts of wicked whoredom than those places and therefore it is necessary that those places and players should be forbidden and dissolved and put down."'

I laughed.

'Oh, there's more,' Father Laurence said with relish: '"In their plays you shall learn all things that appertain to filthiness. If you will learn how to be false, how to play the harlots, how to obtain one's love, how to ravish, how to beguile, how to betray, to flatter, lie, swear, forswear, how to allure to whoredom, how to murder, how to poison, how to disobey and rebel against princes, to consume treasures prodigally, to move to lusts, to be idle, to blaspheme, to sing filthy songs of love, to speak filthily, to be proud, how to mock, scoff, and deride!"' He chuckled again, plainly enjoying himself as he turned another two or three pages. 'Oh, and here Age talks about you!'

'About me?'

'Indeed! He condemns you for being "contrary to nature"!' He gave me a mock-stern look. 'Men attire themselves, he says, "in women's apparel, with swans' feathers on their heads, silks, and golden apparel!" Do you wear swans' feathers on your head, Richard?'

'I wore goose feathers once.'

'What a very bad boy you must be,' he said, and dropped the book back into the basket. 'The city fathers and the Pursuivants, both are Puritans! We can mock them, Richard, but they have power now. Their numbers increase.' He closed his eyes and looked pained. 'The church was corrupt, God knows it was corrupt, but still we fed the hungry, we clothed the naked, and we tended the sick. We did good works, we prayed for souls and we gave comfort. But now the Puritans revile us, they call us the devil's creatures, and they hate us. They hate even their own kind, other Protestants. And they would close your playhouses, Richard, they would strip the churches of what small beauty is left in them, and they would make the world drab.'

'But not yet, father,' I said, 'and before they do I must find those play scripts.'

He looked at me sadly. 'I hope you do,' he said, 'and I think you're right about where poor Simon took them.' I had told him of my suspicions earlier, and he had evidently been thinking about my words. 'It makes sense that the boy would have run to Sir Godfrey. Saint Benet's is very close by. But that was a day and a night ago, Richard. You think the scripts will still be at Saint Benet's?'

'No,' I said.

'Then what can you do?'

'Go to the place where Sir Godfrey will have hidden them,' I said. 'A place no one in their senses would dare approach.'

'But you will dare?'

'I have to.'

'And tomorrow you go there?'

'I do, father, yes.'

He closed his eyes. 'In the name of God, Richard, be careful. Please be careful.'

Because on the morrow I would be meeting Washington.

*　　*　　*

Next morning I went to the Theatre first. It had stopped snowing and the world that dawn was a miracle of whiteness, bright and gleaming, just waiting for sinful mankind to besmirch it. A carpenter was already at the playhouse, his footprints deep in the new snow. He was repairing the tiring-room door, and reluctantly stood aside to let me enter. Once inside I found Jeremiah swathed in the company's thickest cloaks and sitting with his massive German pistol on his lap. 'It's you,' he greeted me morosely.

'It's me,' I agreed.

'Are they rehearsing here today?'

'No, still at Blackfriars. I just came to collect a few things. And I told the Sharers that you couldn't stop the Percies.'

He frowned. 'Well of course I couldn't.' He spoke truculently. 'The Lord Almighty couldn't stop them. They were bloody Percies! They can do what they want.'

'You couldn't stop them,' I said, 'because you weren't here, but the Sharers don't know that.'

He understood then, and understood that I had lied for him and that he would not lose his job as guardian of the Theatre. Gratitude was a stranger to Jeremiah, but he screwed up his face and managed a grimace that was probably intended to be a smile. 'You're a good lad,' he said grudgingly.

'So as thanks,' I said, 'you can lend me a pistol.'

'A pistol?'

'One of those things,' I said nodding at the weapon on his lap.

He frowned again. 'What do you want with a pistol?'

'To frighten someone.'

I could see he wanted to argue, but then he remembered I had done him a favour, and he nodded. 'Hemp seed or a ball?'

'A ball.'

'You want to be careful, lad. You kill someone, and they'll have you dancing on the gallows. Hemp seed does the job well enough! Aim for the bugger's face and you can turn his eyeballs to jelly.'

'A ball,' I said again.

'I hope to Christ you know what you're doing, lad.' He heaved himself to his feet. 'You want spare powder? Spare balls?'

'Just the one ball,' I said. I reckoned I would have no time to reload, indeed I hoped I would not have to use the gun at all, but the place I was going was, indeed, dangerous, and one pistol ball might save me. Or swing me.

While Jeremiah rooted among the weapons upstairs, I changed clothes, choosing thickly lined hose, breeches, and doublet from the costumes hanging in the tiring room. All the garments were in very dark cloth, either woollen or twilled cotton. They were working-men's clothes, the kind that the mechanicals would wear in *A Midsummer Night's Dream*. Most working men wore shoes, but I chose tall, stout boots in black leather. I crammed my hair into a plain woollen cap, then borrowed a thick dark cloak with a hood, and a canvas bag of the sort craftsmen use to carry their tools. My tools would be a chisel, a dagger, and the pistol that Jeremiah had loaded. It was the smallest gun from his armoury. 'Keep it pointing upright,' he advised me. 'I did ram it proper, and it's well wadded, but best to keep it upright so that nothing falls out.' He handed me the weapon that was surprisingly heavy. 'I tested it,' he said, 'and it sparks all right, but the trigger's stiff as a nun's tit. You have to give it a good old tug.'

The pistol was a wheel lock. Pulling the trigger opened a small pan in which gunpowder lay, and, at the same time, drove the flint down onto a serrated steel wheel that spun to produce a small cascade of sparks that was supposed to ignite the powder. I had fired wheel locks before, but only during the battle scenes of a play, and never with a ball in the gun. Three or four of us would stand in the tiring room and, at the right cue, pull our triggers, and inevitably only one or two of the guns would fire, and sometimes none, and if any did fire we would have to stamp on the flaming wadding that vented from the barrels, while other players beat metal on metal and shouted incoherently. 'Don't overdo the battle noise!' Alan Rust would insist to us, but we always did.

I slung the heavy bag across my body, then pulled the cloak's hood over my head. 'You look like a bleeding monk,' Jeremiah said.

'It's cold out there.'

'You think I haven't noticed? They should put a hearth in here. A man deserves some warmth. And don't forget to bring the bleeding pistol back!' Jeremiah shouted as I edged past the carpenter repairing the door.

'I won't!'

I walked westwards, first crossing the Finsbury Fields where the windmills stood motionless with icicles hanging from their tethered vanes, then through the small thatched cottages that lined Chiswell Street. Off to my right, to the north, lay a frozen countryside, while to the south were the gardens, orchards, and houses that reached as far as the city wall. Smoke poured from chimneys and darkened the cloud-grey sky above London. I walked fast except where ice sheeted the roads. I turned north to reach Olde Street, then west again to cross the Saint Alban's road. Cattle were being driven south, their dung steaming. Once over the road I followed a path through a churchyard to the Clerkenwell Road, and there I slowed.

I slowed because the place where I was going lay not far away. It stood in a rough pasture just north of the road, and was surrounded by a fence of wooden palings that was taller than a man. The River Fleet ran to the east of the fenced yard, hurrying south to join the Thames, though on this cold morning the narrow river was entirely shrouded in ice. There were a half-dozen sheds inside the fence, but only a single chimney spewing smoke. I crossed the old bridge that spanned the Fleet, walking slowly and bent over like an old man, the big dark hood shrouding my face. The road was trampled with foot- and hoofprints and I could see someone had already visited the big fenced yard that morning because hoofprints led through the snow from the road to the gate. There was a mess of prints right by the gate where the horseman must have dismounted and someone had come from the yard to greet him, and there was a curved scar in the snow, which showed where the gate had been swung open to let man and horse inside. There were no hoof-prints leading out of the yard, suggesting that horse and rider were still inside. I did not pause, but kept walking. I doubted anyone inside the yard was watching the road, but I did not want to attract attention by appearing curious. Once past the fence's western boundary, I looked for a gap in the hawthorn hedge, found one, and pushed through. I ran now, going to the yard's western wall and heading north until I turned the corner, and only stopped when I was halfway down the fence's northern side. No one could see me here. There was nothing but fields and bare spinneys between me and the smoke that marked the far village of Islington.

The heavy wooden wall surrounded a place called Scavenger's Yard. I never did learn why it was called that, perhaps it had once been a place where the city's scavengers took whatever they swept or scraped from the streets, but now it was owned by Sir Godfrey Cullen, rector of Saint Benet's, molester of small boys, and supplier of beasts for the entertainment of Her Majesty and the populace of London. Scavenger's Yard was where he kept the cockerels, dogs, apes, and, most valuable of all, Washington. Washington was a bear, an enormous beast, scarred and shaggy, who would be chained to a post and then attacked by a pack of mastiffs. The bear was named for the village in the north of England where he had been reared, and he was almost as famous as Sackerson, a monstrous beast who could attract crowds of two or three thousand every time he fought. When Washington fought he would be paraded down the lanes and streets of the city to the Tiltyard, or to wherever else he would be chained that day. He would be muzzled with rusty iron for the journey, led by Buttercup, and guarded by Strawbelly Sam, the animal keeper, who would be armed with a heavy goad. Children would run alongside, daring each other to slap Washington's matted and scarred flanks, and behind the bear would come a horse-drawn cage filled with snarling and howling mastiffs, most of whom would be crippled or disembowelled by day's end.

When I had been a grey-robed scholar at Saint Benet's I would sometimes be sent with a pair of companions to help Sam so I knew Scavenger's Yard well. I had swilled out cages, cut up carcasses, and cleaned the dung from the small arena that lay in the yard's centre, an arena that was surrounded by banked seating for four or five hundred people. The yard lay well north of the city and so was not as popular as the Tiltyard or the Curtain, but on summer Saturdays it made a fine outing for folk, who came to see the dogs attacking Washington, or else, most popular of all, to see a terrified ape strapped to a cheap and doomed horse's back trying to avoid the leaping assaults of maddened hounds. The ape, which would often be dressed as a Roman Catholic priest, died screaming, to the cheers and laughter of the crowd.

That cold morning I was relieved that a horseman had come to the yard because it meant his beast would be somewhere inside, and the dogs which normally ran loose would be locked away so that they could do the horse no damage. Scavenger's Yard was indeed a dangerous place, guarded by a score of animals that were trained to kill.

I reckoned that on the night he had stolen the plays, Simon Willoughby would have fled to the nearest refuge where he would find warmth and sanctuary, and that refuge had to be Sir Godfrey's house, which lay just one street away from the Lord Chamberlain's mansion. My brother had not thought of Sir Godfrey, perhaps not knowing that the priest had agreed to provide beast shows to the new playhouse across the river. If he had suspected that Sir Godfrey was sheltering Simon Willoughby and the stolen play scripts, he would have assembled a group of Sharers, armed them, and gone to Saint Benet's. There would have been an affray, possibly worse. Swords would have been drawn, constables summoned, and doubtless, eventually, Writs of Attachment would have been issued by the magistrates to prevent another such confrontation.

It seemed I was the only person who had understood that Simon would run to Sir Godfrey, but Sir Godfrey could not know that, and he must have feared my brother's wrath. If a group of armed men came to his house and searched it, he would want to make sure that the plays were not there. He would want the precious scripts in the safest place possible, a place that no one would dare search, a place guarded by slavering beasts ready to tear an intruder into bloody ruin, a place called Scavenger's Yard.

And I was the intruder.

There was a small gate in the northern wall which was only ever opened at the end of the Saturday beast shows to let villagers from Islington take a shortcut home. It was bolted shut, of course, but there was no lock. There was no need. No one would ever try to break into the yard except a fool, and that cold morning I was the fool.

I used the chisel, inserting it into the gap between gate and jamb and finding the bolt's barrel which I then tried to edge aside. Except it would not move. The bolt seemed rusted into place, and every time I tried to lever it, the chisel's edge would slip and screech on the iron barrel. The gate creaked as I struggled. I hammered the chisel with my hand and tried again, and at last the bolt moved with a grating noise. I found that slightly pushing the gate inwards made the job easier. The old bolt was still reluctant and stiff, yet, bit by bit, the barrel jarred back until at last it slipped free of its tunnel and the gate sprang open an inch or two. I pulled it half open, flinching at the noise the old hinges made, and just then the dogs started howling.

I crouched instinctively and held my breath. I could see no one. The dogs were baying and yowling, their feet scratching and thumping on the shed walls. I edged inside, pulled the gate shut, and latched the bolt, doing both as quietly as I could, then groped in the canvas bag to find the comfort of the pistol's hilt. In front of me were the rickety benches, snow-covered now, which stood on crude wooden platforms held aloft by rough scaffolding. Beyond the benches was the pit where beasts suffered and died, while to my left, between the fence and the stacked high benches, was Strawbelly Sam's small house from which the smoke rose thick from a brick chimney. Between me and the house, and built against the stout fence, were the beast sheds. 'Quiet, you sodden bastards!' I heard Strawbelly Sam shout inside the nearest shed, then heard him hammer a cage bar with the stick he always carried. The noise quietened a little, though the dogs went on whining. One of the cockerels bred for fighting crowed, but the birds were all kept on the yard's farther side, safely locked away from the dogs. I waited. No one came from the dog shed, but why would they on this freezing morning?

I stood and walked towards the sheds, my boots crunching in the unspoiled snow. I heard the mutter of voices, then a door slamming. The dogs were still restless, whining and growling. Did they sense me? I was close to their shed, edging between its wall and the nearest scaffolding. I wanted to be anywhere but in this place. Why had I not told my brother of my suspicions? Then he could have assembled a half-dozen men, all armed, and we could have come here in force. The noise of the dogs was making me tremble. I wanted to be home or in the great hall at Blackfriars, and that made me think of Silvia.

And thinking of Silvia reminded me of my mother, long ago, when she had been amused by a question I had asked when I was just eleven or twelve years old. How does a man find a wife, I had asked her, and she had laughed and looked at me, her hands white with flour. 'You don't find her, Richard, she finds you!'

'She does?'

'As like as not,' she said. She had been gazing through the kitchen window at the apple tree in our back garden. 'Girls set their caps at a likely man,' she had said, no longer laughing. 'Look at Will and Anne!'

'Will and . . .'

'God help them both,' she had interrupted me, plainly regretting the words. She began rolling the pastry.

'Did you set your cap at Father?' I asked.

'Oh I did, I did! Your father was a fine young man. A very fine young man. He had all his hair back then!' She laughed again. 'I bumped into him leaving the church, and pretended it was an accident, which it wasn't, but it made sure he noticed me. And he did!'

Had Silvia found me? I saw nothing shameful about that, indeed I wanted it to be true. I wanted it desperately. And why was I thinking of marriage? I hardly knew her, I just knew I wanted her. And I had never contemplated marriage before because it seemed something far off that would happen to a person I had not yet become, a person I did not know. My brother had married young, and his experience was no encouragement, but suddenly, in the snow, listening to the dogs as I stepped slowly nearer to their shed, I felt the burden of growing up. I had been a boy in the company, and I had stayed a boy too long. I was a good player, I knew that, but there were few parts like Uashti. The younger boys played the characters I had once portrayed, and I was being stranded, neither boy nor man, and it was past time I cut my hair short and let my beard grow. And that, I thought, was why I was here in Scavenger's Yard, because I would do a favour for my brother that would force him to treat me like a man. I would be Romeo.

I could hear voices now. Bad-tempered voices. There was a woman's voice, and I remembered that Strawbelly Sam had a wife, Marion, who he treated like one of the animals. She was a drab creature with stringy hair and sunken cheeks, but she gave as good as she got from her sullen husband. 'I do feed him, sir!' I heard her say resentfully.

'You feed him slop,' a man insisted, and I recognised the voice of Christopher de Valle, the Earl of Lechlade's man of business, and a self-proclaimed Englishman from scalp to arsehole. 'You feed him the same muck you give to your animals,' he went on harshly, 'so feed him properly, woman.'

The voices dropped, so I heard no more. I was at the door that led into a short passage that connected the dogs' shed to the larder, and then to Washington's lair. The house lay beyond the bear's cage. There were at least three people in the house, Strawbelly Sam, his slatternly wife, and de Valle, and I suspected there was a fourth. I needed the three whose voices I had recognised to leave, and then what? I had not thought it through. When we perform a play we rehearse the moves we will make onstage. The actors move about the stage, and the people watching probably give those moves no thought, they look so natural, but in truth they have been planned and practised, yet now I realised I had not planned at all. I had thought it enough

234

to get inside Scavenger's Yard and then snatch whatever opportunity presented itself. I stood, freezing and uncertain, not sure how I could overcome three, maybe four people.

Get inside the sheds, I told myself. There were places to hide inside. There was nowhere to hide in the snow-covered pit with its scaffolding, and, besides, as soon as deValle left, the dogs would be released.

I pressed the latch on the door. It clicked as the heavy wooden lever inside rose. I stayed still, listening for movement, but heard none. I pulled the door open, flinching at the grating sound of the hinges, and then, my heart beating like a trapped bird, I stepped inside, closed the door, and the stench of dog turds and rotting carcasses hit me.

The dogs saw me through the opening that led from their shed and immediately started howling again. There were at least a score of them, all safely caged, and all snarling and slavering, all barking and howling as they scrabbled with their paws at the iron bars. They were big dogs, with jaws like vices, with yellow eyes and dirty teeth, all malevolence and hunger. They hurled themselves at the bars as I crossed to the larder, and so vanished from their sight. The larder stank. It was where Strawbelly Sam kept food for the animals. There were dead cats, two dead dogs, some stinking cuts that could have come from any beast, all hanging on hooks, a massive blood-stained cleaver on a wooden table, and, at the larder's far end, a small room that was the close-stool built so that it drained directly into the River Fleet. I darted inside and managed to close the door just as Sam burst into the larder and started bellowing at the dogs to be silent.

The smell of the close-stool room would have felled a carthorse. I held my breath as long as I could, waiting until the dogs subsided, and I watched Strawbelly Sam through a crack in the wooden door. He was like a bent gnome, as malevolent as his mastiffs. He had a harelip that his scanty moustache could not cover. He hammered his heavy cudgel against the cage bars, and, when the mastiffs quietened, went back to his house that lay beyond Washington's lair.

I waited until I heard the door shut, then followed him.

The next shed, built alongside the house, was the smallest, and most of its space was taken by the great cage in which Washington lay. In the gloom he looked like a mountainous heap of dirty fur, but he saw me or smelt me, and raised his massive head. His eyes gleamed, looking oddly red in the shadow. He yawned, or perhaps it was a snarling threat, and I could see his teeth, all broken off and filed flat so that his massive bite did not kill his tormentors too quickly. I slipped past his cage and stood in the small passage outside the house.

And knew I had guessed right.

'It's the rats,' Strawbelly Sam was saying, 'they get the dogs excited. Bloody rats.'

'He is not here,' I heard deValle say firmly, 'to feed your damned dogs. He is not your servant, you disgusting piece of gristle! He's your guest. Do you understand?'

'Yes, sir.' It was Marion's voice. She sounded sullen.

'You will feed him,' deValle said, 'and feed him well!'

'Yes, sir.'

'And your job, young man, is to make that copy and to make it quickly!'

'I'm trying, sir.' And I almost smiled, because that was Simon Willoughby's voice.

'Four pages so far?' deValle sneered. 'That's not trying!'

'The candles are bad,' Willoughby whined, 'and the quills are split.'

'Who gave you the quills?'

'I did,' Strawbelly Sam said in his slurred voice, 'and there's nothing wrong with the quills, sir! Made them myself from cockerels' tail feathers. Good quills those, sir!'

'Can you write, man?' deValle demanded.

There was a pause as Strawbelly Sam contemplated his answer. 'Not exactly, sir, no, sir,' he said eventually, 'not write, not as you'd notice.'

'Then what do you know of quills? The boy's right. These are vile quills!' deValle snarled. 'You'll buy him proper quills. Today! Now! And ink.'

'Sir Godfrey sent the ink,' Strawbelly Sam said sullenly.

'It's toad piss, not ink! You'll buy new quills, good ink, and candles. Today! This morning! Now!'

'Yes, sir.'

There was a pause, then the sound of coins being slapped onto the table. Behind me Washington growled and stirred in his cage. I was ready to leap back into the larder if I heard footsteps beyond the door.

'When both plays are done, lad, you'll have the use of his lordship's house,' deValle went on in a kindlier tone, 'but this is the safest place for you till the copies are made.'

'Yes, sir, I know, sir.' Simon Willoughby sounded utterly miserable.

'And buy food,' deValle went on, presumably to Marion, 'something fit for a Christian to eat.'

'My pottage is good, sir,' she protested.

'Your pottage is slop expelled from the devil's arsehole,' deValle said. 'And bake some fresh bread, woman, not that green muck.'

I heard movement, and edged backwards, but it was evident the three were going towards the further door that led to the yard's main gate, where, I assumed, deValle's horse waited. 'I'll come back tomorrow, Master Willoughby,' I heard deValle say, 'and I'll expect progress.'

'You shall have it, sir, I promise.'

'You'll open the gate, man,' deValle ordered Strawbelly Sam,

237

'and then walk to the city to buy quills. We want the first copy this week, not next year!'

'Yes, sir.'

'You're being paid good money for this,' he reminded them.

'Yes, sir,' Strawbelly Sam said again. 'You'd best come and bolt the gate, Marion,' he added, then I heard the creak of a door, receding footsteps, and the slamming of another door. The three were gone, and Simon Willoughby was alone in the room.

Two of Sam's dog sticks were leaning in the passageway. Each was about a yard long, each a stout shaft of wood topped by a rusty iron bracket. They were used in the pit when the dogs had fastened their teeth into the bear's flanks and would not let go. Strawbelly Sam, or sometimes Buttercup, would ram the iron bracket into the dog's mouth and lever it open to force the dog away. I picked one up. It was heavy, then I waited a few more heartbeats. My heart was thumping. I heard the scrape of a chair or stool, and the sound almost made me jump in fear. Then, as if I was going onstage from the tiring room, I took a deep breath and opened the door.

Simon Willoughby was sitting by the fire. He turned. He saw me. His eyes widened, and his mouth opened.

And I hit him with the dog stick before he could make a noise.

I did not think, I just swung the heavy stick, and the iron bracket slammed into the side of his head. In my panic I had swung it too hard because he gasped and fell from the stool, blood oozing from his ear. Then he just lay motionless. Had I killed him? I gazed at him, aghast, remembering Thomas Butler lying bleeding in far Stratford. Then Simon Willoughby twitched and moaned and I reckoned he was alive, but would have a royal headache, and I crossed the room to the table beneath the window, and there were the two plays.

As simple as that! There was a pile of papers that I scooped up, pausing only to look at one random page. I read:

> *Ro: O blessed blessed night, I feare being night,*
>   *All this is but a dreame I heare and see,*
>   *Too flattering true to be substantiall.*
> *Iul: Three wordes good Romeo and good night indeed,*
>   *If that thy bent of loue be honourable?*
>   *Thy purpose marriage*

It was enough. These were the stolen plays, and I pushed the fat sheaf of papers into the canvas bag, then heard movement behind me and turned to see Simon Willoughby trying to stand. Blood dripped from his long hair. 'Richard!' he croaked and I kicked him hard in the head. He gasped, and, to silence him, I kicked him again.

'Quiet, you bastard!' I hissed, surprised by my anger.

I heard the squeal of hinges as the yard's outer gate was pulled open. It was time to leave. I kicked Willoughby again, then left by the door I had entered and ran into Washington's cell, and there I had an inspiration. I unbolted the bear's cage, opened its door, and prodded him with the dog stick. He stirred, lumbered up on his forefeet and I dropped the stick and ran through the larder to the door. The dogs saw me as I dragged it open and began their howling, then I ran through the snow, unbolted the gate and dashed out into the pasture.

I had done it! I had the plays!

I paused, listening. The dogs were howling.

I had done it!

Thy purpose marriage! Silvia!

Then Marion screamed.

And I panicked.

*   *   *

Dogs! Why had I not thought of them before? All Strawbelly Sam needed to do was release the dogs, and I would be hauled down in the pasture and the snow would turn red with blood as the animals tore me apart.

I ran blindly, stumbling westwards across the field, pushing through a hedge and still running, always listening for the howl of dogs getting louder. They did not come. Washington must have saved me, because the dogs were not released, and I reckoned that Strawbelly Sam could not get past the bear to reach the dogs' cages.

So what had made Marion scream? The sight of Simon Willoughby bleeding? Or the discovery of an angry bear loose in the sheds? I ran on, stumbling on snow-covered hillocks. The sky was dark with heavy-bellied clouds. It would snow again soon, I thought, and the sooner the snow covered my footprints the better. Leather Lane was just beyond the next hedge. If I could reach it then I could run south and lose myself in the alleys and taverns of Holborn.

Then I looked back and saw Christopher deValle.

He was on horseback and he was pursuing me. The horse was big and black, deValle wore a great black cloak, and in the snow, horse and rider looked like a dark avenging devil. I could see deValle savaging the horse with his spurs, see the snow being hurled up in clumps by the big hooves, and I knew I could not reach Leather Lane, let alone Holborn, before he caught me.

I stopped. I knelt in the snow and fumbled in the canvas bag. God help me, I thought, but the pistol was pointing downwards. Was it still loaded? I dragged it out. It was heavy. I needed both hands to level it, and my hands shook. The black devil was getting closer. I could see deValle's mouth open as he shouted at me, though I heard nothing of what he said. My ears were filled by a keening noise of fear and despair.

I pulled back the lever that held the flint. It was stiff,

compressing the steel spring that would drive it forward. DeValle must have seen the gun, but he did not stop. I saw his spurred boots savage back against the horse's flanks, saw him draw his rapier, and I was shaking, filled with panic and fear, my eyes half closed against the snow's glare, and when he was close I aimed the gun at the horse, saw the barrel shaking, and pulled the trigger.

It was too stiff. I pulled again, almost screaming with terror, and this time the trigger moved, the flint snapped forward, the pan-lid slid back, the serrated wheel spun around to make the sparks, and nothing happened. I tried to throw myself backwards, away from the horse.

Then the gun fired.

The noise was huge.

Filthy-smelling smoke billowed from the barrel. Wadding burned and died on the snow.

There was a scream.

I thought at first it was me screaming, then realised it was the horse that had swerved and reared. I had fallen into the snow, thrown back by panic and by the surprisingly strong kick of the pistol. I was sprawled helplessly, and saw the glint of horseshoes high above me. I think I did scream then, fearing those bright hooves would hammer me, but then the stallion slewed sideways. DeValle dropped the rapier and clung to the horse's mane as it fell sideways into the snow. He shouted in pain as the horse, which had fallen on him, scrambled to its feet. There was blood on its scalp, more blood trickling down its face, and a few red drops scattered on the snow, but it stood, whinnied, and trotted away, its wound apparently trivial. But deValle was cursing; his right leg bent at an odd angle. His hat, which sported two long black feathers, lay a dozen feet away. 'You bastard!' he said. He lunged towards his fallen rapier, but I kicked it away, and he hissed in pain as he put weight on his broken leg.

I thought about borrowing his horse, but as soon as I approached the beast it trotted away. I took deValle's hat instead, and saw there was a hole through its crown. I dusted the snow from it and walked towards the hedge. DeValle tried to get to his feet, but moaned as his leg collapsed beneath his weight.

'You'll die for this!' he shouted.

Then I was gone through the hedge, the thorns ripping at my cloak. I paused to look back, and saw deValle crawling towards his horse. I was shivering, but it was not from the cold. Then I ran down Leather Lane.

I would play Romeo!

NINE

I REACHED BLACKFRIARS as the church clocks were striking eleven. Snow sifted slow past the city's bell towers and steeples, whitening the roofs and turning to grey slush in the streets.

I had looked behind constantly, fearing pursuit, but none came. How could it? DeValle had a broken leg, his horse had a headache, and Strawbelly Sam was doubtless too busy cornering the bear. I hurried, shivering, not just because of the cold, but because I was reliving the morning, remembering the stench of my hiding place and the terror of the moment when the horse reared above me.

I entered the mansion through the Water Lane gate where the guard gave me a familiar nod. 'It's cold,' he said, stamping his feet. 'Nice hat, Richard!' I was wearing deValle's flamboyant hat with its two long feathers.

'It's got a hole in it,' I said.

'All the best things do!'

I crossed the stable yard, where barrels were being unloaded from a massive wagon. 'More wine for the wedding,' a servant told me.

'If they drink all that they'll fall asleep in the play,' I said.

'More like during the sermon!'

Once in the house, a maid offered me a conspiratorial grin. 'I'll tell her you're here!'

I smiled thanks and walked on, entering the great hall through the door from the scullery passage, though that door now led into the shadowed space that was our tiring room. Three short flights of makeshift stairs led up to the curtained entrances to the stage where the company was rehearsing. I stood for a moment at the head of the central steps, peering through the cloth. Richard Burbage, Henry Condell, Alexander Cooke, and Christopher Saunders were standing awkwardly on the stage, while my brother talked with Alan Rust. It was evident from the conversation that they had finished rehearsing the whole play, and were now discussing whatever scenes needed more work. 'You could move to the right of the stage?' Rust suggested to Richard Burbage.

'But Hermia's on the left.'

'Can she cross earlier?' my brother asked.

'We'll try that,' Burbage answered, 'but what if . . .' then he fell silent, because I had pushed through the curtain.

'What if . . .' Rust began.

'It doesn't matter,' my brother said curtly. He looked at me, plainly angered that I had come so late to the rehearsal. This was the first day the company had performed the whole play, and they would have had to work my scenes without me, which would have annoyed everyone. The rest of the players were gathered on the floor of the hall, and they, like my brother, glowered at me.

I ignored their anger, crossed the stage, jumped down to the hall floor, and went straight to the fire. I crouched there, feeling the heat seep into my frozen bones.

'So good of you to join us,' Alan Rust called to me caustically. Isaiah Humble had not returned, and Thomas Pope was evidently serving as the bookkeeper, the table scattered with the players' parts, because the one fair copy was in my satchel. Will Kemp, lounging in a great chair close to the fire, chuckled, while the other players edged away from me as though they feared contagion.

There was a moment's silence, as if the company was waiting for my brother to savage me for being so late, but when he said nothing Richard Burbage turned back to Alan Rust. 'Where do you want to go from?' he asked.

'Go from "Oh, when she is angry",' Rust said.

'What's the line before that?' Henry Condell asked.

Thomas Pope sorted through the pages. 'It's "No, sir, she shall not . . ."'

'No, it's not,' I interrupted him.

They all looked at me. I could feel their anger, which just needed a spark to erupt. Alan Rust tried to keep the hall calm. 'Go from "No, sir, she shall not . . ."'

I had taken the untidy pile of papers from the canvas bag. I stood, waited for Henry to say his line, then interrupted him. '"Two household friends,"' I declaimed in a loud voice, '"alike in dignity, In fair Verona, where we lay our scene, From civil broils broke into enmity, Where civil war . . ."'

'Give that to me!' My brother came towards me, then stopped, terrified, because as he moved closer I held the thick stack of pages towards the roaring fire.

I waited till I was sure he had stopped, then drew the scripts back from the flames. '"Where civil war makes civil hands unclean,"' I read on. '"From forth the fatal loins of these two foes, A pair of star-crossed lovers,"' I paused, smiling, 'you want me to burn it, brother?'

'Richard!' he pleaded.

'Who plays Romeo?' I asked, again holding the pages towards the hungry flames.

'No,' he said, his eyes on the pages, 'no! Please, no!'

'Who plays Romeo?' I asked again, louder this time.

'What is this?' Richard Burbage jumped down from the stage, but my brother held out a hand to stop him.

'What did you do?' my brother asked quietly.

'I'll tell you what I did,' I spoke loud and slow, making sure every man and boy in the hall could hear me. 'I broke Simon Willoughby's head. I shot a pistol at a man and his horse. I played hopscotch with a bear, and I have brought you these.' I held the pages towards him.

'He's playing Romeo?' Richard Burbage demanded angrily.

My brother ignored the question. He ignored the offered pages too, and I saw, to my surprise, that there were tears in his eyes. He walked to me and embraced me, his arms awkward about my waist. 'Thank you,' he whispered, 'thank you.' He stepped away and took the pages, holding them as if they were the most precious things in all the world.

'He's playing Romeo?' Richard Burbage demanded again.

'No, no,' my brother said distractedly, 'of course not, no.'

'He can't play . . .' Burbage began.

'He's not!' my brother snarled.

'Why not?' Will Kemp asked mischievously.

'Quiet!' Alan Rust intervened, and that tyrant king voice stilled the whole hall. He watched as my brother carried the two plays to the table and laid them down reverently. 'Who had the plays?' Rust asked me.

'Sir Godfrey,' I said.

'Where do you want these?' a voice called from the stage, and I saw a serving man carrying bolts of green cloth. Silvia was just behind him, her arms similarly loaded.

'Anywhere,' Alan Rust said impatiently, 'just drop them!' He turned back to me, 'Sir Godfrey had them?'

'He's providing the beast shows for the new playhouse,' I explained.

'Oh, dear Christ,' my brother muttered, 'of course!'

'And he had Simon Willoughby hidden at Scavenger's Yard,' I said.

'Is that the place they keep the dogs?' John Heminges asked, appalled.

'It's where they keep the dogs,' I said, 'the dogs, the fighting cocks, and a bloody great bear.'

'So what happened?' Heminges asked.

We are players, and we love an audience. Sometimes, if a play is going badly, it is easy to think of the audience as an enemy, but truly they are a part of the play, because an audience changes the way we perform. We can rehearse a play for weeks, as we were doing with *A Midsummer Night's Dream*, but the moment the playhouse is filled with people, so the play is transformed. There is a new nervousness, of course, but also an energy. We often ran a whole play in the Theatre without any audience, simply as a rehearsal, and often it would be dull and dreary, grown stale by too much rehearsal, yet next day, with two thousand people gaping at the stage, it would come alive. I had my audience now, though I pretended to be unaware that Silvia was listening.

I had seen the serving man pluck her elbow, plainly wanting to leave, but she had stubbornly stayed, and the servant had stayed with her, and they both now listened as I described breaking into Scavenger's Yard. John Heminges, God bless him, fed me my lines. 'Weren't you worried about the dogs?' he asked.

'I was terrified,' I admitted, 'so I took this,' I pulled the dagger from the canvas bag. 'I reckoned I might have to kill a couple before I reached the shed door.' That was not true. The mastiffs would have reduced me to shredded meat long before I could have scratched even one of them. I had thought that if the dogs were loose I would have had time to reach the shed before they reached me, and I could have left the yard by distracting them with meat from the larder. As it was, I had been lucky. 'But I was lucky,' I told John.

'Lucky? How?'

'They had a visitor, the Earl of Lechlade's man.'

'You know it was the earl's man?' my brother asked sharply.

'I recognised him,' I said, 'and I listened to them talking.' I put the dagger back in the bag. 'His horse was inside the yard, so all the dogs were locked up.'

'You were lucky,' John said fervently.

'Go on!' my brother urged.

'I sneaked inside,' I said, 'and that started the dogs howling, but I hid while Strawbelly quietened them. Then I went to the house door and heard them all talking. Simon Willoughby,' I offered John Heminges an apologetic glance, 'was supposed to be copying the plays, but they'd given him bad quills.'

'Ha!' my brother said.

'So then Strawbelly Sam and his wife took de Valle back to his horse . . .'

'De Valle?' my brother asked.

'The earl's man of business,' I explained, 'and they left Simon in the house, so I went inside, and I hit him before he could call for help.'

'You hit him?' John Heminges looked anxious.

'He won't know whether it's Christmas or Easter when he wakes up,' I said. 'He was bleeding. I hit him too hard.'

'Good,' my brother said firmly.

'I picked up the plays,' I went on, 'and left. Oh, and I released the bear.'

'Is that Washington?' Will Kemp asked. 'I like Washington. He's a mean old bastard. I saw him finish off a score of dogs in one afternoon.'

'You released him?' John Heminges asked. 'Why?'

'Because I reckoned they'd follow me,' I explained, 'and a bear in their way might slow them down.' The company just stared at me. 'He did too.'

'Did what?' Heminges asked.

'He slowed them down,' I said.

'Wasn't it dangerous?'

'I ran faster than the bear,' I said, as though that explanation was obvious. 'I got out of the yard and kept running, but then de Valle followed me. He was on horseback. I was going towards Leather Lane and he came after me with his sword drawn.'

'Dear sweet God,' John Heminges said quietly.

'But I took this as well,' I said, pulling the pistol out of the bag.

'Dear sweet God,' my brother echoed John Heminges, 'don't tell me you shot the Earl of Lechlade's man!'

'I shot his horse,' I said, 'not badly. I frightened the beast, but it threw de Valle, fell over in the snow, and broke de Valle's leg. So I took his hat, and came here.'

'Took his hat?' John Heminges asked in puzzlement.

'It's a nice hat,' I explained, 'except for the bullet hole.'

Silence. We like it when an audience is silent, when no one coughs, no one shuffles, no one cracks a nut, or uncorks an ale bottle with a sudden hiss. Silence means the play is working, and we have the audience in our power. To a player, that breathless silence is better than applause, and that morning in the great hall my audience was silent.

My story, of course, had been accurate as far as it went, but I had left out rather a lot. My brother, in one of those careless moments when he forgot to be nasty to me, once told me that the art of storytelling was knowing what to leave out, and I dare say he is right, though often, learning lines of his plays, I wish he had left out twenty times more. I had left out my terror, the cringing terror that almost made me piss myself. I left out my heart beating wildly, my panic when de Valle's horse

249

loomed over me and I had just pulled the gun's trigger blindly and the pistol had suffered a hangfire. I did not confess that I had been hurled backwards by the pistol's kick, that I had been screaming in terror and sprawling helpless in the snow, but instead I had made that moment sound coolly deliberate, as if I had aimed, when in truth my eyes had been closed and the shot was effective only by a miracle. I had been whimpering, shivering, scared halfway to death, yet, knowing Silvia was listening, I had painted myself as a hero.

And so I was! My brother looked at me with what might even have been mistaken for admiration and was certainly gratitude, John Heminges beamed, the boys gazed at me with awestruck faces, and even Will Kemp was impressed. He scraped back his chair, stood, then slapped me on the back hard enough to hurt. 'Well done, lad,' he boomed, 'well done!'

Only Richard Burbage was unhappy. He drew my brother away, leading him by the arm to the space beneath the oriel window, and I saw them talking there, and Richard Burbage glanced at me, then seemed satisfied and went back to the new stage. My brother climbed to the window seat from where he beckoned me.

'You can't play Romeo,' he greeted me.

'You . . .' I began.

'You can't,' he said firmly, but surprisingly gently. 'Sit down.'

I sat. He glanced out of the window. The warmth in the hall was melting the frost patterns so that drops of water ran down the outside of the glass to distort the view of the frozen river. 'It's still snowing,' he said. 'A hard winter!'

'You said . . .' I began again.

'I know what I said,' he interrupted me again, 'and it was said lightly. Romeo is a big part, too big, and Richard will play it beautifully. What I will promise you is a man's part of substance, a good part.'

'Substance,' I repeated the word.

'A Sharer's part,' he said, 'I promise it.'

'A man's part? Not like Francis Flute?'

He had the grace to smile. 'Not like Francis Flute. You'll like this part. A proper man's part. You can grow a beard, and you'll be paid well. I promise.' He waited, expecting me to speak, but I said nothing. 'It's a good play,' he said wistfully, 'it's even a very good play, and we can start rehearsals as soon as it's copied. His lordship tells me Her Majesty has been asking for us to perform again, so now we have two plays to take to court. And you will be in both.' He stood. 'And spring will come! We can play both pieces at the Theatre when the weather clears. You will be busy, Richard, you'll be busy and you'll be paid. Now, we needs finish the rehearsal.' He glanced down at the window seat. 'Thank you,' he said, then went down the stairs. I followed his glance, and saw he had left coins on the tapestry-covered cushion. Six shillings!

'What's his name?' I called after him.

He turned and looked up at me. 'His name?'

'The part I'll play.'

'You'll have to use a rapier to play him, so practise!'

'His name?' I asked again.

He pretended not to hear, but just walked on, and I wondered whether I could believe his promise. What had the Reverend Venables said? That promises in the playhouse were like kisses on May Day. I had just been kissed.

And beyond the window the snow fell harder.

There was still time to rehearse some more scenes, and they went well, maybe because everyone was in a good mood except for John Heminges, who still lamented his apprentice's treachery. Even Bobby Gough managed to remember all his lines, though he was still nervous, perhaps because he was a year or so too young to play Titania.

The player who surprised me was Alan Rust. He was a tall man, strongly built, who usually played serious, middle-aged characters. His voice was deep and his presence onstage imposing, which made him a surprising choice to play Puck, Oberon's mischievous servant, whose mistakes and jests propelled much of the play. When I copied the play I had seen Puck as a sprite, an elf, a merry goblin who would dance rather than walk and sing rather than speak. Indeed my brother suggested as much, sometimes calling Puck 'Robin Goodfellow', and there wasn't a man in the company who had not grown up listening to tales of Robin Goodfellow's pranks. He was a trickster, a spirit of the deep woods, a mischief-maker, and it was a part, I thought, which one of the boys would play well, and then the Sharers had given it to a man who normally played kings or lords or tyrants. Yet Rust transformed the part, and in doing that he rivalled Will Kemp as a cause for laughter. He did not try to diminish his stature, though he did make his voice higher than usual, and all his movements were deliberately light. In repose he was all dignity, but the dignity vanished when he moved. He danced, he trembled, he was impatient, he was funny. 'My gentle Puck, come hither,' Oberon called, and gentle Puck skittered across the stage too enthusiastically, skidded to a stop and then stood poised to dart away again.

'Thou rememberest,' Oberon went on, 'since once I sat upon a promontory and heard a mermaid on a dolphin's back,' and Puck nodded too quickly and too eagerly. He was quivering, as if he just wanted to fly away on whatever errand was about to be his. It was plain he was not listening to his master. Oberon wanted him to remember that moment when the mermaid sang and the rude sea grew calm and the stars stooped to hear her music. 'Thou rememberest?'

'I remember!' Puck said too quickly, and it was plain he did not, and that whatever followed would eventually go wrong because he was all energy and no sense. The potion of the magic flower would be poured onto the eyelids of the wrong lover, and the result would be star-crossed couples and confusion. 'Fetch me this herb,' Oberon commanded, pointing to the left of the stage, 'and be thou here again ere the Leviathan can swim a league.'

'I'll put a girdle round about the earth in forty minutes!' Puck said, and fled off through the right-hand door as if pursued by a bear. We all laughed.

Silvia laughed too. She had left the great hall after delivering the bolts of cloth, but had returned soon after with Jean, our seamstress, both women's arms heaped with more fabrics. Lady Anne Hunsdon, grandmother to the bride, had inspected some of the finished costumes, and was now insisting that they be made even more ornate. 'There is money, Master Shakespeare,' I had heard her say to my brother, 'spend it!'

My brother had bowed. 'Your ladyship,' he had responded in amazement.

'Spend more!' she said imperiously. The Theatre had a large stock of clothes, which I regarded as my wardrobe, but other than disguising the boys as women, dressing the noble characters in silks and satin, and the commoners in fustian, we took little trouble over costume. When Richard Burbage played Titus Andronicus, he wore hose, shirt, falling band, and boots, over which a white sheet had been artfully draped to suggest a toga. His troops, all played by hired men, wore battered helmets and dented breastplates that had seen service in Ireland or the Low Countries. The audience never seemed to mind, but Lady Anne wanted better, much better. 'I wish the play to resemble a masque,' she had said more than once.

I had never seen a masque, but I knew they were lavish entertainments staged at country mansions and city palaces for the Queen and her aristocracy. My brother told me they were not so much plays as presentations, replete with gods and goddesses, choirs and musicians, and distinguished by the most elaborate effects and costumes that machinery, cunning, money, and needlewomen could devise. Gods flew, mermaids seemed to glide upon lakes, fountains spouted coloured water, grass was painted gold, cherubs chirped prettily, and, most astonishing of all, women played the parts of women. 'And some do it amazingly well,' my brother had said.

'Then why don't we . . .'

'Because the Puritans hate us enough already! Put women on the stage and the Puritans will burn down the playhouses. If there's one thing a Puritan fears, it's a woman. Besides, they're not real plays.'

'They're not?' I had asked.

'Masques are mere pious recitals,' he said scathingly, 'devised to make the audience feel inspired with unending speeches about chastity, nobility, bravery, and other such nonsense. They're enchanting to look at, but dreary beyond belief to hear.'

So *A Midsummer Night's Dream* would be enchanting to look at. Jean and Silvia had brought yards of white silk gauze, cream-coloured satin, and delicate lace, which would be used to clothe the fairies. The company's youngest apprentice boys had the fairies' speaking parts, but they were accompanied by a half-dozen children from the Lord Chamberlain's household for whom my brother had written three songs that Phil had set to music. The children were the sons of the household's servants, and one, called Robin, turned out to be Silvia's nephew. 'Say hello to Francis Flute,' she ordered him.

'Hello,' the child, six or seven years old, said.

'Hello,' I said awkwardly.

'He's a cheeky little bleeder,' Silvia said, kneeling to drape Robin with gauze, 'and stand still or I'll smack you.' Those last words were addressed to the child, who stared up at me with wide eyes. 'He's my brother's eldest,' Silvia explained. Her brother Ned worked in the stables. The whole family, it seemed, had connections to Lord Hunsdon's household. Silvia's father had been one of his lordship's bargemen before he bought his own wherry, and her mother, like Silvia, had been a maidservant. 'And I expect Robin here will grow up to serve the family,' Silvia went on.

'I want to be a soldier,' Robin said.

'You don't want to be a soldier,' she said, 'because soldiers just get chopped to little pieces. You want to work in the stables like your dad. And stop picking your nose!' She slapped Robin's hand, then draped more gauze around his shoulders before tucking it, pinning it, and adding a silk ribbon. 'There, you look like a lovely fairy!'

'I don't want to be a fairy.'

'Well you are one. And you sing. You're a singing fairy.' She tied the ribbon, then looked up at me. 'He's got a lovely voice. Robin has. He sings like a little bird, don't you? Just like a little robin redbreast.'

Robin said nothing, just stared up at me as if appealing for help against this monstrous feminine abuse.

'So you shot a horse?' Silvia asked.

'Barely.'

'You didn't kill it then?'

'No, I just scared it.'

She grinned at me and was about to say something more when Jean called out to my brother. 'Are we putting rugs on the stage?'

'Yes!'

'So the fairies don't need shoes?'

'Fairies never need shoes.'

'You hear that?' Silvia said to Robin. 'You don't need shoes, so make sure you wash your feet.'

'Why?'

'Because I said so.' She leaned back to look at her work. 'You are a pretty little fairy! Isn't he pretty, Richard?'

'Very,' I said.

'And don't bite your fingernails!' Silvia slapped at Robin's hand.

Robin scowled. 'Aunt Silvia is going to marry Tom,' he said out of nowhere.

My world stood still. I had no idea what to say, because there was nothing to say. Silvia blushed and did not look at me. She was slicing a pair of shears into the gauze costume, and the blades hesitated a moment, then cut again, savagely. 'You're getting married?' Jean, on her knees in front of another child, asked blithely.

There was silence for a moment. Silvia had put two pins between her lips, but took them out. 'My dad wants me to,' she said flatly.

'Who's Tom?' Jean asked.

'A waterman.' Silvia still did not look at me. 'He helps my dad.'

'Nice boy, is he?'

'Do we want to hem this edge with satin?'

'We'll use the blue on the children's jerkins,' Jean, still on her knees, shuffled across the floor to look at Robin. 'Oh that does look nice! That high collar is ever so clever! And maybe the same for Titania? But in gold? Did we bring the gold?'

Silvia had just put the two pins back between her lips, so shook her head.

'I'll fetch it,' Jean said, starting to stand.

Silvia spat the pins out. 'No, I'll go!' She ran across the hall floor and vanished through the large doors. Robin, swathed in gauze and satin, began to pick his nose.

'She's a lovely girl,' Jean said, when Silvia had left. 'That Tom's a lucky man.'

'He is,' I said dully.

'And she can sew!' Jean began hemming the edge of Robin's jerkin. 'She's magic with a needle. I wish she could come work with me.'

'Yes,' I said.

Jean rocked back on her heels and looked at me. 'Lord above, Richard, I don't understand you Shakespeares. Live with your heads in the bleeding clouds, both of you. Stand still, you little bugger.' She slapped Robin's hand. 'Don't pick your nose! You want your brains to leak out? Why do you think your Silvia's not married?'

'My Silvia?' I asked.

'She's sixteen, for God's sake! John Heminges's wife was a widow at sixteen. Silvia should have been wed two years ago.'

'She should?'

'Don't you go listening to none of this,' Jean said to Robin, 'and don't bite your fingernails either, or you'll end up with two stumps like Slippery Daniel. You'll have to eat like a dog if you have stumps. She doesn't want to marry this Tom, does she? And her dad is too soft to make her.'

'Who's Slippery Daniel?' Robin asked.

'No one you know, darling, but he makes a God-horrible mess when he eats. Can't wipe his bum neither, so he smells something awful.'

Robin laughed, and I watched the hall's doors, but Silvia did not reappear. The snow was falling still harder, plastering the oriel window white, and the Sharers decided to call it a day and let everyone go home. 'We meet tomorrow,' my brother announced.

I went home.

The snow lifted. For most of the day it had seemed we would be buried by the big soft flakes, but by the time I reached home the snow had stopped. I paid the Widow Morrison three shillings in rent, and she stared at the coins as though she had never seen such things before. 'A February miracle!' she said, and kissed me on the cheek. 'Have an oatcake, darling. Have two.'

'How's Father Laurence?' I asked her.

'He's busy, darling.' She winked at me, which I suspected meant that the old priest was hearing confessions. 'There was a man here asking for you.'

'For me?'

'A nasty man, too,' she said, and I must have looked alarmed. 'It's all right, darling,' she went on, 'I told him you hadn't paid your rent and were out on the street. That was almost true too, wasn't it?'

I went upstairs to the attic that was dark and freezing. I struck steel on flint, lit a patch of charred linen in the tinder box and transferred the flame to a rushlight. I was miserable. Father Laurence was busy, and I was in no mood to huddle alone in my attic. Silvia! I wanted to believe what Jean had told me, but the mind forever slides downhill to believe the worst. And marrying Tom made sense. He was a waterman, he was young, he would have a trade, he would make money, and why would Silvia's parents ever wish her to marry a penniless player? Perhaps Jean was right and perhaps Silvia did not want the marriage with Tom, but good sense dictated that she should marry him.

I thought of some words that Bottom said to Titania after she had declared her passion for him, a burning passion despite the ass's head perched on his shoulders. Under the influence of Oberon's magic potion she swore undying love, to which Bottom answered, 'To say the truth, reason and love keep little company these days,' and I so hoped that was true! Yet I feared that reason and love would prove bedfellows. In a play anything can happen. Fairy queens can fall in love with monsters, but Silvia's parents would want their daughter married safely, reasonably, to a man who could support her, and keep them in their old age.

I did not want to be alone and cold, but nor did I want to stay dressed in the craftsman's clothes I had worn all day, and so I changed into the finest garments I had stolen from the Theatre. I was angry. I told myself that Silvia had deceived me, and that once I had discovered the deception, she had fled from me. So tonight I would find another woman and squander what I had left of my brother's gift. I chose a doublet cut from the softest Spanish black leather, slashed with strips of dark blue velvet. It had once cost a fortune, but some lordly soul, tiring of it, had donated it to the playhouse. The sleeves were tied at the shoulder with silver cords threaded through silver eyelets, and were padded with white silk, which bunched out of the slits on the forearms. The cuffs were of French lace, and the doublet, in short, was a thing of beauty. Wearing such a garment seemed like a gesture against malign fate, against the reason that had soured love. I hung a sheathed dagger from my belt, covered my finery with a thick, dark cloak, and then, with coins in my pouch, I went back into the cold night. 'Going to the tavern?' the widow asked as I left.

'For a while.'

'You should save your money, Richard.'

That was doubtless good advice, but nevertheless I walked to the Dolphin, hoping that Alice would be alone, but when I pushed through the door into the crowded, smoky, candlelit main room, I saw my brother sitting at a table beyond the big hearth. He was with four other men, none of whom I knew. I stayed in the shadows, watching him. He looked animated, plainly telling some tale, and his companions were laughing. He looked happy too, and why did that surprise me? Perhaps because whenever he was with me he seemed to scowl? I doubted he would welcome my company, despite having restored his

259

precious plays, nor did I want his company, so I shrank further back into the shadows and then saw Alice come down the stairs and cross the crowded room. She looked so slight and pale, her fair hair tousled, but when she saw my brother her face brightened, and my brother, seeing her, extended an arm in invitation. She went to his side, sat on the bench, and snuggled into his shoulder. It was well past curfew which meant the city gates were closed, so plainly my brother had no intention of going home. He would spend the night here. He whispered something in Alice's ear, and she laughed. He bent down and kissed her forehead. She began to talk animatedly, and my brother and his companions listened. They were happy.

I did not want to stay there, but nor did I want to slink home, so with misery as my companion I went to the Falcon, where, as usual, Marie sat by the fire, Dick scowled, and Margaret and her husband squabbled. 'Don't you look grand!' Margaret welcomed me. 'Doesn't Richard look grand?'

'Tie a ribbon round a dog's neck,' Greasy Harold, her husband, growled.

'You miserable old bastard.'

I bought a mulled ale, then sat by the tavern's fire, where I brooded on Silvia, and then remembered the 'nasty man' who had enquired at the widow's house. I suspected he had been sent by deValle. Somehow, in all the day's excitement and disappointment I had not thought about deValle's revenge, but he would want it. He was a proud man, and I had broken his leg and stolen his hat. I shuddered, suddenly realising my danger. 'I might sleep here tonight,' I told Margaret.

'It's stopped snowing, Richard, but of course you're welcome.'

'If you pay,' Greasy Harold put in, 'you can stay if you pay. We're not a poorhouse.'

'We're not? Isn't that a surprise,' Margaret said. 'Of course you can stay, Richard, don't mind him.'

'He might have to share a bed,' John grumbled.

'Share a bed! Who do you think will want a bed tonight?'

'Someone might.'

'Someone who missed the curfew,' Marie put in helpfully.

'No one's travelling tonight!' Margaret said scornfully.

And that was when we heard the hoofbeats. 'Oh no?' Harold crowed. 'So no one's travelling?'

You don't hear horses that late at night, not in Shoreditch, and there was more than one horse, instead it was a whole clatter of hooves that was scarcely muffled by the snow. They came close, and we waited for them to pass, but instead they stopped and there was only silence. Horses mean money, and money means power, and power means trouble, and everyone in the Stinking Chicken knew it. We all looked at the street door.

'Can't be nothing to do with us,' Margaret broke the nervous silence.

The silence stretched.

'They've gone,' Harold said uncertainly.

'I need a piss,' I announced. I dropped a small coin on the table, snatched up my cloak, and went to the still room door.

'Not in there, you dirty bugger!' Harold protested. 'Use the alley like a Christian!'

I pushed through the door. A pair of rats vanished under barrels, and I pulled open the outer door into the stable yard and saw the man waiting there. Or rather I saw the long pale streak of a sword blade, which, the moment I appeared, was raised towards me. The swordsman said nothing. He was dressed in black, and I only saw him because there was a lantern in the back room of Nellie Cotton's house, which overlooked the yard. Nellie never slept. She would be sewing in her back parlour, making endless clothes for her babies, all of whom were in Saint Leonard's churchyard. She was mad.

261

The man moved towards me, the light of Nellie's lantern glimmering on his blade. I went left fast, through the gate into the piss-stinking alley, and there was another man waiting, and he too was dressed all in black, and he too carried a blade, this one a short, wide-bladed knife. 'Mister Price wants to see you,' he said, and the man who had been in the Falcon's yard came through the gate, and his sword tip touched my spine between the shoulder blades.

'Who is Mister Price?' I asked. I was thinking I could jump and catch hold of the wall's coping and be over it into Davy Locket's backyard, but the sword in my spine prodded me. I would never be over the wall in time.

'Mister Price,' the second man said, 'is the gentleman who wants to see you.'

'You've got the wrong man,' I said, and for a moment I even believed that. The only Mister Price I knew sold fish and couldn't raise two pennies, let alone have black-dressed retainers with naked blades.

'No, Dickie boy,' the swordsman behind me said, 'we don't.'

'Come gently, boy,' the knife man said, 'and you might keep your balls.'

'Or one of them,' the swordsman said, then moved his blade so it pierced my cloak and slid between my thighs. He pressed the steel upwards. 'And one's better than none, right lad?'

He was right. So I went gently.

There were six of them, and seven horses. The seventh horse was for me. It was a broken-down jade with a saddle, but no stirrups, and even if I could have kicked it into a gallop I would never have escaped the six men on their sleek stallions. They were Percies. Pursuivants. They did not tell me that, but nor did they need to because they were commanded by the bulbous twins who had been humiliated by Alan Rust in the Theatre.

One twin rode on my left and the other on my right, and both talked across me. 'He's a pretty boy, brother,' one said.

'He is, brother. For the moment.'

'He's got a nice hat.'

'It is a nice hat!'

'He's not very chatty, though, is he?' The twin on my right nudged me. 'Lost your tongue?'

'Very likely he will lose it,' the second twin said, 'if Mister Price decides to tear it out.'

'By the root.'

'Gobble gobble,' the second twin said with a laugh. 'That's what you'll sound like when he's done with you.'

'No,' the first one said, 'it's more like gurgle gurgle, but only after they've stopped screaming.'

'Gobble gurgle then.'

The twins were young. Maybe in their middle twenties. Young and confident. The two men who rode ahead of us and the two behind were bigger, older, and silent. The pair in front listened to the twins' chatter and did not even turn their heads, and I sensed that they despised the brothers.

We went slowly. You cannot hurry a horse in the darkness, not unless you want to break the beast's leg, and especially not when the animal is treading an uncertain road through newly fallen snow. We went north and west around the city, following Hog Lane between hedgerows thick with snow. The city wall was a dark streak to my south, the battlements faintly outlined by the lamps of London. The night's small wind was blowing from the south, bringing the city's reek of sewage and smoke. There was little moonlight; just enough to show the fields smooth and white.

The horses quickened as we reached the houses built north of the Cripplegate. There were lanterns burning in archways here, and dim washes of light from tavern windows. The streets grew narrow, and we had to duck under jutting storeys or hanging signs. We passed the Duck and Drake where I had once won sixteen shillings playing cards with a clothier come from the north. The cards had been marked. For a moment I feared the Percies were taking me back to Scavenger's Yard, but then we turned south towards Smithfield. Watchmen ducked into doorways, and the few other people still not abed scurried out of our way, disappearing into alleys rather than be seen by black-dressed men mounted on powerful horses.

'Perhaps the pretty boy has a sister, brother,' the twin on my left said as we rode into the open space of Smithfield Market. His breath made a cloud in the dim light of a lantern.

'We like sisters, brother.'

'We do.'

'Or a sweetheart?'

'We like sweethearts too.'

'He must have a sweetheart. He's a pretty boy.'

'And we hate pretty boys, don't we brother?'

'We do hate pretty boys.'

I still said nothing, and my silence frustrated them so they too went quiet. We rode on to Westminster, and there came to a massive gate guarded by two men in scarlet livery and lit by a pair of flaming torches that guttered in the night's light breeze. The guards said nothing, they evidently recognised the horse-men, and so they simply pulled their halberds upright and one pushed open the right-hand gate. I knew where we were. This was the palace where I had seen Simon Willoughby kissing his lordling in the rain-soaked courtyard.

'Hop off, pretty boy,' one of the twins commanded me once we were inside the gate, and I obeyed. The twins also dis-mounted, and one plucked at my elbow to take me through a low door into a lantern-lit passageway.

Palaces are like playhouses. In the front it is all gaudy and bright, painted with stars and gleaming with false marble, but go through a door from the stage, and behind it is filth, disorder, bare wood, and cracked plaster. We were backstage in the palace, deep in the bowels where the servants never slept. Firewood was stacked on one side of the passage, and steam came from a door where a laundress thrust a pole into a cauldron poised over a fire. She saw the twins and made the sign of the cross. You could do that in the palace and not face questioning from the constables. Rumour said the Queen kept a crucifix in an inner chamber, a great cross hanging on a wall with the crucified Lord gazing down at her, and perhaps that was true. Men had their guts ripped out and burned before their eyes for less.

'He works late,' one of the twins said to me.

'Mister Price,' the other one explained.

'He works late.'

They spoke with a strange respect, not for me, but for the late-working Mister Price. My hatred for the twins was turning to loathing. They were a head shorter than I, yet everything about them seemed too big; big rumps, big noses, big chins, bushy black hair under their black velvet caps, brawny muscles plump under black sleeves. Bulbous graceless boys who led me across a small courtyard piled with barrels and so into another corridor, where one rapped on a door.

'Come,' a voice said.

'Go,' a twin pushed me through the door.

'Hat off,' the other twin said, and snatched Christopher deValle's wide-brimmed hat from my head. They followed me into the room, and two other Pursuivants came with them. They all nodded respectfully to the man sitting behind a table. 'We have him, Mister Price,' one of the twins said. There was no answer.

The room first. Not large, but large enough. There were

rushes on the floor, and the walls were panelled in dark wood, while the ceiling was painted with a night sky in which ships with wind-bellied sails travelled between the stars. I sensed Mister Price had not ordered that painting, because it seemed too frivolous for the rest of the room, and Mister Price did not look like a man for whom ships would sail across the heavens. He was a man who liked order, and there were shelves against one wall, and those shelves were neatly piled with papers, while more papers were stacked on the vast table that took up half the room's space. There must have been thirty candles on the table; big candles, all burning to make the room bright, and, because there were no windows, the candles must have burned night and day. Beyond the table, and taking up half of the far wall, was a wide stone fireplace in which a fire blazed. Firewood was heaped to the left of the hearth and sea-coal to the right. The heat was intense, yet Mister Price sat close to the fire in a heavy black coat.

Mister Price. He was at the table, writing. The quill scratched on the paper. He did not look up, but kept writing, scratching, dipping the quill in a pewter inkwell, carefully draining the excess from the nib, then scratching again. All I could see was the top of his head, which had a bald patch like a monk's tonsure. *Scratch scratch.* So far as I could tell he was dressed all in black and he wore no ruff. A Puritan? Even the twins wore ruffs, though theirs were poor half-starved grubby things that flopped beneath their too big chins. 'Where,' Mister Price broke his silence, still writing, 'do we obtain our quills?'

'From Mistress Hamilton's shop in Grass Street, Mister Price,' one of the twins answered.

'The proper name is Gracechurch Street, I believe?'

'I meant Gracechurch Street, Mister Price, sorry, Mister Price.'

'You will inform Mistress Hamilton that her quills are insufficiently softened. Ask her if I am expected to suck my own nib?'

266

'I'm sure Mistress Hamilton will suck your nib, Mister Price.'

A silence followed that. The quill paused, and Mister Price went very still. The twins did not move. 'I . . .' the one who had spoken said, then paused, 'did not, I mean. I can . . .'

The quill began moving again, and the twins relaxed. A coal fell in the fire, pushing a puff of smoke out into the room. 'Feed it,' Mister Price said, and one of the twins edged around the table to put more fuel on a fire that was already raging like hell's inferno.

Mister Price took a scrap of rag and carefully wiped the quill's nib. He folded the rag neatly, laid it beside the paper, and put the quill into a pot, then looked up at me.

Pig, I thought instantly, and remembered Lord Hunsdon talking about Piggy Price. And he was right, because George Price was a pig in human form. A smallish, plump man with heavy jowls and a squashed nose and small eyes and a scanty beard and a pursed mouth. How old? Forty years perhaps. Maybe more. He had a weak chin and a petulant expression. An ugly beast, I thought, ugly and angry and dangerous. 'My name,' he said, 'is George Price. George . . . Price.' He repeated the name distinctly, separating the George and the Price with a long pause.

He paused, probably expecting me to speak, but I said nothing. He tapped the table top with his fingers. His nails were chewed, the skin around them torn bloody, but there was no ink on his fingers. I have never seen a writer or a poet or a clerk or a scrivener who does not have fingers smeared with ink, but not the pig-like Mister Price. He was a fastidious piggy. The fire roared behind him, its flames doing as much to light the room as his many candles.

'He doesn't speak much, Mister Price,' the twin standing on the hearth said.

'Quiet,' Mister Price said. Then he looked at me, closed his eyes, and put his skin-bitten fingers together. 'Let us pray,' he said.

'Shut your poxy eyes,' the twin standing beside me growled.

'Oh Lord,' Price said, 'in whose hands lies the safety of this realm, bless, we pray, our labours this night that they may add to Thy glory and hasten the coming of Thy kingdom. We ask this in the name of our Lord Jesus Christ. Amen.'

'Amen,' the twins muttered together.

George Price opened his eyes and looked at one of the two Pursuivants standing by the closed door. 'Fetch the boy,' he said.

The man left, and we stood waiting. The fire crackled. The melted snow from our boots made puddles among the rushes on the wide plank floor.

I heard footsteps. The door opened, and in came the Pursuivant holding a boy by the collar of his jerkin.

It was Simon Willoughby.

'Now,' said Mister Price, 'we can begin.'

TEN

SIMON WILLOUGHBY looked terrified, and whatever beauty he had once possessed was now ruined. The right side of his face was one large purple bruise against which a dark gash of clotted blood ran jagged. It looked as if I had broken his cheek-bone. His right eye was closed, his upper lip was swollen, his long hair was lank, and he was shaking. He looked at me and whimpered, as if expecting me to do yet more damage. 'The boy can sit,' Mister Price said.

The Pursuivant who had fetched Willoughby dragged a chair away from the wall. 'Thank you, sir,' Simon Willoughby whimpered.

'You two can wait outside,' Price frowned at the two men who had been standing just inside the door. He waited for them to go, leaving just myself, Piggy Price, Simon Willoughby, and the twins in the overheated room. One of the twins stood close to me, while the other waited by the fire. 'Are you comfortable, young man?' Price asked Simon Willoughby when the door was closed.

'Yes, sir, thank you, sir.'

'And you recognise this man?' Price gestured towards me.

'Yes, sir,' Willoughby said, 'that's Richard Shakespeare, sir.' His speech was slurred, perhaps because the dog stick had broken a tooth or because his cheek was so swollen, but he still managed to invest my name with venom.

'And he is the man who assaulted you and stole property entrusted to your keeping?'

'Yes, sir, he did, sir.'

'Lying little bast—' I began, whereupon the twin standing beside me slapped me hard on the mouth.

'You will be silent,' Price told me, 'unless questioned.' He tidied some papers on his desk, fussily aligning their edges. He looked up at me when he was satisfied. 'You are a player?' he asked, pronouncing the last word as though it was coated with shit.

I did not answer. He already knew who and what I was, so why speak?

'I can make him squeal for you, Mister Price.'

Mister Price ignored the eager tone of the twin who had spoken. His fingers tapped on the table as he gazed at me. 'Her Majesty,' he said, 'has a liking for masques, for interludes, and plays.' He plainly disapproved of that, but she was his Queen and he was her man and so he uttered the words respectfully. 'Do you believe that gives you privileges?'

'No.'

'No, sir,' the twin beside the fire corrected me. I ignored him.

'She will not protect you,' Mister Price said, 'and do you know why not?'

I said nothing. 'He doesn't know why not, Mister Price,' the other twin said. I could smell a mixture of tobacco, fish, and ale on his breath.

'Because you are a player and a thief and a liar and a rogue,' Mister Price said with sudden malevolence. 'What else are you?'

'A Christian,' I said, knowing it would annoy him.

'Blasphemer!' Price spat. 'Are you a papist?'

'No,' I said.

'No, sir,' Fish-Breath corrected me, 'be respectful to Mister Price.' He drove an elbow into my ribs as he stressed the word 'Mister'. His brother snorted with suppressed laughter. He had put more sea-coal on the fire, then stirred the blaze vigorously with a poker, and his blunt face was now shining with sweat.

'He will learn respect,' Mister Price said calmly. 'Master Willoughby?'

'Sir?' Simon Willoughby said eagerly.

'Is Mister Shakespeare a papist?'

'Yes, sir, I think he is, sir!'

'You little turd . . .' I began, and was again slapped across the mouth by Fish-Breath.

'Why do you say that?' Price asked Willoughby.

'Because before every play, sir, his brother makes the sign of the cross. I've seen him do it often, sir. Often!'

'And if one brother is a papist,' Mister Price said, looking at me, 'then we might assume the other is too?'

'Yes, sir,' Simon said.

'And you piss yourself before every performance . . .' I started, and jerked my head away as Fish-Breath's hand struck me a glancing blow. 'You lying little bedwetter,' I snarled at Willoughby.

'The sign of the cross,' Price said slowly, savouring each word. 'Your brother is unashamed of his foul beliefs, and you share a house with a known Romish priest. It is not enough to be a player, scum though you are, you must also be a stinking turd expelled from the buttocks of the whore of Babylon! Does Father Laurence hear confessions?'

He asked that question swiftly, almost taking me by surprise. 'No!' I managed to answer.

His porcine face betrayed that he did not believe me, but he did not press the question. 'Make it ready,' he said instead to Sweaty-Face, who still crouched by the fire. Mister Price stood, revealing a plump little pig-like belly. He pushed the chair back as far as he could, then edged past Sweaty-Face to come around the table and thrust his snout up into my face. 'Do you believe,' he demanded, his breath stinking of stewed apple, 'in the saving grace of our Lord Jesus Christ?'

There is only one way to answer that question. 'Yes,' I said.

'Yes sir!' Fish-Breath said.

'It's ready, Mister Price,' Sweaty-Face spoke from the fire, which now burned brighter than ever to flicker lurid-edged shadows on the ships sailing between the painted stars.

Price ignored him, staring indignantly up into my face instead. 'Tell me,' he demanded, 'what does a player do?'

'Do?' I asked.

'In the den of iniquity you call a playhouse,' he said, 'what does a player do?'

'We pretend,' I said.

'You tell lies then?'

'We make stories come true,' I said. I had to look down on him because he was a full head shorter than I was.

'You cannot make truth from lies,' he said, 'any more than you can make a custard by stirring the turds in a close-stool.'

'Very good, Mister Price,' Fish-Breath said, chuckling, 'very apt.'

Mister Price ignored him. 'You dress as a woman, do you not?'

'As does Simon Willoughby,' I said.

'Yet the scriptures forbid it!' Price ignored my comment about Simon. He looked up at me, and his face shuddered with distaste as his voice rose in anger. '"Neither shalt a man put on a woman's garment, for all that do so are an abomination unto God." That is God's commandment, from His holy word! You hear what God says? That you are an abomination! You deceive, you lie, you dissimulate, you put on women's garments!' He was really angry now. 'Does Father Laurence hear confessions?'

'No!'

He spat into my face, and then, disgusted, turned away. 'Tell us, Master Willoughby.'

Willoughby shuddered. 'In the new play, sir,' he lisped, his mouth and lips too bruised and bloody to enunciate properly, 'there is a character called Friar Laurence, sir. He talks of confession, sir. Riddling confession.'

'A sympathetic character, would you say?'

'Oh yes, sir.'

'The new play,' I said, 'is set in Italy. There are no Protestants in . . .'

'Did I ask you to speak?' Price turned on me. 'Then be quiet.' He looked back to Willoughby. 'And this play was written by William Shakespeare?'

'Yes, sir.'

'Who makes the sign of the cross?'

'Before every performance, sir, yes, sir.'

'Then how came that play to be in your possession?'

Simon Willoughby could not meet my eyes, while his own good eye gleamed with tears. 'Sir Godfrey, sir, feared that the play would be heretical.'

'That, surely,' Price said, 'is the business of the Master of the Revels?'

'Not if the play is to be performed privately, sir,' Simon said, I suspected they had rehearsed this scene, and Simon, despite his discomfort, was performing well.

'I see!' Price pretended to be surprised. 'Then would you say, Master Willoughby, that the Lord Chamberlain's company is a nest of secret papists?'

'Oh yes, sir!' the little bastard said eagerly.

'The Lord Chamberlain is a Protestant!' I said.

'You . . .' Price began, but I interrupted him for a change.

'His mother was a Boleyn! You can't be more Protestant than—' I had to stop because Fish-Breath hit me.

'Who knows what foul secrets lie in the hearts of man?' Price asked sanctimoniously. 'You say Sir Godfrey feared heresy?'

'And he begged me to discover the play, sir,' Simon said, then added weakly, 'which I did gladly, sir.'

'You did God's work, boy,' Price said piously, 'as did Sir Godfrey.' Piggy Price was no player, and he lied badly. He knew as well as I that Sir Godfrey was a piece of disgusting slime, but for the moment the disgusting slime was an ally. And that, I thought, was interesting. Piggy George Price was not doing God's work, he was doing the Earl of Lechlade's work.

'How much is the earl paying you?' I managed to ask before Fish-Breath punched my cheek again.

'Paying?' Price turned on me savagely. 'Paying? You spawn of Satan! Do you know what the work of this office is? Our task is to eradicate heresy, to root out papists, to destroy the evil of Rome, and to bring to justice those traitors who would kill our Queen and place a whore of Babylon on England's throne! When I am told by an informant that heresy is breeding in a playhouse I do not ask for pay! Even if the struggle impoverished me, I would fight such foulness! It is my duty to God and to the Queen.' He spoke passionately, angrily, and I understood that he spoke truthfully. Someone, plainly the Earl of Lechlade, was using George Price's commitment to eradicate heresy as a tool to destroy our company. And how eagerly Price would accept that task! In his febrile, God-drunken mind he had an opportunity to scotch a nest of papists and, at the same time, close down one of the hated dens of iniquity, a playhouse. 'You think the Lord Chamberlain will defend you against papistry?' he demanded. 'Against treason? Against sedition? Against heresy?'

The inside of my cheek was bleeding. I swallowed the blood. 'Suppose your informant lied?' I asked.

Price held up a hand to check the punch that Fish-Breath was about to deliver. 'If he lied,' he said, 'then I shall uncover his untruths. Or rather, you will.'

'I will?'

'You are a thief. Do you deny it?'

'I do deny it,' I said indignantly. 'I merely took what was our property.'

'You equivocate!' Price spat. 'You are a thief! Tell us, Master Willoughby.'

'Tell you, sir?' Simon Willoughby asked, flicking a scared glance towards me.

'Is Master Shakespeare a thief?'

'Yes, sir,' Willoughby said quietly.

'Be not afraid, Master Willoughby,' Price encouraged him. 'You are under my protection now and no more harm can come to you. Tell us what you know.'

And Willoughby proceeded to tell the story of how he and I had helped the drunken lordling across Finsbury Fields to the Spanish Lady tavern just inside Moorgate, and how we had taken his purse and divided the money between us. We had each made eight shillings that day, but Simon Willoughby claimed we had made eighteen shillings apiece, and he sounded so full of remorse as he spoke, so regretful about his part in the theft. He performed his role well. 'I knew I'd done wrong, sir,' he said to Piggy Price, 'and my conscience began to trouble me.'

'Ha,' I scoffed, and was hit for my pains.

'Go on,' Piggy Price encouraged Simon.

'I had broken God's commandments, sir, and knew I was going to hell. The only priest I knew was Sir Godfrey, so I went to him and he prayed with me. He said I must seek God's forgiveness, sir, so I did.'

275

Dear Lord in His glory! It was mostly lies, of course, but the lies were grounded on a shred of truth, and they were told by a good player, and so the lies were convincing. Simon Willoughby went on to say I had tried to persuade him to steal again and he finished by giving me a vituperative look through his one good eye. 'He's a thief, sir, a thief!'

'As were you once, Master Willoughby!' Piggy Price said sternly.

'Yes, sir,' Willoughby answered miserably, 'I was, sir.'

'But you have come to a saving knowledge of our Lord Jesus Christ?'

'I have, sir, I have.'

'Then like the thief at Golgotha your sins are forgiven and you are washed whiter than snow.'

I would have laughed if I could have endured another of Fish-Breath's punches. Price turned back to me. 'Do you deny Master Willoughby's charges?'

'Of course I do,' I said. 'He's a liar, a pathetic little bed-wetting liar.'

'And you are a thief,' Price said, 'and you will now use your sinful skills on my behalf. Is it true,' he looked back to Simon Willoughby, 'that the company's scripts and documents are concealed in the Lord Chamberlain's house?'

'Yes, sir.'

'And you,' the piggy face turned back to me, 'will bring the offending scripts to us. You will bring me the Romish play and your brother's copy of the *Conference*.'

I had forgotten the seditious book that pleaded the case to make a Roman Catholic princess of Spain into England's next monarch, possession of which was enough to condemn a man to one of London's vile prisons. I looked down at Price. 'You're Pursuivants,' I said, 'so why don't you search the Lord Chamberlain's house yourself?'

He grimaced. He knew the answer as well as I did, that he dared not search Lord Hunsdon's property. His lordship was first cousin, perhaps even half-brother, to the Queen, and much too powerful a man for Piggy Price to attack directly, but a company of players was meat for his appetite. He ignored my question. 'You will bring us those papers and the book tomorrow.'

'Tomorrow!' I was surprised.

'It should be simple enough. You know where the play is concealed?'

'He knows, Mister Price,' Simon Willoughby said.

'And if I refuse?' I asked.

'You won't,' Price said, 'because if you leave the Lord Chamberlain's house without the documents that I require then I shall arrest you and you will be accused of robbery and assault, you will be tried, and, let me assure you, convicted. And the sentence,' he added with relish, 'will be death by hanging.'

Fish-Breath grinned and made a choking noise, pretending to be a hanged man.

George Price frowned at Fish-Breath, evidently unimpressed by the pretence. 'You and your brother,' he ordered the twins, 'will wait at Saint Benet's, and Mister Shakespeare will bring you the papers. Tomorrow!' The last word was spat at me.

'What if I can't bring the papers tomorrow?' I asked. Not that I cared, I was merely trying to find an exit from a stage that appeared to have none.

'Tomorrow!' Price snarled.

'We're not rehearsing tomorrow,' I lied.

'That might be true, sir,' Simon Willoughby muttered.

'Then the next day,' Price said, 'or the day after. But no more! Three days! And if you fail me you will surely hang.' He stepped away from me. 'Bring it,' he ordered Sweaty-Face, then looked at Fish-Breath. 'Strip his left sleeve,' he ordered.

Fish-Breath pulled off my cloak, then gasped, and no wonder, because the doublet of Spanish leather looked fit for a prince, if not a king. Then he grinned, knowing he was about to destroy the garment. 'Let's have your sleeve,' he growled, and drew a short knife to slice the sleeve open from the wrist to the shoulder.

I still had the dagger sheathed at my belt, a dagger that was hidden by the panelled beauty of the doublet's skirt, and both Fish-Breath and Mister Price were standing so close to me that they could not see what my right hand was doing.

Fish-Breath grabbed the wrist of my left sleeve, which was prettily finished with an unstarched frill of white French lace shaped into star points, each point tipped with a pearl, but before he could use his knife to slit the sleeve he whimpered and went very still. 'Take the knife away,' I said.

He whimpered again and pulled the knife back from my sleeve. 'What . . .' Mister Price began, and I nudged the dagger that I had slid into Fish-Breath's groin. Fish-Breath made a mewing noise. 'What is it?' Mister Price demanded, annoyed.

'I have a knife against his bollocks,' I explained.

'He has a knife against my bollocks,' Fish-Breath echoed in a voice so small that it could have passed for the heroine in any playhouse.

Mister Price surprised me then. He might have been a piggy little man with a piggy belly and piggy eyes and piggy jowls, but he moved with a deft swiftness. He seized the collar of Fish-Breath's coat and hauled him hard backwards, away from my blade, so the mewling fool half fell, stumbling against the wall. 'Ruthers! Carson!' Mister Price bellowed, and the door opened to let in the two Pursuivants who must have been waiting outside. They saw the dagger in my hand and drew swords.

'Drop it!' one of the men snarled at me.

I doubted they would use the swords, because Mister Price wanted a man able to answer his questions and steal a play script, not a sword-punctured cripple, and so I held onto the dagger. I said nothing because I did not know what to say. The two men had left the door open and I half thought of making a dash for it, but of course I could never have reached that far. They and their swords barred the way.

'I'll kill him,' Fish-Breath yelped.

A sword reached for me, the blade threatening my throat. Now what could I do? Cut Fish-Breath's throat and have my own gullet slashed open? I lowered the blade.

'You will not kill him,' Mister Price told Fish-Breath calmly, 'you will just strip his sleeve.'

My oldest brother was fond of telling me not to push my fortune past the peradventure, which I am sure is good advice, and, like all good advice, is doomed to be ignored, yet on that evening, faced by two swordsmen and by a knife in the hands of a bollock-pricked fish-eater, I decided the peradventure was far enough. It was time to cooperate, and I pushed Fish-Breath away before he could attack my arm. 'You wish,' I said, 'my sleeve to be removed?'

'I do,' Mister Price said.

'Then I shall strip it,' I said, and so sheathed the dagger and unlaced the sleeve. I like clothes, and had no wish, whatever nastiness the evening had yet to hold, to see a fine doublet of velvet, Spanish leather, French lace, and white silk mangled by a fool. The knots were old and it took time to pick them apart, but no one interfered, and, at last, the sleeve was separated from the shoulder and I tugged it over my wrist.

'The shirt,' Mister Price said, gesturing at my left arm.

'Woven by elves,' I said, 'from linen bleached by the fairies.'

'Bare your arm, you fool,' he growled, then looked at Sweaty-Face. 'Bring it, Thomas,' he said, 'bring it now.'

I am a player and I am a good one. I had been playing to audiences for seven years and had learned the players' tricks, and I confess there is a pleasure in silencing a crowd, in stopping their breath as they wait to watch a murder or witness a kiss. There is pleasure in their wild applause, in their cheers, in their gifts to the players, in their rapt silence. There is no pleasure when they are displeased, when the groundlings jeer and the rotten fruit flies to spatter on the stage, but that is rare. We players can play an audience as a man plays a lute. You have maybe seen us, have paid your pence to stand beneath us or to sit in the galleries above us, and if we did our work well then you thought what we did was easy.

It is not easy. It is monstrously hard. I remember Sir Godfrey, who is as wicked a man as ever sucked the devil's tits, instructing us boys. 'What you do,' he said, cutting the air with the thick birch rod that he loved to lay on our naked arses, 'is unnatural, and I do not speak of your disgusting practices, but of performing. Of being on a stage, it is unnatural, yet you will learn to make it look natural.' And we did.

'It is a deception,' Sir Godfrey would tell us, sometimes standing behind one of us and unbuttoning his breeches, 'as false as the tits on an ingle whore, but the audience wishes to be deceived, and you are their conjurors. And the first step to make the fools believe is for you to believe yourselves! You must believe because if you do not, then they will not believe. In the name of the Father and of the Son, boy, bend over.'

Deceiving is hard work. It might look easy, but you only need watch the mummers in some village fair to know the difference between the men you see on the stages of the London playhouses and the awkward fools who cannot stop fidgeting on their village's wagon beds. And to walk through the tiring room door into the gaze of two thousand people, to face a cliff of Londoners staring from the galleries, and a sea of faces in the yard, all of them watching, is frightening. I have seen men who have been playing all their lives vomit in the bucket by a stage door, others pale as death and twitching uncontrollably or making the sign of the forbidden cross, yet when the cue comes they thrust the door open and stride so confidently into the light. They smile, their cloaks swirl in graceful motion, and the groundlings greet them with gasps, even with applause, and why? Because they pretend.

And that is what I did that night in Mister Price's over-heated chamber. I pretended. In truth I was terrified because I knew nothing good was about to happen, but I am a player, and though my heart beat like a captive bird and though a muscle in my right leg shivered, I pretended to be brave. Then I saw what was in Sweaty-Face's hand, and the pretence was overpowered by the terror.

It was a brand. He carried a long iron rod, held in a thick cloth, and at its tip was a squirl of heated iron. That iron tip glowed red hot, shimmering the already overheated air. 'Bring it,' Mister Price said again, and Sweaty-Face edged around the table. 'Hold him,' Mister Price ordered, and Fish-Breath took hold of me. He held me firmly, turning me so that my left arm was bared towards Sweaty-Face.

'You will be tempted to run away rather than bring me what I require,' George Price told me, holding out a hand to stay the glowing iron, 'so I will brand you with the letter P. It could be P for Price,' he said, 'but it is not. It could be P for Protestant, but it is not. It could even be P for player, but it is not. It is P for papist.'

'I'm not a papist,' I said, no longer pretending. My fear had destroyed pretence, and my voice would not have carried past the wretched groundlings who lean on the stage's edge and crack hazelnuts by our feet. I was whimpering scared.

'P for papist,' Mister Price said again. 'The scum of Rome are our country's enemies and they lurk in the shadows, and I will mark them so they cannot hide.'

'I'm not a papist,' I repeated, scarce above a whisper.

'Maybe not,' Mister Price said, 'but I will mark you as one, and if you fail me, Master Shakespeare, then every constable and every magistrate in England will know your mark and seek you out. Every sheriff's post in every town will have your description. You will be a marked man, and you will be mine!' He nodded at Sweaty-Face. 'Do it.'

Sweaty-Face leered, then thrust the brand onto my forearm. And I screamed.

The pain was instant and terrible. I screamed and wrenched my arm to escape the pain, but Fish-Breath held me too firmly, and then Simon Willoughby intervened.

He screamed as he lunged across the room. 'Let me do it!' he shrieked. 'He hurt me, let me hurt him!' And he thrust Sweaty-Face aside, inadvertently forcing the brand away from the bubbling skin on my arm, and then he seized the iron rod ready to thrust it hard against my flesh again.

Only he forgot that the whole brand, both the P at the tip and the long iron rod that served as its handle, had been heated in the fire. He had no folded cloth as Sweaty-Face did, and the moment his right hand closed about the rod he screamed again. He screamed like a child, he dropped the brand, then thrust his scorched hand between his thighs and crouched, sobbing. 'I'm hurting, oh God help me! I'm hurting!'

The floor rushes started burning. They were bone dry, they should have been changed weeks ago, and the moment the red-hot brand fell they burst into flames that spread fast. Fish-Breath and his companion let go of my arms and started stamping out the fire, Simon Willoughby squealed, and Piggy Price bellowed at Sweaty-Face to pick up the iron. Which he did, but he had dropped the cloth when Simon Willoughby snatched the brand away, and so he also used his bare hand, he bellowed in sudden pain and dropped the glowing iron again to start a new fire. 'Ruthers!' Price shouted. 'Water!'

The Pursuivant ran from the room, leaving the door open. Price was helping to stamp out the flames, Willoughby was crouching in agony, weeping and whining, Sweaty-Face had managed to find his cloth, picked up the brand, and, unsure what to do with it, carried it back to the hearth, while smoke from the charred rushes curled up towards the magical ships on the painted ceiling.

'Are you trying to burn down Her Majesty's palace?' a voice asked from the doorway. A tall, saturnine man stood there, a look of amusement on his face.

'An accident, Sir Leonard,' Price said sharply, 'an accident.'

'Her Majesty will not be pleased by your accident, Mister Price. Palaces cost money!'

'It was an accident!' Price snapped. He was embarrassed.

The stranger, who was plainly but elegantly dressed, and wearing an enamelled chain of office about his neck, stepped into the room and waved his hand to disperse the lingering smoke. 'What clumsy fellows you Pursuivants are. Is this your way of purging sin?'

'The fire is out, Sir Leonard,' Price said.

'And I see you have a guest,' Sir Leonard said, frowning at the wound on my arm. 'Why was I not informed?'

'Our work,' Price said, summoning his dignity, 'is to protect the Queen's Majesty from sedition.'

'By burning down her palace? The Queen's Majesty, Mister Price, is protected by informing the yeomen if any strangers are to be lodged in the palace overnight. The curfew is past, is it not?'

Ruthers, the Pursuivant, edged past Sir Leonard with a pail of water, but the flames had already been stamped out, though the blackened rushes still smoked. My arm throbbed around the burn's agony. The skin was black and red, and blood was already crusting there. Price and his men were plainly discomfited by

Sir Leonard's arrival, so I took the chance of stepping to the chair where my cloak had been dropped. I flinched from pain as I draped it around my shoulders.

'Wait!' Price snarled.

'What is your business with this man?' Sir Leonard asked.

'Our business is finished,' Price said sullenly. The burning rushes and the scorn of Sir Leonard had spoiled his evening, 'Within three days!' he snarled at me. 'You will bring me the book and the papers within three days. Otherwise you hang!'

'I want to kill him first!' Simon Willoughby whined, still keeping his burned hand between his thighs. 'Before he hangs, I want to kill him!'

Price ignored him. 'Ruthers, Carson! See this wretch to the street.'

I snatched up de Valle's hat and walked to the door, which Sir Leonard, who was evidently an officer of the palace, courteously held open for me. It was also evident that he disliked George Price and just as plain that Piggy Price feared Sir Leonard, who offered me an aloof nod when I bowed to him. Ruthers seized my wounded arm, making me gasp with pain, then walked me down the passage. 'Three days,' he growled.

'I heard the man,' I said, then dared a question. 'Who are the twins?'

I thought neither man would answer, then Carson gave a harsh laugh. 'His nephews.'

'Little bastards,' Ruthers added under his breath.

They marched me back the way we had come, opened a small door in the great gate, and pushed me out into the street. 'Three days!' Carson called after me.

And after three days I would hang.

It was cold. Freezing. The night was still, baked with frost. The snow sparkled where lantern light touched it, and my breath made clouds. My cloak was thick, but even so within minutes I was shivering helplessly. Only the wound on my arm was hot, burning and throbbing. I stooped, picked up a handful of snow and clapped it on the burn, and that helped, but still the pain seared.

I stumbled away from the gate. I had a thought to walk home, but I would have died of the cold long before I reached Shoreditch. I needed shelter, but by this time of night the taverns in Whitehall were tight shut, not even a lamp glimmering. I passed Charing Cross, and the snow crunched beneath my boots as I followed the Strand eastwards. I was almost sobbing with pain and cold. At least, I thought, I might find a church porch where, on cold nights, beggars sheltered. Then I saw a flicker of firelight down an alley to my right. The alley, which was bordered by high stone walls, led to the river and to the Yorke Stairs, and the firelight came from a watchman's brazier.

At the alley's end I could see the river skimmed with ice, and, jutting out towards the river's centre, a long wooden jetty. A score of ice-locked wherries were moored to the jetty, while on the bank, at the top of the stairs, was a small wooden hut with one side open to the Thames. Two men sat there, warmed by the sea-coal burning in their iron basket. Such men were employed by the watermen of the Thames to protect their boats during the night, and, when I came from the alley, I heard the grinding click of a pistol being cocked. 'You want to lose your face, son?' a voice asked.

'For the love of God,' I said, 'pity!'

'Pox off, son.' I saw the pistol raised towards me.

'I'm a friend of Joe Lester,' I said on a sudden inspiration.

'Joe?'

'Who lives over there,' I said, pointing to the river's southern bank.

'Who's his bow oar?' the second man asked suspiciously.

'Tom,' I said, 'and he has a son called Ned and a daughter named Silvia. For the love of God, I'm freezing.'

The pistol was lowered. 'There's a stool,' the first man said grudgingly. 'How do you know Joe?'

I dragged the stool near the brazier and felt the blessed warmth. 'I'm Lord Hunsdon's man,' I explained. I made it sound as if I was a member of the Lord Chamberlain's household rather than one of his players. 'So I know Silvia and Ned.'

'Silvia's a pretty one,' the first man said, laying the pistol on the bench next to him. He watched as I shivered. 'So what are you doing out on this godforsaken night?'

I did not want to mention Pursuivants because such a mention might raise suspicion and I needed these men to welcome me. 'I was with someone,' I said through chattering teeth, then gestured towards Westminster. 'Then her husband came home.'

They laughed. 'That'll teach you a lesson, son. Don't plough other men's wives on freezing nights, eh?'

'And now her husband's driving the warm furrow,' the second man said, 'not you!'

'Dear God,' I said in relief as the warmth at last began to seep into my bones. I found a shilling in my pouch and put it on the bench next to the pistol. 'As thanks for your kindness,' I explained. It was an extravagant gesture, and one I could hardly afford, but I would have paid twenty times as much to escape that bitter cold.

'You're welcome, son, welcome.'

And so I was.

'Butter,' Silvia said.

'Ouch!'

'Don't be such a baby, hold your arm out.' She peered down at the crusted wound on my forearm. 'Why would he put an F on your arm?'

286

'It's a P.'

'No it's not, it's an F. F for Francis Flute. Look!'

I looked and she was right. Sweaty-Face had not pressed hard enough, or else Simon Willoughby had snatched the brand away before Sweaty-Face could finish the job, and the curve of the P was missing. 'F for fool,' I said.

'You're no fool, no more than any other young man. Hold still. Butter.' She slapped a handful of butter onto my arm. 'That'll mend it. Butter for burns.'

'My mother always reckons on dock leaves.'

'She's from Stratford. What do they know in Stratford? Keep it still.' She had a strip of linen that she used to bandage my arm. 'So tell me what happened?'

I had left my Thames-side refuge when the bells announced the end of curfew. It was still cold, but a rising sun had offered an illusion of warmth as I walked along the Strand. I entered the city through Ludgate, then turned downhill to the Lord Chamberlain's mansion. The guards knew me now and just nodded a companionable greeting. To my relief the fire in the great hall still burned and I fed it with logs, crouched by its warmth, and waited for the shivering to cease. No one else from the company had arrived, they were not due for at least another hour, and so I had waited, and while I was waiting Silvia had found me. 'Pebble said he saw you arrive,' she explained.

'Pebble?'

'The skinny guard. The one with warts on his nose. Gawd in His heaven, what have you done to your arm?'

Now, ten minutes later, she tied off the bandage. 'So tell me what happened?'

'Tell me about Tom.'

She looked me in the eyes. 'Lord above, are you worried about him?'

287

'You're going to marry him?'

'When the sky turns green, yes. My mum wants me to.'

'And your father too,' I said bitterly.

'My dad wants what my mum tells him to want.'

'What about Tom?' I asked. 'Does he?'

'Does he what?'

'Does he want to marry you?'

'I should bleeding hope so, I'm not ugly! But he never says anything. I think a cat got his tongue when he was born.'

'He'd be a good husband for you,' I said unhappily.

'And why is that, Richard Shakespeare?'

'Because he's reliable. He's a waterman, there'll always be a job for a waterman. He earns regular money.'

'He does,' she said, 'at least when the river's not frozen.'

'So he'd be a good husband,' I said.

'You're right!'

'I know I am,' I said, utterly miserable.

'You're not right about Tom,' she said. 'You're right about F standing for fool. I ain't going to marry Tom.'

'You're not?'

'Of course not! His nose is too big.'

'Will you marry me, then?' I blurted out. I had not intended saying anything so foolish, but I did.

'Probably,' she said, 'I've been thinking about it. Now tell me what bleeding happened!' So I told her, all of it, and she crouched beside me in front of the great hall fire and listened. She frowned at some of the tale, and when she frowned her eyebrows drew closer together. 'Like caterpillars,' I said.

'Like what?'

'Your eyebrows,' I said, touching one, 'they're like caterpillars.'

She rocked back on her heels and gave me a severe caterpillar-frown. 'Maybe I should marry Tom after all.'

'His nose is too big.'

288

'Everyone says mine is too!'

'It's not small,' I said.

'Lord above! Big nose and caterpillars!' She frowned again. 'So the Percies are waiting for you, yes?'

'Yes.'

'Then stay here. They'll not dare come into his lordship's house. He'll have their heads in a bucket. He can be a fierce old bugger when he's crossed.'

I looked into her eyes. She was crouching with me on the hearth, her face lit and shadowed by the flames. She looked so earnest. 'You mean stay here in the mansion?' I asked.

'Of course I mean that!' she said. 'You're not going to give the piggy man what he wants, are you?'

'No,' I said.

'And if you don't give him the play, then the Percies will want to arrest you. But they won't dare come in here. You'll have to sleep here.'

'But what if I'm found?'

'Lord above it's chaos here! More people coming and going than on London Bridge!'

'But where . . .' I began

'Come here,' she said. She stood, took my hand, and tugged me towards the stage. 'Mister Harrison,' she said, meaning the household's steward, 'always looks around the house before he toddles off to bed, but he doesn't look down there.' She had climbed the temporary stairs that led to the stage and was trying to open the trapdoor that was used for some of Puck's entrances. 'Gawd,' she said, 'that's heavy. How's a bleeding fairy supposed to open that?'

'They use magic,' I said, and pulled the trapdoor open.

She peered down into the darkness. 'I hope there are no spiders down there, I hate spiders.'

'You want me to live down there?'

'You can't stay with me,' she said, 'I share an attic with four other girls.' She frowned, pulling her caterpillar eyebrows close together. 'There's all that cloth down there. What we didn't use. It will make a nice bed. And it's warm in here,' she meant the great hall, 'warmer than my attic.'

'You sleep in an attic?'

'Except when the Lady Elizabeth wants me in the ante-chamber, which ain't often.' She frowned at me. 'Once she's married she'll move, won't she?'

'Will she?'

'Of course she will! She'll have to live with her husband, won't she? Probably in Gloucestershire. They have a London house too, on the Strand. But wherever it is, she'll want me to go with her.'

'You can't,' I said.

'Can't? And why's that, Richard Shakespeare?'

'Because we're getting married.'

'Oh, I'd forgotten that!' She grinned, then sat at the hatch's edge and dropped down to the floor beneath. 'You can't have candles,' she called up from the gloom, 'you'll be found, but it ain't bad!'

I followed her through the hatch. The back of the stage was wide open, leading into the makeshift tiring room, but there were plenty of places to hide beneath the stage because the space was being used to store unused timber, empty barrels, crates, and bolts of cloth. 'Here,' Silvia called from the dark-ness, 'you can sleep here. No one will find you. Just don't snore.'

I found her at the front of the stage, between the frame that held the green cloth frontal, and a heap of timber. She could almost stand upright, but I had to stoop low. 'No one will see you,' she whispered, as if she feared someone was already searching for me. 'It's like a little cave, you'll be cosy.'

'And lonely,' I said, thinking I would have to hide in this dark space from nightfall to dawn.

'Don't be such a crybaby,' she said. 'Better to be lonely than dangling at a rope's end.'

'And where do I go when the wedding's over?' I asked.

'Well, we worry about that later,' she said.

'We?'

'We,' she said firmly and I remembered my mother's words that girls set their caps at a likely man. I had been capped.

'The Percies will still be looking for me,' I reminded her. 'They want to hang me.'

'Lord Hunsdon will stop that!' she said firmly.

I shook my head. 'My brother doesn't want him involved.'

'Don't be daft! He's your patron. Only now's not a good time to talk to his lordship on account that he's grumpy because of all the money he's spending. But he likes me. I'll tell him when I ask permission to get married.'

'You need his permission?'

'Of course I do! But he'll say yes. And he gave the last girl fifty shillings when she got married!'

'I love you,' I said.

'Of course you do,' she sat on the floor, 'probably fifty times more than you did a minute ago. I have this idea, you see?'

'Idea?'

'Jean and I have been talking. She's a wonderful seamstress. So neat! I swear that woman could sew up the devil's arsehole and he'd never know he'd been touched. And rich folk pay well for nice things. Hoods, collars, masks, shifts, belts, sleeves, headbands, stomachers, veils, billaments, purses, partlets, garters. We can make them all!'

'You and Jean?'

'I don't expect you to sew,' she said. 'Can you sew?'

'No.'

'Of course you can't. So yes, me and Jean, and fifty shillings would buy us a lot of lovely fabrics.'

'So Jean will leave the Theatre?'

'She likes working at the playhouse, and I'll help her. We can do both jobs. Jean would be making all those things now if she knew where to sell them, but I know lots of the gentry's maids. Her ladyship will buy from me, she likes me, and so will others.'

'I like you too,' I said.

'But you'll have to stop thieving,' she said suddenly. I began to speak, then had no idea what to say, and she reached out and touched my cheek. 'It's all right,' she said, 'I know about you. And I know you've done some stupid things, but we all do stupid things when we're young. You just have to stop. I don't want you swinging off a gibbet.'

'You've done stupid things?' I asked.

'Not yet, but I will.'

'What stupid things will you do?'

'Marry you, of course.' She leaned forward and kissed me, and just then we heard the main door of the hall open, and footsteps sounded loud on the flagstones. 'Someone's already fed the fire,' a manservant's voice said.

'It must be the fairies from the play.' It was Walter Harrison, the steward, who answered. 'The mansion is apparently infested. Go and draw water instead.'

'The house is waking up,' Silvia whispered, 'I must go.' She scrambled away towards the back of the stage.

Reason and love keep little company together nowadays. And thank God for that.

PART FOUR

A
SWEET COMEDY

And, most dear actors, eat no onions nor garlic, for we are to utter sweet breath; and I do not doubt but to hear them say, it is a sweet comedy. No more words. Away! Go, away!

A Midsummer Night's Dream
Act IV, Scene 2, lines 39ff

ELEVEN

LADY ANNE HUNSDON, the bride's grandmother, sat in state at the very centre of the great hall. Two maidservants, neither of them Silvia, sat on stools at her feet, while beside her, on a small table, was an hourglass. We had just finished our first rehearsal in which we had performed the whole play in costume, or at least in as many costumes as we could because many of the elaborate garments were still being sewn, and now the players, all of us, stood awkwardly on the stage, waiting for her ladyship's verdict. It was the afternoon after my encounter with the Pursuivants, the wedding was just six days away, and Lady Anne had demanded that we perform *A Midsummer Night's Dream* for her. 'After that interlude you did at Christmas,' she had announced to the Sharers, 'I want to make certain we do not send our guests to sleep.'

Lady Anne was dressed in fashionable black, her grey hair coiled beneath a French hood. She gazed at us, her jewelled fingers drumming on the table. We had watched her, of course, as we played, and her stern face, scarce breaking into a smile, let alone laughter, had made us all apprehensive. Now she delivered her judgement. 'Almost two and one half hours, Mister Shakespeare, two and one half!'

'Was it that long, my lady?' my brother responded.

'Two and one half!' she repeated, lifting the hourglass as proof.

'Indeed, my lady.'

'His lordship cannot abide two and one half hours,' she said sternly.

'I'm sorry to hear that, my lady.'

'But if we played it to amuse my husband, Mister Shakespeare, we'd scarcely be sat down before the play ended.'

'His lordship was kind enough to say,' my brother began.

'My husband's opinion of plays is of no account,' Lady Anne interrupted brusquely, 'none whatsoever. He likes entertainments in which people die. Gorily and frequently. Write more of those, Mister Shakespeare, and he will be your patron for ever.'

My brother bowed in response.

'My opinion, on the other hand,' her ladyship went on, 'does matter! And I do like this play. I like it very much, and I dare say that if Her Majesty deigns to appear among us, she will like it too.'

'Your ladyship is most kind,' my brother began as he bowed.

'I most certainly am not! As I said, I like the play, but I do not like it at two and a half hours ...' She paused, evidently expecting a response, but my brother said nothing, and the rest of us just shuffled our feet. 'I have a question,' Lady Anne said.

'Of course, your ladyship.'

'The play postulates,' she clearly liked the last word because she stressed it heavily, 'that if the poor girl Hermia does not marry the man of her father's choice then she will face execution. Is that truly the law in Athens?'

'Indeed it is, your ladyship,' my brother said confidently.

'Extraordinary!' she said. 'Quite extraordinary, but of course the Greeks are foreigners, so one can't expect good sense.' She stood, straight-backed and imperious, and her two attendants scrambled to their feet. 'Mark me, Mister Shakespeare. The play is too long at two and a half hours. Consider that we shall already have endured a sermon from the bishop, and God knows that man can preach for ever. You,' she pointed at Thomas Pope, 'remind me what your character is named?'

'Egeus, my lady.'

'He complains for far too long, far too long. The man's a fool, anyway, so the less of him the better. You,' she pointed at George Bryan, 'you play the duke?'

'I do, my lady.'

'Dukes should speak less. In my experience they rarely have anything useful to say, and you are no exception. And you, my child,' she pointed at Bobby Gough who was swathed in Titania's gauze and silk, 'you have one speech of utter tedium. Fairy queens are not bishops, and so should not be tedious.'

Bobby, not knowing whether he should bow or curtsey, did neither. 'I'm sorry, my lady,' he mumbled.

'And learn your lines, young woman!' she snapped, before pointing at Puck. 'What is your name?'

'Rust, my lady, Alan Rust.'

'You are a delight, Mister Rust, a delight, as are you, Mister Kemp.'

'Your ladyship is most kind,' Kemp said, bowing low.

'Kindness is for dogs, Mister Kemp, not for paid players. And no more poems, Mister Kemp, no more poems. And let the play be no longer than two hours, Mister Shakespeare, two hours! Come Caesar, come!' She swept from the hall, followed by her ladies, and by Caesar, a small white dog that had been hidden beneath her long skirts.

There was silence on the stage after she left, a silence George Bryan broke. 'Paid players, indeed!'

'What else are we?' my brother asked.

'A delight,' Will Kemp said angrily, 'we are a delight!'

Will Kemp had played Bottom well, but those of us who knew him could sense the anger that had simmered beneath his performance all afternoon. He was brooding over something, and Alan Rust, fearing an outbreak of Kemp's rage, tried to divert the conversation. 'Is death really the law in Athens for disobedient daughters?' he asked.

'Of course it isn't,' my brother said, 'but if I'd admitted that she'd have demanded accuracy. As if accuracy matters. It's a play!'

'At least she still wants us to perform the play,' John Heminges said gloomily.

'She wants me to perform!' Will Kemp said, letting his anger loose. He jumped off the stage and strode to the nearest table, where he poured himself a cup of the Lord Chamberlain's ale. 'You heard her ladyship. What works in this play, you tell me that?'

'It all works,' Richard Burbage said.

'Then why does she want it shortened?' Kemp demanded. 'What works is the comedy. Nick Bottom works!'

'No one denies that you're good, Will,' my brother said, trying to placate Kemp.

'Good!' Will Kemp spat. 'And you give me how many lines in *Romeo and Juliet*?'

Alan Rust groaned as he realised what had caused this outburst. Kemp had been brooding on the new play for days, and his unhappiness could be contained no longer.

'I gave you sufficient lines,' my brother said curtly.

'God damn your sufficiency!' Kemp snarled. 'God damn it to hell and back.' He drained the cup, slammed it onto the table, and filled it again. 'They come to laugh!' He pointed at my brother with the hand holding the jug, spilling ale. 'They don't come to be miserable. They have enough goddamned misery in their poxy lives already. They don't come to see lovers die, they come to laugh!'

'They come to see you?' Alan Rust asked acidly.

'They come to see me,' Kemp replied bitterly, then glared at my brother. 'You've given Peter thirteen lines. I counted them. Thirteen! That's what you think of me, a thirteen-line serving man. The poxy Theatre will be empty after thirteen minutes.'

'Will—' my brother began.

'Empty after two minutes,' Kemp roared, 'and a pox on you too! All of you!' He slammed the jug down, snatched up his cloak, and stalked out of the main doors to avoid crossing the stage.

'Oh, dear sweet God,' my brother said.

'Is all our company here?' Alan Rust quoted Peter Quince's opening line, but failed to raise a smile.

Billy Rowley, Kemp's apprentice, looked close to tears, uncertain what he should do. 'Go after him, boy,' my brother said. He stared at the door through which Kemp had left. 'It's my fault,' he went on, 'I should never have shown him the script.'

'He had to see it sooner or later,' Alan Rust said.

'Is there a bigger part for him?' George Bryan asked nervously.

'No, there is not!'

'He'll be back in the morning,' John Heminges said anxiously.

'If he's not trotting off to Philip Henslowe and the Rose,' my brother said.

'I'll talk to him,' Alan Rust said. No one spoke to that, no one else wanted to face an angry Will Kemp. 'He'll be back,' Rust said, 'I'm sure.'

My brother gazed up at the hall's beams. 'Nothing else we can do today, and our last rehearsal is tomorrow.'

'Tomorrow!' I blurted out, astonished.

'His lordship needs the hall,' my brother explained. 'The wedding is next Thursday. If tomorrow goes ill, we'll rehearse at the Theatre.' He looked at Bobby. 'Learn your lines, for Christ's sake, learn them!'

'Yes, sir,' Bobby said miserably.

'So go home,' my brother said, 'all of you, go home.'

'Are you shortening the play?' John Heminges asked.

'What her ladyship wants, her ladyship receives,' my brother said, then sat at the table, drew some candles towards him, and opened the box that held his quills.

The players and musicians went home. And just a street away, the twins were waiting for me at Saint Benet's. It was time to hide.

A Midsummer Night's Dream was a wedding play, all its events springing from the marriage between Duke Theseus and his bride, Hippolyta. Their wedding was the cause of Peter Quince gathering his band of Athenian workmen, who hoped to amuse the duke with their play, *Pyramus and Thisbe.* They rehearse the play in a wood near Athens, and most of the play is set in that wood, which we constructed with five hornbeam saplings cut from the northern edge of Finsbury Fields. The saplings, of course, were bare because it was winter, but my brother had insisted that they must have leaves, and so Jean and Silvia had spent hours cutting leaves from green cloth and tying them onto the naked branches. 'You could have used holly bushes!' Jean had complained.

'I want it to look like hawthorn,' my brother had said.

'Don't tell me you want white blossom too?'

'That's a good idea. Yes, blossom!'

'In midsummer?' Jean had protested. 'Hawthorn blossoms in May!'

'It's a magic wood,' my brother had airily explained, so Jean and Silvia had twisted white scraps of wool into tiny blossoms.

The hawthorn wood was where Oberon, King of the Fairies, and Titania, his queen, had their quarrel. Titania was sheltering a small Indian child, who was played by Walter Harrison's grandson, Matthew, whose face would be darkened by burned cork. Matthew, who was six years old, was only onstage once and had no lines to speak, but his grandfather, Lord Hunsdon's steward, had beamed proudly when he saw the lad in costume for the first time. 'He does look good, does he not?' he asked Alan Rust, who had been trying to marshal the small boys into some kind of order.

'When he stops picking his nose, yes.'

Nose-picking Matthew was the cause of the quarrel between Oberon and Titania. Oberon wished the child to be in his entourage, and Titania refused his demand, and so, to punish her, Oberon despatches Puck, his servant, to find a magical flower, which, when squeezed, oozes a juice that Oberon will drop onto the sleeping Titania's eyelids. When she wakes the very first living thing she sees will become the person or beast with whom she falls helplessly in love.

And she sees Will Kemp, wearing an ass's head.

The ass's head was a wicker frame over which we had stretched rabbit pelts. The eyes were oversize glass beads on which were painted a pupil and iris, while the ass's ears were more rabbit skin stiffened with wicker strips so they stood high. The ass's mouth was left open, so the wedding guests could hear Will speak, but we added chunky wooden teeth, painted white, so that the beast looked as if it was braying with laughter. At first Will had found it hard to keep the head on his shoulders because the front part, with the teeth, was too heavy, so Jean had sewn a strap to the back of the wicker frame that stretched down to a belt he could wear beneath his shirt. Kemp loved the head and was reluctant to take it off, delighting in prowling the mansion's passageways to scare unwitting servants.

It was indeed a big play, with over twenty characters. Theseus, Oberon, Titania, Puck, Peter Quince, Nick Bottom, Demetrius,

Lysander, Helena, and Hermia all had substantial parts. Will Kemp, playing Bottom, had the most lines in the play, which he thought was his due, and, before he had stalked out in dudgeon, he had revelled in the ludicrous love scenes he had to play with Titania and with me. The other lovers in the play were even more star-crossed, or rather juice-crossed by Puck. Hermia loves Lysander, but her father insists she marry Demetrius or else face dire punishment, and so she and Lysander elope to the wood of five saplings. They are pursued into the wood by Demetrius, also in love with Hermia, and by Helena, Hermia's friend, who is in love with Demetrius. Oberon, taking pity on the forlorn Helena, instructs Puck to anoint Demetrius's eyes with the magic flower so he will fall in love with Helena, but Puck mistakes Lysander for Demetrius, and so the lovers' knot is tangled and tightened. There were fights, there were quarrels, there were chases, and there was laughter, and in the end Oberon and Titania are reconciled, Theseus marries Hippolyta, Hermia marries Lysander, Helena marries Demetrius, and Pyramus and Thisbe both die.

It was indeed a wedding play.

The preparations for Christmas in the mansion had been hectic, but they were nothing compared to the fuss preceding the wedding. Lord Hunsdon was still not certain whether his cousin, the Queen, would come to the marriage, but he had to assume she might, and so a second stage was built, this one close to the great hearth so that Her Majesty could dine a few feet higher than her subjects, and stay warm. The small tables that had sufficed for the Christmas guests were declared inadequate, and three new tables were made, a small one to stand on the new dais, the other two to match the existing long table, which could seat thirty-six people. Chairs were made, and so the great hall echoed to the sound of carpenters. Swags of white cloth were hung over the hall's panelling, but Lady Anne Hunsdon, inspecting it, declared it to be shabby, and satin was ordered instead. Garlands of ivy were twisted about the new swags and around the ceiling's high beams. Candles arrived by the bushel, and all needed sticks or stands. Lady Anne had declared the stone-flagged floor of the hall to be too cold for aristocratic feet, so rugs were ordered. 'Rushes were good enough in my day,' Lord Hunsdon grumbled.

'Rushes harbour fleas,' his wife declared brusquely.

'And fleas don't live in rugs?'

'Not in my rugs! And Harrison!'

'My lady?' The steward bowed.

'Rats were seen in the scullery passage.'

'So I heard, my lady.'

'It's the river,' Lord Hunsdon grumbled. 'You always get rats by a river.'

'Not in my house!' her ladyship said. 'Get rid of them!'

'I shall, my lady,' Harrison said.

'And what are these?' Lord Hunsdon had found a box and took from it a thin silver stick that ended with two tines. 'And why do we have so many?'

'They are forks,' Lady Hunsdon said.

'Forks?'

'You eat with them. Don't pretend you haven't seen one before! Katherine Howard uses them.'

'What's wrong with a good knife and fingers?'

'We are not peasants.'

'Fork,' Lord Hunsdon had said, flinching as he tested a tine on one finger. 'Fork! Harrison, fork!'

'Indeed, your lordship,' the imperturbable steward said.

Lord Hunsdon turned towards the stage where we were trying to rehearse. Any attempt to keep the play secret from the household had long been abandoned, though such was the chaos that I doubt anyone could make sense from the scraps of dialogue they heard. 'Is that supposed to be a wood?' Lord

305

Hunsdon snarled.

'It is, my lord,' my brother had answered, 'it's a wood near Athens'

'They must have forking poxy woods in Athens! It looks more like a feeble spinney. You couldn't hide a sparrow in those leaves. Green gauze, man, green gauze. Thicken it up!'

The Lord Chamberlain's suggestion worked. We draped expensive green gauze over and between the trees, and the illusion of a thicker wood was instant. It looked even better when candle-stands were put behind the gauze and the light filtered through.

The candles were a problem, though hardly the most severe that we faced. We had often played by candlelight in palaces and mansions, and knew that as the play progressed the candles would begin to gutter and it would be necessary to pause the performance while the wicks were trimmed. 'Three pauses are sufficient,' my brother had said.

'Four,' Will Kemp had said immediately. If my brother had suggested four then Kemp would have wanted three.

'We need music for the candle trimming,' my brother had shouted at Phil, ignoring Kemp, 'three pieces!'

Phil nodded. He was gloomy because the household musicians, who would play during the wedding feast, were insisting on rehearsing in the minstrels' gallery, which meant our musicians were forced to wait while the larger group played. 'They're not even musicians,' Phil had grumbled to me, 'they're more like catgut torturers. God! Listen to that note!'

'It sounds good to me.'

'Thank God you don't sing in this play. I suffer enough.'

The chaos in the hall was so great, that a week before Simon had stolen the two plays we had tried to move the rehearsals to a capacious undercroft beneath the old chapel, but the room was damp, and the weather so cold that ice formed on the ancient stone walls. We did manage to stumble through the first half of the play once, teeth chattering and feet stamping, but the undercroft was plainly inadequate and became even more so when, as the wedding day approached, servants brought hams to hang from the ceiling. The smell of cooking began to pervade the mansion.

Bobby Gough still did not know Titania's lines.

The fairies' costumes were unfinished.

Will Kemp had walked out of the play.

The wedding was close.

And the twins waited for me at Saint Benet's.

'Shouldn't you be going home?' my brother asked me.

The other players had left. A lone carpenter was working at the hall's far end, while my brother sat at the central table and turned pages. 'What are you doing?' I asked.

'Shortening the play as her ladyship insists. And shouldn't you be going home?' he asked again. The coldness in his voice told me that whatever warmth had been generated by my rescue of his plays had vanished.

'I'm going,' I said. I picked up my cloak, found de Valle's hat, and crossed the stage. I opened and shut the door to the scullery passage, making enough noise to convince my brother that I had left, then crept under the stage. I crawled to the front, to the corner where Silvia had made a nest out of the green cloth, and there I settled down. The lone carpenter finished his work and left. My brother worked on. The front of the stage was draped with cloth, and I could just see over the top where the material sagged. The fire lit the hall, flickering its lurid shadows as, one by one, the candles went out, all but for the six surrounding my brother's pages.

I heard the hall door open, and then footsteps. My brother looked up and stood.

'Sit down, man, sit down.' It was Lord Hunsdon, who took a

307

chair opposite my brother. 'There's no peace in the household,' he grumbled.

'Another week, my lord, and it will all be over.'

Lord Hunsdon grunted, then, 'Do you have daughters, Mister Shakespeare?'

'I do, my lord. Two.'

'Two!'

'Susanna is twelve and Judith ten, my lord.'

'Two!' his lordship said again. 'I have eight! I married them all off, and now it's the granddaughters getting married.' He turned in his chair and shouted towards the door. 'Harrison! Someone! Anyone!'

A serving man answered. 'My lord?'

'Sack, man, and two cups. Quickly now!' He looked back to my brother. 'Two daughters, eh? Pretty girls?'

'I think so, my lord.'

'I like daughters! They keep a house lively.' His lordship leaned back in the chair and stretched. 'The Queen tells me she'll be here for the wedding.'

'We're honoured, my lord.'

'God's breath! Honoured?' His lordship laughed. 'She can't abide the groom's mother. I hoped that would keep her away. Maybe the weather will?'

'You hoped, my lord?'

'Dear God, man, entertaining Her Majesty is not easy! And she'll bring Christ knows how many courtiers, who all need wine, food, and flattery. But if the river's frozen . . .'

'Then she might come by coach, my lord,' my brother suggested mischievously.

'She's in Greenwich. It's the river or nothing,' Lord Hunsdon said, then paused as the serving man brought a tray with a jug of sack and two goblets. His lordship waved away the servant's help and poured the sack himself. 'The water under the bridge wasn't frozen the last time I looked. Like as not she'll be here.' He pushed a cup towards my brother. 'She may not stay for the feast. Who knows?'

'If she doesn't stay, my lord, she'll miss the play.'

'My wife says you should play in the afternoon. Before the feast.'

'Really, my lord?'

'She says too much wine makes folk sleepy. And she likes your play.'

'Her ladyship hides her opinion well,' my brother said drily.

Lord Hunsdon laughed. 'She's cracked the whip, eh?'

'Indeed, my lord.'

'Now you know how it feels.'

'Only too well, my lord. I also have a wife.'

'Here, in London?'

My brother shook his head. 'She stays in Stratford,' he said, then paused. 'It's better that way.'

'Yet I doubt you lack for company.'

'No more than does your lordship.'

Lord Hunsdon laughed. 'You knew Emilia?'

'I do know her, my lord.'

'A good woman, a good woman!' Lord Hunsdon sounded wistful.

'And married now.'

'Indeed she is,' his lordship said gloomily, then drank deep from his cup and poured more sack. I listened enthralled. It was plain that his lordship liked my brother, and equally plain that my brother was comfortable with his lordship, and I wondered if I would ever have the confidence to chat casually with a great lord. And Lord Hunsdon, the Queen's closest relative, was indeed great. He leaned back in his chair and looked up at the shadowed beams where the swags of expensive satin hung. 'Eight daughters! Eight weddings! Christ help us.'

'Maybe He could turn the water into wine?'

Lord Hunsdon laughed. 'Gossip says your clown walked out.'

'He did, my lord.' My brother sounded grim.

'A pity! Anne says he's funny. Very funny!'

'Her ladyship is right, he is funny, he also thinks he's indispensable.'

'No one is indispensable,' Lord Hunsdon said, 'except possibly Harrison. Will your fellow be back?'

I saw my brother shrug. 'Eventually, I suppose. He's walked out before. I suspect he'll soak his pride in ale tomorrow, then crawl back.'

'But you need him tomorrow?'

'We do, my lord.'

'Want me to send Ryker to him?'

My brother paused, surprised and pleased. Ryker was Lord Hunsdon's chief yeoman, the commander of his household guards. 'Would you, my lord?'

Lord Hunsdon grinned. 'It would be a pleasure, Mister Shakespeare. Let's remind your fellow that he's one of my retainers, eh? And Ryker can be frightening as hell. He scares me. Where does your fellow live?'

'At the sign of the Phoenix in Lombard Street.'

'A good tavern! Ryker will be there in the morning, and I dare say your fellow will be here soon after.' His lordship pushed the jug across the table. 'I must to supper. I look forward to your play, Mister Shakespeare.'

My brother stood as Lord Hunsdon got to his feet. 'Your lordship is most kind,' he said formally.

'I'm old, that's why. Kindness comes easier when you're old.'

My brother did not stay long after his lordship left. I saw him make notes on the pages, then he put the script into the big chest, locked it, and put the key on the high mantel. He pulled on his cloak and hat, and I heard his footsteps clump across the stage above me. The door opened and closed, and all that was left was the slight crackle of the fire. Occasionally, from somewhere deep in the mansion, I could hear music, and once or twice there were footsteps in the scullery passage. A chill began to seep into the room as the fire burned down. Time crept, marked by the church bells striking the hours through the slow dark. In a moment of silence I pushed aside the fabric covering the stage's front, tiptoed across the floor to the table. I took the jug of sack and carried it back to my lair, where I swathed myself in the spare green cloth. There had been a time when I would have kept the silver jug and sold it, but that time had passed. Silvia, I thought, Silvia.

I fell asleep, only to be woken by footsteps. A dim light showed in the great hall, and I peered through the gap in the fabric to see Walter Harrison attended by a serving man who held a lantern aloft as the steward looked around. 'All is well,' Harrison announced, and the two left. I stayed still, scarce daring to breathe until their footsteps had faded. I pulled more of the cloth about me, cocooning myself, still shivering. It was no colder than my attic room at the Widow Morrison's house, but it felt strange to be so alone in such a great house, startled by every creak, every small noise, every scrabble of a rat in the undercroft beneath the hall. There was still a glow from the fire, but the small warmth did not reach the stage. The church bells were silent, their ringers gone home, and London slept.

I fell asleep a second time, to be woken as a heavy blanket was thrown over me. I cried out, startled, and a voice hushed me. 'Richard! Richard!' It was Silvia, whispering. 'Gawd, it's cold,' she said, and I felt her slide under the blanket to join me. For a trembling moment we just lay there, maybe both

311

surprised by what was happening, but then I reached for her and she made a small noise and came into my arms. 'I couldn't leave you here,' she whispered. The blanket was a thick fur, lined with satin, and taken, she said, from her mistress's closet. 'She has four, she doesn't need this one. And it's warm, we need it.'

It was warm, and we needed it. And later, I do not know how much later, we slept.

There comes a moment in a lot of plays when everything seems on the edge of disaster, and, quite suddenly, a character appears onstage to set it all right. My character Emilia does that in the *Comedy of Errors*. Her long lost husband has been condemned to death, but Emilia enters just in time to save his life. 'Most mighty duke,' she exclaims, 'behold a man much wronged!'

I remember when I first played Emilia thinking that the groundlings would never believe her sudden intervention. She is an abbess, thinks herself a widow, and believes her husband and one of her two sons are drowned. She has mourned them for years, and then, quite unexpectedly, both husband and son are there in Ephesus. Egeon, the husband, is about to be executed, but the Abbess Emilia rushes onto the stage and utters her cry of recognition, 'Behold a man much wronged!' The family is suddenly reunited, the execution averted, a feast is served, and the audience is in tears, but they are tears of happiness, not of grief. I remember Richard Burbage, who played the lost son, scorning the scene when we had first rehearsed it. 'Life isn't like that!' he told my brother. 'It's too pat, too convenient!'

'This is the stage,' my brother had said, 'we traffic in dreams.' And he was right. No audience had ever mocked the sudden intervention of the abbess, instead they gasped with relief, they smiled, they shed tears, they were happy!

I needed an Emilia. I needed a character to exclaim, 'Behold a man much wronged!' I was safe for this one night, but we had only one more rehearsal in the great hall, after which I must leave the mansion and risk arrest. 'I'll think of something,' Silvia had said, but all she could suggest was that I hid in her parents' house.

'Then they'll be arrested too,' I said.

'Dear God, no,' she had whispered.

I needed an Emilia, and instead I was discovered by Fang and Nasty. Silvia had left me in the night's darkness, whispering that she had to light fires. She had kissed me. 'Stay there,' she cautioned me, scrambled away, the mansion fell silent once more, and I fell asleep again. It was the sleep of exhaustion, a deep sleep, so I did not hear the first scrabble of paws, the voices, or the footsteps, but woke abruptly to a dog howling in my ear. A second dog barked. 'They found something!' a voice called.

I was dizzy with sleep, my heart pounding. A faint light showed from the back of the stage. I tried to stand and hit my head painfully on the boards above. 'Go get him, Nasty!' a second voice shouted, and both dogs redoubled their barking. They were high, shrill barks, not the deeper and threatening sound of the fighting mastiffs, but the noise still scared me, and I seized the blanket and pushed out through the fabric covering the stage's front, tearing the cloth from its nails. The morning's first grey light was showing through the oriel window, and a servant was reviving the fire to flicker shadows across the hall. He seized a poker as if to defend himself, then just stared at me as two men crossed the stage, one carrying a lantern. 'That's not a rat!' one said.

'Naked as a rat, though,' the second man said. The dogs, both terriers, proud of their work, howled at my heels. 'Quiet!' the man shouted. 'Down, Nasty! Down, Fang!'

I managed to pull on hose, shirt, and doublet before the steward arrived. More dogs had come to the hall, so there were now six of them running around, yapping in excitement and pissing on Lady Hunsdon's new rugs. They were ratcatchers' terriers, their dirty pelts matted and their muzzles bloodied. 'Let me have silence!' Walter Harrison demanded loudly. 'The family is sleeping, this noise is unseemly!'

Even the dogs quietened. The steward must have been newly woken, yet he still appeared immaculately dressed, his chain of office gleaming over his silver-buttoned doublet. He looked me up and down, from my long unkempt hair to my grubby hose through which one toe poked. 'Mister Shakespeare,' he said, disappointment in his voice, 'explain yourself.'

'He was thieving, Mister Harrison!' a serving man had crawled through the torn fabric at the stage's front and now reappeared with the empty silver jug. 'I found this, sir!' The terriers evidently thought this damning, because they started howling.

'Quiet!' Harrison bellowed. He frowned at me. 'Stealing, Mister Shakespeare?'

'I stole the sack, sir, not the jug.'

He seemed to accept that explanation because he looked me up and down again, then said, 'You are hardly dressed as a thief. Explain yourself, pray?'

There were now six or seven serving men in the hall, together with the two ratcatchers, all surrounding me as I shivered. 'I slept here, sir,' I explained.

'You slept here,' Harrison said flatly. 'Why, pray?'

'I was too late to leave the city, sir.'

'And you purloined one of her ladyship's bedcovers?' he enquired, looking at the expensive blanket of satin-lined fur.

'I found it,' I said weakly.

'Yet I believe the coverlets are kept in her ladyship's chamber?'

Harrison asked, provoking one of the serving men to snigger. Harrison turned on him. 'Begone! You have work!'

'I just found it, sir,' I repeated, unable to think of any other lie.

One of the terriers pissed against the logs stacked on the hearth. 'Take your wretched dogs away!' Harrison ordered the ratcatchers. 'The rats are in the undercroft, not here. Go!' He waited as they left. 'It seems there is no harm done,' he declared loftily, 'and we shall say no more on the matter. Today is your final rehearsal in the hall, is it not?'

'Yes, sir,' I said.

'Then finish dressing, Mister Shakespeare, have your rehearsal, and then make sure you leave.'

'Leave, sir?' I said stupidly.

'Leave, Mister Shakespeare. Remove yourself from the mansion. Depart. Go home. Leave. You cannot sleep here! His lordship's residence is not a common lodging house. You will leave.'

'But he can't!' a voice protested from the door.

'Can't?' Harrison turned towards the door, his voice rising in indignation. 'Can't?'

'He'll be hanged!' Silvia cried.

My Emilia had come onstage.

Will Kemp arrived shortly after the church bells had tolled nine. He came into the hall as if there had been no argument the previous day. 'Good morrow, all!' he called cheerfully. 'A little warmer today, I think.' He was followed by his apprentice, Billy Rowley, and by a tall grim man in Lord Hunsdon's livery who I supposed to be Ryker, the commander of the Lord Chamberlain's guard. The tall man stopped in surprise when he saw that Lord Hunsdon was in the great hall. 'Don't go, Ryker,' his lordship called, 'I need you!'

'My lord?'

The Lord Chamberlain was furious. Silvia had told me he could be a fierce old bugger when he was crossed, and she was right; all trace of his usual geniality had vanished, and Will Kemp, surprised like Ryker that his lordship was present and fearing that the anger was aimed at him, backed away a few steps. 'I will not be defied!' Lord Hunsdon snarled.

'I meant no harm, my lord,' Kemp said in an unnaturally humble voice.

Lord Hunsdon ignored him. No one else spoke. All the players were in the hall, all of us looking nervous. The musicians were peering from the gallery, while Walter Harrison, who alone seemed unmoved by his lordship's anger, stood by the fire with a protective arm about Silvia's shoulders. She looked anxious, glancing constantly towards me. The bandage had been taken from my left arm, and the burn, oozing pus, throbbed. 'A horse, Ryker!' Lord Hunsdon demanded.

'At once, my lord.'

'You're coming with me.'

'Of course, my lord. Where to, my lord?'

'Whitehall, now!' His lordship stalked from the room, and Ryker, still looking astonished, followed.

'God's belly,' Kemp said, 'what is happening?'

'You are!' my brother said. 'All of us are. The Sharers! We're starting the rehearsal at midday.'

'At midday?' Kemp said startled, 'but we . . .'

'We shall be finishing later than we promised, Mister Harrison,' my brother said.

'I am sure you can be accommodated,' Harrison said calmly.

'Don't take your cloak off, Will,' my brother said to Kemp, 'you're coming with us.' He strode to the chest beside the fire and took out a book, a sheaf of papers, his quill box, and ink. He carried them to the big table where the play's properties were piled. 'Swords!' he said. 'If you're a Sharer, get yourself a sword.' He looked at me. 'You won't need a sword, brother.'

He called me brother!

He sat, found a clean sheet of paper, and began writing. 'Ralph,' he called as he wrote, 'practise the dances. Phil? The singers could be rehearsed.' He finished whatever he was writing, sanded the paper, and stood. The Sharers, looking mystified, were buckling sword belts. My brother did the same. 'We'll be back soon,' he announced.

'Where are you going?' Ralph Perkins asked.

He ignored the question. 'We'll be back soon,' he repeated, 'now come.'

We went.

The piece of paper on which my brother had written so hurriedly contained only eight words:

Romeo and Juliet
A Tragedie
by
William Shaksper

Beneath it was a thick stack of more paper, the bookkeeper's copy of a play. I carried the play and the book, which was the unbound copy of *A Conference*, down Addle Hill, while my brother followed with Will Kemp, Alan Rust, John Heminges, Richard Burbage, and Henry Condell. All six men wore a sword or a rapier, the weapons' long scabbards hidden by their cloaks. 'No murder,' had been my brother's last words as we left the mansion.

A small rain was blowing from the south, making the cobbles of the hill slippery. The ice was largely gone from the river, and the wherries were busy again, carrying passengers up and down between the city's landing stages. 'You'll have to talk to my pa,'

Silvia had said in the all too short night, 'if we're marrying.'

'We're marrying now,' I had said, and she had giggled. She had wanted to come with us to Addle Hill, but Walter Harrison had scoffed at the thought, telling her sternly that she had some explaining to do.

'So you were with the girl last night?' my brother asked.

'Silvia, yes.'

He grunted. 'His lordship might not be pleased to hear you seduced one of his family's maids.'

'We're getting married,' I said defiantly. It seemed strange to say that out loud, especially to my brother.

'Dear sweet Saviour!' he said, then chuckled. 'Lord, what fools we mortals be.'

His amusement irritated me because, as so often, he made me feel like a child again. 'You were younger than me when you got married,' I retorted.

'Indeed I was.'

'And Silvia says his lordship won't mind.'

'I doubt his lordship minds whether she marries or not,' he said mildly, 'except he might be sorry to lose a good maid-servant. And from what I hear she is a good girl.'

'Too good for me, you mean?'

'She'll surely be good for you,' he said, and I wondered whether it had been my brother who had told Silvia I was a thief. I was about to ask him, but he had a question of his own. 'You know she and Jean have been talking?'

'I know.'

'Jean wants her to help at the Theatre.'

'She's a wonderful seamstress,' I said, to encourage him.

'There are many skilled seamstresses,' he said dismissively, then suddenly we were at the porch of Saint Benet's Church. 'We'll follow you in,' he said, 'and remember, no murder.'

'No murder,' I repeated, then went down the familiar steps.

318

The church, which Sir Godfrey liked to boast had been there from before the time of the Conqueror, lay almost three feet beneath the cobbles of Addle Hill, and parishioners had to go down four old worn stone steps to reach the door. The entrance to Sir Godfrey's house lay a few yards further down the hill, and that door would be bolted, but the church door only closed at curfew. 'The faithful,' Sir Godfrey liked to say, 'must have access to God's saving grace,' by which he really meant that the faithful must have access to the massive poor box, iron bound and flamboyantly padlocked, that greeted every visitor. Sir Godfrey preached charity, encouraged generosity, and pocketed the coins. I had to duck under the stone arch and so entered Saint Benet's where I had so often chanted the psalms in the white-washed choir. The church had once been painted with scenes from the Bible, it had possessed a handsomely carved pulpit and had boasted silver vessels on the altar, but Sir Godfrey, feeling the chill of a Puritan wind, had made sure that anything beautiful was sold or destroyed. There was no pulpit now, the altar was a plain deal table, and the candlesticks were turned from beechwood. Only the poor box was colourful, its flanks white and its face painted red, with a text from the Book of Proverbs: 'He that hath pity upon the poor lendeth unto the Lord.'

I skirted the huge box, walked up the brief nave, and pushed open the door into the vestry. It was empty. I crossed the room and pushed down the latch of the further door. If Sir Godfrey was home then this door was left unbolted, and it was. I pushed the door open, and Sir Godfrey, sitting at his breakfast table, turned, startled. 'Richard!' he exclaimed.

'It's the pretty boy,' a mocking voice snarled, and I saw that Piggy Price's two bulbous nephews were also at the table. I had thought they might have left after waiting one night, but it seemed they were staying till all three days were passed. The fourth person at the table was Simon Willoughby, who shuddered when he saw me. The four were sharing a loaf of bread, some cheese, a flitch of bacon, and a jug of ale.

'Perhaps you'll join us, dear boy,' Sir Godfrey said, smiling through his black spade beard.

'I want to hurt him!' Simon pleaded. His face was still bruised, his lip swollen and his eye closed. The great blood clot showed dark on his cheekbone, while his burned right hand was bandaged.

'We must be friends,' Sir Godfrey said silkily. 'Did you bring what we wanted, Richard?'

I put the play and the book on the table. One of the twins, either Fish-Breath or Sweaty-Face, snatched up the play and peered at the top page. 'You can read?' I asked him.

His chair scraped as the twin stood, eager to punish my insolence, but Sir Godfrey held out a warning hand. 'I'll have no affray,' he said, 'it seems that young Richard has done his godly duty like a good Christian.' He drew the book towards him, then reached up to fully open a shutter to let in more of the morning's light. The twin, it was Fish-Breath I saw, because the other twin, like Simon, had a bandage around his scorched hand, sat unhappily as Sir Godfrey read the book's title aloud. '"*A Conference About the Next Succession to the Crowne of Ingland.*" Is this your brother's book?' he asked me.

'Yes, Sir Godfrey.'

He smiled wolfishly. 'It seems we have trapped Mister William Shakespeare in sedition!' He chuckled and held the book towards Fish-Breath. 'As we agreed, this is yours, and that,' he took the play script, 'is mine.'

'We can arrest the brother?' Fish-Breath asked, taking the book.

'Indeed you must arrest him,' Sir Godfrey said, and I knew my brother would be listening by now, hearing what he had

320

expected to hear, that Sir Godfrey had made a devil's bargain with the Pursuivants. They would prove sedition, and Sir Godfrey would have a play to sell to a wealthy earl.

Sir Godfrey smiled as he looked at the top page. "'*Romeo and Juliet*,'" he read aloud, "'a tragedy.'" He bared his yellow teeth in another smile. 'Thank you, dear Richard.' He put the top page aside and picked up the next, and I watched as his smile slowly faded. He frowned, then read aloud again. "'Scene one, the English court. Enter William the Conqueror, Marquis Lubeck with a picture,'" he paused and looked up at me, then turned towards Simon Willoughby. 'The English court, William the Conqueror. Was this play stolen from you, Simon?'

'No, sir. That's *Fair Em*.'

Sir Godfrey shook his head sadly and looked back to the page. "'What means fair Britain's mighty conqueror so suddenly to cast away his staff?'" he read, then looked up at me. 'What means young Richard so suddenly to cast away his wits?' he snarled. 'You will hang for this!'

Fish-Breath stood and reached for me, then suddenly went very still because a sword blade was at his throat.

He went still because my brother and the other Sharers were pushing through the door, filling the small room, and my brother was holding the sword at Fish-Breath's gullet.

Sir Godfrey was the first to recover from the surprise. 'Buttercup!' he shouted. 'Buttercup!'

There was no answer.

'You sent him to buy salt, sir,' Simon Willoughby whispered.

'You wanted to hang my brother Richard?' my brother asked Fish-Breath, but the twin had no answer. His head was tilted, forced back by the blade. 'Are these the twins that branded you?' my brother asked.

'Yes.'

'The twins that wish to arrest me for sedition?'

'Yes, brother,' I said.

'No murder, my masters,' my brother said, 'no murder. Now set to.'

We set to.

TWELVE

Now, fair Hippolyta, our nuptial hour
Draws on apace; four happy days bring in
Another moon . . .

W E WERE APPREHENSIVE. We had never rehearsed a play for so long, never seen so much money spent on any play, and had never been so nervous before a performance. Expectations, at least the expectations of the Lord Chamberlain's wife, were high, and we were playing to an audience whose attention was reluctant. Many had seen *Fair Em* and had to be wondering why Lord Hunsdon was inflicting yet more pain on his guests. They had endured the wedding service, endured the bishop's homily, and now had to endure us, and if the Queen had not been present, and everyone in the hall knew she liked watching plays, the noise of conversation would have swamped George Bryan's opening lines. A few guests still whispered as Duke Theseus spoke those first words, but a savage look from Her Majesty swiftly silenced them. Even the servants distributing kickshaws, sweetmeats, and wine dared not move.

We had started almost two hours late. Some said it was because the Queen's barge had to wait for slack water before rowing under the bridge, others blamed the bishop's sermon, while Will Kemp, on no authority but his own, claimed the bride had fainted at the prospect of losing her virginity. My brother tried to calm the company's nerves by saying that all weddings started late. 'Which is why we marry in haste,' he added. No one smiled.

I remembered his wedding. I was eight years old and in awe of him. My father, mother, and I had walked to the church at Temple Grafton on a cold November day. We all wore our best clothes, while my brother had a new dark doublet. His hair was longer then, and my mother said what a handsome boy he was, and he was almost a boy, only eighteen years old, while Anne, his bride, was eight years older. She was dressed in pale grey linen, and had sprigs of holly berries in her unbound hair. A small pot belly pushed at her skirts, and that small pot belly, though I did not realise it for a long time, became my niece Susanna. There were just eight of us in the church, nine if you count Susanna, the ceremony was over almost before it began, and then we had walked back to Stratford with Anne grumbling because showers were sweeping across the fallow fields, though we reached Henley Street before the rain turned heavy. 'Well,' my mother said, taking her usual seat at the kitchen table, 'that's done.'

George Bryan vomited during the long wait. 'Dear sweet God,' he kept muttering, one leg twitching. Silvia, who was helping Jean, looked at him aghast as he puked into a wooden pail held between his legs.

'Is he sick?' Silvia asked.

'He's always like that,' I said.

'Dear sweet God,' George said again. He was dressed in one

of Lord Hunsdon's robes, a gorgeous cloak of dark blue velvet trimmed at the collar and cuffs with heavy drapes of lynx fur. His cap was dark blue velvet, also trimmed with fur and sporting the two black feathers from the hat I had stolen from deValle. He wore a golden chain hung with a badge. He was Duke Theseus, and he was shivering, pale, and vomiting.

John Heminges paced the tiring chamber, sometimes pausing to peer through the curtains that covered the entrances to the stage, but seeing nothing in the hall except servants laying down plates and goblets. I heard him muttering his opening line. "Ill met by moonlight, proud Titania!'" He was Oberon, King of the Fairies, and was dressed in black hose and shirt, covered with a cloak made from real cloth of gold. The cloak was stiff because the gold wire woven into the silk threads made it unwieldy. The cloth had come from Lady Anne Hunsdon's bed hangings, and Silvia had made it into a cloak, adding edges of black satin on which she had sewn white stars.

'You can't sit in it,' she had warned John, 'because it will bend and stay bent.'

'Bend?' he had asked, distracted.

'No sitting, no kneeling, sir!'

"'That very time I saw,'" John Heminges said, one hand gripping the hare's paw that hung about his neck on a silver chain, "'but thou couldst not,

> *'Flying between the cold moon and the earth*
> *Cupid all arm'd! A certain aim he took*
> *At a fair vestal thronéd by the west,*
> *And loosed his love-shaft smartly from his bow.'*

'I have a love-shaft!' Will Kemp boomed, then seized Jean and kissed her on the lips as he did before every performance.

'But you have a helper now,' he said, and took Silvia's arm, turned her, then recoiled as he tried to kiss her, 'what in God's—'

'Pins, sir,' she said, taking two from her lips, 'sorry, sir. I hold them in my mouth.' She had put the pins between her lips when she saw Kemp kiss Jean. She smiled sweetly at him, then stooped to fasten the buckles on his shoes.

Kemp was in buff leather, woollen trews, a simple cap, and a good mood. 'Keep it moving, my masters!' he called. 'Keep it moving!' No one listened. Kemp did not really expect anyone to listen.

My brother turned his back on the company and made the sign of the cross.

'I need to piss,' Thomas Pope said. Richard Burbage drew his sword and kissed the blade.

And I left by the scullery passage door and climbed the stairs. I was wearing a coat of goose-turd green, rough hose, and a woollen cap. My long hair was gone. Jean and Silvia, both of them laughing, had cut it off, then trimmed what was left. 'There's a wigmaker in Old Change who'll pay well for this,' Jean had said as she carefully laid the long tresses onto a piece of linen.

'How much will I get?' I had asked.

'You? You won't get a penny! Silvia will get a few shillings. You won't!'

'Lord above,' Silvia had said, standing back to look at me. 'He looks ten years older!'

The short hair felt strange at first. Father Laurence, seeing it, had smiled. 'A man at last, Richard?' he had said.

Now, a man at last, who waited for the wedding to end and for the guests to come from the chapel, I climbed to the minstrels' gallery. Phil was there with his five musicians. Robert, Phil's friend, raised his crumhorn in greeting when he saw me. 'Short hair!' he said, surprised.

'I've grown up,' I answered.

'Is that Richard?' Phil pretended not to recognise me. 'I don't think I've seen you without a skirt!' His voice was unusually sibilant.

'What's the matter with your voice?' I asked.

'I had two teeth pulled yesterday.'

'What did that cost?'

'Four pence each.'

'God's belly,' I said, 'I'd have done them all for nothing!'

He laughed and struck his fingers across the strings of his lute. 'Why are we late?'

'Because our masters haven't finished the wedding, I suppose.'

I leaned on the balustrade. The candles had been lit on the tables, silverware gleamed, and the fire burned like a furnace. The Queen's dais with its high-backed throne and solitary table was covered by a rich red canopy of state. It was mid-afternoon, yet already the sky beyond the oriel window looked dark. 'You've got a black eye,' Phil said.

'I do.'

'I'd have done it for nothing,' he said, and I laughed.

Sir Godfrey had done it instead.

'Now set to,' my brother had said, though for a moment no one did. Sir Godfrey had begun a halting protest which my brother had ignored, sheathing his sword. No one else had moved, no one perhaps believing that there would be violence. 'There must be a mistake . . .' Sir Godfrey had said nervously.

Fish-Breath had snarled at Sir Godfrey to be silent. 'We serve the Queen!' he had said defiantly.

'You don't,' my brother had said calmly.

'And you'll be locked in the Marshalsea by noon,' Sweaty-Face had finished for his twin.

'At this moment,' my brother had said, still very calmly, 'the

Lord Chamberlain is with Her Majesty. You will find that your employment has ended by noon.' And with that he had punched Fish-Breath in the stomach.

It was a hard, thumping blow. My brother was not a big man like Will Kemp, nor was he agile like Richard Burbage, but he was strong and relentless. I remembered watching him fight Dick Quiney when both boys were about sixteen, and Quiney, who was a head taller than my brother, ended up beaten and bloody. Fish-Breath had tried to hit back, but my brother had parried the fist, then head-butted Fish-Breath, who had whimpered, then put a hand to his dagger. My brother had seized the hand and bent a finger back. Fish-Breath had squealed again, there had been a cracking noise, a louder squeal of pain, then Sweaty-Face had hurled himself across the room to help his twin brother, and that was when the rest of us had set to.

Sir Godfrey had stood and tried to push past me, and I had pushed him back, and he had swung a fist to blacken my left eye. It had hurt and it had angered me. And seven years' of anger had suddenly erupted as I kicked him hard between the thighs, then I had brought my knee up to meet his face as he bent over. I had felt his nose break. I had seized his lank black hair, dislodging his cap, and I had forced his head back against the wall and had punched his face till it was a bloody mess and my knuckles were hurting.

It was all over very fast. Sweaty-Face had put up a fight, but Will Kemp was quicker, taller and stronger, and within a moment Sweaty-Face had become Bloody-Face. 'It wasn't us!' Sir Godfrey had pleaded through bleeding lips. He was on his knees with blood pouring from his nose. 'It was Francis Langley. Talk to him!'

'I will,' my brother had said, and thumped Sir Godfrey around the ear. 'And as for you,' he had stepped over Fish-Breath and advanced on Simon Willoughby, who had whimpered.

'He's mine, Will,' John Heminges had said.

'Leave him to me,' Will Kemp had demanded.

'No, he's mine!' Heminges had insisted.

Bloody-Face had tried to haul John Heminges away from Simon, but Alan Rust and Richard Burbage had taken hold of him and hurled him against the wall. 'The Lord Chamberlain,' Rust had said, 'is unhappy with you. He sends you greetings,' and he had driven a fist into his ribs, 'and asks that you do not steal from our company.' He had driven the fist again, then a third blow into the already broken nose. Richard Burbage and Henry Condell, feeling left out, were dissuading Fish-Breath from trying to help his twin by pummelling him mercilessly, while my brother was staring down at Sir Godfrey, who was on the floor covering his head with his hands. 'We are the Lord Chamberlain's Men,' my brother had snarled at the cowering priest, 'and you do not piss on our stage!'

'No!' Simon Willoughby had wailed, and we had looked over to see the boy on the floor and Heminges, his apprentice master, standing over him with a knife.

'No murder,' my brother had said.

'No!' Simon had wailed again, because Heminges had plucked the boy's cap off to release his long golden hair. Heminges then gathered the hair in one hand and pulled it straight up.

'Wigmakers pay handsomely for golden hair,' he had said.

'No!'

'Stop whining,' Heminges had said, and struck the boy with the knife's heavy pommel. Then he had begun sawing at the hair, slicing it all off, wielding the knife roughly to leave Simon's scalp bloodied. 'You are released from your apprenticeship,' he had said as he worked, then laughed at the mess he had made of Simon's head. 'Are we done?'

My brother had looked around the crowded room where the four men were bloodied and beaten. 'We're done,' he had said, picking up the book and the play, 'and a very good morning's work, my masters.'

We were laughing as we went back up Addle Hill. Will Kemp had his arm around my brother's shoulder. 'You're a good man, Will!' he had boomed. 'A good man!'

'Despite Peter?' my brother had asked.

'It might be a small part,' Kemp had said, 'but I can make something of it.'

'Then let's make something of today's play,' my brother had said.

And we had. The last rehearsal seemed to be infused with the energy of the fight, with enthusiasm, with the laughter that had echoed on Addle Hill. We were the Lord Chamberlain's Men, and no one pissed on our stage.

The first guests arrived in the great hall. They came in small groups, all dressed gaudily in silk, satin, and fur, all laughing or chattering, evidently relieved to have been released from the chapel which must have been cold because they mostly gathered about the wide hearth. I gazed down from the minstrels' gallery, seeing feathered hats and bejewelled headpieces. Walter Harrison, resplendent in his steward's black with a gold chain of office, clapped his hands to summon servants. 'Wine,' he said, 'for the guests. Now!'

'Oh good,' Phil said, 'a drunken audience. We might as well give them *Fair Em* again.'

Walter Harrison turned and looked up to the gallery. 'Music,' he called, 'let us have music.'

'Let us have musicians then,' I said, and skipped sharply away from Phil's retaliatory slap.

I went back down the stairs. 'Not long now,' my brother said as I re-entered the tiring room.

'Dear God,' George Bryan prayed.

'"Ill met by moonlight, proud Titania!"' John Heminges muttered over and over, pausing only to kiss the hare's foot that hung about his neck on its silver chain.

'Doesn't that thing stink?' Will Kemp demanded.

'No worse than you.'

'Gentlemen!' Alan Rust intervened. The noise of the guests in the great hall was getting louder. The boys who played women and girls were sitting on a bench where Jean and Silvia coated their faces, bosoms, hands, and legs with the ceruse that made their skin white. The ceruse was infused with pearls so that their skin would shimmer in the candlelight. One by one they had their lips reddened, then their eyes anointed with belladonna and darkened with soot mixed with pork fat.

'I need a piss,' Thomas Pope groaned.

'You pissed five minutes ago!' Henry Condell said.

'I need another.'

'Piss in George's bucket,' Alan Rust suggested. George, abandoning the bucket, was reaching up to touch the ceiling. Another superstition.

'Time to light the candles?' Richard Burbage, who was stretching his arms, asked.

'Not yet,' my brother said.

'Dear God above,' George Bryan moaned. He could not quite reach the ceiling.

'Jump!' Will Kemp said, and George dutifully jumped and his finger brushed the beam.

'It must be soon!' John Heminges gripped his hare's foot.

'The Queen isn't in the hall yet,' Alan Rust said. He was peering through the central entrance.

Laughter sounded loud from the hall. I joined Rust to spy through the curtain. The guests were taking their seats, and servants were pouring wine. The stage was dark. Folk kept looking towards it, but all they saw were two heavy curtains that

331

hung from the minstrels' gallery, one obscuring the right-hand third of the stage, and the other the left. Each drape had been painted with a pair of white columns that stood at either side of a painted niche in which was a painted statue. The drapes were there to suggest the audience hall of an Athenian palace, and hid the gauze-hung hornbeam saplings.

A servant burst through the door from the scullery passage. 'She's coming,' he hissed, 'she's coming!'

'Oh Christ,' George Bryan moaned. He sat on a tiring chest, rocking backwards and forwards, his hands clasped in apparent prayer.

'Tom, Percy!' my brother called. 'Light the candles.'

Tom and Percy were both serving men of Lord Hunsdon's household, but this day they would be our stage hands. They each lit a taper from the candles in the tiring room, and vanished through the curtained doors. There were fifty candles on each side of the stage; all of them big church candles, standing over three feet high, and all made of expensive beeswax so the Queen would not be assaulted by the stench of tallow. 'Money,' Lord Hunsdon had moaned when the big candles arrived, 'it's only money!'

'I'll tell the musicians she's coming,' I said, and without waiting for an answer I left by the back door, raced up the stairs and onto the gallery, only to hear the Queen's trumpeters announcing her arrival before I had a chance to speak. The guests in the hall stood, the men bowed and the women curtseyed. Phil's musicians stopped playing.

The Virgin Queen! Elizabeth came into the hall dressed in glowing white, the white of silk and satin, her red hair wreathed with a headpiece of bright silver in which rubies glinted. A stole of ermine was loosely draped on her shoulders, not hiding the whitened skin of her bosom against which diamonds gleamed. She walked slowly, head high, not acknowledging the respectful guests, but guided towards her canopied dais by her cousin, Lord Hunsdon. The front of her hair had been shaved to achieve the high, fashionable forehead, and her face was pasted white and smooth beneath the bright red loops and swirls of her thick curls. 'Is that a wig?' Phil murmured in my ear.

'Of course it is,' I whispered, 'she's old enough to be your grandmother.'

'If she was my grandmother,' he said, 'I'd be the Prince of Wales.'

'God help the Welsh,' I said. The Queen's ladies-in-waiting followed her, and behind those four women came the bride and the groom, both quite outshone by their monarch. The bride looked pretty, in pale yellow slashed with purple, while her husband was in dark blue. The families of the couple followed, all stopping and the men bowing as the Queen climbed the two carpeted steps to her solitary table. 'Shouldn't you be making a noise?' I asked Phil.

'Not till Grandma sits,' he said.

The two serving men were still lighting candles, slowly brightening the stage with its painted hangings. The Queen sat, and Phil's musicians began playing again, softly at first, as the guests resumed their chairs and the murmur of conversation began again. I stood in shadow, watching, trying to ignore the nervous beating of my heart every time I thought of going onstage. More wine was served, and silver plates heaped with delicacies were being carried to the tables. The families of the bride and groom took their seats, the bride gazing expectantly at the empty stage. Lord Hunsdon was bending over the Queen's chair, listening, and I saw him straighten, turn, and nod towards Walter Harrison, who, in turn, spoke to Percy, the serving man who was lighting the candles on the left-hand side of the stage.

'We're beginning,' I told Phil.

Percy finished the last few candles and disappeared under the gallery. Laughter sounded in the hall, the voices rising as the wine in the great silver jugs fell. I heard footsteps on the stairs, then the door opened and John Heminges came onto the gallery. 'We can start now,' he told Phil. Heminges, who had shed his great stiff cloth of gold cape, came and stood beside me to look down on the glittering, jewelled audience in the hall. 'God help us,' he said softly.

The music ended. There was silence in the gallery for a few seconds, then the drummer began a slow beat on his largest instrument, the sound reverberating through the hall, and after a dozen of the blows had largely silenced the audience, the trumpeter stood and blew a fanfare that faded to let Phil and the other musicians begin a sweet and melodic dance. And beneath us the boys of the household and the fairies of the company came onto the stage to dance. There were no words, just the boys dancing to the music, and Percy and Tom had come onto the gallery and now hauled on the ropes that lifted the painted screens to reveal the glittering forest behind.

It had been Alan Rust's idea to begin the play with a voiceless dance, a dance to quieten the audience, a dance that would look like something from a masque, something that hinted of the magic to come. The dance did not last long, but it worked, because I could see the audience gazing in silence at the dancers, who were interrupted by a sudden crash as the drummer beat hard on his drum and the two painted screens fell back down to denote that we were now inside the palace. The falling screens made the closest candles shiver, but none went out. The barefooted dancers left through the left and right doors, and heavier footsteps sounded as the players came onto the stage from the big central door. George Bryan, who only a moment before had been quivering in terror, who had

334

vomited in his nervousness, now strode with his head high and his voice full of confidence.

'"Now,"' he said, '"fair Hippolyta, our nuptial hour

> *'Draws on apace; four happy days bring in*
> *Another moon: but oh methinks, how slow*
> *This old moon wanes ...'*

We had started.

George Bryan and Thomas Pope began the play. Pope was another Sharer, a quiet and unassuming man who often took older parts. He had purchased his share in the company on the death of his father, a Puritan wool merchant who had hated the playhouses. 'Every time I walk onstage,' Thomas liked to say, 'he twists in his grave.'

He played Egeus in *A Midsummer Night's Dream*. Egeus was Hermia's father and begins the play by complaining about his daughter. He wishes her to marry Demetrius, but Hermia is in love with Lysander who, Egeus maintains, '"hath bewitched the bosom of my child."' He accuses Lysander of singing beneath his daughter's window and of showering her with gifts; a bracelet fashioned from Lysander's own hair and with '"rings, gawds, conceits, knacks, trifles, nosegays, sweetmeats!"' So now Egeus demands justice. He appeals to the duke that either Hermia be forced to marry Demetrius, or else, according to the law of Athens that my brother had invented, she should be put to death for disobedience.

Our audience in the great hall gave a slight gasp when Thomas Pope uttered the word 'death'. That was a good sign. They were listening. True, some listened only because they feared the Queen's displeasure, but that audible gasp meant that many had already been drawn into the story being told onstage.

It would have been different in the Theatre. The ground-lings there like to let us know their opinions, and doubtless would have shouted a protest at Egeus's outrageous sugges-tion that his daughter should be executed for refusing to marry Demetrius. Playhouse audiences like to talk back to the stage or to argue with each other about what they watch, but that was much less likely in candlelit halls. There is an art to playing in the Theatre. We cannot pretend the spectators are not there, they are all around us, the closest of them sit on the stage itself, while others lean on it, put their ale bottles on it, and crack their nut shells on its boards, and so we often speak directly to them, wink at them, but always try to be ahead of them. 'Keep it moving!' Alan Rust growls before we enter. 'Don't give them space!'

Will Kemp loves to give them space because he sees a comment from the audience as a challenge, as a contest of wit that he is confident of winning. He will even stop a play to trade barbs with the groundlings, cheered on by the many who come just to enjoy his coarse sallies. My brother hates it when Kemp begins inventing lines, but there is little he can do because Kemp is too celebrated. But the rest of us are enjoined to keep speaking the lines quickly and naturally. 'Don't sound like a town crier,' my brother snarls whenever a player slows in a rehearsal to stress the words heavily.

'Don't give them time to think,' James Burbage tells us. 'Lead them by the nose or they'll start throwing things!'

I slipped out of the gallery and went back to the tiring room. The opening scene was going well enough, but the audience was becoming restless as Hermia and Lysander plotted to run away, and Helena, who was in love with Demetrius, vowed to betray their plot to him. It was a long scene, and from the tiring room I could hear coughing from the audience, always a sign that they are losing attention. I was listening closely to

336

Alexander Cooke, playing Helena, and heard the lines that told me the scene was close to its ending.

'Love looks not with the eyes, but with the mind;
And therefore is wing'd Cupid painted blind . . .'

I moved to the right-hand entrance. Will Kemp was already there, and nodded to me. We were the mechanicals, the clod-hopping craftsmen who would present a play to the duke and his bride. Five of us would enter onto the right of the stage, while only Peter Quince entered from the left. 'Let's wake the buggers up,' Will Kemp growled softly to us. 'Enjoy yourselves!'

I stood behind the entrance curtain and felt the fear. The fear of forgetting the words, of being overcome by blind panic. 'If you're not frightened,' Richard Burbage once told me, 'you're not a player.' I was frightened, wishing suddenly to be almost anywhere except in this hall with this daunting audience.

Helena finished her speech, vowing to regain Demetrius's love. She left on the far side of the stage, and Will Kemp, sensing that the audience needed to be stirred, swept the entrance curtain aside and leaped onto the stage. Tom and Percy, up in the gallery, loosed new hangings to hide the painted pillars. The candles again flickered madly as the fresh hangings, both made of plain brown cloth, dropped into place. The plain brown suggested we were still indoors, but no longer in a palace. We appeared between the new hangings, shambling into the candlelight in our dull costumes. I could sense that Kemp wanted to shock the audience, to waken them and make them laugh, but it was my brother who altered the mood in the great hall.

He came onstage slowly and with a puzzled expression. He ignored us, instead he peered out into the hall and looked around, becoming ever more puzzled, and he left a pause so long that James Burbage, who was serving as our bookkeeper because Isaiah was still sick, whispered his opening line. My brother ignored the whisper. He still looked at the audience, still apparently bemused, and then his eyes widened as he gazed directly at the Queen, and at last spoke his first line, not to us, but to the hall, and spoke it in a tone of pure bewilderment. "'Is all our company here?'"

They laughed. It was not polite laughter, instead it was a great gust of enjoyment, almost of relief. Our audience, apprehensive that they were being forced to endure a two-hour ordeal, had realised they might enjoy it instead. We no longer needed the Queen's presence to keep them attentive. We had captured them.

We came offstage exultant. The play might have started slowly, but the mechanicals had warmed the audience. We fed from their enjoyment, finding an energy that had never infused the rehearsals. I had shrieked in pretended horror on the line which had so angered me the first time I read it. "'Nay, faith, let me not play a woman!'" I had not meant to shriek, it just came, and the audience laughed. They kept on laughing, so much that Will Kemp had to pause during his imitation of a lion roaring. Peter Quince had just given the lion's role to Snug, and Nick Bottom wanted it instead. "'Let me play the lion too! I will roar!'" And of course he did roar, bellowing crudely at the audience, who rewarded him with laughter, so Kemp naturally had to embellish the lines to add more roaring. My brother interrupted him to bring us back to the script, not that anyone noticed. They liked us, and as we left the stage, having promised to meet again to rehearse our play in the woods close to Athens, we were all grinning.

The music began and I snatched up a pair of shears. Tom and Percy had lit the candles, but they had to stay in the gallery, so two of us mechanicals took the right-hand side of the stage and two the left, where we trimmed the wicks, cutting off the excess to make a clearer, brighter flame. Guests chatted and drank wine until the drumbeat and trumpet flourish announced that the play was resuming. The two servants on the gallery hauled up the hangings, and the wood was revealed again, sparkling with green light. Alan Rust entered dressed all in green, even his face was green. Jean had spent days boiling woad and green-weed to find a green dye that would mix with the ceruse, and she had added haughty eyebrows in black. Puck, looking ludi-crous, entered with stately pomp and the audience applauded. "'How now, spirit! Whither wander you?'" he began, and the hall fell silent to listen to the play.

'No!' Bobby Gough suddenly wailed in the tiring room. I turned to see that one of the children had stood on his queenly train, Bobby had stepped away at the same moment, and now Titania's gauzy white robe was torn from shoulder to hip.

'Dear Lord above,' Silvia hissed. 'Come here!'

'I have to go onstage!' Bobby wailed.

'You'll go onstage when I tell you,' she said. 'Now don't fidget. And you,' she glared at her nephew, who, dressed as a fairy, stood waiting to follow Titania, 'don't pick your nose.' She plucked an already-threaded needle from her apron. 'Don't move,' she told Bobby, and I watched the needle flash down the long tear. Jean moved in to help, tacking the lower hem with more thread.

"'But room, fairy!'" boomed Puck, "'here comes Oberon!'"

"'And here my mistress,'" the fairy answered onstage.

Silvia snapped the cotton with her teeth and slapped Bobby's bum. 'Go, mistress!' she said. 'Go!'

There was another gasp of astonishment when Oberon and Titania, along with their fairy entourages, entered the stage. The players shimmered, they glowed, they were apparitions in silver and gold. Then they argued, and the audience paid them the greatest compliment of all, they were utterly silent. Not a creak of a chair, the clatter of a plate or a cup, not a cough, nothing. The stage was filled with magical creatures who glittered in the candlelight. The fairy king and fairy queen faced each other, they argued over the Indian child, until Titania, played with a sudden new confidence by Bobby, refused her king's demand and swept haughtily from the stage, and Oberon, simmering with anger, summoned Puck. "'Thou rememberest,'" he said to Puck,

'Since once I sat upon a promontory,
And heard a mermaid on a dolphin's back
Uttering such dulcet and harmonious breath
That the rude sea grew civil at her song
And certain stars shot madly from their spheres,
To hear the sea-maid's music.'

And I wished Father Laurence could have heard John Heminges say those words, because they flowed like the sea-maid's music itself, like a melody with a soft beat, and still the audience was silent, entranced by the poetry. Even in the tiring room we were silent and unmoving as the magic on the stage wrapped about us.

"'I remember.'" Puck said, and then Oberon orders Puck to find the purple flower that would yield the sorcerous juice which, dripped onto a sleeper's eyelids, would cause the sleeper to fall in love with the very next creature that he or she saw. Oberon's revenge on the stubborn Titania would be to squeeze the flower's juice onto her eyelids, and he knew exactly where to find her.

'I know a bank where the wild thyme blows,
Where oxlips and the nodding violet grows.'

And on that bank, where he knew she would be sleeping, Oberon would anoint her eyelids and,

> *'The next thing then she waking looks upon,*
> *Be it on lion, bear, or wolf, or bull*
> *On meddling monkey, or on busy ape,*
> *She shall pursue it with the soul of love.'*

Oberon thus plots his revenge, but is interrupted by the arrival of Demetrius and Helena from Athens. "'I am invisible!'" Oberon tells the audience, and, astonishingly, no one in the hall mocked the claim, no one seemed to think it unlikely, instead they remained silent, watching Oberon as he, invisible to Demetrius and Helena, listens to the two lovers squabbling.

'It's going well!' Bobby Gough, his face glinting with the powdered pearls, whispered to me. He sounded surprised.

I hugged him. 'You're doing well,' I told him. He was too. Of all the players, we had been most worried by Bobby, fearing he was too young for such an important part, but in his first scene he had invested Titania with a sly authority. He knew he could not rival Thomas Pope's Oberon for stature or dignity, and so he had found an insinuating, seductive manner. The men in the audience, watching him, forgot he was a boy. He was a goddess, Queen of the Fairies, slim, beautiful, desirable, and sly.

"'I love thee not!'" Demetrius snarled at Helena, and she appealed to him, reminding him that he did once love her, but Demetrius is in love with Hermia, and so he stalks from the wood, spurning Helena.

Invisible Oberon, who has been still and silent through the quarrel, now stirs and swears he will punish Demetrius for his callous behaviour. He will use the juice of the magic flower to force Demetrius to love Helena, and so he orders Puck to find the callow man. "'Thou shalt know the man,'" he tells Puck, "'by

341

the Athenian garments he has on.'" And Puck, having found Demetrius, will use the flower's magical juice, "'Fear not, my lord, your servant shall do so.'"

Puck and Oberon left the stage, and Phil, above us, started a slow lyrical tune, all breathy flute and delicately plucked strings. The small children of the household ran onto the stage and began their dancing. Two of the company's apprentices, also dressed as fairies, had to carry Titania's bank, where the wild thyme blew onto the stage. It was a very low table with legs scarce five inches long on which were mounted sprigs of cloth-leaved hawthorn and sprays of white-petalled flowers. The boys almost tore the entrance curtain when it snagged on one of the table's nails, but Alan Rust leaped forward and snatched the curtain back, and the two boys, who played the fairies Moth and Cobweb, managed to carry the table to the centre of the stage. There Titania would sleep, but first the boys all sang.

'Dear God,' my brother murmured to no one, 'it's working.'

Silvia had crept to the right-hand entrance and pulled the curtain back a couple of inches to stare at the dancing, singing boys. 'It's beautiful!' she whispered. She turned, and I saw the candlelight reflected in her eyes. 'It's beautiful!' she whispered again. I stood behind her, hands on her shoulders, and just watched as the dance slowly ended, fairy after fairy leaving the stage until finally Titania yielded to tiredness and sank onto the bed of violets and wild thyme. The music faded as she fell asleep, there was a heartbeat of silence, then Oberon appeared at the far side of the stage. He advanced slowly and silently towards his sleeping queen, and I swear we could have heard a mouse squeak in that great hall.

Then Oberon stood above his queen, and the audience gasped as he squeezed the flower over Titania's eyes, then held their breath as she stirred. She moved, she moaned in her sleep, Oberon froze, but she did not wake. The hall was silent, quite silent. The fairy king smiled as he let the magical drops fall on her eyelids. "'Wake,'" he commanded Titania, "'when some vile thing is near!'"

I moved the curtain very slightly and stared across the hall to where the firelight was brightest. The Queen was leaning forward, gazing, her bright red lips slightly parted, her eyes as wide and shining as if they had been anointed with belladonna.

And the confusion began.

Hermia is in love with Lysander.

Lysander is in love with Hermia.

Demetrius is in love with Hermia.

Helena is in love with Demetrius.

And no one is in love with Helena.

But Oberon is determined that Helena should gain her heart's desire, and so he has ordered Puck to squeeze the magic juice on Demetrius's eyes. Puck would recognise Demetrius by his Athenian garb, which, on that winter afternoon in Blackfriars, was doublet and hose of silver cloth over which Henry Condell wore a vaguely Roman toga. Richard Burbage, playing Lysander, wore a black doublet and black hose over which he wore another vaguely Roman toga. Puck, seeing a sleeping man wrapped in a toga, anointed his eyes with the flower, except he squeezed the juice onto Lysander instead of onto Demetrius. Lysander, who has gone to sleep close to his love Hermia, wakes to see Helena, who has just stumbled upon the sleeping lovers.

Now Lysander is in love with Helena.

Helena is in love with Demetrius.

Demetrius is in love with Hermia.

And Hermia is in love with Lysander.

And, as if that were not confusion enough, we mechanicals rehearse our play in the same moonlit wood where Titania is sleeping, and where, not far off, the four Athenian lovers also sleep. Puck has discovered our rehearsal, but, like his master Oberon, he can make himself invisible, so we do not see him. We rehearse, and Nick Bottom goes offstage into a hawthorn brake, which in our case was the tiring room, where Puck magically converts his head into an ass's head. Will Kemp pulled on the wicker and rabbit-skin head and came back onto the stage.

The hall, which had been chuckling at the scene where we rehearsed *Pyramus and Thisbe*, roared with laughter when Will came back.

Those of us onstage fled in terror, leaving Nick Bottom, quite ignorant of his new and monstrous head, pacing up and down in front of the bower where Titania sleeps. Nick Bottom sings to himself.

And Titania awakes.

She sits up, she stretches, she yawns, she hears Nick Bottom singing, she sees him walking, and she freezes.

She stares. Her eyes widen. The audience, knowing what is coming, laughed in expectation. It was a nervous laugh, but in its sound you could sense the great burst of laughter that was waiting to happen. It was like a taut bowstring, held to the ear and quivering with its immense power, just waiting to be released.

Nick Bottom still sings. Then Titania, gazing entranced at the shambling peasant with an ass's head, speaks.

"'What angel wakes me from my flowery bed?'"

And the great hall exploded with laughter. The Queen, usually so careful of her dignity, was laughing as much as the rest. The bride had her hands clasped in front of her mouth, her eyes fixed on the stage, a look of sheer delight on her face.

Will Kemp was in heaven.

Once, a couple of years before we performed *A Midsummer Night's Dream* and at a time when my brother was still speaking civilly to me, a half-dozen of us had gone to the Dolphin tavern after the first performance of *Richard II*. The play had gone well, and my brother was in a generous and expansive mood. Nell, the pretty redhead, had sat next to him, cradled in his arm. He had ordered us oysters and ale, but had said little except to the playgoers who came to our table and congratulated him. To them he was polite, but he did not encourage them to linger. He was happy.

The conversation was loud as players relived their moments on the stage. Augustine Phillips had played Richard, and was chuckling because he had almost forgotten some lines, 'I was in a panic!'

'It didn't show,' someone had said.

'Which lines?' my brother had asked.

'"For now hath time made me his numbering clock,"' Augustine had recited.

And my brother, usually so reticent, had been sparked by the line. Had we seen his lordship's clock in Somerset House, he had asked, and none of us had. He had described it to us, a marvellous invention of dials and wheels, of cogs and chains, which drove a pointer around a dial painted with numbers to tell the time. To make the clock work, he had said, it was necessary to pull a weight upwards, and then the weight, released, slowly descended to drive the intricate mechanism behind the clock's face. 'A play is like that,' he had said.

Will Kemp had laughed. 'My arse it is, Will!'

'Truly!' my brother had said, his right hand stroking Nell's hair.

'And how, my demented poet,' Will Kemp had demanded, 'is a play like a clock?'

'Because we spend the first part of a play pulling the weight upwards,' my brother had said. 'We set the scene, we make confusion, we tangle our characters' lives, we suggest treason or

345

establish enmity, and then we let the weight go, and the whole thing untangles. The pointer moves around the dial. And that, my friend, is the play. The smooth motion of the clock hand, the untangling.'

And Will Kemp, usually so scornful, had nodded and raised his pot of ale. 'Here's to untangling.'

And so, by the time we trimmed the candles' wicks for the third and last time, we had untangled our play. There had been a spectacular fight between Hermia and Helena, a fight that kept our audience laughing, swords had been drawn, because folk liked to see swordplay onstage, but after the fighting and the fury the lovers' confusion had been resolved, and by the time we snipped the wicks for the last time, Hermia was in love with Lysander, Lysander was in love with Hermia, Helena was in love with Demetrius, and Demetrius was in love with Helena. Hermia's father, who had begun the play demanding his daughter's death, was now reconciled to her marrying Lysander. Duke Theseus and Hippolita would marry, Hermia and Lysander would marry, and Helena and Demetrius would marry. Titania, released from her devotion to Nick Bottom, was reunited with Oberon. It was a wedding play. It was nonsense, happy nonsense, lovers soaked in moonbeams, froth, and we had reached the happy ending.

Except the play was not over. The weight had still not pulled the chain all the way down, the clock was still ticking, and the pointer still moving. The lovers' confusion was untangled, but still there was more to come, and, just before Phil's musicians played the music to entertain folk as the candles were trimmed, Nick Bottom, now reunited with the rest of the mechanicals, announced that they would go to the duke's palace in hopes of presenting their play, *Pyramus and Thisbe*. "'And, most dear actors,'" Nick Bottom pleaded with the rest of us, "'eat no onions nor garlic! For we are to utter sweet breath; and I do not doubt but to hear them say, it is a sweet comedy. No more words: away! Go away!'"

I took off my goose-turd green coat, stepped out of my boots, breeches, and hose, then strapped on my false breasts that were linen bags stuffed with felt and stiffened with withies so that they jutted unnaturally. They were bigger, much bigger, than any I had worn before. Silvia laced them at my back, then I sat as she smeared madder on my lips. There would be no ceruse for Thisbe. We were tradesmen playing players, and must look grotesque, not beautiful. I would play Thisbe barefoot and bare-legged, though of course I had not shaved my legs any more than I had shaved my face, on which a day's stubble showed dark. Silvia brought me my dress, a simple dress in straw-coloured linen tied at the waist with a pale blue sash. She giggled. 'You're a pretty girl, Richard Shakespeare.'

"'Nay, faith,'" I said, pulling the dress over my head, "'let me not play a woman.'" I draped a bright red mantle around my shoulders like a shawl.

It was night outside. The dark comes early in February, and the high oriel window at the hall's far end was black. The music was jaunty, befitting the play's ending. In the hall, servants fed the fire, served wine, and trimmed the candles on the long tables. Folk laughed and talked, but fell instantly silent as the music ended, the drum beat and the trumpet sounded to announce that the play was continuing. Duke Theseus, with his bride and his courtiers, went onto the stage.

I sat, listening to the dialogue onstage, as Jean brought me the wig. We rarely used wigs at the Theatre, they were brutally expensive, delicate, and tended to fall apart too quickly, but this wig was a monstrosity. It was made from the tail hairs of a grey horse, dyed a bilious yellow, and then treated with wax so that the strands stuck out in unkempt spikes. Silvia laughed, the boys who were fairies giggled, everyone backstage grinned when Jean slid the wig over my hair. 'How does it feel?' she asked.

I nodded my head and tugged gently at a strand of yellow hair. 'It feels firm,' I said.

'Ready?' my brother called quietly.

'Ready,' I said. I took Silvia's hand, kissed it, and moved to the big central entrance.

The play's weddings were over, and now the newly married couples waited in the duke's hall for their evening's amusement. The painted hangings had dropped again, hiding the green magical wood, benches had been placed on the right of the stage, and there the three newly wedded couples sat and demanded entertainment. "'A play there is, my lord,'" Philostrate, the duke's Master of the Revels, said, "'some ten words long, Which is as brief as I have known a play: But by ten words, my lord, it is too long.'"

"'What are they that do play it?'" the duke asked.

"'Hard-handed men that work in Athens here, Which never laboured in their minds till now.'"

"'And we will hear it!'" the duke said.

"'No, my noble lord! It is not for you!'"

But dukes, like queens and lord chamberlains, get what they want, and so the mechanicals of Athens, hard-handed men, a weaver, a joiner, a bellows mender, a tailor, and a tinker, present their play. And if there had been laughter before, and there had been much laughter, it was as nothing to the laughter that greeted *The Most Lamentable Comedy and Most Cruel Death of Pyramus and Thisbe.*

It began with my brother's stumbling, stuttering, agonising prologue. I watched the Queen through a crack in the curtain and saw her smile. How often had she gone to a town in her realm and listened to some nervous mayor greet her with a prepared speech, but the man was so nervous that his fine words became mangled and his sense quite lost? Peter Quince's prologue was the same, a disastrous introduction to a ludicrous play. And when the prologue was done, we players were introduced, one by one.

Will Tawyer, the trumpeter from Phil's musicians, went onstage first and blew a mighty fanfare. The audience waited, expecting the fanfare to bring on a new character, but no one appeared. There was nervous laughter from the hall as the audience suspected some player had missed his entrance, then Tawyer blew his trumpet a second time and Will Kemp stumbled onto the stage as if he had been violently pushed from behind. He was no longer Nick Bottom, but Pyramus, wearing an ill-fitting breastplate that hung down over his belly, a wooden sword stuck in his belt, and a battered helmet. He recovered his balance and struck an heroic pose, and the laughter broke against the stage like a wave.

A second fanfare introduced Thisbe. I minced on, all shy and modest, glancing coyly at the audience and immediately looking away, hands clasped high to hide my pretty face, my breasts wobbling, all provoking shrieks of laughter from the hall.

My brother had to pause in his speech to let the noise subside. Will Kemp, of course, kept the laughter going by preening, but I doubt my brother minded, then at last another fanfare brought Richard Cowley onto the stage. He was Tom Snout, the tinker, but in *Pyramus and Thisbe* he was playing the wall, and was dressed in a vast swathing robe that Jean had painted with masonry. He spread his hands wide, looked dumb, and there, hanging from his outstretched arms, was a wall, and I heard a woman almost choking with laughter. She was gasping for breath, squawking between each gasp, and every squawk only made the rest of the audience laugh the more.

Peter Quince brought a measure of calm by bringing John

Sinklo onstage. He played Moonshine, because the mechanicals were worried there would not be enough light to illuminate *Pyramus and Thisbe* and so supplied their own moon. John, wearing a night-dark robe onto which Silvia had sewn silver crescent moons, carried a small thornbush, a lantern, and had Caesar, Lady Hunsdon's small yapping dog, on a rope leash.

And last came John Duke, playing the lion. He was swathed in a robe made from rabbit pelts, while on his head was a floppy mask, also of rabbit skin, from which great teeth protruded. He wore gloves that had claws attached. He made a feeble threatening gesture with the wooden claws, which prompted Caesar to bark furiously, and the duke, fearful of dogs, leaped sideways.

We were indeed ludicrous, and our play, of course, was equally ludicrous. I wondered if my brother was remembering *Dido and Acerbas* from so long ago. In that interlude, his very first work, he had tried to make an audience cry with grief as Dido burned herself to death, and instead had made them weep with laughter. Now he made an audience weep again, but this time with merriment and joy. The story of *A Midsummer Night's Dream* was over, the lovers had found each other and had married, and all we did now was to celebrate their love and happiness by telling them a tale of thwarted love and miserable death.

Pyramus and Thisbe must meet secretly because their two families are enemies and so disapprove of their love. The story comes from the Latin poet Ovid, we had been taught it at school, and in Ovid's telling it is a tragedy. The doomed lovers meet at the wall, using a crack in the masonry to talk with each other. Richard Cowley played the wall, spreading his arms so that his stone-painted robe made a barrier through which Pyramus ripped a hole with his wooden sword. He sees Thisbe through the newly made chink. Will Kemp was bending over, his vast rump sticking out to the audience's delight. "'I can hear my Thisbe's face!'" he cried, "'Thisbe!'"

"'My love thou art!'" I called desperately, "'My love I think!'" I bent to the wall.

"'O kiss me through the hole of this vile wall!'" Pyramus pleaded.

I puckered my lips and jammed them into the thickly-painted cloth, while Will did the same from the other side. We gave the kiss a few heartbeats, letting the audience laugh, then I recoiled, pretending to spit out lime. "'I kiss the wall's hole,'" I wailed in grief, "'not your lips at all!'"

"'Wilt thou at Ninny's tomb meet me straightway?'" Pyramus asked.

"''Tide life, 'tide death. I come without delay!'" I said, and with that I ran from the stage, using small tripping steps, while Will exited on the far side.

The story is well enough known. How Thisbe encounters a lion on her way to Ninus's tomb, but escapes the dread beast at the expense of her mantle that she lets fall to the ground, and how Pyramus, finding the mantle, which has been stained with blood by the lion, thinks his beloved is dead and so kills himself. This was Will Kemp's favourite scene, a death he could exaggerate, and he stabbed himself, or rather slid the wooden sword repeatedly beneath his armpit, he staggered about the stage, he recovered, he staggered again, and finally collapsed at the front of the stage and gave the audience a look of utter despair. "'Now die!'" he called, still stabbing himself, "'die, die, die . . .'" and then he stopped.

A look of panic came to his face. This was not Pyramus, this was a frightened player who had forgotten his lines. He froze, the wooden blade poised, and the embarrassing silence stretched, then my brother, pretending that Peter Quince was the play's bookkeeper, hissed the forgotten word, "'Die!'"

"'Die!'" Will shouted.

There is nothing like the laughter of an audience who love

what they hear and love what they see. Some in the hall were helpless with laughter. The Queen watched us avidly, while the bride, I think, was tearful with joy. We were celebrating her wedding.

I died next, slaughtering myself above the body of Pyramus and tugging a scarf of red silk from my bosom to denote blood. My wig fell off, which only added to the mirth as I fumbled it back on. I died. And then the other mechanicals dragged our corpses from the stage, and the fairies returned and danced to the sound of sweet music, and Oberon called down blessings on the house. The audience, all smiling, calmed, and Puck bade our farewell to them in the play's final speech. "'Give me your hands!'" he called, encouraging them to clap, and they clapped.

We lined up onstage as a company. We basked in their pleasure. We had taken Her Majesty and her courtiers from wintry London and transported them to a magical wood in Athens. They clapped, they stood, they cheered, we bowed.

I had rarely been happier. We bowed again. We were a company.

It had been a sweet comedy.

EPILOGUE

I DIED JUST after the bells of Saint Leonard's rang the third hour of the afternoon.

We were back in the Theatre. It was a fine spring day, the sky clear with just a scattering of clouds, the yard was crammed with people, and the galleries were full. From the stage all you really saw were faces, two thousand of them. And all gazing at us as our story unfolded. This was only the second time we had told the tale, yet word had already gone around the city that it was a story worth hearing, and so folk had streamed across Finsbury Fields, too many folk, and some had to be turned away with the promise that we would play the piece next day and the day after that. Others wanted to know when we would perform *A Midsummer Night's Dream* again, a play that also filled the Theatre time and again.

I was dressed in black hose, black boots, black breeches, and the doublet made from the softest Spanish black leather, slashed with strips of dark blue velvet, that I had saved from Fish-Breath's knife in the winter that was past. My white shirt was frilled with French lace, I wore a falling band instead of a ruff, and my short hair was covered with a fine blue hat sporting the two black feathers I had taken from deValle and which I now tried to wear whenever I went onstage. The feathers were my talismans, my magical protection against the devils of the playhouse who would make you forget your lines. My beard was short, trimmed neatly. I was Mercutio, Romeo's closest friend.

It was, as my brother had promised, a proper part, even a wonderful part. Richard Burbage played Romeo, and, in the rehearsals, he and I had drawn closer. He had even taken me to the Dolphin and bought me ale, told me tales of his father, and then, unexpectedly, talked of my brother. 'There's none like him,' he had said.

'None like you,' I had retorted, and that was true. Of all our players, Richard was the most skilful, his only rival being Ned Alleyn who played with the Admiral's Men at the Rose.

'Aye, but we would be nothing without the words,' Burbage told me, 'nothing at all. Folk come to hear a play, and if the words aren't there, nor will they be.'

The words! I had begun to listen more carefully to my brother's words, and, albeit grudgingly, was beginning to understand their magic.

"'I dreamed a dream tonight,'" Romeo said to me.

"'And so did I.'"

"'Well, what was yours?'"

"'That dreamers often lie.'"

"'In bed asleep, while they do dream things true.'"

Romeo and Juliet, those star-crossed lovers, were moving fatally towards their end at which, like Pyramus and Thisbe, each would die because of a misunderstanding. And, just like Pyramus and Thisbe, they came from warring families. Romeo, by falling in love with the thirteen-year-old Juliet, was loving an enemy, and Juliet, in loving Romeo, was defying her family. They both must die, but Mercutio dies first.

I die in a brawl. I used a rapier, fighting against Tybalt, who

354

was played by Henry Condell. Tybalt tries to pick a fight with Romeo for no other reason than Romeo is a Montague and Tybalt is a supporter of the Capulet family. Romeo will not fight because he loves a Capulet, but Mercutio, goaded by Tybalt's challenge, draws.

Henry Condell was no mean swordsman, and our fight, even with the longer rapier blades, was spectacular. We moved from one side of the stage to the other, the blades flickering like snake tongues, clashing, sliding, disengaging. We had rehearsed each move, yet even so I found Condell fast as a viper. The audience gasped at the fight. They love sword fights. Many in the playhouse were swordsmen, they knew what they watched, and we had to make it seem real. The fight finished as I drove Henry back, feinting and lunging, beating off his counters, moving faster than he did, until Romeo, knowing that duelling in the streets is forbidden, tried to end the fight by standing in front of me and so barring my attacks. And then Henry, Tybalt, lunges under Romeo's outstretched arm and pierces me in the chest.

The bell of Saint Leonard's struck the third hour of the afternoon.

"'I am hurt!'" I cry, "a plague o' both your houses.'" I stagger, left hand clutching my wound, squeezing the pig's bladder to ooze sheep's blood. The playhouse was silent, the loudest noise my shoes scraping on the boards of the stage.

"'Courage, man!'" Romeo said to me, "the hurt cannot be much!"

"'No, 'tis not so deep as a well,'" I say, still clutching the wound, "nor so wide as a church door; but 'tis enough, 'twill serve! Ask for me tomorrow and you shall find me a grave man. I am peppered, I warrant, for this world. A plague o' both your houses! 'Zounds, a dog, a rat, a mouse, a cat, to scratch a man to death! A braggart, a rogue, a villain that fights by the book of arithmetic! Why the devil came you between us? I was hurt under your arm.'"

And so I die slowly, and, because it is always difficult to remove a corpse from a sunlit stage, I stumble away to die elsewhere. "'Help me into some house, Benvolio,'" I pleaded to my brother, "'Or I shall faint. A plague o' both your houses! They have made worms' meat of me.'"

And so, my arm about my brother's shoulders and with his arm about my waist, I staggered back to the tiring room, where my wife waits. Silvia now works at the playhouse and we live in the rooms that once belonged to Father Laurence, who is worms' meat himself, though he gave us his blessing before he died on an April evening.

I have not seen Christopher deValle from that day to this. Rumour has it that he has gone to his master's house in Berkshire where he is a steward, while his master, the Earl of Lechlade, who lurked behind our tale all winter, is banished from the court.

George Price, Piggy, has gone from London to God knows where, and his nephews with him. The Pursuivants still ride, but they come nowhere near us.

Francis Langley has found plays, and the Swan an audience. I saw him and my brother walking arm in arm on Bankside, deep in conversation. Peace has broken out between them.

Sir Godfrey, being the parish priest in Blackfriars, was forced to read the marriage banns for Silvia and I, but we were married by the Reverend Venables in his lordship's chapel. The reverend took me aside afterwards and told me I was not much spoiled by having a beard. Sir Godfrey still supplies dogs and the bear Washington to the Curtain, and, sometimes, to the Swan playhouse, but rumour says he will soon retire from London and start a school for boys in some West Country cathedral town.

Simon Willoughby, the right-hand side of his face scarred deep and his blinded right eye milky white, was last seen begging for alms by Saint Paul's Cross. He claims to have been a soldier wounded by a Spaniard in the Low Country, and plays the part well.

Her Majesty has demanded that we take *Romeo and Juliet* to her palace at Richmond. We shall do that soon. We are high in Lord Hunsdon's favour, and even higher in the affections of his wife.

My brother lives with a woman named Anne. She is sociable, pretty, full of laughter, and married to another man. He and I are reconciled, perhaps because he likes Silvia. He kept his promise and gave me the part of Mercutio, and after our first performance he embraced me. 'Well played, brother,' was all he said.

Now he helped me off the Theatre's stage. 'Look at the mess!' Silvia said, brushing at the sheep's blood staining the white of the doublet. 'It won't wash out!'

I silenced her with a kiss.

We are the Lord Chamberlain's players. We tell stories. We make the magical appear onstage. We turn dreams into truth. We are actors.

HISTORICAL NOTE

S OMETHING QUITE extraordinary happened in the last years of the sixteenth century; the professional theatre was born. There had been plays and players before, of course, but those companies had no permanent home. They toured England and Europe, playing in great houses, inn yards, and parish halls, but in the 1570s the first permanent playhouses were built in London. James Burbage, who had begun his career as a carpenter, then became a player, built one of the first in Shoreditch, close beside the Finsbury Fields. By 1595, when the novel is set, the Curtain lay nearby, while across the river on Bankside, the Rose was attracting audiences, and the Swan was being built. In time there would be many more, most famously the Globe, which was not to be built until 1599.

Burbage named his new playhouse the Theatre, a word he plucked from classical Greece and a name that now encompasses a vast and exhilarating profession worldwide. Yet, in 1574, when Burbage leased the land and built the playhouse, he was taking a considerable financial risk. Not all playhouses thrived. The Red Lion had failed, and the Curtain would fall on hard times, but the Theatre and the Rose both proved profitable.

They also changed the nature of the professional companies. Previously, when groups of actors toured Britain, they could present the same play in the different towns they visited, secure in the knowledge that an audience in Warwick would not be the same as the audience that had seen the play two or three nights before in Kenilworth. Thus they could survive on a repertoire of very few plays, but once the playhouse was permanent then they were performing for the same audience week after week, and that audience wanted something new, and so the professional playwright was born. We know, from Philip Henslowe's diary, that the Rose presented around thirty different plays a year, and the Theatre must have felt the same pressure to perform new and fresh material. London, in 1595, had a population of around 200,000, making it by far the largest city in Britain, and a city needed a large population to provide permanent audiences for the permanent playhouses. And those playhouses were large. The Rose and the Theatre each accommodated around 2,000 people, while the new Swan would play to an audience of 3,000. Those figures are comparable with the largest theatres in modern-day London or New York! So, on any given day, a significant proportion of Londoners went to the playhouse, and those audiences constantly demanded new material. Much of it was undoubtedly dross, but those same early years saw the emergence of an astonishingly talented group of writers, among them Ben Jonson, Christopher Marlowe, Thomas Kyd, and William Shakespeare. It is not fanciful to suggest that none of those playwrights would have achieved fame, and few if any of their plays would have been written, let alone survived, if the desperate hunger for new plays had not been dictated by the unrelenting demands of the permanent playhouses. Bricks and mortar, or more accurately, timber and plaster, were the necessary catalysts to give birth to one of the glories of civilisation; Shakespeare's plays.

Yet the acting companies, despite their success, were vulnerable. They were hated by the emerging Puritans, and, famously, by the Puritan-ruled City of London, which was why all the playhouses were built outside the city's boundaries. The new playhouses were popular, attracting enthusiastic audiences, which only exacerbated the Puritan attempts to close them down. What saved the profession was the patronage of Queen Elizabeth and the nobility. The most rancid Puritan was helpless in the face of the Queen's approval of plays and players. When James VI of Scotland became King of England in 1603 that royal support became even more explicit, and the Lord Chamberlain's Men became the King's Men. The world owes a debt of gratitude to England's monarchy and aristocracy because, without them, the nascent theatre might have been throttled at birth, and we would have no Shakespeare.

The boy theatres existed, and, by a quirk of the law, were allowed to perform inside the City of London. One such school was in Blackfriars, though it was not active in 1595. The boys performed adult plays, and, because they performed indoors, were not constrained by weather. In 1596 James Burbage, alive to the advantages of an indoors playhouse, was to purchase a hall in Blackfriars, which, after many legal wrangles, became a playing space for the company. That hall, or perhaps the great halls of the Inns of Court where many of Shakespeare's plays were first performed, is the true ancestor of most modern theatres. The Globe is justly famous, though it should be remembered that many of Shakespeare's finest plays had their first performances in the Theatre, but Blackfriars, a 'hall theatre', changed the profession. In an open-air playhouse, like the Globe, actors shared the same natural light as the audience, and, because the stage was thrust forward into the yard, they had spectators all around them. They had to play to the whole audience, almost half of whom were behind them when they faced outwards at

361

the front of the stage. It was like a modern play presented 'in the round', but a hall theatre placed the whole audience in front of the stage, as is the case with most theatres today. The audience was also protected from the weather, which was good for profits, and, within the limits of candlelight, could sit in relative darkness, while the players were lit. There could be no 'fourth wall' in an open-air playhouse, and there is plenty of evidence that the audience had few inhibitions about talking back to the players. Behaviour in a hall theatre was more decorous. Hall theatres could seat fewer people, but the price of admission was higher, much to the displeasure of London's apprentices.

The play in which Richard acts the part of Queen Uashti was *Hester and Ahasuerus* by an unknown playwright (quite definitely not the Most Reverend William Venables, who is fictitious), which was performed by the Lord Chamberlain's Men in the 1590s. The lines quoted are not from the play, the text of which is now lost, but either from a civil pageant celebrating Hester, which was performed for Queen Elizabeth in the City of Norwich, or else from a play of 1561, *The Virtuous and Godly Queen Hester*, which is also by an unknown author.

We do possess the text of *Fair Em, the Miller's Daughter*, the full title of which is *A Pleasant Comedie of Faire Em, the Miller's Daughter of Manchester. With the Love of William the Conqueror.* No author's name is given in the two editions that survive from the sixteenth century. There have been suggestions that the play was an early work by William Shakespeare, but that seems most unlikely. Nor is there any evidence that the Lord Chamberlain's company performed the play, but that was certainly a possibility.

Scholarly consensus suggests that *Romeo and Juliet* was written after *A Midsummer Night's Dream*. The two plays were certainly written very close together, sometime in the mid-1590s, and I suspect that the Pyramus and Thisbe interlude in the *Dream*, which ends with the grotesque suicide of the two lovers, was Shakespeare's sly burlesque on his own *Romeo and Juliet*. The version of the opening sonnet of *Romeo and Juliet*, the famous 'Two households' speech, which Richard quotes in Chapter Nine, is not a mistake, but rather the version printed in the First Quarto of 1597, and which, I suspect, was the version first heard on the stage before Shakespeare revised the speech into its more familiar form.

The jig *Jeremiah and the Cow* is entirely fictional, but all plays were followed by a jig, which was, in effect, a bawdy playlet tacked on to the main feature. We have the scripts of a few of those jigs, which consist of a simple story, usually about sex, some extemporary jokes, and dancing by the company. The jigs were not staged after a royal command performance, but whether the actors lined up and took a bow as I suggest in Chapter One is not certain. That company bow is certainly recorded after the Restoration of 1660, when jigs fell out of fashion, but it does not seem unreasonable to speculate that it might have derived from the more formal presentation of plays in aristocratic mansions and royal palaces. The poem that I have Will Kemp reciting after the performance of *Fair Em, the Miller's Daughter* is 'Lye Alone', found in the *Reliques of Ancient English Poetry* collected in the eighteenth century by Bishop Thomas Percy. We are also indebted to the good bishop for the text of 'Panche', which is the 'farting song' Will Kemp failed to complete. Kemp was famous as a comic actor, more famous, probably, than Shakespeare to a London audience. Nick Bottom was a marvellous part for Kemp, and perhaps he embellished the role with extemporary dialogue, a practice Shakespeare deplored, 'and let those that play your clowns speak no more than is set down for them,' he writes in Hamlet's speech to the players. The clowns that added their own dialogue are 'villainous', Shakespeare wrote, and show a 'pitiful ambition', and I suspect he had memories of Will Kemp in mind when he expressed that condemnation.

Will Kemp is identified in the Quarto text of *Romeo and Juliet* as the actor who played the serving man Peter, a very small role for such a prominent player, but Kemp would doubtless have dominated the jig following the tragedy. Kemp left the Lord Chamberlain's Men in 1599.

The book *A Conference About the Next Succession to the Crowne of Ingland* was published in 1594, and did, indeed, infuriate Elizabeth I. The pseudonym R. Doleman almost certainly conceals Robert Persons (sometimes Parsons) who was a Jesuit priest and a leader of the mission to convert England back to Roman Catholicism. He was a clever, subtle man, and his book was banned in England. The ageing Queen detested any discussion of the succession. She had no direct heir, of course, and while most people in the 1590s would have assumed that the Protestant James VI of Scotland would succeed her (he was a great-grandson of Henry VII and did, indeed, succeed to Elizabeth's throne), the Queen obstinately refused to name him or anyone else. The moment she did name an heir, of course, power would begin to flow away from her as courtiers sought the approval and patronage of the next monarch.

The spellings in the cast list (Hippolita, Lisander, etc.), which differ from today's accepted spellings, are how the names appear in both the Quarto and Folio editions. I have used the more modern versions except where the novel quotes a document that might have been contemporary with William Shakespeare, or, as he once spelled his own name, Shakspere. We have six surviving signatures of William Shakespeare, each is spelled differently from the others, and not one of them is spelled Shakespeare!

The idea that Shakespeare wrote an interlude called *Dido and Acerbas* is entirely fanciful, yet the notion that Shakespeare had been a schoolmaster before settling in London is not entirely without foundation. John Aubrey, the seventeenth-century antiquarian and gossip, who is usually reckoned to be as unreliable as he is amusing, wrote in his book *Brief Lives* that Shakespeare 'had been in his younger years a schoolmaster in the country', and notes in the manuscript's margin that he had that information from 'Mr Beeston'. Mr Beeston was William Beeston, a somewhat disreputable actor and theatre owner, and the son of Christopher Beeston who had been an actor with Shakespeare in the Lord Chamberlain's Men. The period between 1585 and 1592 is often termed 'the lost years', because we have no records of Shakespeare's activity in that period, but Aubrey's citation of Mr Beeston offers the tantalising prospect that perhaps the recollection was accurate.

Some readers might object to a depiction of William Shakespeare as a man willing to use violence, yet within a year of the fictional events of *Fools and Mortals*, he was bound over by the Surrey magistrates to keep the peace. The episode is shrouded in mystery, but in November 1596 a man named William Wayte had a Writ of Attachment (similar to a restraining order) issued against William Shakespeare, Francis Langley (of the Swan Playhouse), and two women, Dorothy Soer and Anne Lee. Wayte claimed he was assaulted and feared for his life. Wayte, judging by other surviving documents, was no saint, but the event, mysterious as it is, is a reminder that the playhouses of Tudor and Jacobean London lay in close proximity to the world of criminals and brothels.

Silvia's talk of a 'red cross knight' and the dragon is a reference to Edmund Spenser's vast, unfinished epic poem, *The Faerie Queen*. Spenser was distantly related to Elizabeth Spencer, the Baroness Hunsdon, who was married to Sir George Carey, son of the Lord Chamberlain, and the mother of Elizabeth Carey, the bride. Elizabeth Spencer was a noted patroness of the arts, and it is not inconceivable that she would have embraced the first production of *A Midsummer Night's Dream* with enthusiasm. Emilia, briefly mentioned in Chapter

Eleven, was Emilia Lanier, who was Lord Hunsdon's mistress for many years. Forty-five years younger than the Lord Chamberlain, she was the daughter of an Italian-born court musician. On becoming pregnant with Lord Hunsdon's child she was pensioned off generously and married to a cousin. Some scholars believe that Emilia Lanier was the Dark Lady of Shakespeare's sonnets.

The Reverend John Northbrooke's diatribe, *A Treatise Against Dicing, Dancing, Plays, and Interludes, with Other Idle Pastimes*, was published in 1577, not long after the Theatre had been built, and it is one of the earliest Puritan attacks on the playhouses. The excerpts I quote in Chapter Eight have been edited for length, but give the flavour of what was, in the end, a successful campaign to close down London's theatres. H. L. Mencken's definition of a Puritan was someone 'who is haunted by the fear that someone, somewhere, might be happy', and the more happiness the playhouses gave, the more virulent the attacks by Puritan preachers. One declared from his pulpit 'the cause of plagues is sin ... and the cause of sin are plays, therefore the cause of plagues are plays.' In 1594 the Lord Mayor of London, John Spencer, tried to persuade the Privy Council to close all the theatres, describing them as 'corrupt and profane', containing nothing but 'unchaste fables, lascivious devices ... and matters of like sort'. He describes the playhouses as 'places of meeting for all vagrants and masterless men that hang about the city, thieves, horse-stealers, whoremongers, cozeners, coney-catching persons. Practisers of treason and other idle and dangerous persons.' Parliament's victory in the English Civil War brought success to this relentless campaign, and, to the delight of the Puritans, the playhouses of London were forcibly shut down in 1642 and remained closed throughout the Interregnum. They reappeared in 1660 with the restoration of the monarchy, and, happily, have been flourishing ever since.

There has been some debate as to whether the playing companies of the late sixteenth century used a director. They certainly did not call him that, the word did not come into common usage until the nineteenth century, but the evidence that one man took responsibility to direct the players and shape the play is contained within the text of *A Midsummer Night's Dream*. Peter Quince rehearses the mechanicals for *Pyramus and Thisbe*, the play within the play, and behaves as a modern director would. He distributes the parts to the actors, draws up a list of props, schedules their rehearsals, and, in Act III, Scene 1, we see one of those rehearsals. He tells the players when to enter or exit, where to go, what to say, and when to say it. 'Why,' he says to Francis Flute, 'you must not speak that yet . . . You speak all your parts at once, cues and all! Pyramus, enter! Your cue is past, it is "never tire".' That is directing! And it is plainly an affectionate portrait of the process by which a play was staged in 1595. Quince, of course, also appears in the play he is directing, which strongly suggests that one of the principal actors served as the director. I have ascribed much of the directing to the fictional Alan Rust, but Shakespeare, as the author of the Theatre's best plays, must often have taken on the responsibility himself, especially for his own plays.

We owe John Heminges and Henry Condell an unpayable debt, because, seven years after William Shakespeare's death, they produced the famous book known today as the First Folio. Many of Shakespeare's plays had already been published as quartos (the names refer to the size of the books – think of a quarto as the size of a paperback, and the folio more like an encyclopaedia), but if we did not have the First Folio we would not have eighteen of Shakespeare's plays: *Macbeth, The Tempest, Julius Caesar, Two Gentlemen of Verona, Measure for Measure, The Comedy of Errors, As You Like It, The Taming of the Shrew, King John, All's Well that Ends Well, Twelfth Night, The Winter's Tale, Henry VI Part One,*

Henry VIII, *Coriolanus*, *Cymbeline*, *Timon of Athens*, and *Antony and Cleopatra*. Scholars have estimated that London's playhouses performed around 3,000 plays between 1570 and the closure of the theatres in 1642, and of those 3,000 we only have the texts of 230, so it is a miracle that any survive, and even more of a miracle that we have 38 by Shakespeare. The mention of *Love's Labour's Won* in Chapter Six is not an error. It is quite possible that a play of that name existed and, if so, it would be, along with *Cardenio*, one of the two lost plays of William Shakespeare. *Love's Labour's Won* is first mentioned in 1598, and could either be a lost play or, possibly, the name was an alternative title for another play, perhaps *All's Well that Ends Well*, or *Much Ado About Nothing*.

And were those plays cut? Shakespeare's plays, if acted in their entirety, are frequently very long, three, or even four hours is not unusual. Yet, in *Romeo and Juliet*, Shakespeare himself describes 'the two hour traffic of our stage', and I believe the plays were trimmed in rehearsal to run little more than two hours. There would have been no intermission in the Theatre, though there would have been in a candlelit hall to allow the wicks to be trimmed. Purists argue that the whole play should be presented, however long and however obscure some of the sixteenth- and seventeenth-century language, and despite the ordeal it inflicts upon the audience. Yet there is strong evidence that the published scripts do not represent the plays as originally performed onstage. That evidence comes from Shakespeare's contemporary, Ben Jonson, who on the title page of his play *Every Man Out of his Humour*, published in 1600, specifically says that the printed text is the script 'as it was first composed by the Author B. J. Containing more than hath been Publikely Spoken or Acted'. The exigencies of time and the experience of rehearsal would surely have cut a play, as indeed still happens.

Some readers may be disappointed that I have nowhere suggested that William Shakespeare was not the author of the plays ascribed to him. The idea that he was insufficiently educated to write the plays has taken hold in some circles, and the argument about 'who was the real Shakespeare?' rumbles on. The argument is a nonsense. We have overwhelming evidence that William Shakespeare of Stratford was William Shakespeare the playwright. I would refer any reader who wants to examine both the evidence and the arguments to James Shapiro's excellent book, *Contested Will, Who Wrote Shakespeare?* (Simon and Schuster, New York, 2010). It is a pity that such a book ever needed to be written, but as Puck says, 'Lord, what fools these mortals be!'

I am immensely grateful to Amanda Moore, who compiled an enormous dossier of research into the background of Shakespeare's world and the playing companies of the 1590s. She has every right to feel aggrieved that so little of that research appears in the novel, but it nevertheless infuses the whole story and was invaluable. All the mistakes that remain are entirely mine.

I am also indebted to Terry Layman, who, when playing Nick Bottom, invented the business of Pyramus forgetting the last word in the sequence 'Now die, die, die, die, die!' It worked wonderfully!

In *As You Like It*, Shakespeare asked, 'whoever loved that loved not at first sight?' In truth he stole the line from Christopher Marlowe's play *Hero and Leander*, which is all a convoluted way of saying that although *Fools and Mortals* is dedicated to the many colleagues who have made my summers so delightful (and terrifying) at the Monomoy Theatre in Chatham, Massachusetts, I am sure none of them will resent sharing it with Judy, my wife, who makes all things possible. To all of them, and especially to Judy, thank you.

Also by Bernard Cornwell

The LAST KINGDOM Series
(formerly The WARRIOR Chronicles)
The Last Kingdom
The Pale Horseman
The Lords of the North
Sword Song
The Burning Land
Death of Kings
The Pagan Lord
The Empty Throne
Warriors of the Storm
The Flame Bearer

Azincourt

The GRAIL QUEST Series
Harlequin
Vagabond
Heretic

1356

Stonehenge

The Fort

The STARBUCK Chronicles
Rebel
Copperhead
Battle Flag
The Bloody Ground

The WARLORD Chronicles
The Winter King
The Enemy of God
Excalibur

Gallows Thief

By Bernard Cornwell and Susannah Kells

A Crowning Mercy
Fallen Angels

Non-Fiction

Waterloo: The History of Four Days, Three Armies and
Three Battles

THE SHARPE SERIES
(IN CHRONOLOGICAL ORDER)